MISSION
Aurora
Operation Stargate

Herbert Grosshans

[1]

THE SHUTTLE LANDED IN SILENCE INSIDE A SMALL GROVE. According to the map, it shouldn't be more than twenty miles or so to the Scouts Outpost. When the exit door slid open, Major Jeremy Falcon looked back at the pilot, tipped his hat in a sloppy salute, and began climbing down the short ladder.

It didn't matter how many times one set foot on an alien planet, the feeling of elation never really went away.

The ground felt a bit spongy but no different from any other forest floor he'd stepped on. He turned to watch the other member of his team coming down the ladder.

She gave him a little smile as she also stepped onto the alien ground.

The ladder disappeared back into the belly of the shuttle and the exit door slid shut, taking away the light that had illuminated the ladder and a tiny circle on the forest floor.

Neither of them spoke a word when the shuttle rose back into the sky and disappeared in the darkness of the night.

"Well, Captain Alita," Falcon addressed his companion. "Here we are."

Her chuckle sounded amused. "That's right. Here we are. You seem surprised."

"Not necessarily." He switched on his headlamp. "Just a little apprehensive. I'm not sure if it was necessary to land like a couple of thieves in the middle of the night this far away from the outpost. I hope the map they gave us is accurate. I don't feel like stumbling in the dark for the next couple of days to find the place."

"We could always wait until daylight before we get underway," Alita suggested. "We each have a sleeping bag in our backpack to keep us warm. Fortunately, we are in a temperate zone, and it is nearly summer on this planet. The night isn't really cold."

"You are right about the temperature, but I think we should get moving," he suggested. "We don't know if there are any predators in this area. I'd like to get out of this forest as quickly as possible."

"I suppose you are not wrong about that. As far as predators go, what I remember from my briefing there are no ferocious big cats in this part of the land, but apparently, they have giant squirrels in these forests. They are not considered dangerous to the colonists, more like an inconvenient nuisance, but there have been documented cases where humans have been attacked by one of these giant rodents."

"Well, even if one would attack us, I'm not worried. We do have weapons." He adjusted his backpack, picked up the huge leather bag that held the special gear, and looked into the dark sky. It was peppered with myriads of tiny specks of light.

"The night sky looks different from the sky on Goldstrike," Alita observed. "Because of its proximity to the rim, there are fewer stars. At home, I could have told you which direction we should walk just by looking into the sky. Here?" She shrugged. "This sky is alien to me. None of the constellations are familiar."

He slowed down to let her catch up. "Goldstrike? Is that where you were born?"

"Yes, I was."

"I've never been there, but I am not unfamiliar with that planet. I know it is near the Accilla occupied territory. Humans and Accilla live there side by side in peace." He gave her a sidelong glance. "Am I correct?"

"You are."

"Is that one of the reasons you took on human form?" He lifted one hand. "Sorry. I am not trying to interrogate you or pry. Just curious."

"No need to apologize. I don't mind. We should get to know each other better, anyway. Goldstrike is in a way a unique planet. My people started colonizing it about a thousand standard years ago, but we were never numerous. The first human settlers came a couple of hundred years later. I don't know how much knowledge you have about my race. We are quite familiar with humans. Because of our ability to mimic other life forms, people of my race have lived undetected on many planets for centuries, Earth being one of them. It wasn't always a peaceful life. You may know that we need to occasionally drink blood from a living donor. Because of that, we've been hunted and killed. Humans called us vampires, witches, monsters and many other names." She sighed. "We are not evil. Our desire has never changed. Ever since our ancestors landed on a planet alien to them, they tried to blend in with the local inhabitants to live peacefully among them. We did that on Goldstrike."

"Sounds like an ideal planet." He chuckled. "Are you going to drink my blood when I sleep?"

She didn't laugh when she answered. "You don't have to fear that. I drink blood mainly from animals. From a human only when permission is given. By the way, I don't need fresh blood often. For nourishment, I eat and drink the same food humans do."

"That is good to know." He let out his breath with exaggerated loudness and laughed. "Just so you know, I am quite aware of your species' peculiar habit. I was briefed. I have no problem with that."

"You've worked with people of my species before?"

"I've never had an Accilla partner if that's what you're asking, but I have had dealings with your kind on a couple of missions." He stopped and switched off his headlamp.

"What is it?"

"I don't know." He stared into the forest. "I thought I saw light flickering ahead."

"I don't see anything." She followed his gaze. "Of course, that doesn't mean much. Your enhanced vision is superior to mine."

"There." He pointed. "I can't make it out clearly, but I think that's a campfire."

"A campfire means people. Should we skirt it or check it out?" she wondered.

"I think we should check it out. The only problem is getting there. The trail we are following is not exactly without hidden traps. Roots trailing across it, rocks sticking out of the ground, broken branches, or even trees blocking it, can cause a person to stumble and take a nasty fall. It'd be more difficult to walk it without any light. I'm thinking of you because I can see quite well in the dark."

"Don't worry about me. I'll just wear my infrared goggles and I'll be fine."

"Okay."

The trail wound itself through the trees and the thick shrubbery. Even though it didn't run in a straight line, it did lead west, the direction they needed to travel. It had been made by some large animal and was probably still used by the same species and possibly others. Hopefully, the creators of the trail were peaceful should they run across one of them.

The forest was not silent. The denizens of the forest filled the night with their barking, howling, and shrill cries. The occasional roar of a large predator caused some of the sounds to become silent for a short moment, and then start up anew.

"We must be near a swamp," Alita commented. "I can smell it."

"So can I. In addition to the decaying vegetation of the forest. I'm almost tempted to wear a filter." Falcon stopped again and stared into the darkness ahead of them. "The trail must have taken a turn. I can't see anything in the direction we are traveling." He pulled out a direction finder and clicked it on.

"What does it say?"

"I was correct. We are traveling south instead of west. I don't want to get off too far. I'll have to keep a close watch on it. We may have to leave this trail and fight our way through the shrubbery."

"Hopefully, the trail will change direction again soon. Perhaps it is just going around the swamp," Alita speculated.

Falcon didn't answer, but he agreed with her assumption. She was correct. They had barely traveled another fifteen minutes when the trail took a sharp turn, leading them west again. When he saw the flickering flames of a small campfire among the trees, he slowed down and lifted a hand. "We are close. We must be careful. This doesn't mean we'll meet humans. It could be some indigenous hunter or hunters. We don't know if they are friendly or hostile."

Walking on slowly, his keen hearing picked up the cracking of a dry twig and the soft scraping sound of fabric brushing against small shrubbery. He stopped and lifted both arms above his head. "We are peaceful, meaning no harm," he spoke loudly, hoping to be understood.

"What are you doing sneaking up on our camp in the middle of the night?" a sharp male voice demanded. A sudden bright light erupted behind them.

"We are on our way to the Scouts Outpost in Riwarda," he answered, hoping whoever had asked the question knew what he was talking about. He also hoped he was talking to a human. "Who are you?"

"I'm a Ranger and I'll ask the questions. Where are you coming from?"

Falcon allowed himself a small chuckle. "From far away and we've been walking for a long time," he lied. "We are tired and could do with some rest. When we saw your campfire, we hoped to be welcome. Can I put down my arms and turn around?"

"Go ahead but keep them where I can see them. That goes for both of you."

Falcon lowered his arms and turned. Squinting into the bright light, he asked, "Are you human?"

"I am. Are you?"

"I can assure you that I am. Mind taking that light out of my eyes? It`s blinding me."

The Ranger lowered the light but kept it shining on Falcon. "Walk ahead of me toward the fire but keep your hands in sight."

Falcon and Alita walked slowly, senses alert. The Ranger most likely thought he was in control of the situation. What he didn't know was the fact that his prisoners were not normal humans. Even though he walked in front of the Ranger, Falcon, with his augmented abilities, could disarm the man in a matter of seconds.

So could Alita. She was a soldier trained in combat, aside from not being human.

However, neither of them saw any need in doing anything else but following the Ranger's order.

As they got closer to the campfire, Falcon saw two men sitting on logs. Both men were dressed in dark green uniforms, and they wore wide-brimmed hats similar to Scouts hats. Except they were green, like their uniforms. He also saw their rifles lying beside them on the ground.

The Rangers watched them closely but made no move to touch their rifles. Falcon took it as a good omen. These men were not hostile.

"What have you got there, Frankin?" one of them asked.

"A couple of intruders trying to sneak up on us."

"Looks like you got things under control," the other Ranger remarked.

"You can't be too careful," Frankin answered. "We should pat them down for weapons."

"You mean you haven't done that?" the first Ranger chuckled. "Frankin, Frankin. If you want to make it as a Ranger, you have to be aware of every little thing that could go wrong." He looked at Falcon. "Are you armed?"

Falcon allowed himself a little smile. "Of course I am. You don't really think I'd be walking through a forest at night without being able to defend myself should I be attacked by an animal or a human?"

The Ranger shook his head. "I suppose not. Who are you anyway?"

Not detecting any danger from these men, he decided to be honest. "I am Major Jeremy Falcon, and my companion is Captain Alita."

The Ranger nodded. "Off-worlders. I suspected as much."

"What gave me away?"

"Your accent, for one thing. Your clothing is another dead giveaway."

"What's wrong with the way we dress?"

"Your coats are too long, your pant legs too wide, and nobody wears those rimless, round hats anymore. If you want to blend in, you change your coats and wear hats like ours, flatter and with a bit of a rim. In addition to making you look like everyone else, the rim protects your face and neck from the sun and rain."

"That's good to know. It seems the ones that did the research on Aurora studied the wrong century."

The Ranger smiled. "Also, the fact that you're following an animal trail in the middle of the night, taking a chance of getting lost in the swamps or thick shrubbery, when you could have walked in comfort on the road that runs through the forest from Riwarda all the way to Rontini, the next town." He made a motion with his hand. "Why don't you sit down and tell us more about the mission you're on."

Falcon shrugged out of his backpack and squatted down across from the two men. "What makes you think we're on a mission?"

Both men laughed. "We get very few visitors from outside, hardly any, come to think of it. The few that come arrive in the freighters that land in Rima. They have a spaceport, you know. Only the military is dumb enough to drop agents in the middle of the forest during the night."

"It seems we've been unmasked," Falcon said with a hint of sarcasm.

"Don't worry about that. Your secret is safe with us. By the way, I am Sergeant Markus. This guy beside me goes by the name Mel Sarkoni, and the eager fellow that managed to make prisoners out of you is Rookie Samuel Frankin. You must forgive him; he is taking his job very seriously. He may just make a real Ranger someday." His gaze wandered to Alita. She had taken a seat on a log beside Falcon. "You haven't said anything, but it is clear you are a woman. And a Captain to boot."

"Yes, to both observations. Is that so unusual?"

"Obviously not where you come from. Here in these parts, it is. We have no women in the Ranger Service. Neither are there any women in other law enforcement agencies."

"That's your loss," Alita said.

Markus shrugged. "Perhaps it is. I can't judge. That's just the way it is around here. And we're not even religious. Be careful when dealing with the religious fanatics. You may want to hide your identity." He looked back at Falcon. "Where you're headed?"

"Like I told your man already, our destination is the Scouts Outpost in Riwarda."

"Why that one? What I mean, it's nothing but a small office in a run-down old building that should be torn down."

"You're familiar with that outpost?"

"Not really. We have nothing to do with the scouts of which there aren't many in the first place. I believe there's another post in Ontura. Rima to be exact. I've never been there. Like I said, scouts on Aurora are as rare as a raindrop in the deserts of Mangali."

Falcon bent forward. "I'm not surprised to hear that. Scouts are the first ones on a newly discovered planet to map it and to ensure it is fit for human colonists. Once that's done, they don't really have a job on that planet and are sent where they are needed. That's when the military moves in."

"We don't have an army, which means no military men or bases. The majority of human inhabitants on Aurora belong to different religious groups. There is a little friction between them. Whatever problems they have with each other, they solve them. An army is not needed to keep the peace." Markus sounded almost conceited. "I don't like to brag, but we have little crime and violence on our world."

"You must have some means to keep the peace and uphold the law. Do you have a large police force?"

"We do, but then again, what is considered a large police force? Some states may have more police than they need. I have to admit that."

"If there is little crime and violence, a police force wouldn't even be necessary." Falcon couldn't help but do a little bit of needling. "Tell me something else. What is the job of the Rangers?"

"We enforce the law. We do not serve only one state and are not bound by borders. The law of the Rangers supersedes any provincial law. Local police cannot challenge it."

"I see. Another question. What are you doing out here in the middle of the night?"

Markus shifted his position on the log. "I don't know if I

should trust you with that information. After all, I don't really know anything about you. You haven't told me the reason for your presence here."

Falcon tilted his head and stared at the Ranger, wondering what he should tell him. Markus gave the impression of being a person he could trust. "Tell you what, Sergeant. I will confide in you if you answer my question. After all, to me, you're also a stranger. You may be involved in illegal activities."

"Hold it there, Major." Markus lifted both hands. "Everything I told you is on the up and up. If you must know, we are on the trail of a couple of dangerous criminals. You are fortunate we know what they look like, otherwise we may have mistaken you for our quarry and things may have ended not as peaceful."

"How lucky for both of us." Falcon didn't hide his sarcasm. He turned his head and gave the young rooky a closer look. "Hey, Frankin. How would you have handled this had we been a pair of vicious murderers?"

"I had the drop on you and I'm pretty good with my rifle." The young man's words sounded brave, but Falcon detected a hint of fear. And rightfully so. He would have stood no chance against him and Alita, but he didn't have to know that. Neither did the other two Rangers. His gaze moved back to Markus. "Alright. I will confide in you. But first I have to consult with my teammate." He looked at Alita. "Is my trust in Ranger Markus justified?"

She gave him an affirmative nod. "It is, Major."

"Good." Falcon knew he could trust her words. All Accilla were telepaths. However, they did not use their ability to constantly read everyone's mind. They did so only when it was justified.

"We are here to stop the invasion of the Osirians."

"Osirians?" Markus scowled.

"That's what they call their race. Those giant bugs that are trying to colonize one of the islands and are expanding. According to our information, they have set up a garrison in one of the states north of here. Ontura, I believe it is called. Apparently, many soldiers are stationed there. We received reports of small groups of Osirians raiding human ranches and stealing cattle. Don't tell me you are not aware of this?"

The Ranger sat silent for a moment, staring into the flickering flames. When he looked up, his expression was solemn. "I don't know where your information comes from. Yes, there are rumors, but they have not been confirmed. If they are true, we hope they are only isolated incidents. Hopefully, they will stay on that island, if in fact they are there. What harm could that do? There are other aliens living on Aurora, including the indigenous population. We get along fine with them."

"This is different. All reports we have been able to gather indicate the Osirians are not a peaceful race. From the reports we've received, this group seems to be from one faction and doesn't represent the Osirian Empire. Obviously, the Solar Union wants to prevent a full-scale war with the Osirians, which means we can't come here with a battleship, guns blazing. It has to be done on a small scale, but we must and will stop this group before they get too powerful."

Even in the flickering light from the fire, Falcon could see the expression of doubt on the Ranger's face. Markus made a motion with his hand. "You two? You will stop these giant bugs? Is this a joke? I haven't had any encounters with them and don't know anyone who has. I know nothing about them. What I know is from reports only. They are taller than a human. They are fast and strong and possess advanced weaponry. With our primitive rifles that shoot projectiles, we don't stand a chance in any confrontation with them. Not against weapons that fire bolts of lightning."

Falcon smiled grimly. "We won't be using primitive rifles, either. Neither will it be only the two of us taking them on. Captain Alita and I are here on a fact-finding mission. Our goal is to mark their positions on Aurora, find out how many of them are here, weaknesses in their defense system, and anything else we are up against."

Markus shook his head from one side to the other. "Typical military talk. Once you find out all these things, what then?"

"Well, the first thing Alita and I will probably be doing is destroy the garrison they are setting up in the north." He looked at Alita. "What is that state called again?"

"Ontura."

"Right. Ontura. It shouldn't be too difficult. Of course, we'll have to check it out first." He gave Markus a sharp look when the Ranger laughed. "What strikes you as funny in that? I don't see any humor in it."

"Everything you are telling me is beginning to sound funny, starting with that notion of wanting to destroy a garrison that may or may not be there. If it exists, do you really have any idea how many of those bugs could be in that place and what you may be up against? The two of you? I'm starting to wonder about you, questioning your sanity. What military branch did you say you are with?"

"I didn't."

"Well?"

"The ISS."

"Which means?"

"Interstellar Secret Service."

"Sounds very impressive, but it doesn't tell me anything." The Ranger yawned. "I'm getting tired. I think I'll crawl into my blanket and go to sleep. I suggest you do the same thing. I suppose you have blankets in those backpacks you're carrying?"

"Sleeping bags. We expected to spend time in the open."

"We have some of the nicest landscape around here with beautiful meadows and clear lakes. Great for picnics." Markus yawned again.

"We are not interested in a picnic, Sergeant Markus." Falcon spoke with a cool voice. "You may not take us seriously, but mark my words, the days the Osirians will still be here on Aurora are numbered."

"As long as you believe that, and it makes you happy." Markus threw a few more logs onto the fire and got up. "I'm getting my blanket."

Falcon nodded to Alita. "I guess we'll do the same. We'll move on tomorrow morning." He lowered his voice. "I don't trust these men. We'd better sleep lightly."

[2]

Even though Alita had assured him that no dangers lurked anywhere, and they had nothing to fear from the three Rangers, Falcon didn't have a restful sleep. His dreams were filled with giant ants and angry over-sized squirrels. It didn't take much guessing what caused the dreams. He was on an alien planet, not familiar with the weather, the plants and animals, or the people populating it.

He woke up with a start, momentarily disoriented, and still trapped within the last fragments of a dream. As his awareness came back, he saw a pair of scuffed boots standing beside the glowing ashes of a campfire and heard the cracking sound of breaking branches, the cause of his sudden awakening.

"You must have been tired," a voice said. "I've been standing here for at least ten minutes. Had I been a criminal I could have killed you in your sleep."

He recognized Ranger Markus.

Sitting up, he rubbed the remnants of sleep from his eyes. "Not so much tired as maybe feeling safe and relaxed, even though my dreams were not peaceful."

"Perhaps the knowledge that I was nearby could have been another reason that let you sleep this deep," somebody else said with a chuckle. It was Alita. She sat cross-legged and wrapped in a blanket beside the remainder of the fire. "It is cool," she remarked, making shivering movements inside her blanket.

"I'll get this fire going and Frankin can make us breakfast. It's one of the small pleasures we enjoy when we're on the trail." Markus threw some dry branches onto the ashes, bent down and blew into them. It took only a few moments before a few tiny flames licked the branches. Throwing thicker branches onto the small flames he got the fire going again. He chuckled. "Nothing better than a campfire. Maybe it is too primitive for you people out there in outer space, sitting inside your heated spaceships, but we like it."

Falcon got up and stretched. "We're not spending much time in spaceships. I've been on plenty of planets where we had to make fires just to stay warm. I think you have the wrong idea about the world beyond your planet. By the way, what are you offering for breakfast?"

"Well, it may not be up to your standards, but we usually fry up strips of smoked meat and a Lacca-egg. One is big enough for three people. If you want, we'll put another one into the pan."

"What are Lacca-eggs?"

"Oh, I forgot. You're not from around here. A Lacca is a giant flightless bird," the Ranger explained. "They run in large groups and are not easy to catch, but they lay their eggs in tall grass near large rocks. One bird can lay three or four eggs at one time. If you find one nest, you will find more, but we only take as many eggs as is practical."

"I'm not fussy when it comes to food. Sure, I'll take you up on it." Falcon looked at Alita. "How about you?"

She gave a little laugh. "I'm okay with that. It'll beat the dry rations they packed for us."

"All right, then." Markus turned and called, "Hey, Frankin. Let's make breakfast. Do your job."

Falcon looked around. Things looked different in daylight. He saw three horses tethered with ropes to a couple of trees not far away from the camp. "Horses," he commented more to himself than to anyone else.

"You are familiar with horses?" someone asked.

Falcon turned to see Corporal Sarkoni coming up from behind him. He carried a metal grate and a large, deep frying pan. "I've seen them on other planets colonized by humans. They are numerous here?"

"Yes. The early settlers brought a few with them. Now they are everywhere. Plenty of wild herds of them in the prairies. Horses are wonderful animals. They can be used for riding, pulling wagons, to pull plows, and for so many other chores." Sarkoni put the grate on the rocks that rimmed the fire pit but put the pan beside it. Then he asked, "Where is Frankin with the eggs?"

"I see him over there with the horses," Alita said.

"I already told him to get going with breakfast," Markus told him. "You know he isn't the swiftest."

"He sure isn't, but I have to admit, he is trying. He might just work out. We'll see," Sarkoni commented with a sigh.

———

It was later than planned when they carried on with their journey, but the three Rangers had been interesting company and a wealth of information. Besides, they were in no hurry. The road they traveled on was sandy and easy to walk on. However, conditions would not be so pleasant after a rain.

Light wind blowing across the open prairie made the air cool but fresh. The few leafy trees sprouting out of the tall grass didn't provide much cover from the wind. In the distance to either side of the road, stood tall conifer-like trees that would deliver more protection from the elements if they were closer. It didn't matter much now. The sky was clear and without any cloud formations, and it didn't look like the weather would change anytime soon.

"We could have saved ourselves some grief last night had we known that a perfectly good road was so close. I've never enjoyed fighting my way down an animal path in a jungle or in any forest," Falcon complained. "How could they have missed that when they surveyed this part of the region?"

"It was probably done by a drone with minimal intelligence," Alita pondered. "A machine that didn't worry about our comfort."

"Or a drone programmed by someone with a twisted sense of humor." Falcon spit into the dust. "Alita, tell me something. How did you end up with Interstellar Secret Service?"

"How did you?"

"I served in the Solar Union Space Navy for many years. Then I joined Special Forces. From there it was only a short hop to the ISS. Your turn."

"You are asking me because I'm not human, right?"

"You got it."

"Remember, I was born on Goldstrike. I joined a special police force that was made up of humans and Accilla. From there I moved straight to Solar Intelligence. It happened when ISS head-quarters sent a recruiter to Goldstrike to find out firsthand if humans and Accilla can work together in harmony. He liked what he saw and he offered me the job. I jumped at the chance, as you can imagine."

He threw her a sidelong glance. "You make it sound so simple. It isn't as easy as that to join one of the most powerful government services. Something else besides just your beauty must have impressed that recruiter."

She stayed silent for a while before she answered. "I was team leader. My team respected me and so did my captain." She smiled a little. "Perhaps that little nudge I gave the recruiter helped."

"You got into his mind. Not really fair to other candidates."

"There was no competition. I don't like to brag, but I was the best. If you know anything about my species, you know we may be able to read minds, but we cannot force anyone to do anything. All we can do is put a suggestion into the mind we touch."

"That may be just enough. Did the recruiter know you weren't human?"

"Of course he did. He knew the tiniest detail and more about every member in Goldstrike's special police force."

Her chuckle made him look at her. "What are you not telling me? What else was there?"

"Nothing. I find what you said amusing. You really think I'm beautiful?"

"Yes, I find you beautiful. Your human form is perfection. My opinion, obviously, but I saw Sergeant Markus checking you out." He laughed softly. "And don't tell me you didn't notice? I could almost smell the pheromones in the air."

"I did. My olfactory is more refined than yours. I can smell and hear things not even you with your enhanced abilities can." She gave him an impish smile. "For instance, I can smell you if I concentrate."

"I hope it is a pleasant smell." His laugh was almost apologizing. "I admit, I am not immune to your appearance, even though I know it isn't really you that I see."

"You may change your mind if you ever see me in my native form."

"Perhaps, but I do know what your species looks like. It wouldn't be much of a shock."

"Maybe not a shock, but a change in your feelings when you see a shapeless giant slug with short legs and arms and no face waddling around. I speak from experience." She looked into the sky. "That bright ball is going to be a problem. No clouds and the wind seems to be dying down. I'm worried about you."

"Why?" he questioned.

"We drank our water this morning. I have nothing left and

neither have you. I can go without water for a long time, but can you?"

"Perhaps we'll run across a stream where we can fill our canteens. I can last for a few hours." He adjusted his backpack. "Most likely we'll take off our coats if it gets too warm." He grinned. "Apparently, they haven't been in style for decades on this planet. Next time I'll do my own research."

They walked on in silence. There wasn't much to discuss until they had more information. This mission was sprung on him without any warning. When he was told he would be teaming up with a female Accilla, he wasn't overly thrilled. The idea of a female agent on the team was another thing he didn't care for much. He wasn't prejudiced, but he would have been more comfortable with a human partner, preferably a male.

Alita was an unknown factor not only because she was a female, but because she was a member of an alien species. This was his first assignment to go on a mission with a member of the Accilla species.

As he told Ranger Markus, his and Alita's mission was to gather information. Once they had the information they needed, the rest of the team would join them to execute the real mission... to exterminate the invaders of Aurora.

He wasn't happy when he thought about that. His superior had used that exact same word...exterminate. Only he had been more specific. Exterminate the nest of the giant ants infecting Aurora.

Even though everyone knew that they called themselves Osirians, to the humans they were nothing but giant bugs, or more precisely giant insects. Just as the Kraach were Spiders when humans referred to the race of giant arachnids.

Humans didn't practice any commerce or even communicate with the Osirian Empire. Until now, the Osirians had never shown an interest in exchanging goods and information with the humans.

The twenty-two soldiers that made up his team were hiding on one of the three moons. Specially trained and physically augmented, just like Falcon, they were waiting for him to give them the go-ahead to spring into action. In addition to being superior to a normal human, they had a battlecruiser especially designed for combat on the surface of a planet.

Falcon's attention was side-tracked when he spotted a horse-drawn carriage traveling on a side road and heading their way. It was still too far away to make out any details.

"Perhaps we can hitch a ride," Alita speculated, also watching the carriage coming closer.

"My thoughts, also." Falcon put down the heavy leather bag, threw his backpack to the ground, shrugged out of his long coat and rolled it up. Using the coat as a pillow, he stretched out in the grass. Lying on his back, he studied the clear sky above him. Taking a deep breath, he said, "There are so many different scents in this air, but mainly it is so fresh." He took another deep breath and let it out slowly. "You know, I've never been to Earth, and I don't know what the sky looks like now on humanity's birthplace, but according to historians, the sky used to be as blue and clear as this one. That was before Earth became overpopulated by an out-of-control birthrate. All those masses polluted the water, the soil, and the air to a point where the survival of humanity was threatened. It wasn't only the big cities where the air was nothing but smog. People had to wear masks pretty much anywhere. In some cities, they even carried oxygen tanks with them just to get breathable air."

He turned his head to look at Alita who was lying beside him. "Have you ever been to Earth?"

"No, never, but many of my people made it their home thousands of years ago. That was obviously before humans began exploring space. All those humans made it a fertile feeding ground. It is in our records. Humans didn't know about other races, believing they were the only intelligent species in the universe. How egotistic and ignorant. Humans were superstitious. They believed in different gods, ghosts, and demons. Things that did not exist. Many of my people were hunted and killed because of their ability to change their shape. Humans called them monsters, witches, vampires, and a variety of other names."

"I don't know much about Earth's history. It isn't taught in the schools, and I was not very interested. I know the basics but that's all. Our history begins when humans first landed on Icarus. Perhaps someday, I will take a crash course to learn more about the first humans on Earth."

"You should. Maybe you will discover things about humans you'll find difficult to believe, even appalling. The history of humankind is filled with darkness and violence." Alita sounded almost bitter.

"You talk as if you're an expert when it comes to humans," Falcon commented.

"Not an expert, but my knowledge of humans is extensive. After all, my people and humans lived side-by-side on Goldstrike for centuries." She hesitated for a moment. "I don't know if I should tell you this, but I had a human lover once."

"Interesting. Did he know about your real identity?"

"He did. He said it didn't make a difference."

"Did he ever see you in your real form?"

"No. He never asked about it and I was scared he may be turned off." She sat up. "I think our ride is here."

"I know." He sighed. "It was nice to lie here and relax with no worries in the world. Just you and I talking. Like two friends." Falcon got up as well, picked up his backpack but left his coat lying where it was. They had to get new clothing in order to blend in. The carriage was just turning into the main road. He noted that it wasn't a carriage but a wagon with one horse hitched to it.

They waited on the side of the road. A man dressed in simple clothing, wearing a sloppy grey hat, sat on the bench, holding the reigns of the horse casually in his hands. He stopped the wagon and looked down at them. "Are you two lost?"

"No, not lost, just tired," Falcon answered him. "We're hoping to make it to Riwarda."

"What's waiting in Riwarda?"

"We're looking for the Scouts Outpost."

The man pursed his lips. "It's a long walk still to Riwarda. You may not make it before nightfall. If you don't mind sitting on an uncomfortable wooden bench, I'll give you a ride. Just hop on but throw your packs into the box."

"Thank you." Falcon smiled. "We don't mind a little discomfort. Better than walking." He walked to the back of the wagon. The box was loaded with large baskets filled with long tubers and other vegetables. A few held fruit and a few bags containing some kind of food. He put down his pack and bag very carefully in order not to damage anything.

Alita followed his example.

"You're a farmer," Falcon stated the obvious as he joined the man on the bench.

The man chuckled. "Not much guessing there, I suppose. Can't hide my identity. What about you? I can tell by your accent you're not from around here. What brings you to this part of Saskona?"

"As I mentioned before, we are heading for the Scouts Outpost in Riwarda. My wife and I are going to meet up with my cousin. He is one of the scouts, you know. His name is Newman. Wesley Newman. Do you know him by any chance?"

The farmer shook his head. "No, I don't know many people in Riwarda. Only the ones I'm trading with. If you don't mind me asking, where is your origin?"

"My origin?"

"Yes, your origin. What I mean where are you from, originally?" He threw a quick glance at Falcon.

"Originally, we come from Brettany."

"Brettany, huh? Lots of religious nuts living there, I hear. Don't know much about Brettany, though, but there are rumors. I stay clear of those places. Are you following the scriptures?"

"Well, I won't say we don't. I mean, everyone does, to a certain extent."

The farmer through him a sidelong glance. "In other words, not so much."

"Right. Not all of us are religious fanatics. There are still a few decent people living in Brettany, especially in the smaller villages. Not everyone believes the stuff the clergy are forcing us to believe." Falcon knew nothing about that state, and he made a conscious effort to change the subject. "Last night we camped with Sergeant Andrew Markus and his team. You know him?"

"Markus, the Ranger? Sure, I know him. Good man, he is. Knew his brother Albert. Too bad about him."

"What happened to him?"

"Got himself killed in a shootout with the Kimble Gang. Took a couple of slugs to his chest. Yes, he did. Damn shame about him. Let me tell you. He was a tough one, that Albert. Hung in there for three days, before he died. Yes, he did. Damn good Ranger he was."

"Sorry to hear that. Markus never said anything about a brother. How long ago did this happen?"

Clucking his tongue, the farmer looked into the sky. "Let's see. My youngest was three at the time. He's twelve now. That makes it nine years ago. Yes, that's right. Nine years. How time flies."

"It does, doesn't it?" Falcon moved on the wooden seat, wishing for a cushion. "I'm surprised to hear about a gang. Markus indicated there was little crime here."

The farmer chuckled drily. "He did, did he now? I guess it's all a matter of perspective. What is little? By the way, my name is Bob Maller. I didn't catch yours."

"Sorry, how rude of me. I'm Jeremy Falcon and the woman beside me is Alita, my wife."

"Happy to know you, Jeremy." He held out his free hand.

Falcon shook the offered hand, aware of the thick callouses on the palm and the strong grip. This was a man used to hard physical labor. "Happy to know you, too, Bob."

"You never told me what you're up to, Jeremy."

"Up to?"

"Yes. What do you do for a living in Brettany?"

Falcon had to do some quick thinking. From the briefings, he remembered that sheep were an important food animal in some areas of Aurora. However, he didn't remember if Brettany was one of the states where they kept sheep. He took a chance and said, "I'm a sheep rancher."

"Really. I would have never taken you for a sheep rancher."

"Appearances can be deceiving," Falcon chuckled, hoping he had not made a blunder. In a way, it didn't really matter. No harm could come out of it if Maller knew their true identity. The reason he wanted to travel incognito was not to draw any attention to him and Alita. The odd chance of the Osirians becoming aware of their presence might make them wonder why a couple of highly trained soldiers were on Aurora, an unimportant planet that didn't have much to offer that Earth wanted.

Falcon closed his eyes to catch a little shuteye. Even though the ride wasn't smooth, it was monotonous.

[3]

HE MUST HAVE DOZED OFF, BECAUSE HE WOKE UP HEARING VOICES. Opening his eyes, his gaze fell on a horse near the wagon. Looking around, he saw more horses. Each one carried a rider. They were dressed in leather pants and long, black leather coats. Black, wide-brimmed hats covered their heads.

Bandits. Six of them.

The one nearest the wagon held a pistol in his hand. He stared at Falcon. "Sorry to interrupt your sleep, but I need you to climb down from that wagon."

Falcon stared back at him. Wide awake now, he asked, "Why?" He noted that Alita and Maller were not sitting on the bench anymore. He was the only one.

The other man laughed. "Because I say so."

"What if I refuse?" Falcon moved his legs to get the blood flowing.

The man with the pistol turned to his companions. "What do you think? Does this man need to be taught a special lesson or should I just shoot him?"

"Both," one of them said with a laugh. "I suggest you shoot

him in the head, right through that ridiculous hat he's wearing."
The others joined his laughter.

Falcon lifted his hands. You never argue with a man while he
is pointing a gun at you. "Alright, alright. You win. I'll come down,
just give me a moment. I'm suffering from painful joints. It will
take a while."

"He's got painful joints," the gunman said to the others, waving
his gun in the air, his attention momentarily not on Falcon. "Perhaps a bullet into one knee will fix it."

Judging the distance between him and the rider, Falcon
launched himself from the wagon. As Falcon smashed into him,
the man slipped to one side, his foot still caught in the stirrup.
While he held onto the bandit, Falcon pulled his ankle gun out of
its holster and shot the man in the chest.

Jumping away from the horse, he said with a cold voice, "Any
of you heroes want to join your leader?"

It seemed none of the five remaining bandits realized yet that
their leader was dead. Falcon pulled the man's boot out of the
stirrup and gave the dead man a shove. The lifeless body slid
further and fell to the ground, not moving. The fact that he was
dead could not be missed.

Falcon held up his gun. "Don't be fooled by the small size. This
little thing will kill a horse with one shot. By the way, I never
miss."

"We have no quarrel with you," one of the bandits almost
pleaded. "This is all a misunderstanding. We never meant anyone
any harm."

"Well, that is good to know. Now, all of you, throw down your
guns, your knives, and any other weapon you carry on you." He
smirked. "It is for your own protection. I would hate to shoot you
by mistake believing you are still armed and want to use your
weapon to harm me."

"We would never do that. We are just a group of friends out for
a little fun, that's all."

"That's fine by me. Now, hurry up and throw those weapons onto the ground. After that, you'll get off your horses and take off your boots."

They grumbled but followed his order. Once that was done, Falcon told them to move to one side of the road and wait. He then removed the bridle and reins from each horse. After that, he slapped each horse on the rump and watched the horses take off.

Turning back to the bandits standing on the other side of the road, he said, "Better start moving. It's a long walk to Riwarda."

"What about our boots?"

"We'll confiscate them. You can pick them up at the police station in Riwarda. Your weapons, too." He looked at Alita and Maller. "Help me load up those boots and weapons. I'm anxious to get going." He turned his attention back to the bandits. "You may want to bury your fearless leader. Sorry, I can't give you a shovel. You'll have to dig the grave by hand. Or, perhaps, just cover him up with rocks."

"You won't get away with this, you know!" one of the bandits yelled.

"That's right," another one added bravely. "We'll hunt you down. Do you know who you are dealing with?"

Falcon shrugged. "I don't really care, but I'll humor you and let you enlighten me."

"We are known as the Kimble Gang."

"No kidding. The famous Kimble Gang? Now I'm really scared."

"As you should be. Nobody messes with us and goes unpunished."

Falcon threw the last pair of boots onto the wagon and turned around. "Tell you what. I have a wonderful idea. Let's have some fun. All of you, take off those fancy leather pants. Let's go and move it, we're wasting time." He took his gun out of its holster again and fired a couple of shots into the dirt in front of them to show them he wasn't playing games.

After they took off their pants, Alita picked them up and threw them also onto the wagon.

"They'll be waiting for you at the police station." Falcon chuckled merrily. "You didn't think I was going to steal them from you? I'm not a cruel man and I'm not dishonest. But now we must leave. Enjoy the rest of the day." He climbed onto the wagon and took his seat on the bench.

Maller and Alita followed his example.

All three were silent for a while.

"I haven't had this much fun in a long time," Falcon finally said with a chuckle.

"You might have had fun," Maller grumbled. "I didn't. I figured I'd seen the last of my days." He turned his head to look at Falcon. "You made some powerful enemies today. That was the Kimble Gang."

"That's what they said. We left a sorry-looking bunch behind there. Just imagine, walking barefoot all those miles to Riwarda. They'll be mighty sore." Falcon laughed. "And without pants."

"One thing you must know, Jeremy. Those five are only a small number of them. The whole gang is at least thirty-strong. They'll be coming after you."

Falcon waved it off with a casual gesture. "I'm not worried. Actually, you got that wrong, Bob. They don't know that yet, but they are the ones who made a dangerous enemy today...me."

Maller looked at Falcon again. "I didn't believe it when you claimed to be a sheep farmer. Not with those soft hands. The way you're dressed made me think, too. But what you just did isn't something a simple sheep farmer is capable of. On top of everything, you killed a man with such ease and without feeling sorry. What are you, Jeremy Falcon? If that indeed is your real name."

"You're right, Bob. I'm not a sheep farmer. I am Major Jeremy Falcon, and this woman is not my wife. She is Captain Alita."

"You are military people. Not from here, obviously, because we don't have soldiers on Aurora. That means you come from the outside. I should have guessed from your accent. What are you doing here?"

"We're here because of those giant bugs."

"Giant bugs?"

"Yes, giant bugs. To be more precise they are giant intelligent ants. They are supposedly on Drago Island."

"Sorry. I don't know anything about giant bugs."

"We have reports of ranches in Ontura losing cattle to them. Also, some reports claim that they are kidnapping humans. That is serious business. Apparently, Aurora is not the only planet being invaded by the Osirians. That's what they call their race."

"I haven't heard any of that," Maller insisted. "Are you sure your information is correct?"

"We have it from a reliable source," Falcon explained.

"Are there more of you on Aurora?"

"Not yet, but in time there will be."

Maller sat silent for a long time, obviously mulling over what Falcon had told him. "I'm just a simple farmer," he stated. "I am not interested in politics. All I and my family want is to live in peace, plant our crops, and sell them at the market. And I want to be left alone. I am happy with the way things are."

"I understand what you're saying, Bob," Falcon said. "Unfortunately, there are forces out there that are not interested in letting you live in peace. They want what you have; they want what your neighbors have. That is the way things are. The Kimble Gang is a good example on a small scale. Things are much bigger out there among the stars. There are whole empires that will invade another empire just because they can. That is why people like me and Alita exist. We try to keep things peaceful. If it means getting violent to achieve that, we will do it."

"Does that mean you are a violent man? Not peaceful?"

It took Falcon a moment to digest that. "I don't think of myself as being violent, but you may be right. I am a violent man but in the right way, if that makes any sense."

"I don't know if I would want to live out there among the stars if that's the way it is. I could never do what you did. To take another human's life is a horrible thing, no matter for what reason. There are no soldiers on Aurora because we try to live in harmony with each other. To have an army on standby creates the opportunity to need an army. That is a basic and simple law."

Falcon sighed. "If it were only that simple, my friend. I would gladly accept that philosophy. Of course, that would mean I'd be out of a job." He turned to Alita. "You haven't said a word for a long time. I wondered why you didn't take care of the situation when I was still sleeping. I'm sure you could have handled it as easily as I."

She laughed softly. "I wanted to see you in action."

"A test then." He chuckled and leaned back against the hard support, briefly wishing he had a pillow.

They drove the rest of the way in silence. Each one of them lost in their own thoughts.

———

RIDING IN A FARM WAGON WAS NOT A WAY TO CATCH SOME SLEEP, even though Falcon managed to doze off for a short time. The ruts in the road and the small rocks on the surface created a rough ride, especially sitting on a hard wooden bench.

Falcon didn't complain. The alternative would have been walking for hours on the same rough road, wearing boots not meant for a long walk, and carrying a heavy backpack. In addition to the large leather bag he carried in one hand.

It was late in the afternoon when they rolled into the town of Riwarda.

Maller didn't know how many people lived in the town. "A few thousand," he guessed. It didn't really matter to him, as long as he could sell his products.

Their first stop was the police headquarters. Falcon accompanied Maller into the station.

"I'd like to talk to someone in charge," Maller told the officer behind the counter.

The officer looked up from a file he had been studying. "What about?"

"Are you in charge?"

The officer looked him up and down. "I could be if you told me what your problem is."

"No problem, really. In fact, it is quite simple. I'm Bob Maller, a farmer, and I am in Riwarda to sell my vegetables at the market. On the road here, we ran into a few of the Kimble Gang. We've got some of their stuff on my wagon. We want to leave it here."

"What kind of stuff?" The officer looked at Maller with a touch of interest but mostly with confusion.

"Stuff, like their pants and their boots."

"Why would you have their pants and boots?"

"We have more," Falcon volunteered. "We also confiscated their weapons. You know, their guns and their knives." Falcon gave the officer a friendly smile. "By the way what is your name?"

The officer shook his head and stared at Falcon. "I'm Constable Garret. Who are you?"

"The name's Falcon. Jeremy Falcon. Bob here was kind enough to give us a ride. We had..."

Garret lifted one hand to stop Falcon from saying more. "Now stop it right there. I don't quite follow you. What's this about the Kimble Gang? How did you get some of their things and why would they be in Mister Maller's wagon?"

"They tried to rob us," Maller explained. "There were six of them. My friend Jeremy killed one of them and told them to take off their pants and boots, but he promised them they could pick everything up at the police station. And here we are. I'd like you to hurry up because I need to get my harvest to the market. It's getting late out there."

"Whoa, hold it right there. I don't think I quite understood what you said. Did you say you killed one of the Kimble Gang?"

"Not me, Jeremy did."

"Nobody kills one of the Kimble Gang and lives. That is their code. What is this really about?" He moved his gaze from Maller to Falcon and back again.

Falcon's gaze was steady as he looked at Constable Garret. "It's like Bob said. They tried to rob us. One of them threatened us with his gun, so I killed him. I have a short temper when it comes to that kind of stuff. Nobody ever threatens me with a gun and lives. That is my code. Can we get this cleared up as quickly as possible? We are new in this town and have to find a place to spend the night."

"New in town? Don't go anywhere, I have to get the Chief." With those words, he left them standing and disappeared through a door in the back.

"We should have unloaded everything on the road some-where. This will be nothing but trouble," Maller complained, getting agitated.

"It will be alright," Falcon tried to calm him. "I will take full responsibility."

A few moments later Garret came back, accompanied by a tall, older, and haggard-looking man. A big, brassy shield on his chest proclaimed him as 'Chief Harris'.

His grey eyes stared first at Maller and then at Falcon. "What is this nonsense about killing one of the Kimble Gang?" he demanded with a loud voice.

"No nonsense, Chief Harris," Falcon spoke calmly. "I'm sure Constable Garret filled you in. They tried to rob us, I defended myself and my companions, and the rest just fell into place. We have their stuff on Bob Maller's wagon, and we are eager to unload it and get on our way. The five surviving members of the Kimble Gang will probably want to pick their things up tomorrow." He chuckled. "It will take them a while to get here. After all, they are walking without boots and no pants."

"No pants?"

Falcon closed one eye in a wink. "You might want to arrest them for indecent exposure. I'm sure you have a law in the books to justify that."

The Chief stared at him. It was easy to see he was struggling to find words. "Who the hell are you? Some kind of comedian? You come waltzing into my station sprouting all this nonsense. Perhaps I should arrest you for public mischief, sir."

"Like I stated, this isn't nonsense. All true. If you don't want to come and have a look, we'll just unload and throw everything onto the street."

"You do that, and I'll throw your asses behind bars for the rest of your lives," the Chief fumed. "You still haven't answered me. I want to know who you are!"

"I am Major Jeremy Falcon of the Interstellar Secret Service, representing the Solar Union."

"The Solar Union?" Chief Harris's face turned red with anger. "We haven't had contact with the Solar Union for decades. Nobody gives a damn about us. Most people here never even heard of the Solar Union. Now suddenly here you are churning out fancy words to impress me. What are you a major of?"

"The Interstellar Secret Service," Falcon told him calmly.

"Whatever that is. How did you get here? I haven't heard of a spaceship landing in Rima or even Shangdu recently."

"We didn't land on any spaceport. Our mission is still a secret."

"A secret? How convenient. I might be inclined to believe you, but that far-fetched story about disarming the Kimble Gang, killing one of them in the process, just takes it all." He suddenly held a gun in his hand. Then he turned to Constable Garret and snapped, "Get those handcuffs. I've had enough of this crap. We'll throw this idiot in jail until we find out who he is."

"You're making a huge mistake, Chief. If anyone had enough it is me." Without any effort, Falcon disarmed Harris. Throwing the gun onto the counter, he suggested, "Let's all go peacefully outside and have a look at the wagon. Perhaps that will convince you." He made a motion with his hand. "After you, Chief Harris."

It didn't take more than a look at the pants, boots, and weapons to convince the Chief. His only comment was, "This is not a good thing."

"I never said it was," Falcon agreed with him. Then they unloaded the wagon and carried everything into the police station. By the time they finally left, it was getting dark.

"I'll have to get going," Bob told them. "My brother will wonder what happened to me."

"Your brother?" Falcon inquired.

"I will stay overnight with him. Tomorrow, I am going to visit my customers to get rid of my vegetables and fruit. I can't wait to get back home again." He held out a hand for Falcon to shake. "I wish you good luck. You will need it."

"Thank you, Bob. Do you know of a place we could stay overnight?"

Maller shook his head. "Not really. You should ask the Chief."

Chief Harris was not a happy man when Falcon walked back into the station. "Any more bad news?"

"Not yet. Perhaps you can help me out. Is there a good place we can spend the night nearby?"

"I'm reluctant to recommend a place. You might just create trouble for them."

"I really don't know why you have such a low opinion of me, Chief. We didn't create the problem with the Kimble Gang. They were the ones attacking us. I only defended myself and Bob Maller's vegetables. You would have done the same thing."

Harris shook his head. "No, I wouldn't, not with that gang. You have no idea what you've done. It's been peaceful around here. We had an understanding with the Kimble Gang. That's out the window now. I'm scared of what will happen tomorrow."

"You worry too much, Chief. If it makes you feel any better, I will check in with you tomorrow. To come back to my question. What place do you recommend?"

"There's a nice place just a block away if you turn right," the Constable informed them. "Tell them I sent you."

"It's your funeral, Garret. I wouldn't have told them," The Chief growled.

"Thanks, Constable." Falcon tipped his hat. "Be seeing you." As he walked out, he thought he heard the Chief say, "That's what I'm afraid of."

"Did you get any info?" Alita had been waiting patiently for him to come back out.

"Apparently, there is a place close by." He turned to look at the entrance to the police station when he heard a loud click and saw Constable Garret through the glass window of the door. He grinned when he realized the sound he had heard was the sound of a bolt being thrown to lock a door. "It's that way."

It was as Garret had said. About a block away from the police station was a small building with a sign above the entrance door that read 'Vacancy'.

The room they were shown was not fancy but clean and roomy with two beds. They decided to take it. The attendant behind the counter gave them a curious look when Falcon put two pieces of gold on top of the counter. He didn't say anything, but he took the gold and put it into a wooden box which he secured with a large padlock. He hung the key around his neck for safekeeping.

"Security surely isn't the way it is on technically advanced planets. It would be easy to rob this place," Alita stated as they walked to their room. "He didn't comment on the gold. You didn't even ask how much the room cost for a night."

"Probably not as much as I paid him. Actually, I am glad he

took the gold, but not really astounded, either. Most colony planets take gold as payment. It is a common currency everywhere in the Galaxy. Local money is no good if you want to trade with other planets. Without gold, they couldn't even do business with visitors from the outside."

[4]

THERE WAS A SMALL EATERY NEXT DOOR TO THE ROOMING HOUSE. They served a simple but descent breakfast. Two cooked eggs and a couple of slices of fresh-baked bread with a coat of marmalade. It was accompanied by a cup of tea. At least that's what it said on the handwritten menu. Falcon didn't expect it to be real tea. The leaves that floated in the cup did come from a plant, but he was certain it wasn't a tea-plant.

Alita watched him take a sip from the cup. "I don't have to read your mind, but it won't poison you. It isn't that bad." She drank from her cup and chuckled. "Reminds me of a beverage we drank on Goldstrike. They didn't call it tea, though."

"I shouldn't complain. One thing about being on these backward planets, the food is wholesome, and it is real. No synthetic meats or vegetables. Even the beverage is brewed from real leaves. It takes a little time to get used to that." He emptied the cup. "The only danger may be a physical reaction to an unknown plant."

"Didn't you get your shots to protect you from that and from diseases?"

"Sure, I did, but I'm always a little leery. I don't completely trust those robotic MDs. They were programmed by humans. What if the programmer made a mistake?"

Her blue eyes studied him, curiosity clearly visible in her expression. "I didn't take you for being paranoid. I understand you've been through an enhancement program. They made changes to your physical body and your mind. You're supposed to be a superior human, physically and mentally. Did someone make a mistake with that?"

"I am superior, but that doesn't mean that I lost my humanity. I can still question things. They did not program that out of me. I'm not a robot."

"No, you're not, but in order to make your mind stronger and faster they had to remove some of your basic human traits. You need to be able to react without thinking too much, or not at all, without doubting if your decision is the correct one. You killed that bandit leader in cold blood, without hesitation. Would a normal human do that? Had you been a normal human you may have hesitated, perhaps let him live. A decision that could have cost any of us, including you, our lives. You are a soldier, used to killing, but being augmented changed you into an emotionless robot, a killing machine." She didn't smile when she looked at him. "You have to accept that, Falcon. You are not a basic human anymore. You are human-plus."

"I'm not sure if that is a compliment or not." He grinned as he looked out of the window onto the street outside. "This sure isn't a town filled with life. Hardly anyone on the street. Strange, on a beautiful morning like this."

"It is still early. Not everyone gets up at dawn." She wiped her mouth with a cloth napkin. "I'm ready to go. Are the Scouts expecting us?"

"They know we're coming, just not when." He looked around and waved to the girl behind the counter. She waved back with a little smile and went back to wiping the countertop. "I guess she isn't coming. Looks like I have to go to her."

He got up and walked to the counter. "I'd like to pay," he told the girl.

"That'll be five kouras."

"I only have gold." He took a couple of gold pellets out of a small leather bag and put them on the counter. "Is this enough?"

Without answering him, she picked up the pellets, pulled a drawer from underneath the counter and put the pellets into it.

"You probably paid too much again," Alita commented as she met him by the door.

"I suppose. We'll have to do a little research to find out how much one of the pellets is worth in local currency. We don't want to run out of money."

"If that happens, we may have to look for a job," she said with a laugh.

"It may be easier to rob a bank."

The street wasn't exactly dead, but they saw only a few people walking on the dirt-packed sidewalk. The street itself was paved with cobble stones. It reminded Falcon of Perseus. The same type of houses.

"I wouldn't want to walk this street during or after a rain," Alita commented.

"Have you ever been to any of these more primitive planets?"

"Only to a couple of them. I spent quite some time on Virgil. You may have heard of it. It was colonized a few centuries ago by humans. Only by accident, I have to add. One of Earth's many colony ships crash-landed on Virgil. The survivors fell back into savagery. A couple of centuries later, one of our colony ships drifted off its programmed course and landed on the same planet. The drive of the Accilla ship was damaged and there was nobody on board capable of repairing it. The distress signal the survivors broadcast was not detected by any of our ships until centuries later."

"I find it odd that nobody ever picked up that signal," Falcon stated.

"Actually, it was a miracle it did get picked up at all because it was broadcast by a tiny exploration satellite used only for short distances. I was among the crew of the rescue ship sent to investigate what happened to our people."

"What did you find?"

"They had survived and thrived, along with the humans. They also had adapted to the primitive conditions on Virgil. The planet was not an ideal planet, plagued by violent weather and extreme temperatures. The Accilla and the humans lived in small villages with only dirt-roads that were muddy most of the time. They had forgotten about wheels because they had no use for them. Everything they transported was carried or pulled behind them with a rope. Even though it reminded me of Goldstrike, I was not sorry to leave that place." She turned to look at Falcon. "How about you?"

"I've been to a few. My last assignment was a planet called Perseus. The conditions there were similar to what we have here on Aurora. In fact, this street could be in one of the villages on Perseus. In some parts of the planet humans and Tangari live peacefully together. You must be familiar with the Tangari race."

"I am. Humanoids with wings."

"That's right. The young females are comely looking, according to Earth standards. Immature Tangari have no wings. They are hidden under a hump on their back. However, once their wings unfold and the hump disappears, the females are extremely beautiful." He paused and spread his hands. "Again, according to what we humans consider attractive and beautiful."

Alita smiled. "Humans can be very superficial. They judge everyone by the way they look."

"You might be correct with that assumption," Falcon laughed. He stopped and admired one of the houses. "Everyone and everything. Judging by this building's attractive outside appearance, it must be beautiful inside. It has to be. Much thought has gone into the architecture, and I assume who designed it put also a lot of thought into the inside design."

"One would assume so," Alita agreed.

As they walked, they saw not only houses but also small stores and eateries. Some vendors displayed their wares in front of their stores. They came upon a market and Falcon wondered if Bob Maller had a stand somewhere trying to sell his vegetables.

People got around by walking or by sitting in small carts pulled by a couple of goat-like animals. Some carts with only two wheels used large birds with long necks and strong legs to pull them. They did see a few people on horseback or in wagons with one horse hitched to them.

Falcon looked at the Primary in the sky. "I think we should try to find the Outpost."

"Good idea. We don't even have any clue where it could be." She gave a small chuckle. "I hope it is in this town."

They both turned when they heard the racket of a horse-drawn coach coming down the road. It stopped near them, and the driver called, "I am for hire. Why walk when you can travel in comfort? Where can I take you?"

"We're looking for the Scouts Outpost," Falcon informed him.

"I know where it is. It'll cost you seven kouras for the both of you."

"Alright." Falcon climbed up the two steps and handed the driver a couple of gold pellets. The driver looked at them, nodded, and pocketed them, confirming Falcon's suspicion that he paid too much for breakfast.

Alita had already entered the coach. It looked clean and comfortable inside, but the padding on the seats was thin, and worn out.

"Not as soft as I hoped," Alita complained.

"Can't argue that, but it's better than walking." Falcon relaxed against the padded back. "This is probably the most comfortable way we'll be able to travel on this planet."

Cobblestones are not the ideal road surface for creating a

relaxing ride, especially in a vehicle with only primitive springs to soften the jumping of the wooden wheels across the stones.

"I'm almost convinced it would have been better to walk," Alita groaned after a short time. "This is agony. I remember traveling like this only once and that was on Vesta after having been captured by a renegade group of Mollards. They threw us into a wooden box with no wheels, pulled by a couple of giant elephant-type animals. That was some kind of torture, believe me."

"It doesn't take much imagination to realize that it was no soft ride," Falcon agreed.

The coach came to a halt not soon enough as far as Falcon was concerned. He got up from the bench and moved his legs before climbing out of the coach. Alita was close behind him. He looked around and saw a row of old houses on both sides of the road.

"Which one is the Outpost?"

The driver pointed at one of the houses. "The one with the faded hat nailed onto the wall above the door."

Falcon recognized the Scout hat. Its brown color had faded to grey, but it was still recognizable. He turned his attention back to the driver. "Thanks for the ride. Perhaps we'll run into you again."

"I'm always around," the driver assured him. He made a clucking sound with his tongue and the horse began to move. Falcon looked after the disappearing coach, listening to the clanking noises the wheels made. 'I've always wondered why the majority of colonized planets revert to this backward stage in the history of Earth. Why not the twentieth century, at least? Why this horrible time?' He was ripped out of his contemplation by Alita.

"Are you coming?"

There was no way to announce their arrival except for banging on the wooden door, which Falcon did. After a while he heard some movement behind the door and then the scraping sound of a bolt being pulled back. The door swung open, and he looked at a young woman with copper hair and green eyes. He observed that small detail about her because the bright light from the Primary reflected in her eyes.

Before he could introduce himself and Alita, she queried, "Can I help you with something?"

"You sure can," Falcon beamed, trying not to show his impatience. "I am Major Jeremy Falcon, and this is Captain Alita. This is the Scout's Outpost, isn't it?"

Her eyes widened. "Yes, it is. My apologies, but we didn't expect you yet for another week or so. I am Mirna Madison." She moved aside. "Please come in."

"Thank you." Falcon let Alita go first before he stepped over the threshold. As he walked down the narrow corridor, he became aware of a musty smell. He realized what it was. It was the scent of old age. Decaying wood smelled like that. This was an old house and everything in it was old, also. The sterile walls inside a spaceship and buildings of glass and steel had no smell, no age. They were dead, unlike the walls of an old house. They had been part of a living organism at one time. In many ways, they were still alive, eager to tell what they had seen.

There was an open door at the end of the corridor. The room they entered was fairly large. The two men sitting at a large desk in the center looked up as Mirna with the two guests in tow walked into the room. One of the men sprouted a thick mustache.

"Major Falcon and Alita," Mirna announced them.

The one with the mustache rose from his seat and came around the desk, his hand out. "I am Scout Carlos Martinez. Welcome to our outpost, Major."

Falcon shook the offered hand. "Apparently, we're not supposed to be here, yet."

Martinez waved it off. "Don't worry about that. We didn't think you'd be here so quickly." He gave a little chuckle. "Bureaucracy, you know. Here on Aurora nothing moves that fast. I'm afraid we've already succumbed to local conditions."

Falcon looked around. He had expected dusty shelves,

perhaps filled with old books and statues like on similar planets he'd been. Instead of shelves, he saw metal filing cabinets and wooden chests with drawers against one wall. The other wall held a large display screen. A couple of outdated computers sat on the desk.

"Not what you expected?"

Falcon turned to the second man who had spoken. He appeared younger than Martinez. "You must be Wesley Newman if my information is correct?"

The man grinned. "That's me. Unless I've been replaced and haven't been informed by anyone." He looked at Alita. "We haven't been introduced."

"I am Captain Alita."

"Alita?" His eyebrows went up. "No last name?"

"No last name," she confessed. "It isn't a tradition among my species."

"From that I gather you're not human." He tilted his head. "You appear to be human. Is this your natural shape?"

She shook her head.

"You're a shapeshifter, which can only mean Accilla. The only known species that can mimic a human being so perfectly." He gazed at her with a thoughtful expression. "We were not informed of an Accilla agent."

"Will that create a problem?" Falcon queried.

"I hope not." He looked at Martinez. "What is your take on this, sir?"

It appeared the older man was in charge of the team. He rubbed his chin. "I don't foresee any problems with us." Looking at Alita he asked, "How often do you change back to your original form?"

"Never, unless I have to. I grew up with humans and am used to this body. I wish all of you will accept me as another human female. To be sure, I am a female."

"I don't know much about your species, but as far as I know, Accilla are vampires, which means you drink blood." Martinez gave her an inquiring look. "Am I wrong?"

"Not wrong," she admitted, "but don't worry, I won't attack you in the middle of the night and drain your body dry. I drink the occasional blood from animals. My species has evolved."

"Like I said, your presence here won't create any problems for us, but I'd like to caution you. The people on this planet are not like colonists on more advanced planets. The majority of them are stout believers. Some might even be called fanatics. They believe in the existence of witches and wizards. They are scared of demons and other creatures that live in the dark. Vampires would be among them. If they suspect you of being any of those, you may end up tied to a tree on top of a pyre or at the end of a rope."

"That's horrible," Alita exclaimed. "I thought humans have evolved and outgrown that kind of barbaric behavior centuries ago."

Mirna, who had been silently following the conversation, laughed. "I'd hate to disappoint you, Alita. The human race hasn't evolved at all. Basically, we are still the primitive ape that will smash in another ape's skull with a rock, because he watched the other ape make fire by knocking two pieces of stone together. That must be some kind of witchery. What we don't know we must kill."

"Come on, Mirna," Newman chimed in. "Give us some credit. We managed to come down from the trees, even ended up in space and on other planets."

"That we did, but is that really such an accomplishment? Even here on Aurora, they still hunt anyone suspected of being a monster with pitchforks. Let's face it, these people have moved back in time to the Middle Ages on Earth."

"Why is that?" Falcon wondered.

"Aurora was first colonized by humans about six hundred standard years ago," Newman ventured. "The first wave of colonists consisted of different religious groups. They came here to escape persecution on the planets they came from. They blamed technology and alien races for their problems. Their descendants have not evolved but reverted back to living in primitive conditions. The second wave happened about two hundred years later. Most of them came for political reasons. Very few settlers came after the second wave. Because this planet is too far away from the trade routes, only the odd freighter will come here. Even now, we seldom see a ship land on one of the spaceports. The population here has lost touch with the rest of the Galaxy."

"How about you? How do you cope with all that?" Alita questioned.

Newman chuckled softly. "We do like the modern comforts. This house may look old and neglected on the outside, but inside we have all the luxury we can afford. We have running water, indoor plumbing, and electric lights. We also have heat when it is cold and air-conditioning when it is hot outside."

"What is your source of power?"

"We have a power cell in the basement strong enough to power a village. I had it installed the same year I came to this place," Martinez explained.

"How long have you been here?" Falcon inquired.

"Well, let's see. I was thirty-three standard years old when I arrived," Martinez speculated. "I turned forty-five a couple of weeks ago. That means I've spent twelve years on this god-forsaken planet."

"How did you end up here?" It was an innocent question, but Falcon was more than just curious.

"How should I answer that?" Martinez looked out of the window. "Let's put it this way, I stepped on the wrong toes. Somebody wanted me out of the way."

"Didn't you ever want to leave and get back to civilization?"

"The first years I did, but now?" He shrugged. "I don't really care anymore. Nothing and nobody is waiting for me."

Falcon's gaze wandered to Newman. "And you? Similar story?"

Newman laughed. "No. Nothing like that. I've been here for five years now. I'm an analyst and also a history buff. The Middle Ages of Earth have always fascinated me. What better place to study them than on a backward planet like Aurora? I actually volunteered to be stationed here, and my superiors approved my request."

"I guess that makes a lot of sense." He looked at Mirna. "May I ask you the same question?"

"Sure. It's been a little over two years now since I came here. I didn't volunteer like Newman. Why did they send me? No special reason. It is just another assignment. Possibly because I am a communications expert." Her shrug seemed innocent enough, but it made Falcon wonder. He could ask Alita to snoop around in Mirna's mind, but it would not be ethical and there was no reason for doing that.

Martinez looked at a clock on the wall. "It is close to lunch. Let's all go into the dining room, spend a bit of time getting to know each other better, and wait for lunch."

"Great idea," Falcon agreed. "We had an early breakfast and lunch would be welcome."

He didn't expect the spacious room they entered with a large table in the center and eight chairs.

"Sit anywhere you like," Martinez urged them. "We are not formal here."

Falcon sat down and ran his hand over the tabletop. "Real wood," he commented, "and superb workmanship."

"Everything is real here," Newman said. "The people on this planet may not be technologically advanced, but they are gifted artisans. And they take pride in their work."

When Falcon looked around the room, he noticed paintings decorating the walls and statues standing on shelves and on the floor. He had to agree with Newman. The paintings and statues were testaments to the enormous talent of their creators.

Martinez was watching Falcon. "I'm a bit of a collector," he explained. "You won't find original creations like this anywhere on the so-called enlightened and advanced planets."

"I can't say I'm a connoisseur of fine arts or antiques, but I do recognize talent when I see it. You are correct about not being able to find original art on most modern planets. Much of what sells as art is mass-produced in factories, mainly by robots. Human hands don't even touch anything. Even if you do find original pieces, they are unaffordable to anyone but the super-rich." He frowned. "As a soldier with no home, I can't even think about ever acquiring any collectables. Where would I put them? However, I can appreciate fine art. Nobody can take that away from me."

"Perhaps now you understand one of the reasons I am staying here," Martinez professed. "I consider this my home." He looked up and smiled. "Here comes the other reason."

Falcon turned his head to watch another person coming into the room. There was no doubt it was a female. She was slim and tall, and she walked with graceful movements, almost like a ballet dancer. Even though the plain dress she wore covered her from her neck to her knees, it couldn't hide the curves of her body.

She wasn't human. She had the eyes of a cat and when she smiled, she exposed two thin canines. It only added to the beauty of her delicate face.

"This is Irida," Martinez introduced her. "She takes care of the kitchen and the rest of the house."

Seeing her made Falcon wonder about something. Looking at Martinez, he asked, "What did you mean when you said she is the other reason?"

"She is my wife."

"Your wife? Nothing in my files says you're married."

"No. There is no record of it. I met her the second year after arriving here. I know you're wondering where she came from."

Falcon watched the alien female put the plates she'd been carrying onto the table. She saw him watching her and turned to look at him. "My people are called Suries. We were here already before the humans arrived." She spoke Inglis with hardly an accent. Her voice was soft and pleasant.

It was clear to Falcon why Martinez would be attracted to her, especially after living alone on an alien planet. Bored and lonesome. And longing for female companionship.

"Are you saying you are a native of Aurora? If you are then the information I received about this planet was not complete." According to what had been in his briefing, the indigenous people were primitive, stone-age humanoids living in small tribes scattered all over Aurora.

"No, I am not. My people came to this planet just like the humans but earlier."

"Are there many of you?" Her presence added another element to the problem on this planet. Nothing in the reports he'd been reading mentioned the existence of an alien race.

She shook her head. "We do not breed like the humans. We are not many."

His attention moved back to Martinez. "You say she is your wife. Does that mean she lives here with you?"

"That's what it means. Of course, we are not married in the conventional way. She moved in with me and that was it." He looked at Irida and smiled. "I love her, and she loves me."

"Your colleagues don't mind?"

It was Newman who answered. "We don't. She is part of the team." He chuckled. "Wait until you taste her cooking."

Irida left the room and came back a few moments later, carrying a large platter with steaming food. Setting it on the table, she said, "I hope you like it. It is a combination of fowl, tubers, and steamed leaves. Carlos tells me it is one of his favorites."

Everyone had taken their place at the table by now. "As our guest, you should begin taking some of the food. Please, go ahead," Martinez told Falcon.

He was reluctant but then ladled a few pieces onto his plate.

He waited until everyone had taken some before starting to eat. After a few bites, he had to admit, the food tasted delicious, even though it had a strange flavor, probably due to unknown spices.

"Well?" Martinez looked at him expectantly.

Falcon nodded appreciatively. "Very good. That food we get on the ships can't compare with a home-cooked meal."

"Do you spend all of your time on a ship?" Mirna queried.

"Actually, I spent very little time on a ship. Most of the time I am on some obscure planet. The food I get to eat in those places is barely good enough to survive. Sometimes it is best to go without instead of worrying if that might be the last meal you eat. Just because the locals eat it doesn't mean it is safe to eat for a human."

"Well, you don't have to worry here," Mirna assured him with a smile. "I've been eating the food Irida cooked for us since I came here two years ago and I'm still alive."

"That's good to know. I believe I will help myself to a little bit more." Before taking another bite, he looked at the fork in his hand. "This cutlery is well made."

"It is," Martinez agreed. "Not only do we have gifted artists on this planet, but we can also boast to have skilled metal workers."

"Let me ask you another question. I talked to a farmer, and he told us that the people living in Brettany are extremely religious. You mentioned the same is true everywhere on Aurora. How much truth is in that really and how bad is it?"

It was Newman who chuckled. "It is different in every state. You have to tread carefully in most places. Saskona isn't as bad as some of the other states. Actually, Riwarda is a pretty safe place to live. You won't see as many churches here as elsewhere. Ontura is probably the most advanced state when it comes to technology, but even there you have to watch yourself."

"We haven't talked about the reason Alita and I are here. We didn't come here to enjoy a holiday or to investigate any of the religions. Our mission is to gather information on the Osirians. The request came from your office. Can you give us more detailed information?"

Martinez rubbed his chin. "We don't really know much, because we haven't had any direct experience with the Osirians. We received a communication from the Outpost in Rima. According to them, the Osirians are building a giant dome on Drago Island."

"What about the reports of them raiding ranches and stealing cattle?"

"Rumors. We have found no evidence of that."

Falcon looked at Alita. "That's what the Rangers told us. I hope we're not barking at a dead moon. We have a team of highly trained troopers with a small battlecruiser on standby on one of the satellites. They could have been deployed somewhere else, including us."

"I would not kill the fire yet, Major Falcon," Martinez cautioned. "We have an old saying: A small tendril of smoke may reveal a large fire. You might as well investigate the rumors. You'll never know where it will lead."

"I guess you are right," Falcon conceded. "Something else has made me wonder. We landed in the middle of the night in a forest. From there we had to make our way here. We were lucky to run across a friendly farmer who gave us a ride in his wagon, which by the way was not exactly a fun trip. Why couldn't we have landed during the day in Rima, which has a spaceport, especially since there is another Scouts Outpost in Rima? Why here?"

"That is a valid question," Martinez twirled his mustache. "I don't have a good answer to that, and I wondered about that myself. We received a communication from Rima informing us to expect two agents and to tell them to make their way to Rima for more instructions. Why did they want you to come here?" He lifted his shoulders. "I don't know. I'm sure you'll get more information when you get there."

"Alright." Falcon wasn't happy with the explanation, but it would have to do. "One more question. How do you get around? Obviously, not on foot."

"On horseback." Newman grinned. "I hope you are familiar with that type of traveling."

[5]

As it turned out, there was a stable not far away from the outpost where they kept their horses. Horses could also be rented from the stable owner.

Falcon had ridden a horse when he was young. That was, of course, many years ago. The saying goes that one never forgets things like that, but he wasn't sure and didn't look forward to riding one again. Alita had never been on horseback, but her species had the ability to adapt to a situation much better than humans.

"You'll get used to it," Newman assured him. "I've seen horses on other planets, but never as many as here. Never rode one, either. Before I became a scout, I had never even seen a horse in my life. You learn quickly when you have no choice."

"Obviously, you didn't come from one of the more primitive colonies. Where is your home?"

"I was born and raised on Sheffield's Planet."

"I've never been there, but I am quite familiar with Sheffield's Planet," Falcon said. "One among the highest developed planets in the Solar Union. It is home to Starshield Innovations, one of the largest and most influential companies on that planet and beyond. Many other large companies are located there. If my memory serves me right, over a billion people call Sheffield's Planet home. Only humans are allowed to settle there. Aliens can get work visas but cannot own property."

"That is correct. No aliens and no large religious organizations," Newman acknowledged. "Other than that, the citizens enjoy more freedom than on most other planets."

"There must have been opposition when they brought in that law."

Newman chuckled. "It goes back many centuries, but from what I can recall about our history there was plenty of opposition and much bloodshed when that law was introduced. Many humans had taken partners from alien races, like Anorians and Tangari. They were forced to either leave Sheffield's Planet or separate from their partners. Neither option was desirable or even feasible in most cases."

"That brings us to Martinez," Falcon followed up on the subject. "I'm not trying to judge here. I am curious. What's the story with Martinez and Irida?"

"You'd have to talk to him about it. They are happy together and that's all that counts. We don't judge him, either."

"I'd like to hear it from you. How long did you say you've been here?"

"Five years." Newman gave him a curious look. "Where are you going with this?"

"I am just wondering. From what I understand, most people here on Aurora are religious and probably frown on humans fraternizing with members of a non-human race, especially when it comes to sexual relationships. What about her people? How tolerant are they?"

Newman cleared his throat. It was apparent to Falcon that he was reluctant to talk about the subject. "Let's sit down over there on that bench. We'll be in the shade under those trees. We can look at the horses later."

Falcon looked into the cloudless sky and nodded in agreement. He was still wearing that rimless hat, not having had a chance to go and purchase clothes in fashion in this part of the planet. Once seated on the wooden bench, he said, "Alright, fill me in on local sentiments."

"It is not an easy question to answer. People on Aurora are quite conservative when it comes to relationships. Liaisons of a human and someone from an alien race are frowned upon in some areas and condemned in others. People in this part of Saskona are more tolerant than in others, but there are still many who are against this sort of thing. As far as the Suries go, they are no different from us humans."

"Does it happen often that humans and Suries marry or live together?"

"It isn't uncommon. It is usually men that enter into these relationships. Men are attracted to Suries females." Newman smiled. "You've seen Irida."

"I have to admit she has something about her that is bewitching, if I may use that word," Falcon agreed, returning Newman's smile. "Tell me, are there ever any offspring?"

"There are. Children from those relationships are called Suman. Sadly, these hybrids are not accepted by humans or Suries. They don't have an easy life."

"It doesn't surprise me. Throughout history, children of mixed partners always had a difficult time. Not so much in more advanced societies but especially on planets like this one where humans have reverted back to more primitive times."

Newman looked at Falcon. "Let me ask you a question. What is your relationship with the Accilla female?"

"None." Falcon shook his head. "We are colleagues, that's all. We are still strangers to each other and are trying to get to know each other more. I've never seen her before this mission."

"She is very attractive."

"No argument from me. Don't forget, it isn't her natural form. If you are implying that something may develop between the two us, forget that notion. My policy is never to get involved with a member of my team. When I say trying to get to know each other, I mean I need to know if I can rely on her when things get rough. As far as I'm concerned, she is just another member of the team, female or not. Makes no difference."

"Then you know how I feel about Irida. She was already here when I was assigned to this post. As far as I was concerned, she was part of the Scouts Base here in Riwarda and I didn't question it." He grinned. "Besides, you tasted her cooking. I'd be a fool to challenge her presence. She is good for Martinez and that is good enough for me." He rose. "Let's go and introduce you to a horse."

Falcon selected a white horse with a long mane. He didn't know why, except that he had a good feeling when it came to the fence to let him touch its head. Perhaps he wasn't the one choosing the horse; it was probably the other way around. He watched the attendant saddle the horse, hoping everything would turn out alright.

The horse didn't protest when he climbed into the saddle, except for one little snort.

"Take it easy on the reigns," the attendant advised him. "She won't give you any problems."

Newman was already sitting on his horse and waiting for him when Falcon left the stable. They rode slowly to give Falcon an opportunity to adjust to riding a horse.

"After a while, it will become second nature to you," Newman reassured him.

Falcon grimaced. "Try to tell this to my thighs."

"Our bodies are funny that way. You may think you're in good shape until you have to do something you aren't used to and your muscles protest." He gave Falcon a sidelong glance. "You seem to be in good physical condition. It shouldn't take long for you to adjust unless you've been sitting behind a desk with no exercise."

Falcon didn't tell Newman that his body had gone through an enhancement program and was already adjusting to this new position. "I can assure you that I'm not a desk-hugger. I think I'll be alright."

"That's good to hear because if you want to get anywhere on this planet, it is either walking or riding a horse."

"I saw people using a big bird to pull their cart. Two men even rode them."

"Ostras," Newman explained. "It takes a little bit more skill to ride those, but they are strong and can run as fast as a horse. Some people even prefer them to a horse. They are easier to take care of and need less space to keep. They are only good for small tasks. Horses are still the more popular animals with farmers and suppliers; also, for long-distance travel."

"I think I prefer a motorized vehicle," Falcon said it as a joke, but he actually meant it.

"You won't find those on this planet." Newman stopped and pointed at a house. "That's the house of a man by the name of Jon Haggard. I don't know if that is his real name. He is what you would call a newcomer. Came here about twenty years ago on one of the trading ships. He never said, but I believe he's a fugitive after committing a crime somewhere. Keeps to himself most of the time. He said he was an engineer. He tried to build some kind of mobile once, but it didn't go anywhere. He couldn't get the power modules he needed to make it work."

"I can imagine that might be a stumbling block. Wonder why he would pick a backward planet like Aurora to spend the rest of his life."

"The most logical and ideal place to disappear. No computers to register your name and whereabouts. Nobody has an identity chip or any other way to be identified."

"That brings up another question I have. I'm talking about money. How do people make a living here?" Falcon wondered.

"Like anywhere else. They either work for it or they trade. You've met a farmer, but there are all kinds of jobs anyone can do. Horses need to be shooed and taken care of, for instance. We need metal workers, bakers, butchers, and other tradespeople. There is a need for grocers, restaurants, you name it."

"Where do you get the local money from?"

"The bank." Newman laughed loudly when he saw Falcon's perplexed face. "Don't mind me. I like to kid. As you know, gold is accepted pretty much on every planet. We brought enough gold to last us for a long time. We just exchange gold for kouras."

"I'll have to find out how much a pellet of gold is worth," Falcon said.

They rode on in silence for a while. Mentally, Falcon registered the most important places and buildings to become familiar with the layout of the town. He became aware of the many different smells and sounds assaulting his senses. The air was laden with the stench of animal and human wastes, but it would be difficult to miss the presence of a place dealing with food, be it an eatery or a store selling baked goods and other prepared foodstuff. The barking, screaming, and chattering sounds of animals were everywhere.

Falcon remembered the sounds and smells of the huge cities on advanced planets, even in smaller towns. They were vastly different from what he experienced here. Not necessarily more pleasant, but less pungent. Even though he had been to planets similar to Aurora, it was going to take some time to get used to this different environment.

"Something is going on there," Newman said suddenly and brought his horse to a halt.

Falcon took his attention away from the backyard of one of the houses he'd been studying, curious to see fowl, dogs, and other domestic animals behind the fence. Looking ahead, he saw a crowd of people gathered around. He noticed the building he looked at was the police station. Then he saw Chief Harris, Constable Garret, and another policeman confronted by a group of men on horseback. All of them wore black, wide-brimmed hats, leather pants, and long leather coats.

"Crap," Newman exclaimed. "That's the notorious Kimble Gang. I wonder what that is all about. Nothing good, that's for sure."

Falcon chuckled. "They want their stuff back."

Newman gave Falcon a puzzled look. "What stuff?"

Falcon shrugged. "I never told you. We had a run-in with some of their members on the way to town."

"A run-in? I have a feeling you are going to tell me something I may not like."

"They tried to rob us. They made a big mistake by pointing weapons at us. I'm a soldier and I don't react kindly to a threat. I killed their leader while defending myself, Alita, and Farmer Maller." Falcon smiled grimly. "I guess they are not happy because I made them walk barefoot back to town. We left their stuff with Chief Harris."

"You killed one of their men? That is bad news, Falcon. Nobody messes with the Kimble Gang."

"Chief Harris told me as much. Well, I am partially responsible for this mess, I'd better clean it up." With that, he gave his horse a gentle kick and rode toward the police station.

"It's your funeral," Newman commented and followed him.

When Falcon was close enough, he called out in a loud voice, "Trouble, Chief Harris?"

Harris turned to look at Falcon. "It's you. Look at the problem you've caused."

"They caused it, not me. They attempted to rob me. It didn't end well for them." Falcon was already in combat mode. He knew this whole thing was not going to be deflated peacefully. People were about to die, but he wasn't going to be one of them. Without conscious thought, he marked each member of the gang. His mind was clear and sharp and without mercy. These men didn't deserve any.

"That's the bastard who made us walk without boots and pants. I'm going to kill him." The man yelling pulled out a gun, but the man standing beside him shook his arm. "Not so fast, Hart. Let's have some fun with him first."

One of the men on horseback caused his horse to move forward, toward Falcon. He was a big man with a thick beard and bushy eyebrows. Falcon instinctively knew he was the leader of these men, and it wasn't unexpected when the man said with a deep, rumbling voice, "You must have a death wish, Mister. Not only did you shame some of my crew, but you also killed my cousin. That will not go unpunished. Do you know who we are?"

Falcon played the innocent man. "Should I?"

"We are the Kimble Gang, you moron. Everybody knows us."

"Not everyone. I don't. I don't actually care what you call yourself and those losers you call your crew. All I see is a bunch of cutthroats dressed in fancy leather outfits terrorizing people that want to be left alone and go about their business."

"You don't know what you're talking about! We protect them."

Falcon laughed. "Protect them from other gangs? I'll bet there are none around."

"Because we are keeping them away. Nobody dares to enter our territory. They all know that you don't mess around with Alfred Kimble and his brothers." He stared at Falcon. "Judging by the way you dress and your accent you are not from around here. I guess you didn't know about us. Too bad for you. Killing my cousin and shaming my men can't go unpunished."

"I think you have this all backward, Alfred. Your men waylaid us on the road with the intention to rob us. I couldn't let that happen." As he was talking, he had been watching the man who had threatened to kill him. Shaking off the arm of his companion, the man leveled his revolver and aimed it at Falcon.

Falcon reacted automatically. He drew the laser from the holster under his arm, squeezed the trigger that released a flash of energy and partially melted the revolver in the man's hand. Letting out a scream of pain, the man dropped the weapon and stared at his injured hand. Falcon didn't have the luxury to watch him or even comment on what happened. From the corner of his eye, he saw Alfred Kimble draw his revolver, but before he could get it in position to fire off a shot, Falcon's laser beam drilled a neat hole into his chest, toppling him from his horse.

Things happened fast after that. The two men beside Kimble drew their weapons, but a .45 Colt is no match for a laser. Falcon shot both men before they could clear leather. More revolvers were being drawn. He killed another man, but he didn't want to shoot every man if he could avoid it. He slid from his horse. Reaching the closest member of the gang, he grabbed him, spun him around, and put his laser against the man's head. "Lay down your weapons or he is a dead man."

The man in his grip struggled, trying to get free. Falcon pushed the laser into his neck. "Stop struggling or you'll join your friends," Falcon warned him. Then with a loud voice he said to the others, "You have six bullets in your guns, but mine has an unlimited supply of power and I don't have to reload."

"All we need is one bullet to kill you," one man shouted.

"You killed the Kimble brothers," another one yelled.

"Yes, I did because it was either them or me. I don't want to kill another man, but I will shoot every one of you unless you follow my order. Don't try to be heroes."

One of the men close to him threw his colt to the ground. "You have the upper hand, Mister," he grumbled, "but you won't get away with this. You'd better look over your shoulder from now on. You are one, we are many."

"So, you are. What's your name?"

"Otto Hamlin. Perhaps you should remember it. What's it to you anyway?"

Falcon gave him a cold smile. "Well, Otto. You know nothing about me, and I don't blame you from threatening me. Don't confuse me with Chief Harris here or Constable Garret. They might be intimidated by you, but I am not. By the way, I am a soldier trained to deal with situations more dangerous than this one. Your threat means nothing to me. If an attempt is made to harm me, it will fail, but you will be the first one I seek out. Guilty or not. It might be in your best interest to keep your friends from doing something stupid."

"I can't influence all of them," the man protested.

Falcon looked at the others. "What I told Otto goes for all of you. I may not know your names, but your faces are burnt into my memory. From now on, if I hear that any of you harass the people in this town or beyond, I will find you. Believe me, you don't want that to happen. One last warning: The Kimble Gang is no more. Don't gather anywhere in their name, or plan something malicious." He gave the man in his grip a shove.

As the man stumbled away, Falcon kept his attention on the other. Satisfied that all of them had thrown their weapons away or shoved back into their holsters, he sheathed his laser.

"He is a demon, not a man," someone in the watching crowd said loud enough for him to hear.

"Maybe he's the Evil One himself," another one suggested.

"I don't really care," a third one commented. "If he keeps the Kimble Gang from robbing us, that's good enough for me."

Falcon turned to the police chief. "Chief Harris, I believe the situation has been defused. These men won't give you any more trouble."

"You killed four men in cold blood," the Chief accused him.

"Not in cold blood," Falcon corrected him. "It was self-defence. There is a difference. Besides, I don't have to justify anything to anybody. I am here in the name of the Solar Union and therefore outrank anyone on this planet. You have no authority over me."

"From what I just saw I don't have the desire to associate

myself with you. You are a walking disaster waiting to happen. I don't want to be around you when it does."

"I'm not forcing you to do anything." Falcon gave the assembled members of the Kimble Gang one last glance. "I would suggest you tell them to take their dead companions out of here and clean up the mess. Also tell the spectators the show is over. I'll take my leave now. Got things to do. Have a pleasant day." He tipped his hat and mounted his horse.

Newman had been watching everything from a safe distance. When Falcon rode up to him, Newman said, "I have to admit, I was ready to bury you, but judging by what I just witnessed, I don't believe I have to worry about that ever again. Chief Harris was right. You are a hazard to be around."

Falcon gave him a grim smile. "That seems to be a soldier's destiny. Violence and death follow him wherever he goes. My mission did not include this kind of work, but I can't walk away from it. It needed to be done."

"You are cold," Newman remarked. "Four men dead in a matter of minutes, actually seconds. I am glad I am a scout. I don't envy you. I couldn't deal with that kind of violence."

"Not everyone can. In my early years as a recruit, I wasn't sure if I could, but like anything else, if you deal with it nearly every day it becomes second nature. You get used to it. After a while, you don't think about it. Violence becomes part of your life. You are probably fortunate to be stationed on a planet like Aurora. Perhaps, if you would be surrounded by a violent environment, you might accept it more readily."

"I think I understand what you are talking about. Before I was sent here, I spent a short time on Helios. I was under the command of Major Anton Moretti. He is a scout, by the way. I'm not saying it was a dangerous assignment, but we did face a few close calls while mapping the planet. I admit, being here is almost like being on a holiday." He smiled. "I am not complaining."

They had been riding slowly down the now almost empty street.

"I love the architecture in this town. The combination of wood and stones gives you a warm feeling, although some of the houses could use a little paint and other repairs," Falcon observed.

"The wood is real, so are the stones, unlike on many other planets where all the buildings are as tall as mountains and all you see is glass and steel," Newman agreed. "I love this place."

Falcon watched a cart pulled by one of those goat-like animals coming out of a side street. "You forgot to mention the thundering sound of a rocket blasting into space on a low-technology planet."

"Or a vehicle powered by an internal combustion engine rumbling down the street. The noise and stink can be more than annoying."

Falcon chuckled softly. "It is true, on planets like this one you don't have the noise, but I am not sure what is preferable, the stink of those engines or the combined aroma of animal droppings and human waste."

"I guess it all depends on how tolerable your sense of smell is."

There were more people on the street now. They came upon a large open area. It wasn't empty. People thread their way through an array of stands and tables where merchants sold their wares. This market was much larger than the one he and Alita had come across the day before. They hadn't seen Bob Maller at that market, but Falcon doubted finding him at this one.

"Come down from your horse. I want to do some shopping here," Newman told him.

[6]

AFTER SPENDING A FEW DAYS ON THE BACK OF A HORSE, FALCON WAS getting used to it and found it an almost pleasant way to get around. Alita's ability to change her shape made it much easier for her to adapt to sitting on a horse.

They had decided to take a trip north toward Ontura. It was time to find out more about the Osirians and to see if the rumors were true. Newman insisted on coming with them. 'After all, I am a Scout. It is my job to guide you and keep you from getting lost' was his argument. He also reminded them that they were supposed to go to the Scouts Outpost in Rima where they might receive more information.

"We can follow the map you gave us. I know it is crude and not precise, but it shows the towns and some of the villages. Most importantly, it has the roads marked."

"This map is a few years old. That is another reason I want to come with you so I can update this map," Newman argued.

Falcon would have preferred to travel without him. He might get in the way when things became tough, but Newman wouldn't take no for an answer.

To divert attention from themselves they needed to blend in. It meant dressing in local garb, which consisted of plain pants and a simple shirt. However, Falcon still wore the leather jacket he brought with him, instead of a local jacket made from cloth and hardly any pockets. It allowed him to wear his laser under his arm. He and Alita also wore hats purchased from a merchant in Riwarda.

Newman was satisfied with the way they looked. "As long as you don't open your mouth and talk, nobody will suspect that you aren't locals."

They brought an extra horse to carry their gear.

To get to Ontura they had to travel through Brettany, the nearest state to the north. The border between Brettany and Saskona was about three days away, but to get to Rowarra would take at least another four days on horseback. The road was great and easy to travel when the weather was dry. Even a short downpour wouldn't do much damage, since the soil was quite sandy, and water drained away fairly quickly. However, a rain that lasted three or more days turned the ground muddy and unfit for travel with a carriage.

On horseback, of course, was a somewhat different story. All they had to do was get off the road if it turned into mud, but it wasn't smooth traveling, either, because of the uneven ground and the giant and small rocks dotting the landscape in some places. There also were forests to travel through and a swamp to cross.

Newman had been in Brettany a couple of times and once in Glasca, the state to the east. It was the reason he wanted to accompany Falcon and Alita. He knew the road and the people. "They have strict rules and are overly zealous when it comes to their religion. They believe in demons, witches, and ghosts. The creatures that roam the night are real. Be careful what you say and do. Alita, for heaven's sake, don't even mention that you are not human. They've never heard of your kind. Remember, these are the descendants of a religious cult."

"I will try to control myself," Alita said with a little smile. "How about Ontura? Are people there also a bunch of fanatics?"

"They are religious, but they are more tolerant. However, I suggest you refrain from broadcasting you are Accilla and what you are capable of, even in Ontura. There are still plenty of radicals and they'll nail your hide against a wall if they smell something unholy."

———

THE WEATHER WAS DESCENT AT THIS TIME OF YEAR, AT LEAST FOR the meantime. There was a good chance it would hold until they reached the border. If luck stayed with them, they might even be able to stay dry for another day. The two tents they brought along were rainproof, but sitting inside a tent to wait out a rainy day was not desirable.

The landscape was mainly grassland. They passed a couple of farmsteads. Judging by the large herds of cattle grazing, it was not difficult to guess what business they were in. They saw a few men on horseback protecting the animals from predators and keeping them from going astray.

"What kind of predators do they have to worry about?" Falcon asked.

"Not many, but there are enough. The Tiger-wolves are the most dangerous. They run in packs, and you don't want to find yourself surrounded by them. They'll bring down a cow or even a bull with ease. The best thing is to just leave them alone and let them have their kill. Then there are the Shramps. Bony, long-legged creatures with claws as sharp as giant scissors sprouting from their heads. They walk on two legs, but don't let that fool you. They are fast and dangerous. We don't have any Sabre-tooth-lions in these parts, but if you ever end up in Mangali, they have plenty of them. There are a few smaller critters roaming around looking for a meal, but they are easier to handle. You still have to be on guard, though. Even they can get nasty."

"Any good animals?"

Newman laughed softly. "Plenty of them. I'm sure we'll run across some. This planet is not as populated as many of the other ones and the woods and grasslands are teeming with wildlife. Big and small. Not all are native to Aurora. Many of them have been introduced by the Suries and quite a few by humans. We can thank the humans for letting their dogs breed uncontrolled and letting them run around free. A pack of wild dogs is as dangerous as a pack of Tiger-wolves. However, there are other, much more harmless animals humans brought with them. To witness a herd of wild horses galloping across the prairie is a beautiful and exhilarating sight. Watching these majestic, beautiful animals running free is something you don't easily forget."

"I heard horses are pretty much extinct on Earth."

"Not extinct, but you'll find them only in sanctuaries. There is nothing useful to do for them on Earth. No room for them, either, like for most animals. Too many people. That's why it is so important for colonists to take animals with them and give them a chance to keep their species alive." Newman sighed. "Most people don't care about animals. I do."

"I like animals. In fact, when I was a little boy, I had a dog."

"A dog?" Newman sounded surprised. "I never asked you about your birth planet. For some reason, I assumed you were born on Earth. Where were you born?"

"My birth planet is called Icarus, a planet much like Earth. My father was a farmer. He grew different types of grains and vegetables. He also raised fowl for eggs and meat."

"Interesting. Your father didn't insist you become a farmer also?"

"He would have liked that, and I almost did, but my younger brother, Connor, was more interested in farming than I. Even though he became a biologist, he stayed on the farm. He will eventually inherit the farm and carry on with what my great-grandfather started."

"How many brothers and sisters do you have," Newman inquired.

"Only the one brother, but I do have two sisters. Emily. She's one year younger than I. She is a zoologist."

"I guess I don't have to ask if she likes animals. Married?"

"Her husband is a detective with the police department in Little Paris on Icarus. My little sister, Julia, is studying archaeology. Her husband is also an archaeologist." Falcon turned to look at Newman. "How about you? You told me you were born on Sheffield's Planet. No horses there, I assume, since you've never seen a horse before. Not too many other animals, either. Where does your love for animals come from?"

"That's easy to answer. The first time I saw a herd of wild horses running free, they stole my heart, and the first time I sat on one, I was hooked. Aurora is a paradise for animal lovers. There are so many beautiful animals here." Newman smiled. "Even dogs."

They rode on in silence. Newman's remark took him back to his youth. Rocky had not been a purebred. His ancestry was a mystery. Not a large dog, but he held his ground and protected Falcon when they were attacked by one of the Kluugers, a large cat-like predator roaming the forests and mountains in certain areas on Icarus. Rocky gave his life that day, but not before ripping out the large cat's throat. He lived for a couple more days, but his injuries had been too extensive. For a ten-year-old boy to lose his best friend is a devastating experience. It took Falcon a long time to get over Rocky. His father was going to get him another dog, but Falcon declined. He knew nothing could ever replace Rocky.

Sighing, Falcon brought his mind back to the present. He had never been one to lose himself in sad memories. It did no good, anyway. They were memories, that's all.

There was a forest ahead and the road would lead them right

into it. Somehow, being inside a forest made him always a little weary, especially on an unknown planet. Anything can hide in low-growing shrubbery, the branches of trees, or behind their large trunks.

As they entered the forest, the road seemed a bit narrower but still wide enough for Falcon and Newman to ride side-by-side. Alita rode behind them, the reigns of the packhorse tied to her saddle horn. The canopy above them kept the rays of the alien sun from illuminating the road. It would be dark inside much sooner than in the open.

They took a break around noon to let the horses rest for a while before moving on. It was close to sundown when the road suddenly widened, and they came upon a fairly large clearing. A narrow brook cut through the clearing and there was a small pool on the other side. The bright light illuminating the clearing revealed a group of travelers sitting around a small fire. The aroma of roasting meat drifted across the clearing.

Falcon knew they had come across a tribe of natives. He counted eight of them.

They appeared to be humanoids. At first, Falcon thought they were wearing furs, but upon closer inspection, he realized they were naked. What he had mistaken for clothing was in reality thick, red-brown hair covering the upper half of their body. When they turned their heads to look at what must seem like intruders in their resting spot, he saw somewhat brutish faces with thick eyebrows, a flat nose, and thick lips.

He had seen similar humanoids on other planets. Most of them looked like the apes that still existed in zoos on Earth. So did these, but their lower body, starting just below their chest, was completely bare of any hair, except for their calves and top of their feet. Their blue eyes protruded from under the ridge of their forehead. Their ears were long and thin, almost like the ears of a donkey.

The white skin of their hairless faces and lower bodies had the appearance of smooth leather.

"Relax," Newman told him in a low voice. "They look shy and harmless, but I never take things like that for granted. Aurora's indigenous people are gatherers and hunters. They do have weapons. As primitive as their weapons are, they can kill you as easily as a rifle or laser."

"I'll talk to them," Alita said behind them.

"You speak their language?" Newman turned around to look at her.

"No, I don't speak their language, but I can talk to them with my mind."

"Oh, I forgot that you can read minds."

"Which I am not in the habit of doing," she assured him. "However, in this case, it will be warranted." She slid from her horse and slowly walked toward the group of natives, her arms and hands open to let them know she wasn't carrying any weapons.

They watched her coming closer. None of them stood up or made any threatening moves. She stood for a moment beside them, and then she squatted down.

The humans, of course, didn't hear anything, but it was obvious she was talking to them in the silent language of the mind.

One of them moved and touched her forehead with his right hand, gently and carefully. She did the same thing to him. Suddenly, all eight of the natives made grunting sounds, touching their foreheads and then each one of them reached out with a long arm and gingerly put a finger against her forehead. She laughed softly when one of them pulled back his arm as if he had been given an electric shock. Then all of them emitted short, barking sounds, exposing their teeth.

"I think they are laughing," Newman speculated.

"I hope so." Falcon was more cautious about making assumptions. He had been watching carefully, his hand on his laser.

A couple of the natives rose to their feet and turned toward Falcon and Newman. Falcon noted that they wore small loincloths to cover their genitals. Their teeth gleamed white between their wide, dark lips. They waved, indicating to them to come closer.

"They are inviting you to share their food with them," Alita told them.

Both men jumped from their horses and followed the invitation, still a little wary. The natives made room for them around the fire. Falcon looked at the roasting small body of an animal pierced by a stick that rested on two forked branches pushed into the ground. The meat looked charred, and Falcon hoped it would at least be edible.

He studied the eight natives, trying not to make it too obvious. Three of them were females. Their white breasts were sticking out from their hairy chests. He noted the long nipples. It was clear these three were mature females. Then he noticed the small breasts on one of the others. If it hadn't been for their white skin, they would not have been visible inside the dark thick hair on her chest. Her nipples were short and thick. Clearly an immature female. She saw him looking and smiled. There was no mistaking that. He hoped she didn't mistake his interest in her as something sexual. One never knew the customs of indigenous races. He didn't smile back at her, just in case, just bowed his head. Of course, that could be interpreted as something else, also.

He also noticed that the females had long hair, whereas the males had a thick crown of red hair on top of their head.

His gaze moved to the male sitting beside the immature female. Pointing at his chest, he said, "Falcon," hoping the meaning would be understood. He was encouraged when the native said in a more or less grunting voice, "Arrlas," touching his own chest.

Falcon pointed at Newman. "Newman."

Arrlas smiled, looked at Newman and again touched his own chest and said, "Arrlas." Pointing at Falcon, he uttered, "Falcon". Then pointing at Newman, he said, "Newman."

It was clear to Falcon that these people might look primitive, but they possessed an intelligence that shouldn't be compared to that of apes. They should not be classified as savages because of their appearance and way of life. A few species he had met on other missions walked around naked. The Anorians did, and they had space travel when humans still killed each other with clubs and jawbones from large animals.

Arrlas reached out and sliced a small chunk of slightly charred meat with a flat shard of stone from the carcass sizzling over the fire. He offered it to Falcon, grunting as he did so. Falcon took it from him and blew on it because it was hot. Then he bit off a tiny piece. It was tough and tasted somewhat gamy and charred, but he chewed and then swallowed it down. "Thank you," he said and gave Arrlas a nod. He touched his belly and smiled, nodding again.

Arrlas grunted and smiled back. Then he helped himself to a piece of meat. He cut off more pieces and handed them to the others. He also offered a piece to Alita. She took it with a grateful nod.

"He must be the chief," Falcon said to Alita.

"He is. It seems he is in charge of the food," she murmured. "A few spices might do wonders to this meat," she said around the piece she was chewing.

"Nobody can argue with that," Newman agreed.

Falcon took another bite from his piece. *It is a good thing I have strong teeth, otherwise, I may have to swallow the whole damn thing without chewing it.* Memories of the rodents he ate on Perseus popped into his mind. He had almost forgotten about that.

Alita chuckled softly and looked at him with a smile. It was obvious, she had picked up his thoughts.

Unfortunately, he had to accept another slice Arrlas offered him. It wasn't charred but not thoroughly done, either. Somehow, it didn't seem as tough, though. Probably because it wasn't dried out from the hot flames. He hoped the meat didn't have any parasites that would make him sick. Raw meat was not something he enjoyed.

When Arrlas sliced off another piece and held it toward him, he put his hands together and shook his head. "Thank you, but my belly is full. It was delicious." Then he said to Alita, "Please, explain that to him."

She snickered and turned to the native. Arrlas emitted a few grunts, and then he put his hands together, imitating Falcon, and inclined his head, exposing his teeth in a smile.

"He thanks you and all of us for sharing food with him. He feels honored. Not all of the intruders to his world are accepting his people when they meet," she told Falcon. "He also says that lately a few of his people have been abducted by new strangers to this world. Abducted and never seen again."

"Is it possible he is talking about the Osirians?" Falcon wondered.

She shook her head. "I can't get a clear picture from him. It is possible."

"I hate to break up this party, but I think we should set up our tents while we still can see a little," Newman suggested. "The sun has disappeared, and it will be even darker once it has sunk beneath the horizon."

"I agree." Falcon turned to Alita. "Tell them we will spend the night here. Ask them if they object."

After Alita had informed the natives, they grunted and nodded.

"They have no objections," she told Falcon and Newman.

All three of them got up and walked back to their horses.

"We should water the horses," Newman suggested.

Once the animals had been taken care of, they removed their

saddles and unloaded everything from the packhorse. They put on their headlamps and then they set up their tents.

Alita's tent had more spare room, so they put all their stuff into her tent, to keep it dry in case of rain, but that wasn't the only reason. Even though the natives had been friendly and peaceful, Falcon did not trust them enough to leave their belongings outside.

"We don't know anything about them," he said. "Remember the old saying: Caution costs nothing, regret everything."

Newman agreed. "This is not my first encounter with indigenous people on this planet, but my knowledge about them is not extensive. Actually, I know nothing about this particular group. There are stories about bands of natives coming at night to human settlements and stealing items out of storage sheds and anything they can find without being seen. I don't know if those stories are true or just rumors, or even fabrications. It is best to eliminate temptation."

The tents were just that—plain tents. They didn't have any way to create heat or cool air. Falcon had been on planets with frigid temperatures where a heated tent was essential for survival. The climate on Aurora was moderate in these parts and regular tents were just fine. They had sleeping bags and blankets to cover their bodies should the temperature drop to uncomfortable levels during the night. However, this was still summer, and the nights didn't cool down much, if at all.

"I hope they don't invite us for breakfast," he said to Newman as both of them lay inside their sleeping bags.

Newman chuckled. "Whatever it was we ate, it wasn't so bad. I've eaten worse."

"So have I, but that doesn't mean I want to repeat it." He turned onto his side and closed his eyes. "It's been a while since I slept in a tent and in a sleeping bag," he mused. "Another thing I don't necessarily want to make a habit of. Hope I can sleep."

"I thought you military types are tough and used to living in an austere environment." Newman laughed. "In fact, you make a habit of doing it. It is part of your training."

"Rumors, Newman. Rumors. It's nothing but propaganda." Falcon turned to his other side, trying to get comfortable. Good thing at least the floor of the tent was inflated to avoid sleeping on a hard ground. "Good night, Newman. Pleasant dreams."

[7]

HE DIDN'T KNOW HOW LONG HE HAD SLEPT. HE WOKE UP WITH THE urge to go outside and get some fresh air. The air felt sticky inside the tent. Crawling out of the opening, he took a few deep breaths, but it wasn't cool, fresh air he inhaled. The air was humid and warm. When he looked into the sky, he saw two moons, both of them full. In their eerie light he could see the natives huddled together not far away. The campfire was still alive, flaring up once-in-awhile when a small gust of wind blew against the glowing embers.

Walking away from the campground, he moved deeper into the surrounding forest to relieve himself. The ground was cool on the naked soles of his feet. When he returned, he thought he saw movement on the other side of the clearing.

Then he saw her. One of the females.

She stood in the pool, her face upturned to the sky. When she slowly turned around, he saw it was the young female. Her small breasts protruded further from her chest and appeared larger because of the wet hair plastered against her skin.

Then she saw him standing there, watching her.

She came out of the pool and walked toward him. Her hairless lower body gleamed pale in the light of the two moons. He noted the dark mound of her sex-organ below her smooth belly. Her face was in the shadow hidden behind her long hair that had fallen across her face. When she reached him, she put one hand on his chest, while her other hand moved down his body, touching his crotch. She searched with her hand until she found him.

Her fingers closed and his body reacted to her nearness and her touch. She smiled, emitting a soft grunt when she felt his hardening member. Boldly, she reached into the top of his pants and let her hand slide down his naked belly until she touched his now hard penis. She sheathed him with her soft hand and gently milked him, causing him to let out an involuntary groan.

Releasing him, she removed her hand, clutched his arm and pulled him toward the trees, seeking a more sheltered spot. He didn't fight her, just let her guide him away from camp, like a buck in heat. When they were far enough, she fell to her knees and pushed up her rump, presenting her naked white buttocks in an invitation that could not be misinterpreted. The puffy lips of her vagina were clearly visible below her buttocks.

With frantic haste, he removed his pants. Then he cupped her small body, put his hand between her legs and gently stroked her. She pushed back against him, letting out a soft whimper. When his engorged penis touched the entrance to her vagina, he found her ready to receive him. She gasped loudly as he slid with ease into the soft interior of her sex-organ. He reached under her and cupped her small breasts. They were firm and solid but felt soft and pliable in his hands.

How long he moved behind her, he didn't know. He lost all sense of time. When his release finally came, her sheath constricted tightly, keeping him prisoner inside her. Her body shook violently, and she emitted a series of whimpering soft cries. When she was done, she released him and collapsed. Breathing harshly, he fell on top of her, trying to catch his breath. They lay unmoving like that for a while, her buttocks like soft pillows in his groin, until she moved under him. He rolled to one side of her and watched her rising up. Bending over him, she pressed her lips against his forehead and gently touched his cheek with one hand. Then she rushed away on silent feet.

He lay there and stared at one of the moons that was still visible through the canopy of the trees. The moons had moved a considerable distance from their position in the sky.

What did just happen? He had sex with an alien female of an undetermined age. How old was she in human terms? Judging by her small breasts, she was probably still an immature female, but there had been no resistance when he entered her tight sex-organ, indicating she had not been a virgin. She had seduced him with such ease, knowing exactly how to turn him on; it was clear it wasn't the first time for her. Human morality did not come into play here.

He sat up and slipped into his pants. Then he walked slowly back to the clearing on weak legs. Silently, he crawled into the tent and lay down, on top of the sleeping bag. The air was still warm and sticky inside the tent. He wished they had one of those modern tents with climate control.

Newman lay unmoving, his soft snoring the only clue he was still alive.

He didn't go back to sleep. He lay there, puzzled at how easily he had let himself be lured into having sex with an alien female without resisting even just a little. How was that possible?

He must have dozed off after all, because the next thing he became aware of was Newman getting up and crawling out of the tent, murmuring something about following the call of nature. There was no sense in staying in the tent any longer. Getting up, he also crawled outside. The air was crisp, a welcome change from the night.

Looking around, he saw the natives already moving around. One of the males, he wasn't sure if it was Arrlas, left the group and came toward him, making him wonder if he knew of the incidence with the young female, who might possibly be his daughter. If that was the case, Falcon hoped he had not broken some taboo. However, his fears were put to rest when the native pointed at his chest and said, "Arrlas." Showing his teeth in a smile, he pointed a finger at Falcon and said, "Falcon."

"Yes." Falcon returned the smile. "Arrlas and Falcon."

Arrlas made a gesture with his hand, indicating the other members of his group, and then he pointed east, moving his hand up and down like a slithering snake or a wave in a body of water. Falcon knew the ocean lay in an easterly direction and figured Arrlas meant to tell him they were traveling toward the ocean.

Nodding to let Arrlas know he understood, he touched his chest and then pointed north.

Arrlas reached out and gripped Falcon's lower right arm. Falcon instinctively did the same to Arrlas. It was a universal gesture of saying farewell.

"I wish you a safe journey," Falcon said, even though he knew he wouldn't be understood. Perhaps his tone of voice conveyed the meaning of his words. Primitive people could read more into gestures and voices than more evolved individuals. Arrlas looked into Falcon's eyes and spoke a few words in his language before releasing his grip on Falcon's arm and walking back to his people.

The group of natives began entering the forest. They had bags made from animal skins hanging on straps from their shoulders. The females carried spears and the males held short bows in their hands. They also had quivers filled with arrows slung across their backs. Before they all disappeared into the trees, one of them turned to look back. It was the young female. Her eyes focused momentarily on Falcon. He could see the flicker of a smile on her wide lips. Then she turned and joined the others.

"It seems you made a new friend."

Falcon turned around to see Alita standing not far behind him. "You mean the young female?"

"No. I mean Arrlas."

"It seems so. He'll probably forget about me before the day ends." *Arrlas may not be so friendly if he knew I fucked the youngest female in his group last night, possibly his daughter.* He avoided looking at Alita and gazed at the pond instead, eliminating any possibility she may pick up his thoughts. He wasn't quite sure if he could believe her when she told him she didn't snoop around in other people's mind without their permission. He had no way of being certain. "I guess we should pack up and get going also."

"Good idea," Alita agreed. "However, before we go, I may just take a short dip into that pool. The water looks inviting. We don't know when we'll get the opportunity again."

"I think I'll join you." It was Newman who came out of the forest.

Falcon hadn't seen him when he came out of the tent. "Where have you been?"

Newman gave him a somewhat sheepish look. "I think the meat our new friends shared with us last night doesn't agree with my stomach. I feel a bit queasy this morning. And my legs seem kind of weak."

"Sorry to hear that. We have pills for that. The queasy stomach, I mean." Falcon grinned. "I've had my share of dubious appearing and tasting food on my missions. I've learned the bitter way." He looked at Alita. "I guess it won't hurt to splash some water on our bodies. After that, I'll have breakfast, though."

"Sounds like a good plan," Alita agreed. She turned to Newman. "That water may help you." With a look at Falcon, she asked, "Didn't you sleep well? You look tired."

"I had a bit of a restless night," he admitted. "My stomach is okay, but my legs are also somewhat rubbery. Perhaps it was the meat, like Newman said." He knew it wasn't, but he had a suspicion about what it could be. Not could be, most likely was. That young female had sucked his energy right out of him. Too much of a good thing, even though it had been pure pleasure.

"Then that fresh water will wake you up. Come on. Let's do it." With that she began to take off her clothes. Completely nude, she sprinted toward the pond and jumped into it.

Falcon heard Newman moaning beside him and then blurting out, "Perfection."

Falcon knew what he meant. Alita's body was flawless. Narrow hips and perfectly formed plump buttocks. Her breasts were round and full. "It isn't her real body. Remember, she is a shapeshifter, not human. She could have turned herself into an ugly, old hag."

Newman sighed. "I know, but it is hard to imagine her looking like anything else but this lovely picture of a woman."

"I know what you're saying. I've only known her since this assignment started. The way she looks is the only version I know of her. This is Alita. Should she change her body she'd be a stranger to me." He watched her washing herself in the pond and he had to admit Newman was right. She was like a beautiful vision out of a dream. Not only was she gorgeous but she was also extremely sensuous. Shaking his head, he had to remind himself that she wasn't real.

"I think I need to immerse myself in cold water to cool down." Newman chuckled. "It's been quite a while since I saw a naked woman. She'll be in my dreams from now on, even though she isn't human." With that he undressed and ran toward the pond, making a splash as he jumped in.

With a shrug, Falcon slowly shed his clothes. When he immersed himself to his neck in the cool water, his thoughts wandered to the young native female and what happened the previous night. Her body had been real, not as perfect and beautiful as Alita's, not even sensuous, and yet, something about her had turned him on immensely. He still could not come to grips with that. Even thinking of her naked body, the look of her round white buttocks and her young sex-organ beckoning, caused a gentle throbbing in his loins.

This was not normal behavior for him. Damn it! He was a soldier, trained to keep his emotions under control, even his bodily desires. There had to be more to it than just seeing her naked body in the pale light of the alien moons in the middle of the night.

He watched Newman splash Alita and heard him laughing, like a teenage boy in the presence of a teenage girl. He had to smile. Even a man like Newman was not immune to the charms of a beautiful woman, human or not. It seems a man's rational thinking went out of the window in the presence of a beautiful female.

He chuckled grimly. Not only Newman's it seemed.

"Hey, Falcon, don't just stand there like a lost little bird," he heard Newman calling. "The water is wonderful once your body adjusts. Splash around a little. I feel better already."

Falcon gave him a crooked grin. "Remember, I'm a man who spends much of his time inside the confines of a military space-ship. Pools of water are not standard equipment in those ships, unlike in pleasure cruisers. Large bodies of water are not something my body craves for. Besides, water is a precious commodity on a spaceship. I almost feel guilty."

"Excuses, excuses. This is your opportunity to enjoy that luxury without feeling guilty. If you're scared of drowning, don't worry. This pool is not very deep."

"You are right." Falcon sighed and ducked under the water. He couldn't swim, but he wasn't worried about drowning. He had to admit, the cool water seemed to make him feel better.

———

THEY ATE HOME-BAKED BREAD AND COLD, HARD-BOILED EGGS FOR breakfast. Irida had wrapped everything in cloth to keep things fresh. She had even supplied them with narrow-necked clay containers filled with juice. They still had food for lunch and two suppers. After that, they had to be content with smoked bacon and a basket full of biscuits. Of course, there were always the dry rations they carried in their packs.

"What do you know about the natives?" Falcon gave Newman an inquiring look.

"Not much, actually. In fact, nothing. Like I said before, I've never ran across this particular kind. The only ones I am familiar with are the Moyans. They have nothing in common with our new friends. The Moyans are much closer to us humans in appearance. Their brown skin is smooth like ours. The only hair they have is on the head and on their bushy tail. They are also quite primitive. Some live in small communities as family units. Some are nomads. All are hunters and gatherers. The ones living in communities also practice simple farming by growing certain foods. They keep animals and they live in huts made from branches and reeds, depending on where they live."

"Sounds like many primitive societies I came across on the planets I was on. Some were humanoids and others were not, but most of them lived as family units, either in small groups or in larger communities. One more question: How peaceful are these Moyans?"

Newman shrugged. "They are peaceful, but they will defend themselves if attacked."

"What kind of weapons do they have?"

"They are not stone-age people, even though they utilize stones in their weapons. They have bows and arrows, which they use expertly to bring down their quarry. They also use spears. I'm not really an expert when it comes to the Moyans. All my information is second-hand."

"Perhaps we'll get a chance to meet them." He turned to Alita. "Let me ask you something. When you communicated with these natives, did you get a glimpse into their lives? Possibly learn something about them?"

"Not really. Their minds seemed closed. I did detect some

almost sinister darkness below their consciousness, but nothing concrete. I had no problem communicating with them, though." Her chuckle was almost apologetic. "I value the privacy of others and I don't force myself on them."

"But you could if you wanted to. Am I right?" Falcon was more than curious. He needed to know as much about her as possible. It wasn't that he didn't trust her, but she was from an alien species, and not human. It was in his nature to be cautious at all times.

She nodded. "I could."

"If you did, wouldn't you reveal your ability to read minds?"

She hesitated before she answered. "Possibly."

"In other words, it isn't only out of respect for keeping the thoughts of other beings private but also for your own protection. That makes sense, but also limits the use of your capability." He stared at his hands for a moment, thinking about the implication of what she told him, and then he looked up. "Would I be able to sense it if you tried to read my mind?"

Her smile seemed forced. "Is there a reason for this interrogation?"

"It isn't an interrogation, more a quest to understand you and the limits of your talent." It wasn't a total lie.

"I see. To answer your question: A sensitive would be aware of my mind-touch, but you probably won't be. Your mind is too busy analyzing the information your senses transmit to your consciousness, you'd never notice my probe."

"That makes me feel so much better knowing somebody with your ability could snoop around in my mind without my knowledge. Is there any way I can protect myself?"

"If you know how to create a mind shield you can, or if you wear an electronic shield around your head, that'll work, but without that you are fair game." She laughed when she saw his expression. "Don't worry. I will leave your mind alone. What exciting stuff would I find in there anyway?"

He smirked. "Plenty, but you'll never find out, I hope."

Her eyes studied him with a thoughtful expression, but she didn't respond, instead she said, "I'd say we get going. Lounging around like this won't get us anywhere."

———

THEY WERE ON THEIR WAY SHORTLY. THE SKY CLOUDED OVER JUST before noon, but the expected rain didn't come. The wind blew from the north, cooling down the temperature a little. As long as they didn't get any rain, the road would be alright for travel, especially on horseback. Falcon was glad they didn't get a carriage to travel in, as Mirna Madison back at the Scouts headquarters had suggested. "Why not travel in comfort," she said with a little smile. "And you'll need only two horses instead of four. When it rains, you'll stay dry and comfy inside your carriage. Something to think about."

He did. Just for a short moment. It sounded tempting, but that cozy ride would end the moment it started to rain. Sure, they'd be dry inside, but that wouldn't be much comfort when the carriage was stuck in the mud. Besides, somebody had to control the horses. Whoever ended up sitting outside would be exposed to the weather.

They left the forest behind shortly after noon. The horses needed to be watered and when they came across a small lake, they stopped for a short break.

They were about to leave again when Falcon heard the sound of hoofs not far away. Looking ahead on the road they traveled, he saw two riders closing in fast. At first, he thought they were going to race by them, but they brought their horses to a halt when they reached them.

The two men were dressed in leather pants and leather jackets, the usual clothing cattle-herders wore. One of the men tipped his wide-brimmed hat and jumped from his horse. "Ho, travelers," he said, "where are you headed?"

"We are hoping this road leads us to Rowarra." It was Newman who answered his question.

The man chuckled. "You're in luck. If you stay on this road, you will indeed get to Rowarra. What's waiting for you in Rowarra?"

"A friend, I hope." Newman smiled. "I haven't visited him for quite some time. Hopefully, he hasn't moved, or worse, died."

"So, you have been to Rowarra? The people in Brettany are a little different from us. They are, how should I put it?" He hesitated with his answer.

"Religious?" Newman volunteered.

"More than that. Be careful. By the way, my name is Rolland. My brother's name is Herm." He pointed at the other man, plainly a younger version of him, and then he looked at Newman, obviously waiting for him to introduce himself. "What are your names?"

"I am Newman, my silent friend here is Falcon, and she is Alita."

"Your wife?"

Shaking his head, Newman said, "She is nobody's wife. We are just good friends. I notice the heavy rifles you have slung across your shoulders. Are you on a hunting trip?"

"We are. Hoping to get us a Shramp."

"They are vicious beasts," Newman said. "That's what I've heard. I've never seen one."

"Pray you never run across one without a reliable weapon. Their claws are as sharp as a pair of scissors. They can take your head off with one bite. Fortunately, they stay mostly in the forest. You'll be safe as long as you are keeping to the road. One more thing. There's a band of Arbeenians roaming around. Be careful and stay alert." He tipped his hat again. "Pleasure chatting with you, but we must go on. Not much daylight left for the hunt. The best time to hunt Shramp is just before the sun disappears."

They watched the two men take off, heading for the bush.

"Good luck," Falcon called after them, but he was sure they didn't hear him anymore. He turned to address Newman. "He said *sun*, is that what they call the Primary here?"

"Yes, they do."

"Good to know. Most planets I've visited call it something else."

It was late afternoon when they came across a small bluff beside a narrow river. It didn't seem deep, but the water was clear. It would provide water and the treetops were thick enough to protect them from the worst should the clouds decide the night would be a good time to start watering the ground below.

They began setting up their tents, when Alita said, "We're about to get visitors."

Looking east, Falcon saw a flock of giant birds emerging from the forest that grew alongside the mountain range between Saskona and Glasca, heading their way. He remembered Newman telling him the birds were called Ostras. Watching them coming closer, he saw riders on their backs. Falcon removed his rifle from its scabbard and held it casually in his hands. It never hurt to be cautious.

He counted nine riders. They brought their Ostras to a halt not far from them, spreading out as they did. Falcon noted that instead of wearing hats they had cloths wrapped around their heads. Wide-sleeved jackets covered their upper bodies, and their pant legs were puffy at the top but narrow at the ankles.

Leather belts circled their hips and the large pistols attached to them could not be missed. None of them acted hostile. Not yet anyway. Falcon kept his rifle pointing to the ground, but his finger near the trigger.

The riders were human, but then he noticed something else. All nine seemed to be women.

One of them moved forward. Even sitting on the big bird, she appeared tall. "You are traveling through our land," she said, her voice resonant and deeper than a normal woman's voice. "Who are you and what is your destination?" Her accent was thick and difficult to understand.

Before Falcon could answer, he heard Alita's voice, "Let me talk to her." He realized she had not spoken aloud. The voice had been inside his head. Startled, he turned his head to look at her.

She nodded to him but didn't say anything. Then she took a step toward the woman on the bird. "We are just simple travelers and on our way to Rowarra."

"Where are you from?"

"We come from Riwarda."

"What is your reason for traveling to Rowarra?"

"It is only a stopover. Our destination is the shrine of Mommet in Akloma." She made a sign in the air with her hands. "My companions and I are students of the Great Mommed."

Falcon had no idea what she was talking about. If she did, he wondered how she got her information.

The other woman tilted her head. "Why do you want to visit the shrine of Mommet? You are not one of us."

"We believe his teachings have great merit." Alita lifted a hand. "We don't want to become followers, but we are anxious to learn from him."

"Why?"

"We study the soil and the clouds, the water and the air, the light-giver, the night companions, and the stars. We study the creatures that live in this world and beyond. We want to know about the past and what may lie ahead. We are students thirsty for knowledge. That is why."

The woman thought this over for a moment, and then she said, "Did you say you are coming from Riwarda?"

"Yes, I did."

"Are these two males your mates?"

Alita laughed. "No, they are not my mates. I am an independent woman."

"Do you couple with them?"

"No."

The woman smiled for the first time. "You said you are thirsty for knowledge. Shouldn't you be curious what it feels like to have a male's organ enter your body?"

"I have experienced that with another male. I know what it feels like." Alita seemed to get impatient. "Why these questions? Have you ever coupled with a male? All I see is females in your group. Are there no males in your tribe?"

The woman's laugh was mocking. "Even though there are no males allowed in our tribe, we couple with males when we want to increase our numbers and when we feel the urge to do so." She pointed at Falcon. "I want him. He looks capable."

Alita looked at Falcon. "Don't accept. As tempting as it is, they cut the throats of the males after they've coupled with them and drink their blood." Her lips had not moved, but her voice had been loud and clear in his head. And urgent. Aloud, she said to the woman, "I cannot speak for him. It is his choice."

The woman's gaze was still on Falcon. Obviously, she waited for an answer from him.

"I am honored by your proposal," he told her. "But I have made a vow of abstinence and must therefore decline."

She seemed disappointed. Her gaze wandered to Newman. "How about you?"

"My faith does not allow me to engage that way with a woman. It would make me unclean." He put his hands together in front of him and made a little bow. "I wish for you that your quest for fulfillment ends with success."

She threw her head back and laughed. "It is not a quest I am on. It only occurred to me this moment that I haven't been with a male for quite some time. Had one of you accepted my request and given me pleasure, I may even have let you live. Are you sure you won't change your mind?"

Falcon shook his head, while Newman said, "I cannot."

"You heard them," Alita spoke up.

"Too bad. Tell me, what is your name?"

"I am Alita, and the males are called Falcon and Newman. What is yours?"

"My sisters call me Seldani." She laughed. "Seldani, the Ravenous."

"The Ravenous? I am afraid to ask what it means."

"You may get a chance to find out." Seldani made a loud clucking sound with her mouth.

Falcon had let down his guard, but somehow the feeling that something was wrong had not left him, sadly too late. So was Alita's silent warning. When all the Ostras took off like one unit, he reacted, but he was taken by surprise. Something settled around his shoulders and around his legs, and then he fell to the ground. He lay there flopping around like a fish that had been pulled out of the water onto land.

He couldn't move his arms or legs. He realized that a tight rope pinned his arms against his upper body and his legs were tangled up in another rope. Tanglers. He was familiar with those primitive weapons. Once caught in them, there was no way of getting out of one without somebody else's help.

Moving his head, he saw that Newman and Alita were suffering the same fate.

One of the women slid down from her steed and kicked him with her foot. Fortunately, she wore small boots made from soft leather and it didn't hurt too badly.

"What do you want from us?" He tried to get free, but the more he struggled the more he became entangled in the ropes.

The woman laughed and when she spoke, he recognized Seldani, the leader. "What do you think?"

"There are many ways to get a man to couple with a woman willingly. Capturing and forcing a man is not the way to get much pleasure from such intimacy," he told her.

She bent down and looked into his eyes. "We have our own ways to make you comply with our wishes." She smiled. "Your desire for any of us will drive you out of your mind. Once your rod enters me, you will be under my spell, and you will not be able to stop before you are so exhausted and weak your heart will burst inside your chest."

Rising, she gave a few commands to the others. Before Falcon realized what was happening, he was lying across the back of one of the horses, strapped down securely without any hope of wiggling free.

Alita and Newman suffered the same fate.

When they started moving, Falcon could see his now useless rifle lying on the ground. The women didn't bother taking anything. They even left the packhorse and the tents.

[8]

It was still light when they entered the forest, but by the time they arrived at the camp of their captors, it was quite dark. Falcon assumed it was a camp because he saw only tents, no permanent dwellings. There were more females there. Some sat around small fire pits while others were busy with chores.

Falcon and his companions were dumped unceremoniously onto the ground and left lying unattended under one of the tall trees.

"Everybody alright?" Falcon craned his neck to get a glimpse of Alita and Newman.

"I'm fine," Newman answered. "Actually, I am not fine. I am spitting mad to have been so stupid to let them capture me. By the way, this is the band of Arbeenians the two brothers warned us about. These women use their beauty to ensnare unsuspecting men, have sex with them and then they kill them."

"Alita warned me already about that barbaric practice. I should have been more alert. Somehow my mind seems a bit foggy today," Falcon admitted.

"Mine too. I don't even remember that Alita warned us."

"I only warned Falcon," Alita said.

"That conversation you had with Seldani. How did you know all that stuff?" Falcon wondered.

"Do you have to ask?" Alita said aloud, but added silently, "It is best if Newman doesn't know."

Falcon could feel a tingling in his arms as they were going to sleep. The rope wrapped around his chest was so tight, it made breathing difficult, and he could barely move his arms to get some circulation back into his hands at least. He felt like a mummy wrapped in strips of cloth. When his ears picked up the crunching of leaves, he knew someone was coming. He craned his neck to see who it was.

It was a young girl, carrying a torch. She stuck the torch into the ground, knelt down and brought her face close to his. Her long hair covered her face partially, but he could still see that she was quite pretty. "Hello," she said with a smile. "Are you a man?"

"I was, the last time I looked." Falcon couldn't help but chuckle, even though he didn't feel cheerful. "Are you a girl?"

"Of course I am." She brushed a strand of hair out of her face. "I guess it is true. Men are stupid."

"You can say that again." Falcon grimaced. "I wouldn't be lying here feeling like a caterpillar inside its cocoon if it weren't so."

"The mothers say men are only good for one thing."

He was reluctant to ask but did it anyway, curious to hear the answer. "And what would that be, little girl?"

"I'm not a little girl anymore." She pulled her hair back with both hands and bunched it together behind her head. "Look at me. Is this the face of a little girl? Soon I'll be old enough to find out how it feels to have a baby made by a man." She giggled. "Wouldn't it be funny if it were tonight? With you?"

"That would be really funny. What's your name?"

"I don't have a real name yet. I'll get my name when I've been with a man."

"What do they call you in the meantime?"

"Mostly 'Little Flower'." She pulled her fine brows together. "Actually, they call most of the other girls 'Little Flower.'"

Falcon grinned. "And here I assumed women were smarter than men. That doesn't sound very smart to me. Listen, can you do me a favor and loosen these ropes? I can barely breathe because they are so tight."

"I can't do that. I'm not even supposed to be here talking to you." She giggled again. "The mothers say I am too curious for my own good." She pulled the stake with the torch on top out of the ground and moved over to Alita. "You are not a man." She sounded confused.

"That's right," Alita chuckled. "I guess that makes me a woman. Why is that so strange?"

"Are you a prisoner of these two men?"

"No. I am a free woman. These two men are my friends."

"Are you a mother?"

Alita laughed. "No. Why do you ask?"

The girl scowled. "I am confused. You are a woman but not a mother. You are friends with two men. How is that possible?"

"Well, Little Flower, that's how the world outside your tribe lives. Men and women live together in peace." She let out a sigh. "Not always, unfortunately. There are places where females are kept as slaves. In other societies, females keep males as slaves. This universe is not peaceful."

"What do you mean by universe?"

"The points of lights you see in the sky at night. They are called stars. There are millions of them. They are like the bright orb that brings light and warmth to your world during the day. Many of those stars have worlds like this one. Some of them are populated with people like you and me and on some live intelligent beings that may look strange, even scary to you. Although all of them may look different from each other, deep down they are all the same. They love, they hate, and they have dreams."

"I'm afraid I don't understand anything you are telling me. How can anyone live on those tiny lights?"

Alita chuckled softly. "Those twinkling lights are far away from your world, that's why they appear so tiny, but in reality, some of those lights are much larger than the orb that warms this world. Some of the worlds, we call them planets, that circle those orbs, are also much larger than yours."

"I don't know if I can believe your story. How do you know all of this?"

After a long pause, Alita sighed and said, "Because I am from one of those worlds. In fact, the ancestors of your tribe came to this world in a big ship that traveled among the stars. The world they came from, is very far away from here."

"Are you certain it was smart to tell her that?" Falcon wondered.

"Smart or not, I hope it puts a tiny seed into her mind that makes her question the world around her. She seems inquisitive and intelligent. Sometimes, you have to rattle a society from the inside to cause a change."

"I feel confused, and my head is spinning," the girl said. "The mothers don't teach us those things. We learn about plants and animals, which ones are edible, which ones are poisonous and which ones are medicine. They teach us how to make fires and build shelters, things like that, but nothing about other worlds." She ran her hand across her face. "I have to go." Then she grabbed the torch and ran away.

"I wonder what she is going to tell them," Newman said. "It is plain whatever you told her, Alita, went over her head. This is a primitive tribe of man-haters. They know nothing about their ancestry. Those twinkling lights in the night sky are just that... lights."

"I know, but it is amazing how one new piece of knowledge can change a world, or how a tiny spark can cause a fire to grow so large it consumes a whole forest."

Falcon heard voices and craned his head to look toward the camp. He saw a torch coming closer. It was one of the women with the girl in tow. She stopped in front of Alita. "What are you trying to do by filling this innocent girl's head with that nonsense you've been sprouting?"

"It wasn't nonsense. It was reality, something you and your sisters are either purposefully ignoring or actually are ignorant of."

"You claim to come from one of those worlds?" The woman pointed one finger into the sky.

"Not claim. It is the truth. Where we come from, males and females live together as family units. They have children and raise them together. They have sex whenever they want to, and they certainly don't murder the males they have sex with." Alita spoke sharply, almost angrily.

"How do you know we kill males after copulation has taken place?"

"It is known. You are not the only ones living on this world. There are many others, different from you. They don't condone such practice."

Falcon let out a breath of relief. At least she hadn't told the woman about her ability to read minds. He didn't think a confession like that would go over well in a primitive society, especially on this planet, where the people believed in the supernatural, in ghosts, and witches.

"We don't kill males, at least not as a rule." The woman's voice challenged Alita.

"But you admit you do?"

The woman hesitated before answering. "It has happened. When we capture a male for the purpose of breeding, he is not always willing to perform. To make him pliable, we give him a brew we make from certain plants to drink. It gives a male stamina and endurance. Sometimes, they collapse and just die."

"Their heart gives out," Alita commented.

"You see, we don't kill them on purpose. They just happen to die."

"What about male children that are born from these unions? What happens to them?"

Again, the hesitation. "We cannot raise them. Our tribe is made up of females only."

"What happens to them?" Alita insisted.

"They are sacrificed in the Holy Flames to honor the Great Mommet. They don't suffer. Their death is quick. It is a great honor, and their spirit joins the Great Mommet in his kingdom."

"That is a barbaric practice," Newman said. "These are innocent children. It makes me sick to listen to that. Do you ever 'honor' adult males by throwing them into the fire?"

"Not on a regular basis."

"But you have done it?" Newman's voice trembled as he said that.

"I admit it is true. It only happens when we celebrate the day of the Great Mommet's arrival on our world. It is done in a humane way. The males are not aware of it."

"Because you drug them, damn it," Newman swore. "It is murder. Plain murder."

"We are not monsters," the woman defended herself. "We treat them well. We let them couple with the youngest and most beautiful females. After that they are served a delicious meal, bathed, rubbed with oils, and decorated with flowers. They are served the sweetest juices, which are laced with the starflower-root extract. It relaxes their body and lets their spirit become one with the spirit of the clouds. They don't feel any pain. They are happy."

A strange suspicion rose in Falcon. "When do you celebrate this special day?"

"Tomorrow night."

"I don't think I have to ask what your plans are for us." Falcon cursed under his breath. They had to do something, but he felt helpless. He could barely feel his hands and arms, and his chest was aching. So much for being augmented. They never counted on him being trussed like a chunk of meat ready to be roasted over an open fire. That thought didn't make him feel any better.

He became aware of the sudden silence near them and realized the woman had left.

"It doesn't look good," Newman commented. "I wish we could do something."

Finding Newman's remark amusing, Falcon chuckled and said, "So do I, but if they don't loosen my bonds soon, they might as well amputate my arms and legs. I don't know if I still have any, because all feeling in them is gone."

He didn't know how much time passed, but again he could hear voices coming closer.

"This one," a woman's voice said.

He felt many hands lifting him off the ground and then he was carried away toward the area that was lit by a number of torches stuck into the soil. There was a large fire burning, but his fear was unfounded. They dropped him beside the trunk of a thick tree. Looking up, he didn't see any branches, but at the top of the trunk they had carved out a face. It was crude, but it was clearly the representation of a male face.

He didn't have to wait long for anything to happen. Two burly women approached him, grabbed the rope that bound him, and stood him up. He would have collapsed had they not held him.

"He isn't going anywhere," one of the women laughed. "I think it is safe to unwrap him."

The other woman chuckled, produced a knife, and cut the rope. They untangled the rope and used it to tie Falcon against the pole with his hands tied together behind the pole. He wished they had left him lying on the ground. Had they not wrapped the rope around his legs and around the pole, he would not have been able to stand straight.

The two women checked everything over and made sure he was securely tied against the pole. Then they left.

His hands and arms began to tingle as the blood rushed back into them. The same thing happened to his legs. Focusing on the pain, he managed to suppress most of it.

Another woman came. She carried a small flask which she lifted to his lips. "We don't want you to die of thirst," she said with a little smile, letting him drink from the flask. The liquid tasted tarty, but it was welcomed by his parched throat.

After that, a few young girls circled the pole, poked him with their fingers, and giggled. One bold one grabbed his testicles and squeezed. "That hurts," he told her. She giggled and let go.

Then they danced around the pole, singing a strange melody. When an adult woman told them to stop their dancing, they left laughing, but only after each one poked him again.

He tried to get his hands free, but he still felt weak and gave up struggling, wondering what made him so weak. As he watched the dancing flames of the fire, his mind drifted into some kind of dream world. The flames became naked women writhing in front of him, beckoning him to join them in their dance. "I can't," he cried out. "I am bound to this dead tree."

They laughed and danced and touched him with their ghostly hands. Even though their hands were tendrils of fire, they didn't burn.

"Come," the dancing wraiths teased him, touching his body and his mind. "Come, dance with us."

He didn't know how much time had passed. The dancers began to fade as the fire burned down. Finally, only dark embers remained, glowing and blinking like the eyes of a dozen ghouls.

The dancers were gone, but their shadows still danced in his mind. When something touched his hands, he became aware. He felt a tugging on the rope that held his hands together, and then suddenly they were free. The rope that had kept him bound against the tree trunk loosened and fell away. He was free, but his legs were still weak, and he began to slide toward the ground.

As he lay there, strong arms wrapped themselves around his

body and lifted him off the ground. He was lying on something soft that began to move away from the glowing embers, carrying him toward the forest.

The movement stopped and he heard a familiar voice. "What is wrong with him?"

"They drugged him," a woman said. He knew that voice also, he just couldn't put a name to it.

The arms that held him let go of him. He rolled from the flat surface that had brought him and sat up. "Take it easy," a man's voice said. He recognized it now. It was Newman.

He saw a flat object lying on the ground. It moved, changed, became round. When it rose he saw it was a woman. She was naked.

"Here, chew on this," the woman said and pushed something between his lips. It tasted sweet. Not unpleasant.

"What are you giving him?" It was Newman asking the question.

"Leaves from a plant they call Crimson Death. They will neutralize the drug in his body."

"How do you know that? Who told you about this plant?"

"Leave it be, Newman. You've learned too much already. I'd better get dressed."

Newman shook Falcon. "Better recover fast. We need to get going before any of them find out you're gone. Can you get up?"

Falcon's mind seemed to clear fairly quickly. Carefully, he stood up, swayed a little but managed to keep his balance. "I'll be fine," he assured Newman, his voice still weak. Looking around for Alita, he saw her nearby getting dressed. He knew what she had done.

"We'll have to get the horses," Newman said, looking at Falcon. "Are you up to it?"

Falcon nodded. "I am." His mind was clearing fast now. He looked back at the camp. Everything was quiet. He could see the tree trunk with the carved face at the top, the one he'd been tied to. The fire in front of it was only glowing embers now. A thought popped into his mind. "Didn't they have anyone guarding the camp?"

"I took care of them," Alita told him. "Now, let's get going."

They found their horses tied to a couple of trees not far away. They would have to ride bareback. The saddles were back at the camp.

Falcon was still too weak to get onto the horse. "I need some help," he said, a little sheepishly. He was supposed to be stronger and faster than any normal man, but here he was asking a normal man for help.

Newman folded his hands to make a swing. "Here, step into it. I hope you can do that."

Falcon managed to get onto the back of the horse but just barely. He watched with mixed feelings as Newman swung himself onto the horse.

Alita had already mounted hers. They rode away in silence, hoping they wouldn't be discovered before they got far enough away.

[9]

By the time they reached their camp, Falcon's mind had cleared, but when he slid from his horse, his legs were still weak. By the light of the satellite, they saw that the camp was undisturbed. Their saddles still lay beside the half-erected tents. Even Falcon's rifle still lay where he had dropped it. The pack horse neighed when it sensed the other horses nearby.

"I think we should not camp here," Alita said. "I don't think they will follow us here during the night, but they might at early dawn. I'd like to be far away before morning."

Falcon and Newman both agreed.

They packed up everything as quickly as possible, loaded the stuff on the pack horse and the saddles onto the ones they rode, and left.

Riding in silence, Falcon tried to figure out why he was so tired when Newman suddenly asked him how he was feeling. "I'm tired and I'm aching," Falcon answered. "My body is screaming for rest. How about you?"

"I could do with some rest. My stomach is bothering me a little and my legs are still somewhat soft. I woke up like that this morning. I thought it might go away, but it hasn't. I have a suspicion it was the meat we ate last night."

Falcon had been wondering about that himself. "Maybe it was. Possibly some kind of bacteria or even a parasite. The meat wasn't quite as well done as I would have liked. I've got some antibiotic pills in my pack. Once we stop, I'm going to take some. I suggest you do the same."

After riding for about three hours, Alita, who rode ahead of them, stopped near a grove of trees. "We won't be spotted as easily as in the open. I think we should set up camp in there," she suggested.

Falcon didn't object, neither did Newman.

By the time they had everything unloaded and their tents erected, both men nearly collapsed.

"I hope I feel better in the morning," were Newman's last words, but Falcon was already half-asleep.

───────

ALITA LET THEM SLEEP. FALCON LOOKED AT HIS WATCH AND SAW IT was already past eight when Alita woke them. "We are in no real hurry," she said. "I wanted to make sure you got enough rest."

She already had a small fire going and was boiling water to make tea. "There is a small creek that way," she told them and pointed. "The water looks clear and fresh."

Falcon found the creek and washed his face with the cool water. He felt better but still not his old self. When he sat down for breakfast, he popped one of his antibiotic pills into his mouth, hoping it would clear up whatever he suffered from. Newman accepted a pill from him, even though he said he felt much better.

They spoke little while they ate their biscuits and dried bacon.

"Something is bothering you, isn't it?" Alita gave Newman an inquisitive look.

"Is it that obvious?"

She smiled. "It is written all over you. Go on, ask?"

"Last night, I saw you change into some kind of giant worm. I knew about your species' shape-changing ability, but it was my first time to see it actually happen."

"It was the only way to free myself from my bonds. I hope you weren't freaked out watching me change. Usually, I like to avoid being observed."

"It was somewhat disturbing. I admit that. Was that your real shape?"

"No, it wasn't." Alita chuckled. "Obviously, you don't know what I really look like. Seeing my true body may shock you a little. Or perhaps a lot." She looked at Falcon. "Are you aware of my natural shape?"

"I am. However, only from briefings about your kind. I've never seen a live Accilla in his or her natural shape."

"Would you be bothered if you saw me the way I truly look?"

With a shrug, he said, "I can't say, but I don't believe it would bother me. As I said, I've seen holograms, which is to say I am familiar with your true shape."

"Good." She rose and began taking off her clothes. When she stood naked in front of them, she looked at Falcon and then at Newman. "Take a good look and tell me how seeing me in the nude in this body affects you."

"How do you think?" Falcon stared at her. "I'm a virile man and looking at a beautiful woman with a body like yours does awake certain feelings in me."

"Even knowing this is not my real shape?"

"I've seen plenty of women that had their body surgically altered from unattractive to ravishing. Their appearance before the surgery didn't really matter to me or other men. We only saw what they looked like after the surgery." He smiled. "Men are shallow."

"It certainly seems that way. What about you, Newman?"

Newman chuckled. "I guess I'm as shallow as Falcon and all

the other men." It sounded like an apology. "Let's face it, basically, we are still animals. We respond to what we see, hear, taste, and smell."

While Newman talked, Alita's body began to change. Her legs and arms shortened, her body lost its shape and then both men stared at the giant slug standing in front of them. There was no neck between the head and body, and the face was flat and shapeless without a nose or mouth. Only two dark eyes moved at the top of the elongated ball. Then two lips appeared under the eyes. They moved when she spoke. "Does this body arouse you sexually?"

It sounded surreal to hear the words in Alita's voice forming between the two colorless lips.

Falcon wasn't shocked by what he witnessed, actually it was more of a surprise to know he wasn't looking at a hologram. This was a body that would feel real when touched.

"Go ahead and touch me," the lips encouraged him.

He did. Her skin felt smooth and soft but solid at the same time.

"I am not repulsed," he said. "If you were worried about that."

The eyes shifted to look at Newman. "Do you want to touch me to see what my body feels like?" the lips asked.

"It isn't necessary." Newman just stood there. He seemed uncomfortable.

The slug waddled on short legs toward Newman. "I want you to touch me, Newman. This body is real. This is my true form. It is just a shell; inside, I am still the same person I was before."

Newman reached out, touched her with one finger and then with one flat hand. "You are warm."

The lips laughed. "I hope so. I'd be dead were it otherwise." Her body began to quiver, change. Her limbs lengthened, her legs formed thighs and calves, her buttocks became small and round, and her breasts grew out of her chest. Within moments she stood before them, again as a beautiful human woman.

Alita's radiant smile seemed to mock them. "I hope I didn't ruin your dreams."

"Was there a purpose to this demonstration?" It was Newman asking the question.

"Actually, there was. If there ever is a reason for me to change openly in front of you again, you will know what to expect. It will not interfere with anything that caused me to change in the first place." She looked toward the tents. "I believe it is time we moved on. I want to be gone in case those bird-riding women decide to hunt us down."

"This time we'll be ready." Newman patted the revolver on his hip.

———

THEY DIDN'T KNOW WHEN THEY CROSSED INTO BRETTANY. THERE was nothing there to mark the border. No fences, rows of trees, or buildings. They knew they were in Brettany when they saw a church and then a few houses scattered on either side of the road. After a while, the houses became more clustered, and side roads led away from the main road. Another church and a small store beside it confirmed they had arrived in a village.

"This isn't Rowarra or is it?" Alita wondered.

"No. Rowarra is still another four day's ride from here, aside from being much larger," Newman said. "I think this place is called Warnon, a town in Brettany, if I remember correctly."

The majority of houses looked old and weathered. They saw an old man with a white beard sitting on the wooden steps in front of one of the houses. He didn't wave or say anything as they passed the house. He just watched them, his eyes squinting against the sun.

"I hope the rest of the populace is friendlier," Falcon remarked.

"Don't hold your breath. The people in these villages are

suspicious of strangers. They don't welcome them and hope they only pass through. Strangers just might corrupt their minds with new ideas and upset their way of life," Newman told them. "You'd be lucky to get a drink of water."

"That friendly, huh? Where are all the people anyway? This looks like a ghost town."

"Many of these people are farmers and are most likely working in the fields. Some are probably hanging out in the store or in the tavern. There could be some action at the marketplace, which is usually in the center of the village."

Warnon was not big, and it didn't take long to reach the center. Even before they got there, they could see a large crowd in the square.

"Looks like the whole village is celebrating some event," Falcon remarked.

When they were close, they could see the reason for such a large crowd. In the center of the courtyard, they had erected some gallows. From the gallows hung three bodies. When Falcon saw their naked bellies and thighs shine white in the bright rays of the sun and the shaggy red-brown hair that covered their chests and upper bodies, he felt a cold shiver running down his backbone.

One of them was a male, the other two were females.

His voice was hoarse, when he spoke. "Why would they do that to these gentle people?"

"Perhaps because they are different. Not human," Alita speculated.

"Barbarians!" Falcon cursed. "Sometimes, I hate the assignments on these backward planets. Instead of evolving and becoming enlightened, they revert back to a time when the human race lived with superstitions and hatred for anyone or anything different. They become savages."

"You just described Aurora with great accuracy," Newman remarked.

"I want to get closer and get a better look." Falcon climbed from his horse. "Also, I'd like to find out why they were murdered."

"There is nothing we can do," Alita told him.

"I know, but I need to find out."

They tied their horses to a couple of trees growing in front of one of the houses and joined the crowd. Working their way closer to the gallows, they managed to get fairly close. Falcon was relieved when he saw that the three corpses were not from the same group he and his companions had met a couple of days before. However, it did nothing to make him feel much better.

Even though his memory was vague and spotty about what exactly transpired the night he had sex with the young female, the image of her was clear enough as it sprang unbidden into his consciousness.

...Her naked white buttocks rotated lazily in his lap as he moved behind her. She held his engorged member prisoner inside her tight sex-organ as she milked him fiercely...

Shaking his head to get that picture out of his mind, he stared at the three corpses, consumed by a sudden rage. What did they do to deserve being strangled to death by the noose at the end of a rope? What horrible crime could they have committed to be hanged by an angry mob?

Somebody touched his arm. "Let's go. There is nothing we can do for them," Alita told him a second time.

"You are right," he agreed. "We can do nothing, but I still would like to know why they were condemned to such a cruel death."

"They were hanged because they are Dreel. Soul-stealers. Vampires that suck the very soul out of any man unlucky enough to be ensnared by them."

Falcon turned to look at the speaker beside him. He saw an elderly man with a thick mustache and a pipe between his lips. "I'm not sure I follow you."

The man gave him an inquisitive look, took another puff from his pipe, and took it out of his mouth. "You must be a stranger," he observed. "I've never seen you in this town before." He held out a hand. "My name is Steward Maldor. I own the tavern at the end of town."

Shaking the offered hand, Falcon said, "Honored to meet you, Steward. I am Jeremy Falcon, and you are correct, I am a stranger. Just traveling through. What do you mean by calling them Soul-stealers?"

"You don't really know, do you?" Maldor lowered his voice. "From what I hear, copulating with a Dreel female gives a man unbelievable pleasure. Much greater than any human woman can give a man, but it comes at a cost. She not only sucks his sperm out of him but also part of his soul. She leaves her victim exhausted and empty. Even though his memory of what happened is nothing but ghostly images, his longing for her is so strong he goes crazy in the end."

"Really? That sounds scary."

"It is. Just one coupling with a Dreel female leaves a man tired and listless, with weak and wobbly legs." Maldor took a couple of slow puffs from his pipe. "That's what I hear." He glanced at the woman beside him. "I have, of course, never been with a female Dreel. Just pray you never get caught in the web they spin."

"It does give a man stuff to think about. Is there a cure?"

"Some say there isn't, but there is a way to protect yourself if you're worried you may fall victim to one of them. You'd have to go and talk to Miriam Collar. She sells cures for all kinds of ailments. She mixes them herself from herbs and plants she collects."

"There are rumors she may be a witch," the woman standing beside Maldor whispered confidentially. "But you didn't hear that from me."

"Just rumors, Hallen. They are just rumors." Maldor seemed suddenly uneasy. He looked at Falcon. "Forget what my wife said. She's talking nonsense. Miriam Collar is a good and knowledgeable woman. Her herbs cured my injured shoulder. She is a healer."

"Where would one find this woman?"

"If you follow the road, she lives in a small house at the end of town. You can't miss it. There is a tall Liiril tree growing in her front yard. Apparently, she planted it herself. If you go and see her, tell her Steward sent you."

"Thanks for the advice, Steward. I might just pay her a visit." Falcon smiled. "I've got some back problems. Perhaps, she can help me out with that."

"You won't be sorry." He turned to his wife. "What is it, Hallen? Why have you've been poking me?"

"I want to go home, Steward. These dead Dreel make me feel uneasy. They'll give me nightmares. I know that already."

Falcon gave the man a pat on the shoulder. "Thanks again. You'd better take care of your wife. Nightmares are nothing to laugh at."

When the couple was gone, Newman said beside Falcon, "I think we should leave, too. Looking at these poor creatures doesn't make me happy. Damn superstitions! I feel like hanging a few of these people right beside them."

"Keep your voice down and that thought to yourself," Alita whispered. "You are beginning to draw attention."

When they were back with their horses, Newman looked at Falcon. "You aren't really serious about visiting the charlatan to have your back problem treated?"

"My back is fine. It's my legs. They are weak and wobbly. In fact, my whole body feels weak. I need to talk to that woman."

Newman pulled his eyebrows together and gave Falcon a more than curious look. "I don't want to jump to any conclusion, but I wondered why you got so upset when you saw those three hanging there. It didn't seem like you. I'm sure you've seen worse than that. Is there something we need to know?"

"Actually, come to think of it," Alita said, "I was curious about that also. Whatever it is, Falcon, you owe us the truth. No matter how embarrassing it is."

"I have a feeling you already know."

Newman nodded solemnly. "I'd prefer you tell us."

Falcon knew, eventually he'd have to tell them. His condition was not getting any better. The truth was it was getting worse. The desire for the young Dreel female filled his mind, he couldn't stop thinking about her. His body was getting weaker, even his augmentation didn't help him. "I had sex with one of them."

"Which one?"

"The young female."

Alita didn't act shocked. "How did it happen?"

"I remember going outside during the night to catch some fresh air. I saw her standing in the water. When she saw me, she approached me. My memory of what happened after that is foggy. I remember unbelievable pleasure like I've never experienced before. It didn't seem real, like a dream. When she left me, I felt exhausted, drained, and unable to form coherent thoughts." He wiped his forehead. "Now she's in my head. I want her badly, and I can't control it." He gave Newman a pleading look. "Are you sure you know nothing about these Dreel? You've been here for five years. You must have heard something."

Shaking his head, Newman said, "Until now, I've never seen them or heard them discussed. I didn't even know they were known as Dreel. This is all new to me. I'm sorry. Had I known, I would have warned you."

"Don't feel guilty. I am not sure if knowing about them would have prevented it."

"It seems to me they use a form of mind control to trap their victims. Like a flower attracts an insect with the aroma of its nectar," Alita speculated.

"I suppose I am the insect, and that young female was the flower?" Falcon smirked.

"You may think that is funny, but have you ever heard of Star-cross?" She didn't smile.

"Can't say I have."

"It is a jungle planet, populated by intelligent plants," Alita explained. "One mother plant has many shoots. In a sense, the shoots are shapeshifters, similar to us Accilla. They are also telepaths. The shoots have restricted movement, but they can move around. They attract their food by taking on different shapes and sending out mental emanations, just like a plant will grow beautiful flowers with sweet nectar to entice an insect."

Falcon grew impatient. He was eager to get going and find this Miriam Collar. "I appreciate what you are trying to do, but it doesn't help my condition. The sooner we get to that healer, the better."

They had no trouble finding the house with the tall tree in the front yard. Beautiful flowers grew in a flowerbed in front of the house. On the side were shrubs; some of them in bloom. When they knocked on the wooden door, a small, thin woman opened it and peered at them. "How can I help you?" she asked with a surprisingly strong voice.

"Are you Miriam Collar?"

The woman looked Falcon up and down. "Yes, I am. Who wants to know?"

"My name is Jeremy Falcon. Steward Maldor suggested we should pay you a visit. You might have something to protect a man from being ensnared by a Dreel female."

Falcon felt a strange sensation rising inside him when he looked into the woman's eyes. It was like the gentle touch of a feather that lasted for only a moment. "Steward was right to send you here," she said. "I can and will help you."

Before he could say it was only a preventative measure, she smiled. "The telltale signs are all over you. There is no denying it. You are infected. A Dreel female demands a high price for the

exquisite joy she gives you when she allows you into her body."
She opened the door. "Before you come in, my services are not
free."

"I understand. We can pay."

"Good." She moved back into the house to let them enter.

Falcon had expected to step into a room with shelves on the
walls filled with jars. Perhaps a big cauldron on a stove where she
boiled her potions and the air laced with the aroma of steaming
plants. He was disappointed. The room he entered didn't look any
different from any other room where people spent part of their
daily activities. There was a couch, a couple of chairs, and a small
table. Pots with plants growing in them stood near the window. A
couple of vases displaying flowers sat on the table, a small stand,
and the walls were decorated with a few pictures.

"Sit down," the woman invited them. "I will go and mix you
the medicine."

Falcon looked after her when she disappeared through a door.
"Nice place," he remarked for lack of anything else to say.

"She looks just like an ordinary older woman," Newman
observed. "Like somebody's grandmother."

Alita chuckled softly. "What did you expect? An old hag with a
wart on her nose, straggly hair, and a tall, pointed hat?"

Falcon lifted his shoulders. "Not that, but I envisioned
different surroundings."

"So did I, actually," Newman admitted. "The old hag you
described in such detail appears in ancient folklore on Earth. I
came across that in my research. They called them witches in
those days. They also owned what they called *familiars*, which
usually was a black cat. To be honest, I did not expect to find
someone looking like a regular woman. I am almost disappointed."

They stopped talking when she came back into the room,
carrying a wooden tray with three steaming mugs. "I hope you

enjoy tea. You'll have to be patient; it will take a while to mix all the ingredients together. I'll have to go into my garden and harvest a couple of the plants I need." She put the tray onto the table. "Don't worry, it won't poison you. This is just some mint tea."

[10]

AFTER GIVING FALCON A CUP OF SOME BITTER COCKTAIL MIRIAM Collar had mixed and brewed in her kitchen, she warned him not to expect immediate relief. "It will take a couple of days, but it will cure you. I guarantee it," she promised. "You will be as good as new. Good luck with your mission."

Before they left her house, the woman looked at Alita and said, "They burn or hang the ones they suspect to be different. To survive among these people, you must never give them reason to suspect you. Be careful."

Alita nodded. "Thank you for the advice."

They decided to stay until the next day in Warnon. They had supper in Maldor's tavern.

The food was simple but a welcome change from their rations. Maldor even served them wine, which was surprisingly great tasting, not sour as Falcon secretly had suspected. Somehow, the man didn't seem to fit the type of people Falcon saw gawking at the three corpses hanging from the gallows. His demeanour was open and friendly.

He watched a couple sitting at one of the other tables. They sat with folded hands and were, as far as Falcon could tell, praying before they started eating. Looking into their faces, their expression was dark and bleak. It was obvious they fitted into the mold Falcon had envisioned the inhabitants of Brettany to be after the farmer Bob Maller had described them as religious nuts.

"What was your impression of Miriam Collar?" He looked at Alita.

"Either that woman was just trying to sound mysterious, or she has a true gift. You heard what she said to me. I almost suspect she knew my true nature," Alita answered.

"I am inclined to believe that, also. She wished me good luck with my mission. I think there is more to that simple-looking woman than appears."

"She could be nothing more than a 'Sensitive', which means she sensed something odd about us but doesn't really know anything tangible. She's guessed the rest," Newman suggested.

"That, of course, is possible," Falcon agreed. "There definitely was something peculiar about her, even though she behaved like a normal person."

"At least she didn't make you get on your knees and pray before she made you drink that concoction, she brewed for you," Newman joked.

"I suspect she is not one of those religious fanatics. As a healer with an extensive knowledge of plants, she'd better stay watchful to avoid people accusing her of being a witch. She warned Alita to be careful. I'm sure she knows that she is walking on thin ice. Is it possible she is a relative newcomer to Aurora?"

"It is possible." Newman leaned back in his seat. "This planet would not be my first choice if for some reason I was told to settle somewhere. I don't know if I would choose a highly advanced planet, either. I like the easy-going life on the colonized planets. I'm not saying a newly opened planet. I've been to those. Life there is hard. There are colonies out there where the people didn't fall back to the times when everyone was superstitious and where technology was an evil word. I would choose one of those. Like everything else, there is always a middle way."

Alita smiled. "From what I saw you don't really suffer here, Newman."

"No, I don't, but I'm only a guest on Aurora, not a permanent resident, and someday I will leave here. I am also glad the outpost is in Saskona and not here in Brettany."

"Have you been in Warnon before?" Falcon asked.

"Only once, and that was three years ago. We never stayed here, only passed through."

"That reminds me, did anyone see a hotel where we could stay the night? I never paid attention, because staying here was never the plan." Falcon looked around for the proprietor. He found him cleaning the counter. "I'm going to talk to Maldor. He might be able to suggest a hotel."

There were only two in town. Maldor suggested they try the smaller one. It was not fancy, but the proprietor was honest and would not cheat them.

———

THEY LEFT AT FIRST DAYLIGHT. IT WAS CLOUDY, BUT THERE WAS NO indication that it may rain during the day.

"How are you feeling this morning?" Alita gave Falcon an inquiring look.

"Still tired, but my mind is much clearer. That strong desire for the young female that tortured me these last couple of days seems to be gone. Her image is still there, but it is fading away."

"Maldor called them soul-stealers." Alita recalled." Of course, we have to remember that these people here are a superstitious lot. You said that you were left tired and exhausted after your encounter with the young female. Also, your mind was cloudy. It leaves me to assume only one thing, while you were having intercourse you absorbed some of her body fluid, which to you is like a powerful drug."

"You may be right, but I believe there is more to it," Falcon speculated. "I think the Dreel, especially the females, have the ability to influence another mind. How else would you explain my obsession with her? You of all people should understand that. I know only little about your species. I know you can communicate with others by entering their mind. In fact, you know what that person is thinking. I don't know what else you can do. Can you control others with your mind?" He lifted a hand. "I may not want to know."

"Most of us cannot, but there are some that can," she admitted. She didn't elaborate if she was one of the ones that could.

"You may be on the right track," Newman cut into the conversation. "Have you ever heard of the planet Epsilon?"

"I haven't," Falcon confessed.

Alita only shook her head.

"I've never been there, but the legendary Colonel Stonewall spent some time there when he was a young scout. I don't know much about the planet itself, except that the mushroom jungle is teeming with giant reptiles. Among the diverse lifeforms that make Epsilon their home, there are intelligent telepathic ants that have the ability to cloud your mind and make you see things that aren't there."

"I don't doubt for a moment that among the multitude of intelligent species in this galaxy there are a few with great mental abilities," Falcon agreed with Newman.

"I guess we can add the Dreel to that list," Alita commented. "Unless what happened to you has nothing to do with any special mental abilities. Perhaps, as I suggested, it is just the drug you absorbed when a part of your body was inside her. It is not a farfetched idea. I know of small reptiles that carry a poisonous substance on their skin. Just touching them can be deadly. It is strictly physical."

"I don't want to find out." Falcon sighed. "I'm glad we stumbled across someone who knew how to treat this thing."

"Me, too." Newman looked down the road and then into the sky. "There are some clouds in the west which I don't like, but the wind is blowing from the east, and they may just blow them away."

"How far to the next town?" Alita inquired.

"Still a few hours. It depends on the weather, of course."

To their left, heads of grain swayed gently in the soft breeze, like a sea of gold. A herd of cattle grazed to their right. Everything looked peaceful and serene, but Falcon was not lulled into carelessness. A peaceful scene could explode with violence when least expected.

He could see a forest of tall trees in the distance. Behind the forest, a mountain range rose into the sky. The tops of the mountains disappeared in the clouds.

"We might get that rain after all," he commented.

The road curved gently toward the west. They'd be closer to the forest than he had assumed. Anyone or anything could hide among the trees. He lifted the field glasses hanging around his neck to get a better look when he noticed movement on the road ahead.

"There are people on the road. It looks like they are walking."

"Perhaps a farmer with his family," Alita ventured. "It is a nice day to go for a walk and enjoy the countryside."

"I don't think so. I don't see a farmstead anywhere nearby. I advise caution." Falcon touched his sidearm. "I won't take anything for granted again."

"Let us not get paranoid," Newman spoke up. "Not everyone is violent."

"It never hurts to be prepared," Falcon defended himself. He looked through his field glasses again and cursed when he saw a wagon with a cage standing not far from the group of people.

"Something is not right here." He spurned his horse on to move faster.

The group of people stopped and turned around to watch him coming closer. He counted ten people. Four were human men. The others were not. There was one female. She was an older version of Irida, the Suries female living at the Scouts Outpost. The other five were children. Two girls and three boys. They were neither human nor Suries. Hybrids. Falcon recalled Newman telling him back at the outpost that they were called Suman.

One of the human men, the Suries female, and the children had ropes around their necks. The ends of the ropes were held by one man. The other two men carried short whips.

"What the hell is going on here?" Falcon demanded with a loud voice.

"None of this is your concern," one of the men said. "Just move on."

"Help us, please." The man with the rope around his neck gave Falcon a pleading look. His voice was weak, and his face swollen. One of his eyes was closed shut. There was dried blood on his face and forehead.

He flinched and cried out when one of the men laid the whip across his back.

"Shut up, you miserable piece of dung!" his tormenter bellowed.

Falcon jumped from his horse. Five steps took him to the group. With an angry shout, he smashed his fist against the offender's head. The man collapsed without a sound. Drawing his pistol, Falcon aimed it at the man holding the ends of the ropes. "Release these people immediately!"

"They are not people," the man shouted defiantly. "They are abominations, spawn of demons, cursed by God."

"If you don't drop those ropes I'll put a bullet into your brain," Falcon growled between clenched teeth. He kicked the man with the whip into the chest with his right foot when out of the corner of his eye he saw him pull a knife. The man fell backward, clutching his chest.

The other man dropped the ropes and glared at Falcon. "Who are you and what are these...these creatures to you?"

"They are not creatures. They are living beings, and they have the right to live just like you. Who am I?" Falcon's laugh sounded evil in his own ears. "I am the demon that will haunt you in your dreams. I am the one who will send you to hell if you don't drop those ropes." He put the gun against the man's temple. "Now!"

Reluctantly, the man dropped the ropes. Falcon hit him with the gun, hard, and grunted when he crumpled to the ground, joining his friend. The man with the knife was on his knees, still clutching his chest. When Falcon looked at him, he said with an accusing voice, "You broke my ribs."

"I'll break your neck if you make one wrong move. Where were you taking them?"

"To Rowarra."

"Why? What's in Rowarra"?

"The slavers."

"Are you telling me you are selling these people into slavery?" Falcon felt the anger growing inside him again.

"You are calling them people. They are not people, not human." The man paused. His breathing was labored. "I am in great pain," he moaned and looked at his friends lying in the dirt. "You killed them."

"I could have, but I didn't. I am not a monster like you." Falcon spoke calmly. He looked at Newman who had come down from his horse also. "Keep an eye on this bastard and his friends. I want to talk to the man. He doesn't look too good."

Falcon walked over to the man they tormented. "Are you okay?"

The man nodded.

"Where were you headed before these men took you prisoner?"

"We were on our way home." He pointed to the forest. "We call our community 'Sanctuary'. His swollen lips formed a crooked smile. "We feel protected there."

"Are there many of you?"

"About two hundred."

"Is this your family?"

He nodded again. "My wife and my five children. People like us are not welcomed anywhere else." He gave Falcon a questioning look. "Why are you helping us?"

"Because you needed help. I have no love for people like them. What they are doing is wrong."

"It is obvious you are not a resident of Brettany. All of them are righteous fanatics. They preach love and tolerance, but only for people of their kind. They hate men like me and they hate the Suries. We were lucky they didn't hang us from a tree." He spat into the dirt.

"Well, I am not like them. Neither are my friends."

"Where do you come from, if I may ask?"

Falcon pointed into the sky. "From up there."

"That's what I thought. Your manner of talking is unlike the way people talk in this world. I've never met an out-worlder before. What's it like out there among the stars?"

"Diverse, but if you believe things are different from the way things are here, I'll have to disappoint you. There is plenty of violence everywhere. That's why people like me exist."

"What are you?"

"I am a soldier. I am not a stranger to violence. I've lived with it most of my life, but I am trying to stop it when I can. By the way, my name is Jeremy Falcon. What is yours?"

"I am Mal Chabot."

"Okay, Mal. Let us get you to safety. We'll take you and your family home."

"I don't know if I can walk that far." Mal looked at the two smallest children. "They won't make it, either. Yer is only three and Zil is four."

"Don't worry. We'll borrow their wagon."

Mal looked suddenly uneasy. "I'm not traveling inside that cage."

"I understand. We'll remove the door. Your oldest boy can sit in the driver's seat. We'll ride behind you to make sure you are safe until you get home."

Looking at the three men on the ground with his good eye, Mal said, "They will seek revenge and hunt us down."

"We'll make sure they don't," Falcon said grimly, hoping he wasn't making a promise he couldn't keep. He turned to Alita who had been standing beside him. "Any suggestions on how we can prevent that?"

"I think I can help out," she said. "It goes against our principles, but in this case, it will be justified. There is only one problem, it won't last, but it will give us enough time to get away and cover our tracks."

Mal looked from Alita to Falcon. "I don't want you to kill them. I don't believe in violence, and it would make matters only worse."

"Don't worry," Falcon assured him. "We should but we won't kill them. We have other methods."

Visibly relaxing, Mal gave Falcon a grateful look.

Mal's wife touched Falcon's arm. She gave him a shy smile. "Thank you for helping us." She spoke Inglis with an accent, but Falcon still understood most of her words.

"You are quite welcome. Do all of you speak our language?"

She shook her head. "No, not all of our children. Only our oldest son and the two girls. Not very good, either." She lifted her slim shoulders. "We will teach the younger ones later."

"I heard what you suggested," Newman said. "I don't know if we can take off the cage door. Those bars are solid iron."

"Let's go and try. Maybe between the two of us we can do it."

He inspected the hinges. Made from iron, they looked solid.

Falcon opened the door and pulled on it. It didn't budge. Then he climbed into the wagon and told Newman to close the door and the lock. Lying on his back, he pulled back his legs and kicked hard. The first time nothing happened. Closing his eyes, he took a few deep breaths, concentrating on his legs. When his feet made contact with the iron bars of the door again, he felt it give. The next kick ripped off the hinges and the door tumbled to the ground with a loud clang.

He jumped down and looked at the door. It was bent out of shape so badly it would never be used as a door again. "I think we are ready to leave," he said to Newman. "Tell them to climb onto the wagon."

"How are your legs?" Newman inquired.

"They are fine. I think I'm back to normal."

"Whatever normal means for you. No wonder you broke that guy's ribs. He seems to be in great pain. Should I at least have a look at his ribs?"

"If you want. I don't feel sorry for him or his friends. Ask Alita to give him some painkillers."

Newman scratched his head. "What are we going to do with them?"

"We'll leave them here. I hope they don't have a long walk home."

"Okay. You're the boss. Somehow, I don't feel right about it, just so you know."

Falcon gave Newman a hard look. "It is more than they deserve. They are heartless bastards with no compassion for others. I hope this is only an isolated event."

Newman made a face. "I'm afraid it isn't. Suries and humans basically get along with each other, as long as they keep to themselves. Interactions between the sexes is a different story. Sadly, the offspring, the Suman, are not loved by either species. I mentioned that already back at the outpost."

"I remember. I'll have to check with Alita and see how she is coming along." Falcon walked over to where Alita was having a mental conversation with the three men. All were standing now, looking somewhat confused.

"Ah, there you are," Alita said cheerfully. "These fine people are heading for the town of Winnira. They asked me if I knew in which direction Winnira lies. I told them I don't know. We'll have to ask Newman. Tomm here injured himself. He doesn't remember how. Looks like he's got a couple of cracked ribs, possibly broken. I gave him some painkillers. That should take care of the pain. I also gave pills to Kerry and Howerd. They are complaining about having a headache. It probably stems from the bruises on the side of their head. They don't know when they got those. How are you doing with the wagon?"

"It is fixed. We'll be ready to move once everyone is on the wagon. I should go and see if they need help. I'll send Newman over." He headed back to the wagon.

Mal had trouble climbing into the wagon. Falcon helped him with that. The oldest boy took a seat on the bench and grabbed the reigns of the horse. The others joined Mal inside the open cage. As soon as all were seated, the wagon began to move.

"Ready to get going?" Falcon called out to Newman and Alita.

He waited until they had mounted their horses and then they followed the wagon.

[11]

THE SMALL VILLAGE OF SANCTUARY WAS SITUATED ALONG THE shores of a lake deep in the forest. The road leading there was narrow and bumpy, but they didn't have too much trouble getting through with the wagon.

The farmhouse of Mal and his family was the first building in the village. It was not a fancy house, but it looked well taken care of. There was another building and a small shed in the yard behind the main house. That's where they kept a couple of milk cows and a flock of poultry. In a pen, about a dozen sheep-like animals were grazing. Falcon also saw a garden in which vegetables grew.

"Looks like you are doing alright for yourself," Falcon remarked to Mal after getting off his horse.

Mal nodded and smiled. "I am a lucky man, Jeremy. I have a beautiful wife who loves me and five wonderful children. What more does a man want?"

"Perhaps a peaceful life?" Falcon suggested.

"I have that, too. As long as I stay here in Sanctuary. Out there..." he pointed in no particular direction. "...out there only violence and hatred wait for someone like me. I don't understand that world."

"It is not easy to understand," Falcon agreed. "Let me ask you a question, Mal. Where you born on Aurora?"

"Yes, I was. Why are you asking?"

"I detect a slight accent when you talk. Unless that is the way people in another state talk. Remember, I don't know much about life on this planet."

"My parents immigrated to Aurora before I was born. The planet they came from was not a peaceful world. Humans were embroiled in a war with the original inhabitants. They fled with a handful of other humans. They came here hoping they would finally find peace. They stayed in Rima for a few years. Later they moved to a small village in Glasca. That's where I was born."

"Sounds interesting. I'd like to hear more of your story."

"And you will, but first let us go into the house. My children are very tired and so is my wife. They need to get some rest. To be honest, I also need the rest. Tell your friends to join us inside. You may want to stay the night."

"If you don't mind, we would like to take care of our horses first."

"Of course. The animals are important. What should we do about the wagon and the horse?"

"I'd say keep the wagon and the horse. Those men may not remember you or anything that happened." Falcon smiled grimly. "They are suffering from memory loss. Hopefully, their memory won't come back, perhaps only part of it. Even if it does, there is a good chance they won't know what happened to their wagon and horse."

"I don't quite understand. How?"

"It is better you don't ask questions. Just accept it. You'll probably want to get rid of the cage. The wagon and horse will come in handy and make life a little easier for you."

Mal gave Falcon a puzzled look but didn't say anything. Then he shrugged. "I'll see you inside."

"I'll come with you," Alita said. "I think the men don't need me to look after the horses." She looked at Falcon. "Is it alright?"

Falcon nodded. "Sure, go with him."

He and Newman took off the saddles and rubbed down the horses. Then they led them down to the lake.

"There is plenty of grass and even some weeds for the horses to eat," Newman remarked. "We can leave them here tied to these trees."

"We should take them into the yard later on," Falcon suggested. "Even though they are probably safe down here near the lake."

As they walked to the house, a man's voice called, "Hello. Did something happen to Mal and his family?"

Falcon saw a man coming toward them. He was dressed in loose coveralls. A sloppy hat covered his head. He carried a rifle, but he didn't appear to be hostile.

"I am Mannie from next door. I saw you people coming with that horse and buggy. What happened?"

"They had a run-in with some slave traders. We rescued them. They are fine."

"You rescued them? What happened to the slave traders?"

"We convinced them to lend us their buggy and horse. Mal's family was in no condition to walk all that way home."

Mannie looked at Falcon with narrow eyes. "I have a feeling there is more to this story than what you're telling me. We may have to expect trouble coming our way. Who are you people anyway?"

"I am Falcon, and this is Newman. We are on our way to Rowarra. We just happened to stumble across these slave traders as they tried to do harm to your neighbors, so we decided to interfere."

"Like I said trouble is on its way." Mannie looked suddenly worried. "They won't let it go."

"If it helps, we'll be staying until tomorrow, possibly even longer, to make sure Mal's family is safe."

"I'll be talking to some of the other neighbors. We may have to put the village on alert. Tell Mal we'll be seeing him tomorrow to discuss strategy. In the meantime, thanks for rescuing them. They are good people."

When they entered the house, Mal wasn't there, but his wife sat in a chair at a table. Looking around, Falcon noted that the room was a fair size. The table and the chairs were plain but solid. The two windows were partially covered with cloth curtains. He saw a counter in the part of the room that was the kitchen. A wood stove stood in the corner and a basin beside it on a wooden bench.

There were plates on the table along with a couple of loaves of bread, also three clay cups filled with water.

"We ran into one of your neighbors. Mannie. He was curious to learn about your well-being. He'll be talking to Mal tomorrow. By the way, where is he?"

"Mal is resting. He wasn't feeling well, but I thought you probably would like something to eat. We don't have much but still enough to share with you. I boiled a few eggs. They are fresh from today, but the bread and the biscuits are a couple of days old. I will bake some tomorrow."

"The bread looks delicious." Falcon smiled. "You wouldn't believe what we have to eat sometimes. Bread only two days old is like freshly baked for us." He put down his backpack, pulled out one of the chairs, and sat down. Alita and Newman followed his example.

There was a knife on the table. Falcon used it to cut off a slice of bread. When he saw the small bowl with what looked like butter in it, he spread some of it onto his bread. Biting into it, he found the bread somewhat stale but tasty.

The woman had been watching him. "Is it alright?"

"As good as fresh," he said. "By the way, you never told us your name."

"I am sorry. My name is Eldira. Your name is Jeremy, yes?"

"You have a good memory. Yes, I am Jeremy. This is Alita and he is Wesley."

She nodded to Alita and Newman. "Thank you for rescuing us. I am so grateful. You saved us from a terrible fate."

"Those men said they were going to take you to Rowarra to sell you to Slavers? Did they tell the truth?"

"They did. Our family would have been broken apart. Mal would have ended up working somewhere in a mine. Females of my race are made to serve men. The fate of my children, because they are Suman, would have been a life of servitude until they died." She put her face between her hands and sobbed. "I do not want to think about it."

"You are back in your home now, Eldira," Falcon said soothingly. "You and your family are safe."

She looked at him, her blue cat's eyes moist with tears. "Why are some people so cruel? We don't hurt anyone."

Falcon reached across the table and touched her hand. "I cannot give you the answer."

She wiped a hand across her face to dry her tears. "I am sorry. I need to be strong for my children and Mal. He is a good man and takes care of us. He would give his life to protect us, but he is not a fighter."

"Not everyone is. To be violent is not desirable." Falcon sighed. "Some of us have no choice. I am a soldier, trained to be extremely violent if the situation warrants it, but I find no enjoyment in that. Sometimes, I wish I had chosen a different path and become a farmer like my father or a scientist like my brother."

"I am glad you didn't." For a moment her beautiful face looked feral as she exposed two small but pointy incisors, betraying her ancestry.

His mind conjured up the image of a wild and fierce jungle cat ready to pounce on his ancestor thousands of years ago, armed only with a dry branch. It only lasted as long as the blink of an eye.

As if reading his mind, she lowered her long lashes over her eyes. "I am sorry, but I am not as peaceful as my husband," she said with a barely audible voice. "Whatever you did to those three men was justified. I feel no remorse inside me."

"And you shouldn't have to." He picked up one of the biscuits. "I think I'll try one of these. They look delicious."

"I forgot about the eggs," she exclaimed. Getting up, she rushed over to the stove and came back with a bowl. She handed him one of the eggs. "I hope you like them hard-boiled. Mal likes his soft."

Mal joined them a couple of hours later. He had washed his face and put on a fresh pair of pants and a shirt. His one eye was still swollen shut, but he looked better overall. "You must forgive me for neglecting you," he apologized. Then he looked at his wife. "You look tired. I think you should go and lie down. I'll take care of our guests."

She didn't argue. "I put out some blankets for you. I hope you all sleep well," she said and climbed up a set of stairs in the corner of the room.

"She is the best thing that happened in my life," Mal said, looking after her. "I don't know what I'd do without her." He sat down on one of the chairs. "I'm sorry we have nothing to offer you but bread and eggs. Tomorrow, you can drink a cup of fresh milk for breakfast. I'll kill one of the chickens and we'll have lettuce from the garden."

Falcon made a dismissing gesture. "You don't have to make a big fuzz over us. No need to kill one of your chickens. Fresh milk for breakfast and a couple of biscuits will do. We'll be leaving in the morning."

"Where are you headed?"

"Rowarra. From there we'll take the train to Rima. You told me that's where your parents lived for a few years."

"They did. Of course, I know nothing about those years or the city of Rima. Why Rima?"

"There is a Scouts Outpost there. My friend Newman is a scout. However, he is stationed in Riwarda. That's where his outpost is located. You might be interested to know that one of his teammates is married to a Suries woman."

"It is nothing unusual." Mal smiled. "Suries women are very beautiful and passionate, and they make good wives. Does this scout in Riwarda have children?"

Falcon shook his head. "No, he doesn't."

"Tell me what it's like on the world you come from?"

"I was born on a planet called Icarus. My world is much like yours, except the people living there have embraced technology. They don't live in primitive surroundings like the people here. Even though there is plenty of freedom, extreme religions are forbidden. We have a central government that makes the laws. The laws are the same all over the planet. Mixed marriages like yours are accepted and not condemned. Everyone has the same rights, no matter what race they belong to."

Mal stared at the tabletop, a wistful look in his eyes. "That must be wonderful. Why did you leave such a world?"

"I became a soldier. I wanted to make a difference and fight for justice."

"Have you ever been sorry you chose that path?"

Falcon didn't answer for a moment. "I have in my weak moments, but most of the time I am glad I did. Especially, when I can help people like you and your family. That's when I know I did the right thing."

"You must have had a more important reason than helping people like me to come to Aurora."

"I have. I don't know how aware you are of the things

happening on your planet, since you are tucked away deep inside this forest."

"We try to stay informed," Mal assured him. "Some of the human men in our village travel to Winnira to stock up on supplies and do a little trading. They catch up on what's new by listening to the patrons in one of the taverns."

"Then you must perhaps have heard about some aliens building a giant dome on Drago Island. Also, about the disappearance of people in Ontura?"

"We have heard such rumors, but nobody knows anything tangible. Stories abound about giant bugs kidnapping and eating little children. We don't know if they are true." Mal looked at Falcon. "People are making up stories like that about the Suries. They call them witches, devils, and demons. None of them are true, of course. The Suries are people just like us."

"We are here to investigate the rumors and to make sure the Osirians, that is the name of their race, are not setting up a military base on Aurora, or worse, trying to colonize this planet."

"Just the three of you?" Mal looked doubtful.

"Actually, only Alita and I. Newman is a scout. He is our guide." Falcon couldn't help but chuckle when he saw Mal's face. "You are not the first one to question our success in this mission."

"I don't question your possible success. I question the mission you say you're on. It seems to me you don't really know anything about these aliens or what they are doing on Aurora, if they actually exist. What are they supposed to look like?"

"Like giant ants. You know what ants are?"

"I do. We have lots of them in the forest. They live in colonies and are very organized. Some of them are quite aggressive and warlike. Not all of them, though. How do you know the Osirians are hostile?"

"We don't know. It is an assumption, judging by what little we know about them. The Osirian Empire does not take part in the commerce between most of the races in the Galaxy. They are keeping to themselves. We know very little about their race. Hearing that they are trying to establish a colony on Aurora makes us nervous. What planet will they land on next?"

"It seems to me you are panicking without having any facts. How do you know they are trying to colonize Aurora? Perhaps one of their ships experienced problems. They may have landed here to fix their ship."

"I rule nothing out. That is the reason Alita and I are here to find out what exactly is going on." Falcon pursed his lips. "We have to tread lightly. Nobody wants to start a war with an enemy we know little about."

"Forgive me if I don't panic about an alien race trying to settle here. We have our own problems to deal with." Mal yawned. "I think I will retire. My body aches, and my face is burning. I can only see out of one eye, so worrying about those oversized ants is the last thing on my mind." He tried to smile but managed only to grimace. "I would offer you beds to sleep on, but we don't have any to spare. Take those blankets Eldira put out for you and find a place to sleep. Don't worry about the plates. We'll clean them up in the morning." With that, he rose and slowly walked up the stairs to the second floor.

Falcon also got up as well. "We should get the horses and move them into the yard."

"Good idea," Newman agreed.

The temperature had dropped outside, but it was still a pleasant night. The forest was not silent. The creatures that preferred the night made their presence known. A hunter barked nearby, and a night-bird was calling from somewhere on the lake. There was only one of the three moons visible in the sky. It looked full, but a closer examination revealed a tiny sliver missing on one side.

A slight breeze blew across the lake. The humid air it brought with it smelled of decaying vegetation laced with the fishy scent of water-dwellers.

Falcon took a couple of deep breaths and stared at the moon, alien and yet so familiar in appearance. He couldn't tell if it was the one where his team was hiding out. "It is peaceful here," he murmured, almost to himself. "One could easily forget the violence out there."

A roar and a loud scream that ended abruptly in a gurgle seemed to challenge his words.

Newman chuckled softly. "The violence is everywhere, my friend. Sometimes it takes a breather but only for a short time."

"So true, so true." Falcon sighed.

They led the animals to the back of the house where they tied them to posts driven into the ground.

There was a wooden, weathered bench in front of the small building.

"I don't feel like going to sleep yet," Falcon said and sat down on the bench. "What about you, Newman?"

Newman sat down beside him. "Might as well. I couldn't sleep anyway."

[12]

FALCON WOKE UP WITH HIS BODY ACHING. SLEEPING ON A HARD wooden floor, even with a rolled-up blanket, was not the most comfortable place to get a good rest. Getting up, he saw Newman and Alita were still sleeping. Not wanting to wake them he moved as silently as possible.

Opening the door, he stepped outside. The air smelled humid, and he noticed the wet ground. It must have rained during the night. It wasn't daylight yet, but the red sky in the east announced that it wouldn't be long before the sun was going to make an appearance.

He walked over to the horses to make sure they were alright. Their coats were still wet from the rain. The stallion snorted softly and nodded its long head when he patted the horse's flank.

"We'll be moving on today," Falcon spoke soothingly. "I know you're getting restless. Perhaps we'll let you stretch your legs once we hit the open prairie again."

A noise from the direction of the barn made him look up. Somebody came out of the door. It was Eldira. She carried a metal can in one hand and a basket in the other. When she saw him, she smiled. "The cows need to be milked early in the morning."

"I'm not familiar with cows, but I know about chickens," Falcon said. "I grew up on a farm. My parents had chickens."

"I've already collected all the eggs." Eldira chuckled. "The wife of a farmer can't afford to sleep in." Her cat's eyes studied him. "I hope the night wasn't too uncomfortable for you. A wooden floor is no substitute for a soft bed."

"No, it isn't," he admitted but smiled. "At least I stayed dry. I've slept on bare rocks during a storm, got rained and snowed on, pummeled by falling branches and other debris, so sleeping inside a house is considered a luxury."

"I am happy to hear that. Having you stay in our house is a small price to pay for what you and your friends did for us."

"It was our duty to help you. What those men did to you and what they planned is unforgivable."

"Yes. It is. I will never forgive them for that." She put down the can with the milk. "It is getting heavy," she said with a little smile. "Last year, one of the families in our community disappeared when they left to purchase a few things in Winnira. They never came back. They had one daughter. The man was a good friend to Mal. It would not be a coincidence if they were abducted by the same three men." She bent down to pick up the can with the milk. "I'd better get back into the house. Much to do today. I want to make some butter."

Falcon took the can from her hand. "Please, let me carry it for you." He smiled. "After all, I'll be drinking from the milk and probably eat some of the butter."

Eldira didn't argue. She just smiled and said, "Don't spill it now, otherwise we'll have to wait until tomorrow to get more milk."

"Don't worry. I promise I won't spill a drop." The can was heavy. He was surprised how easily she seemed to have carried the nearly full can. It revealed the strength members of the Suries race obviously possessed.

As they walked side-by-side toward the main house, Eldira suddenly stopped walking. "Did you hear that?"

He stood listening for a moment but heard nothing except the usual forest noises.

"There it is again. It sounded like a short squeal. The sound a horse makes."

Straining his ears, Falcon listened more carefully. "I am not familiar with the sounds a horse might make, but I think I heard something like a groan."

"Definitely a horse."

The sudden deep hooting of an animal could not be ignored.

"Danger is heading our way." Eldira looked at Falcon, her eyes large. "That was the warning cry of one of our sentries. We must get back into the house to warn the others." She sounded urgent, even a little scared.

Falcon became aware of the drumming many horses produce as their hooves strike the ground. There was no mistaking that sound, even for someone not familiar with horses.

Before they reached the house, a large group of riders burst out of the forest. They brought their horses to a sudden halt. One of the horses, a big black stallion, reared up on its hind legs, front legs pawing the air.

Falcon automatically reached for his weapon when he recognized the rider, but his hand found only emptiness. His gun was safely stowed away in his backpack, which was in the house.

"What a pleasant coincidence to find you here." The man on the horse grinned. His chest was wrapped with a few strips of cloth. "You broke two of my ribs, you filthy bastard. Seems to me you're just another Suries-lover." He jumped from his horse and moved closer. He carried a large revolver in his hand. "You're not such a big man now without your gun, aren't you?" he sneered, waving the revolver in front of Falcon.

Falcon could easily have taken it away from him, but he had to consider the other men. They were watching closely. Most of them carried rifles. He also had to worry about Eldira. She was standing exposed and was the most vulnerable right now.

"Look at you. My friend Tomm. It appears you got your memory back sooner than I hoped. If you think holding a gun in your hand makes you a big man, you are suffering from an inflated ego," Falcon said calmly, putting down the can with the milk. "To me, you're still nothing but a worthless piece of shit hiding among a bunch of common thugs. What do you think you're going to accomplish by threatening a family of peaceful people that was never a danger to you or your loser friends?"

Aiming the gun at Falcon, Tomm shouted angrily, "I could make your head explode like a ripe melon right now, you stupid fucker. Who do you think you are talking to me like that?"

Falcon's chuckle was anything but pleasant. "Like I told your friend already, I am the demon that will haunt your dreams at night, the one that will cause you to look over your shoulder during the day and make you afraid to walk in the dark."

Spitting like an angry snake, Tomm lifted his revolver to strike Falcon, but Falcon moved aside and forward. Grabbing the weapon, he twisted it out of Tomm's hand. Aiming it at his head, he said loudly, "I suggest all of you come down from your horses and throw your rifles onto the ground."

When nobody followed his order, he fired a shot into the sky. "The next one kills your friend here," he shouted. "Perhaps a few of you, also."

One of the men laughed. "You'll be dead a moment later. You might be able to take a couple of us with you, but you only have five bullets left and we have twenty rifles with many bullets." He pointed his rifle at Falcon. "I suggest you throw down the gun and get onto your knees unless you have a death wish. I can put you out of your misery right now."

Evaluating the situation, he was confident he could kill a few of them with Tomm's revolver if it came down to it. Their horses were much too close to each other, which would be to their disadvantage. If he took away a rifle from another man, there was a distinct possibility he'd be able to kill all of them. Unfortunately, the presence of Eldira made that impossible. She would not survive the skirmish. A stray bullet could kill her.

Then there was the other reason. Morally, he could not justify killing so many civilians without more provocation, unless they started shooting at the house or killing Eldira without just cause.

Falcon whirled the gun around his finger and then threw it onto the ground. "You win," he said, "but only for the moment." He was wondering why nobody came out of the house to see what was going on. Were all of them still asleep?

"What is your purpose for coming here?" he asked, looking at Tomm.

Tomm's laugh was ugly. "We came to wipe this nest of the devil's spawn off the surface of Aurora once and for all."

"Are you telling me you want to kill all the people living in this community?"

"You heard me correctly. Kill them and burn down their houses of sin. Actually, we won't kill all of them. The lucky ones we spare will end up as slaves somewhere."

"You realize there are over two hundred innocent and peaceful people living here. Most of them women and children."

"No women and children. Whores of an alien race and their brood. I will enjoy their screams as their soulless bodies burn in the Holy Fire of our Lord, and I will laugh watching the men that created this cesspool swing from the highest trees." His eyes had a wild look to them as he shouted these words.

"You are a sick man," Falcon said from between clenched teeth. He barely could contain the urge to shoot Tomm where he stood. He looked at the men sitting on their horses. "You heard him. Is that why you came here? Are all of you carrying such hatred inside you that you would murder all these people living in this peaceful village in cold blood? People that never did you any harm?" He spoke with a loud voice, hoping all of the men could hear him.

"That's what we came here for," the nearest man said. "But before we burn them we'll have some fun with those bitches from hell. One thing cannot be denied. They are beautiful and supposed to be wild when they fuck." He grinned widely as he spoke.

"This son-of-a-bitch probably found that out when he fucked that bitch standing behind him," another rider sneered.

"What are we waiting for?" one of the men in the back yelled. "Let's kill him and get started. I want to be back home before evening. I promised my wife to go to the Evening Service with her. Brother Dawson is presenting a sermon about the wages of sin."

"Me too," another man said.

It took all of Falcon's efforts to stay calm. He knew now how all of this would end. Nobody would go to listen to Brother Dawson's sermon tonight. As far as he was concerned all of them were dead already. None would leave here alive.

Where the hell were Alita and Newman? What about Mal?

The morning silence was shattered by a gunshot. One of the men fell from his horse. Falcon saw movement in the forest behind the intruders. More shots rang out. The horses became agitated and whinnied. Two more riders collapsed in their saddles and hung lifeless at the side of their steeds. Suddenly, Mal was there. He grabbed his wife's arm and pulled her toward the barn to safety.

Angry barking sounds erupted behind the house and half a dozen wolf-like beasts, displaying long teeth, loped on powerful legs toward the riders and were among them in moments. Horses screamed as other horses tried to push them aside. Some went down as the beasts sank their teeth into their legs and hinds. The sound of rifle shots and the cries of wounded men added to the chaos that ensued. Some of the horses bolted and headed for the lake, the only, apparently, safe spot. Their riders collapsed as bullets cut them down.

Falcon reacted instinctively when a screaming man ran at him wielding a long knife. The man went down when Falcon smashed his fist into his neck with full force. Only subconsciously he registered that the man was Tomm.

Suddenly it was over. The rifles stopped firing. The only sounds interrupting the silence were the moans and cries of wounded or dying men and horses. Falcon bent and turned over Tomm's unmoving body. He was dead. Falcon had broken his neck.

From the forest appeared men. Falcon counted seven, he had expected more. They carried rifles. Their faces were grim as they surveyed the scene. Two shots rang out in quick succession when one of the men lifted his rifle. The moaning stopped. Falcon knew the man had given two of the men still fighting for their lives the killing shot, the way you would with a wounded and dying animal.

Another man fired his rifle a few times, his targets the injured horses, and then it was finally over for good. The sudden complete silence was almost painful.

Falcon looked for the six beasts but couldn't see them. Newman came stalking toward him, a look of sadness on his face.

"This was not necessary," he said with a toneless voice.

"They were here to murder the people in this village, the men, the women, and the children," Falcon told him. "They made their choice. The men from the village only defended themselves and their families. The blame does not lie with them."

"I am not blaming the villagers. They did what they had to do. I am blaming the stupidity and narrow minds of the people living on Aurora. I am blaming the religion that causes them to hate anything and anyone different from them and their beliefs."

"I can understand that it makes you sad, even angry, but we must face this reality, both of us. As a soldier, I cannot allow myself to feel pity or regret." Falcon looked around. "Have you seen Alita? I hope she is alright."

"She is. You saw her." Newman looked stressed.

"I don't think I did, but then again, everything happened incredibly fast." He spotted Alita coming out of the forest. She walked slowly. He wondered why she was naked.

When she was near, she gave him a tired smile. Then she looked at the dead bodies, human and animal. "What a mess," she said, her voice weak and as tired as her smile.

"What happened to you? Why are you naked?" And then the truth dawned on him.

She must have seen it in his expression. "You know what I am. It shouldn't be too hard to figure out, Falcon."

"The wolves," he said. "How?"

"All six of my manifestations were connected to each other with a thin tendril. It took a lot out of me. I am exhausted and dirty. I think I'll go down to the water and wash myself."

He watched as she walked down to the lake, wondering what else she was capable of.

"What do you suggest we do with the dead men and the horses, the dead and live ones?"

He turned to look at the speaker. It was Mannie, the neighbor he met the day before. He ran his hand over his hair, trying to think. Why would Mannie ask him? "I suggest you burn the dead bodies, men and horses. Burn the saddles and all personal belongings. If you're not sure, burn it or get rid of it."

"What about the rifles?"

"I see no reason not to keep them unless they have personal markings on them. You don't want to keep any evidence of what happened here. You may have to bury some of the stuff that can't be burned. Bury it deep in the forest, away from the village."

Mannie shook his head, his expression troubled. "This is a bad thing that happened here. How can you hide the disappearance of so many people? There will be questions."

"That's why you must get rid of everything that can be recognized as something that belonged to the men who died here. Don't push it off. Do it as soon as possible."

"Where can we burn such a mass of bodies?"

"Don't you have an open field that can be plowed after it is done?"

"Good idea." Mannie took a few deep breaths. "The horses will be a big job. We may have to cut them up. What should we do with the live ones?"

Falcon looked at Newman. "What do you think?"

"I think it is a big problem. As tempting as it is to keep them, I suggest you don't. There is a good chance someone might recognize at least one. Burn the saddles and set the horses free. Horses can swim. Take them across the lake and, if possible, as deep as you can into the forest on the other side. Then let them go. They'll find their way into the prairie where they can join a herd of wild horses. I can't think of any other way. Maybe some of you can come up with a better idea, but I wouldn't wait too long. Time is of the essence."

"I'll run it by the others, but I think your idea has merits." There was a determined look on Mannie's face. "Yes, I think it can be done. I need to go and talk to the others. And then we'd better get started with the cleanup."

"There is one more thing. I've noticed that some of the horses are shoed. You'll have to remove the shoes before setting the horses free."

"I'll make sure it is done."

Falcon studied the carnage. Dead men lay either on top or under the dead horses. A couple of the men were beginning to take the saddles off the horses, while another led away the live ones.

"Do you think it will work?" Newman sounded doubtful.

"It will have to, otherwise this village and the people living in it are doomed."

"What can we do to help them? I hope you agree that we should stay."

"Of course, we'll stay. I wouldn't feel right leaving them now with all this mess." Falcon looked down at the can of milk. Miraculously, it still stood where he had put it. The basket with the eggs Eldira had been carrying had not fared that well. It lay upturned on the ground. Some of the eggs were cracked. He looked for Mal, wondering if he and Eldira were safely inside the house.

As if on cue, he saw Mal coming out of the house. He came over to where Newman and Falcon were standing. "All of this is my fault," Mal blurted out.

"Why would you say that?"

"Had we not left our village we wouldn't have been captured by those three men. None of this would have happened."

"Don't even think that for one moment. Those are not healthy thoughts," Falcon warned. "From what I witnessed here today, it would have happened eventually. These men were filled with hatred for you and your families. I don't know why. Probably, because you don't fit into their image of how the world should be. They feel threatened by you."

"We are no danger to them. The only thing we want is to be left alone and live in peace. Why doesn't anyone understand that? Killing these men will lie heavy on our conscience and will be hard to forget, if not impossible." The agony he felt was visible on his face when he looked at Falcon. "We may not be religious in the eyes of the people living in this world. Even though we don't worship their god, we do believe in a higher power. We are not evil. We are not the demons they think we are. We are good people."

Falcon didn't know what to say to that. He reached out and put his hand on Mal's shoulder. "When we rescued you, I told you I was a soldier. My life is ruled by violence. I have seen more than my share of it, and I have hardened my mind to it. Your world does not have the monopoly on intolerance and maliciousness. The evil is everywhere and sometimes it touches us when we least expect it. We can't let it overpower us. We must fight and conquer it. It is the only way to survive."

"I am not a soldier, and I don't envy you and your way of life. I cannot even condone it, but I don't judge you and I accept that people like you have their purpose in this universe." He gave Falcon a sad smile. "I know without you my life and that of my family as we know it would have been over. I will forever be grateful to you for that."

"It was our duty to help you. Perhaps, whatever gods rule this universe led us to you." Falcon removed his hand from Mal's shoulder. He picked up the can of milk. "I'm going to take this can of milk into the house. I promised your wife I wouldn't spill a drop."

"Then you'd better not break that promise." Mal managed to laugh. "Eldira's wrath will be terrible. She's quite fond of that milk."

"I'm going to check on Alita," Newman said. "She went down to the lake to wash herself. With those men around, she may want her clothing, naked as she is."

"You do that," Falcon agreed. "She'll appreciate it. Possibly, she may need your help anyway. The fight took a lot out of her." He glanced at Newman. "I assume you know what I'm talking about."

"I saw," Newman said gravely.

Falcon followed Mal to the house.

Mal's children sat at the table, eating breakfast. It took only one look for Falcon to know they were traumatized and scared. Eldira saw the milk can in Falcon's hand.

"I can't believe it didn't get spilled," she said as she took the can from him.

"I told you I'd bring you a full can," he said with a little smile. "I never break a promise."

"The children already wondered what happened to the milk." Her expression became sad. "I guess the eggs are lost."

"I managed to rescue a few," Mal said from the door. He put the basket onto the counter. "There should be enough whole ones for everyone."

"We'll harvest more tomorrow." Eldira looked into the basket. "More than I expected." When she looked at Falcon, he saw the tears in her eyes. "Thank you for everything," she whispered.

He just nodded and said, "It will get better."

[13]

ALL THE CAPABLE ADULTS WORKED AROUND THE CLOCK TO CLEAN UP the mess. To burn the bodies of the dead men was a priority. They loaded the corpses onto wagons and took them into the middle of one of the fields that had been harvested. The young men and the boys old enough to help dragged dry branches and old wood into the field and made a huge brush pile. Then they threw the bodies onto the pile. Once the bodies of the men lay on the brush pile, they brought the saddles and other stuff that needed to be disposed of. The stench of burning flesh and leather was unbearable, but nobody complained.

Because of their size, the bodies of the dead horses presented a bigger problem. They had to be cut up, but they got it done with the help of some of the women. Fortunately, there were only six dead horses to get rid of.

In the end, they decided to distribute the meat of two of the horses among the villagers for food.

The scavengers didn't wait too long to make an appearance. They came already the first night, but the fires that had been lit around the corpses kept them at bay.

"We have to get the horses away from here," Mannie reminded them. He and two other men took over the job. They roped the horses together and used two boats to guide them across the lake. Once on the other side, they took off the ropes and fired a few shots into the air to scare the horses. Most of them disappeared into the forest. Only two seemed reluctant, but eventually, they followed the others.

After four days there was no evidence left of what had taken place in front of Mal's house. However, the fire in the field was still burning. They wanted to make sure that absolutely every scrap of cloth and leather had been turned into ashes. Anything made from metal had been buried somewhere deep in the forest, away from the village.

Even though a dark shadow hung over the village, the Elders suggested they celebrate. Most of the people living in Sanctuary had at one time or other gone through a period of hardship before they settled in Sanctuary. They had proved to each other again that they could persevere if they stood together in the face of danger.

Near the center of the village was a piece of land the mothers and children were using as a spot to get together on nice days to let the children run around free and play their games. It was decided it would make a great place to celebrate. The men set up fire-pits to roast chunks of meat and the women brought plates with vegetables and other foods. They spread blankets on the grass for everyone to sit on.

As the men and older boys and girls sat around the fires watching the meat sizzle and keeping the flames from dying, they talked about other events that had threatened their way of life. They were also interested in hearing Falcon and Newman tell stories of other planets they had visited and what it was like to travel among the stars.

"Are there people like us somewhere?" one boy wanted to know. Falcon saw it was Milber, Mal's oldest son.

"Do you mean people that look like you?"

"Yes. Are there?"

Falcon shook his head. "I don't know. Until I came here I've never met any of your mother's people, but I don't doubt that on some planet there are people just like you. We humans have colonized many planets, and it is quite possible that humans have met members of the Suries race. The chances of a human man falling in love with a Suries woman are pretty good." He smiled. "After all, from what I see, Suries women and girls are very beautiful."

"What about a human woman falling in love with a Suries man?"

"I'm sure there are plenty of those, also." Falcon noticed that the man who had asked the question was not human. "There are many different races in this galaxy of ours and mixed liaisons are not uncommon. Take Perseus, for instance, which has been colonized by humans and humanoids with wings. They call themselves Tangari, by the way. There you will find many couples where the men have married human women, or the other way around. Unfortunately, that is also a planet where mixed marriages are frowned upon, because many Tangari look at humans as being handicapped since they lack wings."

"Are the children of those marriages hated like here?"

He looked at the girl asking the question. "No, not hated, tolerated but pitied if they are born without wings."

"Then why do the humans on this world hate us to the point where they want us dead?"

"I cannot answer your question. I don't think they know the answer to that, either. Maybe they are scared of you because you are different. You may change their way of life if they accept you. People don't like changes."

"We won't make them change," a little girl piped up.

"It is not that simple," Falcon said with a smile. "I wish it were."

"I believe this meat is finished," one of the men declared. "Who wants to be the first to eat a piece?"

He carved off a few pieces, pushed them onto sticks and handed them out. Some of the women brought wooden plates with vegetables on them.

"This horsemeat tastes quite good," Newman remarked. "I've never eaten horsemeat before."

"Neither have I," Falcon admitted. "I agree, it tastes better than some of the meat I ate on my other missions. A shame we had to kill these majestic and beautiful animals to find that out." He looked around and felt a sadness inside him. The children chased each other, laughed, and played games. Everybody seemed to enjoy the cookout. These people were so happy, even though they had just spent days working hard to clean up the evidence of a tragedy not of their making.

"It's a shame that things had to come to this," Newman said as if reading Falcon's mind.

"Yes, it is. By the way, have you seen Alita?"

"Not since this morning at breakfast. She told me she was feeling tired."

"She hasn't been herself these last few days. I hope there is nothing wrong with her." Falcon looked at Mal's son. "Milber, do you know if Alita, my friend, is somewhere in the park?"

"She isn't here. She told my mother that she was tired and would be resting in the house."

"Thank you." Falcon rose. "That isn't like her at all," he said to Newman. "I'm going to check up on her." He hurried across the park and then down the road, an uneasy feeling in his stomach.

He found her lying on the Chesterfield in the living room, her eyes closed. When he stepped closer, she opened her eyes. Recognizing him, she gave him a feeble smile.

"What is wrong?" he asked.

"I've underestimated my ability," she said. "I think I overdid it. Now my body is paying for it."

"You've lost me there, I'm afraid."

"The six beasts. It was too much for me. They sucked all my energy out of me. Just to move around takes a lot of effort." Her smile was weak. "Sorry, I am missing the celebration."

"Is there anything that will bring back your energy?"

"There is. I need fresh blood."

"How about one of Mal's sheep? I'll carry you outside, if necessary."

"I won't work." She shook her head. "It has to be human blood."

"Alright then. I'll let you drink mine."

"It isn't that simple. I didn't tell you everything when you asked me about my requirements. There is more to it than just your permission. We have to become intimate you and I."

"You mean having sexual intercourse?"

She nodded. "The energy I need from you can only be transferred at the moment of your climax. When you reach your orgasm the pleasure you experience creates endorphins in your brain and metaphysical energy in your blood which will resonate inside my body when I drink your blood and absorb your seminal fluid. Don't ask me to explain all that."

"Sounds simple enough."

"It does, doesn't it? However, there is more to it than just the clinical explanation of what happens. It isn't just a cold mechanical joining of our bodies. I will experience an orgasm at the same time you are. At that moment it won't be only our bodies that are joined together but also our minds. Our minds and bodies will become one." Her hand touched his face. "There is the danger having sex with me will leave you with strong feelings and desires for me. The pleasure human women you may have been intimate with gave you cannot compare with the joy you will find in my arms as together we climb to the peak of our passion. And passion it will be, I promise you that."

He bent down to kiss her on the lips. "The pleasure we will

experience will be a bonus. Helping you to gain your strength back will be the main objective."

She sat up and began taking off her clothes. "We might as well be naked," she said with a wicked smile. "I want to feel your skin on mine."

"I wouldn't have it any other way," he said, grinning, and slipped out of his own clothes.

"I need to be on top," she told him. "It will make it easier." She came into his arms and looked up at him. "I don't want you to feel obligated," she whispered, molding her naked body against his.

She was warm and soft in his arms. The apprehension he felt at first melted away and he pulled her close. Suddenly, he wanted her badly. His body reacted to her nearness. Grabbing her full buttocks, he kneaded them gently.

She put her hand behind his head and lifted it to kiss him. Her lips opened and she sucked his tongue into her mouth, kissing him with great passion. Pulling back, she whispered, "Come, lie down."

He stretched out on the Chesterfield and watched her straddle him. Her white skin was smooth, without a blemish and her breasts were full and perfectly formed. There wasn't a trace of hair on her puffy mound. Smiling, she grabbed his erect penis and guided him. With almost agonizing slowness, she sank into his lap, taking him deep into her.

The pleasure began from the moment he entered the slippery entrance to her sex-organ and increased in intensity the deeper he slid into the tight, hot sheath that molded its walls around his engorged penis. No human woman had ever felt this way. Closing her eyes, she gyrated her hips, partially releasing him and then taking him back into her with every stroke. Her whole body undulated like a boneless serpent above him, and her alien vagina seemed alive as her inner muscles rippled along the length of his penis. He lost all sense of time as he swam in a sea of pure pleasure.

There was a sudden moment of disorientation and then his mind seemed to expand. He knew she was there with him; he felt her presence. Their bodies and minds became one. He heard her silent voice, "Now...Let it happen...now..."

He felt a faint sting and a roaring sound echoing through his mind, but there was no pain, only joy, nothing but joy, and it consumed his whole being. He was aware of her warm naked body pressing against him, her breasts soft on his chest, her sex-organ milking his gushing penis as her mouth drank his blood from a vein in his neck. He didn't care. He knew there was no danger when she soothed him without words.

When it was over and her mind left him, he felt empty and alone. She still lay on top of him, still felt soft and warm in his embrace, but that intimate feeling of complete joy was gone.

He held her to him, not wanting to let her go, not wanting to lose that feeling of intimacy two lovers feel when their naked bodies touch, when their limbs are entwined, but he knew that this moment would end. Sighing, he ran his hands over her body, enjoying her soft, smooth skin one last time.

She lifted her head and looked at him. He barely noticed the thin fangs in her open mouth, he saw only love and gratitude in her eyes. "Thank you," she whispered and kissed him. Not with passion but with great tenderness.

Then she slipped out of his embrace.

He looked up at her as she stood beside him, like a vision out of a beautiful dream, one that would fade in a short time. "I love you."

She smiled down at him, but there was sadness in her smile. "You cannot love me."

"Why not?"

"We are partners on this mission not lovers. I warned you that having sex with me will create a strong desire in you for me. Nature has cursed my species with the need and desire for fresh blood to survive. It had to be consumed during sexual intercourse with the donor. While drinking the blood we gave the donor great pleasure. Another survival trait. We have evolved and don't need to have sex to get our blood, which makes it possible to get blood from animals. However, in matters of life and death situations, we must join our bodies and minds with the donor. I hope you understand."

"Why would it be so wrong to love you?"

"You don't love me, Jeremy. You love this body but not me. What you feel isn't actually love, it is an obsession. Another design of nature to make it easy for me to drink your blood when I need it again. You and I can never be real lovers because our species are so different. Our couplings, no matter how wonderful they feel, will not produce any offspring. Ever."

"Two people can still love each other without creating children," he protested. "Take, for instance, when members of the same sex fall in love with each other."

"Of course, they can, but usually they are members of the same species. This is different."

"Since I am so obsessed with you, tell me, is this the same thing I went through with that Dreel female? Do I have to drink a special plant concoction to cure my obsession?"

"This is not the same thing. The Dreel female infected you with some kind of virus that needed to be treated. I didn't infect you with anything. You are attracted to me because I made you feel good physically and mentally, that's all there is to it. It will fade in time." She laughed softly. "There is nothing wrong with you having feelings for me. Just don't expect to have sex with me whenever you feel horny."

He stood up. "Now that we cleared that up we should get dressed." He smiled. "I was attracted to you from the first time we were introduced. Now that attraction has turned into love. I can live with that." He reached out and pulled her to him. "Isn't it better than hating you?"

"I suppose it is." She put her hand on his chest and gently

pushed him away. "I am grateful to you for what you did, but let's keep this professional. Just so you know, I don't have feelings of love for you, but I like you. Be satisfied with that."

Sighing, he let her go completely. They both dressed in silence.

"Are you feeling alright?" he asked when they were dressed.

"I am feeling much better, but it will take a little time to be my old self again. Thank you for caring."

"You want to go to the park and join the festivities?"

"I would like to," she said with a little smile. "I hope there is still some food left. I am starving." She chuckled. "I still need real food to get my strength back, just so you know."

"I'm sure there will be enough for you. By the way, the horse-meat tastes quite good. You should try some."

When they got to the park, they heard music. Somebody played an instrument, and a few people even sang. They saw couples dancing in the grass, adults and children.

"Everybody looks so happy. It seems I missed a lot," Alita said and grabbed Falcon. "Come, dance with me."

"I can't dance," Falcon grunted. "When it comes to dancing, I have two left feet."

She laughed merrily. "I'll teach you. Don't be a spoilsport. I feel like dancing."

Had it not been for Newman, she might have convinced him to dance, or at least try. He popped up from nowhere. "I wondered what happened to you." He sounded concerned.

"I just took a little nap," Alita explained. "I felt tired and wasn't feeling good, but I'm okay now." She glanced at Falcon with a smile. "Falcon can be very entertaining when he wants to be. He gave me some pep-talk and brought me a cup of milk to drink. I may have been a bit dehydrated."

Newman looked at her. "You look better than when I saw you last. The important thing is you're fine. I was getting worried when Falcon didn't return. I was just about to come and look in on you."

"I appreciate your concern, but I'm alright. By the way, is there some food left for a hungry person?"

"I'm sure there is. You'll have to look for a bunch of people sitting around a fire pit. That'll be your best chance."

"Thanks, Newman. I'll do that. I think I've spotted a place. See you later." She walked away, leaving both men standing.

"Weird," Newman commented. "She looked quite bad before and now she is so chipper." He pulled his eyebrows together. "I suppose it is just her alien identity. Her metabolism is different from ours."

"I suppose that's it," Falcon agreed. "I was going to talk to you about our next move. There is nothing we can do here anymore. These people will be fine without us. I think we should leave tomorrow. What do you think?"

"I am all for that. We've done more than enough for them."

[14]

IT RAINED DURING THE NIGHT, WHICH WAS A BLESSING IN MANY WAYS. It washed away most of the evidence the riders and horses had left behind on the road to the village. Overgrown with weeds and small shrubs, the road had never been great to begin with.

Once they left the forest, they could ride a little faster to gain back the time they had lost. It took most of the day to reach Winnira, but there was still enough daylight left to search for a place to stay.

The hotel was not fancy, in fact, it was quite shabby looking, but it would do until the next day.

"We need two rooms for one night?" Falcon put two pellets of gold onto the counter.

The old man behind the counter looked at them, swallowed, and said, "One more pellet."

"Too much," Falcon told him. "We'll take one room then. With two beds. We paid two pellets of gold for that in Riwarda."

"This is not Riwarda. Even though, you can't have just one room. It is immoral to have two men and one woman in one room. That's the law."

"Not the law where we come from." Falcon reluctantly fished another pellet out of his leather bag. "You are robbing us, old man."

"You can always leave and find a hotel somewhere else," he challenged Falcon, giving him a defying look. "This is a respectable place. We follow the word of the Prophet. Are you denying the Word of the Prophet?"

"Your Prophet is not mine." Falcon felt irritated. "His Word means nothing to me."

"You'd better watch your tongue around here, Mister. We've strung up people for less." The hostility in the old man's face was quite clear.

"No need to become argumentative," Newman said soothingly. "My friend here had a bad day. He didn't mean what he said."

"If you don't mean what you say don't say it at all." He glared at Falcon. "The mood in this town is gloomy. Everyone is on edge. We've lost twenty good men lately. One of them was my son-in-law. We don't need no stranger coming in here and criticizing the Word of the Prophet. Remember that!"

"What happened to those men?" Newman inquired.

"Nobody knows. They went on some secret mission days ago and never came back. Not one of them. No men and no horses. Even Kerry, my own son-in-law, didn't tell me anything except they were going to do the work of God. I have no idea what he meant."

"Perhaps whatever they were going to do took longer than expected. How do you know they are lost somewhere or dead?"

"It's been too long since they left. Besides, most of them had families to take care of and work to look after. They couldn't afford to stay away this long. No, we have accepted the fact that they are dead."

"That's not a good thing. Losing a member of the family is always sad. You have my sympathy."

"It won't bring him back." The old man made a dismissing

gesture with his hand. "To tell the truth, he was not really an upstanding citizen, anyway. Gave my daughter a lot of grief. She may be better off without him. He did stuff I didn't always agree with."

"Like what?"

"Apparently, he and a couple of his friends were involved in smuggling. They waylaid people, robbed them, and sold them as slaves." He bent across the counter. "I'm not saying they were completely wrong doing that. From what I heard they were only Suries and Suman."

"Am I wrong to assume people in this town don't like Suries and Suman?"

"Who does? The Suries women are evil. Daughters of the Dark. They seduce good men, have sex with them, and produce creatures neither human nor Suries. The Suman are the brood of the Dark One. There's a whole nest of them deep in the woods. We should burn down that whole forest and the whole lot of them with it. That's what we should do."

"Wouldn't that be murder?"

The old man stared at Falcon with narrow eyes. "What do you care? You don't honor the Prophet's Word, so why would you worry about a bunch of alien witches and their spawn?"

The old man's words irked Falcon. One thing he couldn't accept, and that was intolerance and species hatred. "Have you ever met members of the Suries?"

"I haven't. All I know is what I hear, and it isn't anything good."

"Then let me tell you that the Suries are no different from humans. The only difference is they don't look like us. They are no more or less evil than we humans. Did you know that the Suries came to Aurora as colonists? In fact, they were here before humans came to settle on this planet. There are plenty of other species out there that don't look at all like us. That doesn't mean they are evil. You should remember that, Mister!"

The old man looked from Falcon to Newman. "What's wrong

with your friend? I think he is a Suries-lover. Don't let nobody hear this crazy talk of his, or they'll hang you right along with him." Then he pointed a finger at Alita. "Same goes for you."

She put a hand against her chest. "Me? I haven't said a word. However, since you pick on me let me say this. It seems there is something wrong with you and this town. Are you in the habit of hanging anyone that criticizes you and your religion? Perhaps you should realize yours is not the only religion on this world and out there among the stars. There are literally thousands of different versions. Most of them believe theirs is the only one. All others are wrong. You need to respect other people's beliefs. No need to murder everyone that doesn't agree with you."

He stared at her for a moment. "You sure have a sharp tongue, woman. This is our town and we do what we want. Our town, our laws. Simple as that. You sure you want to stay in my hotel?"

"Let's just all calm down now, people," Newman said sharply. "We came to stay one night and get some rest before we move on. Let's do that. I don't feel like wasting hours looking for a suitable hotel. Besides, it is getting dark outside." He turned to the proprietor. "We'll take the two rooms. Are you serving food here?"

"Yes, I am, but not to you people. You'll have to find another diner or a tavern. You've given me enough grief. Don't need more. Checkout time tomorrow is nine in the morning. I hope I'll never see you again." He handed Newman two keys and walked away.

"What about breakfast?" Newman called after him.

The old man just lifted an arm. He didn't even bother answering or turning around.

"I guess not."

The two rooms were on the second floor. They actually had a connecting door. Falcon wondered if the proprietor was aware of that.

After entering their room, Newman threw his backpack onto one of the two beds. Then he turned to Falcon. "What's eating you, Falcon?"

"What do you mean?"

"The things you said to the proprietor. They could land us in hot water. These little towns have their own laws. Each village and town is run by its own council. I wouldn't count on the local police force to come to the rescue if things go sideways. The chief is probably a member of the council. I was somewhat disappointed to see you act so hostile to the old man."

"Yeah, well. Perhaps I've seen too much of the same stuff that is going on here. These backward planets sometimes rub me the wrong way. I told you about Perseus, my last mission."

"Yes, you did," Newman confirmed. "Humans are sharing the planet with Tangari colonists. You said they were getting along fine."

"For the most part that's true, but there are places where that is not the case. Like here on Aurora, some of the villages make their own laws, especially the ones in the backwoods, away from civilization. The places where no lawman ever goes. I was sent to Perseus to track and apprehend a dangerous criminal."

"They don't have their own police force on Perseus?"

"They do, of course, but this man was not a local. He was already a wanted man on Icarus for committing crimes against humanity. I won't go into details here." Falcon didn't think it was necessary.

"Weren't you born on Icarus?"

"I was, that was the main reason they sent me to Perseus. Once there, I was partnered with a local detective. He was familiar with the backwoods areas, having been raised in one of the little towns. He was the son of a human father and a Tangari mother. His name was Marcello. We clicked immediately." Falcon paused for a moment, taking his thoughts back to the incident.

Then he continued. "We became friends in the short time I knew him. I don't make friends easily, but there was something about him that made you like him. He was easy to get along with and he had a great sense of humor."

"Did you ever catch the criminal you were after?"

"I did, but that was not of importance. Marcello and I spent a few days in one of these small towns. Actually, more a village than a town. People for the most are quite tolerant on Perseus when it comes to mixed couples. It is different in these small towns and villages that exist in those areas that have little or no contact with the outside world. I mentioned that Marcello was a hybrid. Half Tangari and half human." Falcon paused again as painful memories flooded back.

"What happened to him?" Newman's face was serious. He probably had an idea of what Falcon was going to tell him next.

"As it happened, people in this small village had never seen someone like Marcello before. People stared at him, but we didn't pay any attention to that. When we had supper in the only bar a group of young men did more than just stare. They made offensive remarks and wanted to know what kind of weird mutation he was. Marcello didn't take it seriously. Neither did I. He told them that his father was human and his mother Tangari. They knew nothing about the Tangari race."

"That is not uncommon," Newman interrupted. "The Tangari are not very active on the galactic stage. They do keep to themselves."

"That is correct, but remember, this happened on Perseus. Many colonists are of the Tangari race," Falcon continued. "That night it happened. Marcello loved nature. He went outside to look at the stars. When he didn't come back before we usually retired for the night, I went outside to look for him. I found him lying unconscious in the dirt. I could tell he had been beaten. There was no hospital in that town. I carried him into our room and made a call to Marcello's head office. He regained consciousness for a short time. Long enough for him to tell me what happened. That same group of young men from the bar had attacked him. They beat him unconscious with fists and clubs just because he was different. He died before he could be taken to a hospital."

"That is horrible." Newman was visibly affected by the account. "What happened to his attackers? I hope they were held responsible for his murder."

"Nothing happened to them. When I reported the incident to the local police force, they told me there was nothing they could do since there were no witnesses to the attack. They couldn't take the word of a dying man. He may have fallen and injured himself to the point of having brain damage. He was probably delirious and didn't remember things clearly. Besides, the young men I blamed for beating Marcello were upstanding citizens in the town. Arresting them for a crime they were accused of would ruin their promising future careers."

Newman stayed silent, and just nodded. "I guess now I understand why this whole thing with the Suman upsets you," he finally commented. "I can't blame you for that."

There was a knock on the connecting door. It opened and Alita stepped through. "This is nice," she commented with a smile. "I wonder if that miserable old man remembers this door," she said, echoing Falcon's earlier thoughts.

"Perhaps he does and intends to spy on us, hoping we commit an indecent act," Falcon said with a grin.

"An indecent act?" Alita gave him a questioning look. "Is that what you think an intimate moment between us would be?"

"I would never think that if it should happen," Falcon hastened to assure her. "Which it won't."

"Would you cherish such a moment?"

"Of course, I would. But you don't have to worry. I won't break down this door in the middle of the night to take advantage of you and I'm sure neither will Newman." He glanced at Newman. "Right?"

"I have no idea what even brought this up. Obviously, I'm not that kind of a man. I respect a woman's right to sleep in her room without having to worry if she is safe or not from being violated."

He looked at Alita. "In fact, I would defend you with my life should you be in such danger."

Alita walked further into the room and sat down on one of the beds. She gave Newman a calculating look. "You know what I am. Which means you are aware of my need to drink fresh blood once in a while. Doesn't that make you worry I might come through that door when you are asleep and sink my fangs into your neck to sample your blood?"

"Is there a chance that can happen?"

Falcon wasn't sure if Newman's question was serious or not.

Alita's laugh seemed to mock him. "Unless I want to have sex with you...no. Remember, I told you back at the Scouts Post that I get my blood from animals?"

"I remember." His look questioned her. "You mentioned sex again? Why?"

"No reason. It isn't important." She looked at Falcon when she said it. "What about you? Are you concerned?"

"About what? That you may want to have intercourse with me?"

"That and my taste for fresh human blood?"

"Should I?"

This time her laughter was in his head, but aloud she said, "You are safe, Falcon. I can control the urge should it come over me, unless it is a matter of life and death."

"Why do I have the feeling I am missing something here?" Newman looked from Falcon to Alita.

"Only in your imagination. I think we should go and look for a place to have something to eat." Falcon suggested.

"Now that is the first sensible thing I've heard since we came in here," Newman said, shaking his head. "Sometimes I wonder if I am actually part of this team."

They didn't have far to go to find a place that served food. The sign above the door proclaimed, 'The Best Food in Winnira'.

When they entered the dining room, the aroma of cooking

food was promising. A few of the tables were already taken, but they did find one for four people against the wall.

The walls were decorated with mounted animal heads. There was even a whole stuffed wolf-like animal standing in a corner. Falcon wondered if those long teeth in the open jaws were real, or just something from the imagination of the man that stuffed the predator.

"Looks like a successful hunter decorated this place," Falcon commented.

"Probably the reason they have the best food in town." Newman studied the handwritten menu. "I was right. They feature mostly wild meat." He looked at Alita. "I hope that doesn't present a problem for you."

She shook her head. "If you can eat it I can eat it."

A young girl came to take their order. Falcon and Newman ordered a meat dish and a tankard of ale, hoping it would taste as good as the sign said.

"One thing with these backward places, people seem to have more time. The sense of urgency that exists in most advanced societies is missing," Falcon commented and leaned back in his chair.

"That's true," Newman said with a laugh. "Except these wooden chairs are not as comfortable."

Looking around the room at the other patrons, he noticed that even though he and Alita had changed into local clothes, they couldn't hide the fact that they were strangers in this town. Even Newman didn't quite fit in. Of course, their accent gave them away the moment they started speaking.

Falcon sensed an uneasiness in the room. There were mostly men sitting at the tables. They spoke in subdued voices. One of the tables was occupied by five women and one older man. Falcon tried to filter out the voices from the other tables. He wanted to hear what the women were talking about. A couple of the younger women sat silent. It was one older woman that did most of the talking.

"I warned Brat against joining that group," she said. "He wouldn't listen. Said somebody has to do something about them. He wasn't going to sit back and do nothing anymore. Said besides there was money to be made."

"That's what he said," the old man rumbled. "He also said the mission was sanctioned by God. Pastor Sanchez said so himself. God commanded him in a dream to collect willing men to do his work."

"Manny never told me anything," one of the other women spoke up. "All he said was they'd be celebrated as heroes after they came back."

"Well, they haven't returned from that secret mission," another woman said. "I don't know what I'm going to do without a husband." She put her face between her hands and sobbed.

Falcon turned his attention back to Newman when he said, "That guy in the long coat standing by the counter is not a local. Aside from the long coat he is wearing a red belt. If you are looking around, you will notice that all of the men in here are using suspenders to keep up their pants."

"We aren't. I'm wearing a belt."

"So am I, but our belts are not red. They don't make red belts anywhere on this planet. All of the belts here are made from real leather."

Falcon turned his attention to the man by the counter. "I see what you mean. That means he isn't even a native of Aurora. I wonder what business he has here in this forsaken town."

While they watched, another man, this time a resident of Winnira, joined the stranger at the counter. Falcon's interest was aroused. "I'm going to find out what they have to talk about," he told Newman and rose from his chair.

Casually, he walked to the counter. When the man behind the

counter asked what he wanted, Falcon ordered a mug of plain water.

"Water?" The bartender gave him a curious look.

"Yes, water. I am thirsty."

While he waited for his water, he paid attention to what the two men were discussing.

"I traveled a long time to get here." The stranger was clearly annoyed. "It took three days sitting on a horse to get here from Rowarra. Using this primitive way of getting from one place to the next is such a waste of time. Now you tell me you can't deliver? I'm not leaving here without at least part of a shipment."

"You have to understand the situation," the other man said. "The men that left to fulfill the order, haven't returned. We fear they're lost."

"Then send more men on that mission."

"We don't have any. Not everyone in our town agrees with what we planned."

"That is too bad. I am not interested in excuses," the stranger said sharply. "We had a contract. There will be consequences. Listen Hanker. It is Hanker, isn't it? I don't think you have an idea who I represent. If you don't honor our contract, we will come with many men and take what we want and need. I'm sure you still have plenty of young males and females you can spare."

"You can't just kidnap any of the young people in our village," Hanker protested, his voice raised.

"Keep your voice down," the stranger warned him. "No need to advertise this thing. Just so you know, we can and will do anything to achieve what we want. You can't stop us." He threw a look at Falcon who had moved closer to the two men as they argued. "Can I help you with something?"

Falcon gave him a little smile. "Perhaps it is I who can help you with what you're after. I couldn't avoid listening to your conversation. It piqued my curiosity."

The stranger's eyes narrowed. "What makes you think you even know what our conversation was all about?"

"Unless I am wrong, which I don't think I am. You are after slaves," Falcon said in a conspiratorial tone of voice.

The stranger looked him up and down. "It is obvious you are not a local resident of this town. Who are you?"

"I'm not telling unless you tell me who you are." Falcon lowered his voice. "I am not comfortable discussing business in here. Too many ears. Why don't we meet outside after I finish my supper? We can get to know each other then. It's been a long day for me and I am tired and hungry."

The stranger looked at Hanker. "It seems my journey won't be in vain after all. Don't think you're off the hook, though. You still owe me." He turned back to Falcon. "You'd better deliver what you are promising. I am warning you, if you are planning something malicious you will be sorry."

Falcon lifted both hands. "You have nothing to fear from me. I'm a stranger here on a mission, just like you. Perhaps we can help each other."

He put the empty mug onto the counter and walked back to his table.

"What did you find out?" Newman asked.

"Not much, yet." Falcon sat down. "We will be meeting him outside after we finished eating. All I can tell you is that he is after slaves. I told him we can help him with that."

"You've lost me there," Newman said. "How can we help him?"

"Obviously, he is a slave trader. I want to find out more about him."

"There is something odd about him," Alita ventured. "I can't put my finger on it, but I sense something menacing, something unfamiliar and disturbing."

"I see our food and drink arrived." Falcon took a swig from his mug of ale and wiped his mouth. "Let's eat. I am hungry."

[15]

IT WAS DARK OUTSIDE WHEN THEY LEFT THE DINER. THERE WAS ONE gas lantern lighting up the immediate surroundings. The stranger was a dark shadow leaning against the pole, waiting for them.

"I was just about to leave," he grumbled. "I don't like waiting."

"We have a saying: Patience is a virtue. Sometimes you miss a good opportunity when you are impatient," Falcon told him.

"We have no such sayings where I come from," the stranger said.

"Where do you come from?" Falcon quizzed him.

"You first," the stranger countered.

Falcon didn't see a reason not to tell him at least one fact. "Originally, I am from Icarus. That's my birth planet. And you?"

"You wouldn't know it. Let's say it is far from here. Very far from here." He chuckled. "But then again, it could be close. Depending on your mode of travel. Now, let's get down to business. You claim to be able to help me to get slaves. Can you?"

Falcon held up a hand. "Not so fast. First, tell me your name. I don't like to deal with anyone without knowing at least his name."

"You can call me Ipar. Yours?"

"I am Falcon. The names of my associates are Newman and Alita. Are you alone?"

"Right now, I am, but that will change as soon as the deal is made. Let me ask you a question. What are you really doing here on this backward planet? I am not comfortable dealing with people I know nothing about. You have to give me more information about you and your associates."

"We will, as soon as you do the same about yourself. To know your name, if that actually is your name, is not enough."

"So far, you'll be dealing only with me. I am the one making the deals. My only purpose for being here is to buy slaves. What we do with them is not your business."

"That's where we don't agree. What you do with them is very much our business. We must be assured that any slave you purchase from us is not killed or mistreated. They feel pain, physical and mental. They are intelligent beings and deserve to be treated with dignity. Am I making myself clear?"

Ipar's laugh was mocking. "I can tell you anything you want to hear. Once they are in my possession you have relinquished your rights to them. However, I assure you we will not mistreat them. I can promise you that."

"How will we know? Perhaps if you tell me which planet or which part of the Galaxy they'll be taken, we can come to an agreement?"

"I could, but I am quite positive that you are not familiar with the star system of my home world. I come from a region far away from here. We don't associate with any of the major races in this part of the Galaxy."

"What do you call your species?" Falcon was hoping for more details. So far Ipar had told him very little.

"I suppose it won't hurt to give you that information. I come from a planet called Apovi. I am an Apovian. That's what we call our race. Mine is an old race and dying. We collect members from many different races, searching for one that is compatible with ours in the hopes of saving our race from extinction."

"You are telling us that you use the slaves for breeding?"

"That's what I'm telling you. None of them will suffer. We will mate with them, hoping for offspring to keep our race alive."

"On the surface, it sounds like a noble undertaking," Newman said. "It all depends how they will be used as breeders. Will they be free to move around, or will they be kept in pens and bred until they are too old to bear children?"

"I cannot give you details. I am only a negotiator. What happens after the slaves are delivered to my home planet is out of my hands." Ipar moved farther away from the light. "Enough empty chatter. Can you deliver or are we just wasting time?"

"These things take time," Falcon said, stalling. They really didn't know anything about the stranger. He had called his species Apovians. Falcon had never heard of his race. If there was such a race, it must indeed be far away from this region of the Galaxy.

Ipar suddenly stiffened. "I think you are not telling me the truth. I sense deception." The last two words came out in a hiss.

"It is you who is trying to deceive us," Alita countered. "You are not what you pretend to be."

"Neither are you. This is not your true form." Ipar moved further away from the light. "I know you are not like me. What are you?"

"I am Accilla," she told him.

"Are you a telepath? I sensed your mind touch."

"If you can sense me, you also have the gift."

"Show me your true form," he demanded.

"It would serve no purpose."

"I do not trust you." The Apovian reached into his coat. His hand came out holding an object, obviously a weapon, one unfamiliar to Falcon. His hand went to draw the gun from the holster under his arm. Things happened fast after that.

Falcon and his companions had one thing in their favor. They stood in the shadow, while the Apovian stood near the gas lantern, an easy target. "Gun!" Falcon's warning shout was not necessary. Alita was already on the move. He hoped Newman was taking evasive action. Throwing himself to the ground, his gun came up. The flash of a lightning bolt from a laser beside him lit up the night for a short moment. He didn't know if it hit its target, but he knew his own did.

The spear of light from his laser hit Ipar in the chest, but the Apovian was already on his knees. Alita's shot had been true. The ear-deafening explosion from a weapon shooting bullets shattered the silence of the night.

Newman.

His bullet hit the stranger between the eyes. Collapsing, he lay unmoving on the ground. He never had the chance to fire.

Falcon rose and slowly walked over to the still figure, watching for signs of life. Bending down, he pried the gun from the lifeless hand and shoved it into his pocket. As he went through the Apovian's coat, a sudden shudder went through the dead body. He jumped up and stepped back, his gun pointing at the convulsing figure.

The form began to change shape, the clothing ripped in various places until only tatters of cloth covered part of what once had looked like a human.

What Falcon looked at was the body of a giant snake. A flat, triangle-shaped head topped a sinuous, thick trunk. In the open maw teeth as long as daggers gleamed in the dim light of the gas lantern and a long, thin tongue lolled between the teeth. The body had no legs but two arms with five-fingered hands.

"What am I looking at?"

Falcon turned to Newman who had asked the question. "Your guess is as good as mine." He looked at Alita. "Have you ever seen anything like this?"

She shook her head. "Not until now. Obviously, this is his true form."

"According to what he told us he is an Apovian. I don't believe he lied to us. The question is: where does he come from? He hinted that there are more of his race on Aurora."

"Did you find anything in his pockets?" Alita wondered.

"I didn't have enough time to search before he began changing. The only thing I have is his gun. I've never seen one like it."

Newman knelt beside the now unmoving body. He pulled out a flat metal box. "I've got something. Perhaps there is something inside."

"What's that on his wrist?" Alita pulled on it but it wouldn't budge. "It appears to be some kind of communication device." When it didn't come off, she lifted her laser and cut off the wrist.

Falcon heard the creaking of hinges and then he saw light flooding out of the opening door to the diner. Three men stepped out and looked around. "We heard a gunshot," one of them said.

"You heard right," Newman told them.

"What happened out here?" The three men left the circle of light and came closer. As their eyes adjusted to the darkness, they spotted the body of the Apovian on the ground. "What in the Dark One's name is that?"

"Looks like a giant snake." All three men made the sign of the cross in the air.

"Must be a Demon," one stated. "Look, he's wearing clothes."

"There is blood on the ground," another one observed. He looked at Newman. "Did you kill this thing?"

"I sure did," Newman bragged. He patted the colt on his hip. "Not the first time this little pistol saved my life."

"Not so little if it brought down this creature. We heard the shot. Shook up everyone inside. We are not used to violence in our streets."

"He won't hurt nobody anymore, thanks to my friend," Falcon said. "If you excuse us, we'll be leaving now. We have a long day ahead of us tomorrow."

"Aren't you the strangers staying at Old Melbur's hotel?"

"We are. Just passing through. We will be moving on tomorrow. By the way, nice town you've got. We loved the food we had in the diner. That sign above the door does not lie."

"Yes, Ben's food is the best. Usually, you'll have trouble finding a table, but right now people aren't in the mood to celebrate anything, because of those missing young men."

"We heard about that," Newman commented. "Terrible tragedy."

"Certainly is," Falcon agreed. "Well, nice talking to you. We'd better be going now. Hope things turn out okay with those missing men."

Once out of earshot, Falcon said, "Too bad we couldn't get away before those three came outside. That creature will be the talk of the town by tomorrow and they will wonder why we killed it. I want to be gone before dawn. We'll catch a few hours of sleep and leave as early as possible."

"I had the same thought," Alita agreed. "We don't want to draw any more attention than necessary by hanging around too long."

———

THERE WAS NO HINT OF DAWN YET WHEN THEY LEFT WINNIRA. THE darkness would protect them from being discovered. The streets were quiet, and they tried to make as little noise as possible, even though the echo of the clip-clop sounds of the horses' hoofs on the cobblestones seemed much too loud.

They breathed sighs of relief when they finally left the last house behind without attracting any attention from anyone.

Fortunately, the weather was in their favor and when dawn finally broke it greeted them with a bright sky. The rising sun painted the sky red at first, but it didn't take long before it turned blue. No clouds were to be seen and Falcon hoped the weather would stay like that for the rest of the day.

The dirt road was dry, and the hooves of the horses created

small clouds of dust behind them. It was close to noon when they came upon a tiny village. There were no more than a dozen or so houses, but they saw one building that clearly was a church. They were more interested in a store than a church and when they saw a small rundown building with a faded unreadable sign above the door, they assumed it had to be a store.

"I'll check it out," Newman volunteered and climbed down from his horse.

"Looks like a ghost town," Falcon observed. "I wonder where all the people are."

"Probably working in the fields," Alita guessed. "It is a beautiful day. Perfect for doing some work outside."

Newman came back out of the door. He waved and called, "It is a store. For a pellet of gold, the proprietor will even make us a few sandwiches."

When Falcon and Alita entered the store, he saw shelves filled with clothing and all kinds of stuff farmers would buy. One wall was covered with farm tools and equipment. There was a counter. Behind it stood an old woman.

Newman was busy talking to the woman. He turned around when Falcon and Alita approached the counter. "This is Melanie Snydor," he introduced the woman. "She said she'll make us something to eat."

Falcon saw loaves of bread, buns, and small cakes on a counter behind the woman. From the ceiling hung different sizes of sausages and smoked meats.

"That would be very much appreciated," Falcon told her.

"Why don't you just browse the store while I make the sandwiches," Melanie suggested. "Perhaps you'll find something you like." She disappeared through a door that probably led into the kitchen.

"Strange, how things are so different on these backward planets," Falcon commented. "Can you imagine a store like this on Easter or on Earth itself?"

Alita laughed. "It would be condemned by the first government agent coming into the store. They'd close it down before it saw any real customers."

"I find it has a certain charm and brings back memories of my childhood. I'm not saying we had stores like this on Icarus, but my father used to take me shopping for supplies sometimes. You may recall me telling Newman that my father was a farmer. Of course, the equipment he used was a bit more modern than what you see here. The clothing is another story."

"We should buy something," Alita suggested. "This woman looked so happy to see us. Finally, customers. I have a feeling she sells very little of her merchandise in this little village."

"What would you buy?" There was really nothing Falcon found interesting.

"How about this knife?" Alita pointed to one of the shelves.

Falcon took it off the shelf and touched the blade. "Not very good steel."

"Buy it as a souvenir." She laughed. "Some day when you're old and grey you can take it off the shelf in your little retirement home, fondle it and remember this day."

"In my line of work, I doubt if I live long enough to enjoy a retirement home. In any case, I might just move back to Icarus and move in with my brother Connor on the family farm and tend to the chickens."

Alita laughed again. "Pardon me for laughing, but I cannot see you looking after chickens. Perhaps, this little old knife will come in handy cutting the head off the chicken."

"Very funny, Alita. Very funny."

"What's funny?"

Alita looked at Newman. "Falcon wants to raise chickens when he retires."

Newman grinned. "Chickens, huh? Inside a spaceship?"

"So, you're a comedian, also." Falcon showed Newman the knife. "Alita suggested I buy this knife to remember this day. I think I'll do that. No snide remarks about that from you. Understood?"

"Loud and clear." Newman lifted both hands. "All that over an old rusty knife. Actually, I was also thinking of buying something. What do you think about this?"

Falcon looked at the item Newman held in his hand. "What is it?"

"This, my friend, is a wallet for carrying money, like gold pellets. Hand-made by a human from genuine leather. You can't buy these things on a civilized planet. Everything there is made from synthetic material in a factory run by robots. No human hand ever touches those things."

"Can't argue that." Falcon looked at the opening door. The old woman came out, carrying a cloth bag. "Fresh bread and sausages. I bake the bread and my husband makes the sausages himself."

Alita took the cloth bag from the woman. "Where is your husband, Melanie?"

"He and our son went to Harristown to pick up some supplies. They won't be back until the day after tomorrow."

"How far is Harristown from here?"

Falcon wondered when Newman asked that question. He had assumed that the Scout knew his way around.

"With the wagon, it takes nearly a day to get there." The old woman explained.

"What is in Harristown?"

The woman looked surprised. "Harristown is our capital. It is the largest settlement in Brettany. That's where our government is situated. You don't know?"

Falcon gave her an apologizing shrug. "I am a stranger in Brettany. I know very little about your state."

"All the big companies have their headquarters in Harristown. It is the place where everyone buys their supplies. Granted, we could get some of the merchandise in Rowarra, but Hank likes

Harristown better. Rowarra has already been invaded by too many non-believers."

"I see. We are on our way to Rowarra. Will we travel through Harristown?"

"No," she said with a shake of her head. "Harristown is north of here, while Rowarra is in the east, close to Ontura."

He looked at Newman. "I assume my partner here knows."

Newman smiled. "I've never been to Harristown, but I've been to Rowarra. Don't worry, I'll find our way there."

"May I suggest something?" Melanie gave them a questioning look.

"Sure. We are always open to good advice," Falcon said.

"To get from here to Rowarra you will have to travel to Sandogo. The road from Sandogo to Rowarra is fraught with plenty of danger. Why don't you go north to Harristown instead? Distance-wise it will be longer, but from Harristown to Rowarra will be much more comfortable, because you can take the train."

"I wasn't aware of a train connecting Harristown with Rowarra," Newman admitted.

"They finished building the tracks just last year. There was a lot of opposition to that. Some people predicted it would bring undesirables into our state, but you can't stop progress."

"Sometimes progress is a good thing. It brings a welcome change. Things can become stagnant and boring," Falcon commented.

"I have no problem with the train." Melanie chuckled. "I actually don't care either way. I'll never use it because I never travel anywhere. However, Hank thinks differently. He mentioned many times how great it would be if we had a train connecting Harristown with Warnon. With a station here in Sunup, of course. It would be much easier and more comfortable for him to get his merchandise."

"I imagine it would. By the way, how is the road from here to Harristown?"

"It isn't bad. Not much different from what you've experienced until now. You will come to a bridge that crosses the Stony River. From there it is still about three hours until you get to Harristown. It is not a bad place to set up camp and spend the night if you have to. Just for your information."

"It is appreciated," Falcon told her. "Thank you for making us something to eat."

"Oh, it is no trouble. As long as I get paid for it, I'll do anything." She gave him a toothless smile and a wink. "Perhaps I should say 'almost anything' if you know what I mean. I'm too old for certain things."

Falcon smiled and returned the wink. "You are never too old. If we weren't in a rush to get going, I might just be tempted."

She gave him a slap on the arm. "I can tell you're a charmer. If I may ask, where are you coming from? I know you are not locals."

"We come from Riwarda," Newman said.

"A long way from here. People in Saskona are different from people here in Brettany. I believe you know what I'm talking about. Here you have to be careful what you say, especially to strangers."

Falcon was curious about something. "Let me ask you a personal question, Melanie. How does a store like yours survive in a village like this one?"

"It doesn't, not on its own. That is the reason we also run a farm. This store was founded by my grandfather. We only inherited it and are keeping it going."

"What about the bread, the sausages and the other food stuff? Won't it spoil?"

"Not really. When it comes to harvest time, we get a lot of farm workers coming from Harristown to help out. They need to be fed. We clean out one of the small sheds and set up tables and chairs to give them a place to eat. They always have a good time experiencing life on a farm."

"That's at harvest time, but what about now?" Falcon still didn't really see it, but he was curious.

"Now? We have the only oven that bakes descent bread in Sunup. They bring me the flour and I bake whatever they want. Of course, they compensate me." She smiled. "We all work together. It is the only way to survive in this village."

"The only way to survive anywhere," Falcon said. "People working with each other can perform miracles." He looked at Newman and Alita. "I suppose we should get going. I see you have our food, Alita."

She nodded. "Don't forget to pay."

Falcon took out his little bag and counted out two gold pellets. Handing them to Melanie, he said, "This should cover it."

"You are very generous," she said with a grateful smile. "I wish I had more customers like you."

They stopped half an hour later when they came across a narrow stream with clear water. After watering the horses, they relaxed in the grass near the stream to eat their sandwiches.

"Life in the countryside is so much different from living in a city," Newman remarked. "I am glad I came with you. To be honest, I was getting bored in Riwarda. I needed a change."

"Why didn't you volunteer to join an exploration team on some newly discovered planet instead of being stuck in a boring job with no future?"

"Good question, Alita, and I believe I explained that when we first met."

"I remember, but wouldn't you want to move on after five years on this forsaken ball?"

He smiled sadly. "That is the reason I joined you two. It is also the reason I am coming with you to Rima. I am planning to apply for transfer away from this boring planet."

"And here I secretly thought you joined our team because of our charming personalities," Falcon said with a grin.

They were attacked a short time later.

[16]

THERE WAS NO WARNING.

Newman, who had been lying on his back looking into the sky, was the first one to spot the disk-shaped craft as it appeared seemingly out of nowhere. Losing altitude with incredible speed, it landed in the field to their right. An opening appeared on one side of the craft and a dozen armed men, dressed in camouflage fatigues, jumped out. Obviously, soldiers. Forming a half circle, they advanced toward them, weapons drawn.

When Newman reached for his colt, Falcon cautioned, "Don't. They have us outgunned and outnumbered."

"I am curious who they are," Alita said. "I am not familiar with this type of aircraft."

The group of soldiers stopped a short distance away, their short-barrelled rifles aimed at them.

Falcon rose from his sitting position and put up his arms. "Who are you and what do you want?" he called in a loud voice.

"We want the communication device you took from one of our own." The speaker spoke with a harsh, demanding tone.

"I don't know what you are talking about," Falcon told him.

"The one you shot without provocation."

"I still don't know what it is you are accusing us of."

"He means that giant snake disguised as a human," Alita said in a low voice.

"Are you talking about the shapeshifter in the shape of a man?" Falcon asked.

"His name was Ipar. He didn't act aggressively toward you and yet you murdered him."

"He went for his weapon."

"It was not a weapon. It was his communicator, which you took from his dead body."

"How could we know? He should have told us of his intention. It appears this is a matter of miscommunication. I am sorry that happened. We felt threatened and we took defensive action." It occurred to Falcon that these twelve men most likely were also shapeshifters, pretending to be human. "Are you like him? If you are not, what do you call your species? Where do you come from and what is your reason for being on this planet?"

"So many questions?" The speaker chuckled. "It is obvious you are not natives of this planet, either. Why are you here?"

"We are human and have every reason for being on Aurora. That's what we call this planet. It is part of the Human Empire. Our mission is to stop the invasion of Aurora by an alien species." It was Falcon's turn to talk sharply.

"If you mean us, you have it wrong. We are not here to invade this planet, whatever name you call it. Our purpose for being here is our business, not yours."

"If you are here to capture human beings and turn them into slaves it is our business," Falcon told him.

"It looks like Ipar told you all about it. Then you must also know that it is not slaves we are after. You don't know the whole truth and I am not about to confide in you." The speaker took a few steps forward. "I will take the communicator from you now."

"I would feel much better if you would stop threatening us

with your weapons unless you plan to shoot us. If that is your plan some of you will die with us," Falcon warned.

"We have no intention to shoot or kill you unless you give us a good reason."

"We are not the ones pointing weapons at you. I'll be lowering my arms now and I will reach into my backpack for that gadget. I'm hoping you will not repeat my mistake."

"We won't but we'll be watching. One wrong move and it will be your last one." On command, the other soldiers lowered their rifles, but the speaker didn't.

Falcon opened his backpack and removed the device he took from the alien they shot in Winnira. At closer inspection, it was obvious that it was not a weapon. There were a couple of dials and a few buttons, with markings that most likely were letters or numbers. He held it up. "Here it is."

"We want everything you took from him."

Newman brought the other two items and handed them to Falcon. "This is all we took," Falcon said.

The speaker of the aliens gave one of the others a sign. Falcon watched him coming closer, alert for any sign of betrayal. The soldier looked at him with a stoic face. Taking the items from Falcon, he turned and walked back to his companions.

"You still haven't told us what you call your species," Falcon said. "Are you like Ipar or are you from a different species?"

"We are Apovians, like Ipar, which means you know that this is not our true form. He may have told you that our home planet is called Apovi."

"He did. We've never heard of a planet called Apovi. In what region of space is it located?"

"That is something I won't tell you. Just being aware of our presence here is already more information than you should possess about us. We are no threat to you, be satisfied with that. I already told you we don't intend to invade this or any other planet. Our numbers are much too low for that. All we want is for our species to survive." He gave the others a sign.

They walked backward to their aircraft, weapons at the ready. One after the other they disappeared into the craft, with one of them standing guard. The last one finally climbed in, and the door closed. The craft shot into the air and disappeared into the clouds.

"Not a trusting bunch," Newman remarked.

"Did they think we were going to attack them? Three against twelve?" Falcon laughed. "I also wonder why it was so important to them to get those devices back. If one of them actually was a communicator. Perhaps it was something of great value to them."

"I guess we'll never know. How did they know what went down in Winnira?" Alita wondered.

"There might have been a witness. Another one of them," Falcon speculated. "Their leader insisted on telling us they have no interest in invading any planets, but if they are kidnapping people they must have a way of getting them off planet. That means a large ship. There are no reports of any large interstellar ships in the area. Also, they must have a base somewhere. Very curious."

"Perhaps we'll find out more in Rima," Newman mused. "There is a spaceport there, you know. Their ship may just be parked there in plain sight."

"I doubt that, but nothing is impossible," Falcon said. He shouldered his backpack. "Time to get going."

When they came to the river with the bridge there were at least a couple of hours left until the sun would disappear, but they decided to spend the night and move on the next day. It was not a bad spot to set up camp.

They finished erecting their tents and were about to sit down and eat the rest of the sandwiches when they saw two riders coming down a side road. They wore dark-green uniforms and wore wide-brimmed hats.

Rangers.

The Rangers stopped and slid off their horses. "Mind if we join you?" one of them asked.

"Not at all." Falcon grinned. "Sadly, we can't offer you any food. We barely have enough for us."

"No problem," the other Ranger said with a smile. "We have enough smoked meat to share with you." He looked at his partner. "What do you say, Randolph? Shall we pitch our tent here? I know it is still early, but I don't feel like riding all night again. Sandogo can wait until tomorrow."

Randolph shrugged. "Fine by me. You're the captain."

"Good, then it's settled." He laughed jovially. "You're probably getting sick by now listening to my stories, Randolph. It is time for a new audience."

Falcon looked at Newman and Alita and smiled. "A storyteller," he mouthed.

"We'll have to look after our horses first," the captain told them. "Then we'll put up the tent. We'll join you after that."

It didn't take long before the two men squatted down by the fire Newman had made. "My name is Ted Munroe, Captain Ted Munroe," the older Ranger introduced himself. "And this young feller is Ranger Randolph Small. May I ask where you folks are from?"

"I am Scout Wesley Newman. I'm stationed at the Scouts Outpost in Riwarda."

"A Scout? That means you're not a native of Aurora." He looked at Falcon. "Are you also a scout?"

Shaking his head, Falcon decided there was no purpose in hiding his identity from a Ranger. "No, I am not. I am Major Jeremy Falcon of the ISS."

"A soldier." Munroe nodded. "What does ISS stand for?"

"Interstellar Secret Service."

"You're a lawman. May I ask what someone like you is doing on a planet like Aurora?"

Falcon smiled grimly. "To be honest, I don't know anymore. Our mission was to stop this planet from being invaded by the Osirians, a bunch of giant intelligent ants, but so far we haven't seen any evidence of them even being here."

"Giant intelligent ants invading Aurora," Munroe repeated. "This is the first I hear of that. Whoever fed you that information sure gave you a bunch of crap. Pardon my saying so."

"Well, something is going on here, we just don't know yet what," Falcon uttered.

"Whatever you think might be going on, it isn't giant ants, I can tell you that. We would have heard about that by now. We may be living in our own little world here, away from all the violence apparently going on in the rest of the galaxy, information does get passed around," Munroe stated. "As a Ranger, I see and hear more than most people. The majority of the people living on Aurora are not interested in what happens out there among the stars, but I am. I've been in Rima, and I have talked to travelers from other planets. I am not just some ignorant local."

"I would never assume that, Captain Munroe," Falcon assured him. "Aurora is not the first backward planet I've been on, if I may use the term backward. Life out there moves fast, while time on a planet like yours seems to stand still. With every century you fall more and more behind. Aurora is different from most other planets I've been on. You have no central government, for instance. Every state makes its own laws and follows different customs. You have no army, which means Aurora is an easy target for any hostile species to invade and take over. You would not be able to defend your world against anyone."

"You mean giant intelligent ants." Munroe chuckled, somehow finding humor in that idea.

"If not ants then another species. You have one thing going and that is the fact that Aurora is far away from all trading routes, and you really don't have much anyone would be interested in."

"Like what?" Munroe challenged.

Falcon shrugged. "I don't know. Agricultural products maybe, or natural resources desperately needed on other planets?"

"In other words, we are quite safe from any invasion," Munroe countered. "We have nothing anybody wants."

"I'm not so sure." Falcon bent forward. "A few hours ago, when we stopped for lunch, we had visitors. An alien aircraft landed in the field not far from us, out came a dozen soldiers. They looked like humans, but in reality, they were from a race of shapeshifters, which means they can take on any shape they want."

"You mean they were Accilla?" Munroe interrupted.

"No, they were not." Falcon was surprised to hear the Ranger say that. His knowledge extended beyond what the majority of colonists on low-tech planets possessed. Some of them weren't even aware that the planet they lived on was not their original home world.

Munroe obviously interpreted Falcon's expression correctly. He smiled and said, "Just because people in Brettany believe in demons and witches doesn't mean I do. I've never met someone who was Accilla, but I am aware of their existence." He paused to let that sink in and continued. "If they were not Accilla, what were they?"

"They called themselves Apovians. By the way, in their original form they are giant serpents," Falcon explained. When he said it, he knew it sounded like some made-up story.

Munroe gave Falcon an unconvinced look. "First it's giant ants, and now it's giant serpents. Any other species you can think of?"

"Not so far." Falcon didn't care if the Ranger believed him or not. "There is something else, though. On your travels between the states, have you heard farmers complaining about having their cattle stolen or about people disappearing?"

"Farmers always complain about losing cattle. Some of those cattle roam around freely. They wander off or get killed by predators. As far as people disappearing? I haven't heard anything specific, but people always disappear. They get lost in the wilderness, of which we have plenty of; they run away or just move into another state. Nothing mysterious about that." He looked at Alita. "You must forgive me for ignoring you. We haven't been introduced."

"I am Alita," she said with a smile.

"Alita. Beautiful name befitting a beautiful woman. How do you fit into this little group?"

"I am a captain with the ISS. Major Falcon and I are partners on this mission."

"I am well aware that it is common for women on many planets to join the military. Here on Aurora women don't become Rangers or policemen."

"I've heard. It seems the further backward people slip on the colonized planets the more primitive they become. With the loss of technology, they lose their common sense." She spoke calmly, but the sarcasm in her voice was easily detectable. Falcon couldn't agree more.

Munroe didn't seem to notice. If he did, he didn't let on. "Different planets, different customs. Why would a woman want to do a man's job anyway?"

Before Alita could give a possibly biting answer, Falcon said, "If I may change the subject, I remember you offering us some of your smoked meat."

"Sorry about that. I offered, didn't I?" He turned to his partner. "Randolph, go and break open that package. I'm getting hungry, anyway."

The meat was dry and had a strong smoky flavor, but when you're hungry everything tastes good. The rangers even shared a bottle of fermented juice with them.

Newman got up and brought a few pieces of wood to throw on the fire. The sun had disappeared, and darkness was quickly approaching. Falcon shivered as the temperature dropped a little. This was going to be the first night in days they would be spending inside a tent. 'We've been spoiled,' he thought, smiling to himself.

"You never told us where you're headed." Munroe belched and wiped his mouth with the back of his hand.

"We're hoping to get to Rima," Falcon told him.

"What's in Rima?"

"Scouts Headquarters."

"I wasn't aware of that, even though the Ranger's headquarters is also in Rima. Then again, we don't really communicate with the scouts." He looked at Newman. "What exactly is the purpose for scouts being here on Aurora?"

"We are observers."

"What do you observe?"

Newman smiled. "Everything. I am an analyst and I study the way people live on Aurora. I record for instance how they cope with living in primitive surroundings and how it affects them."

"Are you saying we are like lab rats to you?"

"I wouldn't say that. I don't only observe, I also live that life."

"Were you born on a planet like Aurora?"

"No." Newman shook his head. "I was born on Sheffield's Planet, one of the most advanced planets in the Human Empire."

"Why Aurora?" Munroe sounded baffled. "Why would you want to spend part of your life on a planet like this one?"

"Living on a high-tech planet is not what it may sound like. Life moves fast and furious. People seem to have no time for anything. Crime is rampant on the ones where people enjoy freedom. Planets that are free of crime are ruled by tyrants and dictators." He laughed. "Freedom comes at a price. Living on Aurora is not so bad."

"I agree, but this is the only life I know." Munroe pulled a pipe out of his pocket and filled it with some leaves. He put it into his mouth and lit it. Puffing away, he stared at the blue smoke. "Yet sometimes I wonder how it would be out there, and I feel the urge to book passage with one of the freighters that come here from another world."

"I know the feeling," Falcon said. "My home world is called Icarus. To call it high-tech would be bragging, even though it uses technology. I grew up on a farm and life was peaceful and comfortable. However, as I grew older, it pulled me to the stars. I became a soldier because that was one way of experiencing exotic worlds. At least that's what I thought. It did turn out different from what I envisioned, but I have few regrets."

"I assume you are not married?" Munroe queried.

"You assume correctly. What woman would want to marry a man with no home, very few possessions, and never stays long in one place? How about you?"

"The same. Even though I share a house with my sister in Mosk, I'm seldom living in it. I travel from one place to another, trying to hold up the law."

"A while ago, we spent one night sitting around a fire like this with one of your Rangers. His name was Sergeant Andrew Markus. Do you know him?"

Munroe chuckled. "That is a strange question, Major Falcon. Of course, I know Markus. I know all the Rangers on Aurora."

"He was as skeptical as you when we told him about our mission."

"I'm sure he was. You are chasing something that doesn't exist. Face it, Major, somebody played a cruel joke on you. There are no giant ants here, and neither will you find giant snakes disguised as humans."

"You may be right when it comes to the giant ants, the Osirians, not being here on Aurora, but they do exist. They are not some made-up race. And who knows? Perhaps they are here, after all, keeping a low profile." Falcon paused, thinking about what to tell the Ranger next. "However, we are not making up a story about the serpents in human form. We killed one of them. He told us that his home-world is called Apovi, and they are the Apovians.

His race is dying, and they are here to buy or capture slaves for the purpose of breeding to keep their race from extinction. We did have an encounter with twelve more of them. They were in human form, but they indicated they were just like the one we killed."

"What did those twelve want from you?" Either Munroe was beginning to believe Falcon, or he was just playing along.

"We took something from the one we killed. They claimed it was a communication device, but we suspect it was more than that. They wanted it back."

Munroe puffed on his pipe. "You know, you sound convincing, and you probably believe everything you told me, but I am doubt-ful. Why haven't we heard any of this?" He blew a ring of smoke and watched it dissipate. "I wish you good luck with whatever you find. I hope you are not wasting your time." He looked at his part-ner. "Randolph, bring me that other bottle of juice. All this talking has made me thirsty and my mouth dry."

They emptied the second bottle, and everyone felt happy. When everyone's words were beginning to come out a little slurred Falcon knew it was time to hit the sack.

Alita had already gone into her tent a while back since she didn't drink any alcohol and wasn't interested in listening to the stories the men told.

"Your female partner doesn't like the company of men?" Munroe asked when he noticed Alita was gone.

"She does," Falcon told him. "But we've had a long day and she told me she was tired and needed some rest." He yawned. "Actu-ally, I am quite tired myself. As much as I'd like to talk more with you, I think I will crawl into my tent and get some shuteye."

"I'll stay up a little while longer," Newman said. "I'm interested in the stories Ranger Munroe is telling. It's been some time since I had a good conversation with another person."

"I'm happy to hear you say that. I don't always get a captive audience." Munroe glanced at his partner who sat slumped over, snoring. "I have a feeling Randolph is getting tired of listening to me talking all the time, and I admit I do have the tendency to ramble on."

Falcon crawled into the tent and under his blanket. He never heard Newman come in.

He woke up early, which was normal for him. He was an early riser and not much for sleeping in. However, Captain Munroe was already busy fanning the flames of a fire under a metal pot.

"I hope you like mint tea," he said when Falcon came up to him.

"Not my favorite, but I don't mind it," Falcon told him. He looked at the fog rising from the ground and shivered. "Nippy this morning."

"That it is," Munroe agreed. "It's that time of year." He looked at his companion who sat cross-legged beside him. "Right, Randolph?"

The young Ranger nodded. "Right, Captain."

A short time later, Alita joined them. Staring at the flames for a little while, she announced, "I'm going down to the river to wash up. I'll expect bacon and eggs when I come back," she said with a little laugh.

Munroe watched her walking away. "Is she serious?"

Falcon laughed. "She referred to the rations we carry. We have all kinds of flavors. All made from the same artificial crap, but it is nourishing. At least that's what we are told."

"That doesn't sound appealing to me. I think I'll stick to the real thing. Eggs from fowl and bacon from pigs." Munroe grinned. "Unfortunately, all I can offer you is smoked meat and stale bread."

"I'll take that," Newman said from behind them. He squatted down beside the fire and sniffed. "Smells like mint tea."

"It is," Munroe informed him with a smile. "The leaves come from a real plant. My sister grows them in the backyard."

"I am familiar with it. We drink mint tea at the outpost in Riwarda."

"How about you?" Munroe looked at Falcon.

Falcon shrugged. "As I said, not my favorite. I prefer a cup of kafii in the morning."

"I'm afraid I don't even know what kind of tea that is."

"It isn't tea. Kafii is black and it is brewed from roasted kafii beans. I'm not even questioning the fact that the plants are not grown on Aurora. It isn't the only colonized planet where that is the case. Some colonists consider the beans an addictive drug and put them on their list of forbidden plants. It seems the early colonists on Aurora decided not to import the kafii plants."

"I'd like to know the real reason," Munroe stated. "There are plenty of wild plants growing on this planet that produce fruit or berries that can be brewed into a drink that may kill you outright, lets you see things that aren't there, or once consumed, make you want more."

The three men turned their heads to look at Alita when they heard her coming back. "I need to warm up by the fire," she announced. "That river is cold."

"Did you submerge in the water?" Newman asked.

"Yes. I felt I needed a bath. You men should do that."

"No thank you." Newman shook himself. "Just seeing you shiver is enough for me."

"I'll be taking my bath in Sandogo," Munroe remarked. "In a tubful of hot water in the hotel where we will sleep in a real bed. I can't wait." He sighed deeply. "And we'll eat fresh food. No more smoked meat and stale bread for a while."

"How long have you been on the road, Captain?"

"Nearly two weeks, Major. Two long weeks of sleeping in a cold tent at night, spending the days on the back of a horse, freezing our butts, eating smoked meat and stale bread, and drinking mint tea. I'm not saying I hate this job, but on occasions like this, I wish I were a baker baking fresh bread. I love the smell of freshly baked bread. My sister is a good baker. You like your job, Major Falcon?"

Falcon chuckled softly. "I do most of the time, but I must admit, sometimes I feel like you. It happens to all of us. Take Newman for example. He's been here five years and is getting restless. He wants to put in for a transfer."

"Only to another planet," Newman protested. "I like being a Scout."

"Everyone ready for a cup of tea?" Munroe reached for the pot.

"I'll get the mugs," Alita offered.

[17]

THEY WERE ON THE ROAD AN HOUR LATER. A FEW CLOUDS WERE beginning to gather in the sky, and they hoped to make it to Harristown before it began to rain. They had been lucky so far with the weather.

Harristown was situated beside a large lake, which meant thriving fisheries. The road into Harristown led them right to the waterfront at the shore of the lake. It had begun to drizzle, and they decided to look for a place to spend the night and possibly another day to explore a little of the city.

The hotel they found looked rundown, but it featured a stable where they could keep the horses. The old man working in the stable promised to look after the animals. In his younger days he had been working as a farrier and, for a price, he would take care of the horses' hooves and shoes.

The two rooms they booked were certainly not luxury suites, but they would do for a couple of nights. The locks on the doors were solid and strong, quite important for this area of the town. After checking out the food the hotel offered, they decided to go and find a place with better food. They found a small restaurant that served seafood and they went inside.

The young girl that served them, suggested fresh caught Skywing, a fish with delicate white meat. She said it was sought after and usually very expensive, but today it was on special, and they wouldn't be sorry.

"Can we afford it?" Newman wondered.

"It isn't a matter of affording. Remember, it isn't our money we are spending," Falcon said. "The question is do we want it?"

They decided they did.

As it turned out, the fish was delicious and neither of them felt cheated or disappointed.

"This is the most expensive fish I ever ate," Newman stated after they finished eating.

"I believe we deserved it," Falcon pointed out. "We don't know what lies ahead."

"I hope no smoked meat and stale bread." Alita voiced what Falcon was thinking. They had a good laugh and ordered another mug of ale.

A group of fishermen at the table next to them bragged about the size of their catches. Falcon wasn't interested in their conversation, but they reminded him of a group of spacers he ran across on his last assignment. Different topics but the same way of telling tall tales.

His interest was roused when one of them mentioned disappearing cattle and giant ants. However, that's all the man said because another one began talking about strange flying objects he saw.

Falcon decided to talk to the fishermen. He got up and approached their table. "I apologize for interrupting your conversation," he said. "I am interested in talking to the man who mentioned giant ants and disappearing cattle."

"What's so interesting about that?" The man gave him an annoyed look. "Who are you anyway?"

"Sorry about that. My name is Jeremy Falcon. My colleagues and I are investigating the reports of missing cattle. Apparently, it is happening in other states, also."

The man looked him up and down. "You are not a Brettan. Where are you from?"

"We come from Saskona."

"Saskona. No wonder you talk so funny."

Falcon laughed. "You sound funny to me, also. Let me buy all of you a drink and perhaps I can persuade you to talk."

"That is different. Now you are talking our language."

Falcon waved to the man behind the bar. "Bring us seven tankards of ale for my friends here," he called. Turning his attention back to the fishermen, he said, "If you'll make room for me at your table it will make it easier to converse."

He pulled a chair from another table, went to get his mug, and sat down. "We just arrived in Harristown this afternoon. Are you by any chance the men that caught the delicious Skywing fish they serve here?"

"We are," one of them told him. "We were lucky."

"Luck has nothing to do with it," another one bragged. "You have to know where and when to throw your nets. That's the secret."

The server brought four large mugs and went back to get three more. Falcon took a mouthful of ale from his own mug and wiped his mouth. "Nothing better than a couple of these after a day of hard work," he declared.

"I can't agree more." The man who spoke put down his mug. "Alright, what do you want to know?"

"Are you the one who saw these giant ants?"

"No, but my father and brother did."

"That's good enough for me. What's your name, by the way?"

"Vic Mallory."

"Okay, Vic, tell me more about those vanishing cattle and the giant ants."

"Well, my parents have a farm near Stoneridge. One night, when my father and brother were out rounding up some cattle that had wandered away, they saw four man-shapes butchering two of the steers and then loaded the meat onto some kind of cart with no wheels. It just floated in the air. One of the moons was out and it was clear to see that they were not human but giant ants."

"Interesting. Was that the only time they witnessed something like that?"

"Yes, it was, but one of their neighbors reported something similar." The man nodded. "Nobody believed them. People around here are quite religious and superstitious. They accused my father and brother of collaborating with demons and the Dark One, and of having been seduced by the dark spirits. Most likely though, they consumed too much fermented juice and chewed black adder leaves. It makes people see things. My father and brother and their neighbor swore they had nothing to drink that evening. They never mentioned that incident anymore after that."

"I am inclined to believe them," Falcon said. "Those giant ants are Osirians. They exist." He looked around the table. "I overheard one of you mention strange flying objects before I came to your table. I'd like to hear more about that, also."

"Then let me tell you my tale," a young man with a round face and dark, almond eyes spoke up.

"You are no Brettan, either" Falcon observed.

"That is correct. I come from a small village in Mangali. My people raise Swamp-buffalo. They are vicious and unpredictable beasts with sharp horns. It takes a brave person to even approach one," he said with a proud voice. "Swamp-buffalo have long shaggy hair and thick skin which can be worked into strong leather."

"Everyone knows that, Cliff. You've mentioned that many times. We know you are a tough man. Carry on with your story about flying objects." The man who spoke was older than the others. His weather-beaten skin was burned brown by the sun.

"I've seen many things in my life on the sea, but never objects floating in the air. I'm also interested in hearing what you saw."

"I was still young then and working for my parents," the young fisherman began but was interrupted by the older man.

"That couldn't have been very long ago. You're not old."

"Can I tell my story?" Cliff smiled but the annoyance in his voice couldn't be missed. "One evening after we rounded up the animals for the night, a disc-shaped object as large as a hut came shooting across the sky at high speed and landed somewhere in the nearby mountains. My brother and I were curious. We knew the place it landed couldn't be very far, so the next day we saddled up our horses, packed some gear, and rode off toward the mountains. After three days we came across something peculiar. We didn't find the object, but we found a camp with people."

"What kind of people?" one of the other fishermen asked.

"There were Suries, Sumans, Arbeenians, and humans. All were young. They were kept behind a fenced-in area. We knew we had stumbled upon a slave camp. As we watched, one of those disc-shaped flying shiny objects landed near the camp. It rested on three thick poles. An opening appeared on the underside and a ladder was lowered to the ground. A few big men carrying strange weapons climbed out and began gathering most of the slaves and herding them into the disc. Then the disc rose up into the sky and disappeared into the clouds."

"Strange story," the older man commented. "Did you say it was a large as a hut?"

"Much bigger. Much, much bigger."

"I don't know what to say. How can something as big as that stay up in the air? Was it carried by a nest of flames?"

"There were no flames. In fact, there was no noise at all. It landed and took off again in complete silence."

"Are you sure you didn't see all this in a dream?"

"I am quite sure. My brother saw it too. We didn't hang around after that. We got away as fast as we could." Cliff looked at Falcon. "I am not making this up. It really did happen."

"Witchcraft," another fisherman said. "What you saw was the workings of the Dark One. They were sinners and he took them straight to hell."

Falcon didn't know how to react. These people had never seen any aircraft. They were ignorant and superstitious. They believed in evil spirits, demons, and the devil. How could he explain anti-gravity or magnetism to them? To them, anything like that was magic and witchery.

"Has any of you ever been to Rima?" he asked.

Only two of them lifted their hands. One was the older fisherman.

Falcon focused his attention on him. "Did you visit the spaceport?"

When the man nodded, he said, "Then you must have seen at least one spaceship on the tarmac, possibly even seen one landing or taking off. They come here from other worlds, and they go back there when they leave here. They don't go to hell. There is no magic involved."

"I never thought of that," the man said. "Our ancestors came to Aurora in a ship like that. It is easy to forget that. Most people don't talk about how we got here."

"Things are different in those worlds or on those planets as they are called," Falcon explained. "Many different species live on those planets. Not all are human. And not many believe in demons and evil spirits."

"Don't you?" one of the younger ones asked.

"Actually, I don't."

"That doesn't mean they don't exist." The young man insisted.

"To me, they don't exist. I'd like to come back to the story Cliff told us. What you saw was real. You are correct when you deducted what you stumbled upon was a slave camp. The people that came in the flying disc are Apovians and the planet they come from is called Apovi." He didn't tell them about the Apovians' ability to change their appearance. It would have really freaked them out.

"How do you know all this?" The suspicion in the older fisherman's voice was clear.

Falcon decided to tell them the truth about himself. "I am not a native to Aurora. I came here in one of those spaceships to investigate what is behind the kidnappings. My job is to make sure that nobody invades your planet and to protect the people living on Aurora. And to stop these kidnappings."

"How are you going to do that? One man against many with powerful weapons?"

Falcon smiled grimly. "I am not alone. I can bring a whole army to your planet in a short time." He emptied his mug and stood up. "Thank you for trusting me with your reports. They are more helpful than you might think. They may be the first concrete evidence that the rumors we heard are true. For a while, we thought our presence here had no purpose."

He grabbed his chair and walked away to join Newman and Alita, leaving the seven fishermen wondering if he was for real or just another storyteller. Before he sat down, he called to the bartender, "Bring another seven tankards over to that table."

"We overheard," Newman said. "Lots of material to sort out."

"We still don't know much," Falcon cautioned. "However, we know now that the reports of cattle being mutilated and stolen are true and that the Osirians are involved. We also know that the Apovians abduct people and take them somewhere. Where? We have to find out."

"That's two problems we are facing," Alita mused. "Of course, we still only have second-hand knowledge."

"That is why I would like to take a ride to that farm in Stoneridge and have a talk with the farmer that witnessed the Osirians butcher those cattle. Apparently, they loaded the meat onto a cart that floated in the air. It is clear he was talking about a platform that used anti-gravity to make it float. Their base must be close to that town, but far enough away to keep it from being discovered."

"Where and how far is this town?"

"I'll go and find out." Falcon got up and walked back to the fishermen's table. "One more question. Where can I find the town of Stoneridge?"

"It is north of here. About a day's ride," Vic told him. "Are you planning to go there?"

"Yes, I am. I want to talk to your father about that incident with the giant ants."

"There is really no more to tell than I already did. Don't you believe me? I'm no liar."

"I am not accusing you of that, Vic," Falcon assured him. "I believe you. That is the reason we want to go find out more. We need to investigate where they are taking that meat."

"It may be your funeral," Vic warned him. "If those ants are from another world, they may have destructive weapons."

Falcon gave him a smug smile. "So do we, my young friend. So do we. Have you forgotten where I come from?" He tipped his hat and went back to his table.

"Putting on a bit of a show, aren't you?" Newman commented.

Falcon just grinned. "I feel good today. It seems we are finally making some progress. Anyone for another round of ale?"

They spent two nights in Harristown and left early in the morning. It rained during the night. The morning greeted them with a cloudy sky, but the clouds dispersed as the day went by and it turned out to be a nice day. The road they traveled wasn't as good as the one from Sunup to Harristown. Obviously, it didn't get much traffic. The rain of the night kept down the dust. They met the odd farmer with their carts on the road, but on the whole, it was quiet. Once, they overtook a group of natives walking on the road in the same direction. The resemblance to the long-extinct Neanderthals of Earth was uncanny. There was one difference. They had long, bushy tails.

They saw only adults; males and females. All wore skimpy clothing made from animal skins, and they carried short spears.

Falcon wasn't worried about being attacked by them, but it always paid to be on the cautious side. They gave the group a wide berth as they passed them, alert for any signs of hostility. The natives didn't stop but kept on walking, by all appearances ignoring the humans. Falcon had no illusions that the group wasn't acutely aware of them and ready to take defensive action should Falcon and his companions decide to attack any member of their group.

Once they were out of earshot, Newman said, "That was a group of Moyans. They are most likely on a hunting trip."

"They seem friendly enough," Falcon remarked.

"They are. Like most natives on Aurora, they want to be left alone and go about their ways. I don't really know much about them."

It was close to sunset when they arrived in Stoneridge. There wasn't much there. It was easy to see it was a town of farmers. The houses were built from wood with fronts of field stones and the yards were large. There was the usual church, which most likely also served as a meeting place.

They didn't see anything that looked like a hotel or restaurant.

"I guess we have to talk to one of the farmers to see if they let us sleep in their barn and sell us some food," Newman suggested.

"I would say we should find the farmer Mallory, the one who witnessed the Osirians that night," Falcon said.

"You are right. Then it should be you who goes knocking on doors," Newman proposed.

Falcon spotted a woman in front of one of the houses. He climbed down from his horse and headed for the house. When the woman saw him approaching, she watched him coming closer. The way she gripped the spade she was carrying made it clear she was uneasy, possibly even scared.

He stopped far enough away from her to indicate he didn't

mean any harm. "I am sorry to bother you," he called, "but we are looking for the Mallory farm."

She relaxed visibly. Then she pointed down the road. "The fifth house to the left. I believe the old man is at home. He hasn't been well lately."

Falcon tipped his hat. "Thank you very much. I appreciate your kindness." Then he turned and walked back to his companions. "Down that way," he told them and climbed back into the saddle.

The house had a veranda in the front. An old man with a beard sat in a wicker chair watching them closely as they stopped their horses in the yard.

"I think I should be the one who goes and says hello," Falcon said. Without waiting for an answer, he got off his horse and walked toward the house. He stopped at the bottom of the stairs.

"Is this the Mallory Farm?"

The old man squinted at him. "Who wants to know?"

"I am Jeremy Falcon. I spoke to your son Vic in Harristown. He told me about your encounter with the giant ants. I am very interested in finding out more."

"Vic is my grandson. You'll want to speak to my son Eric. He and Dean, my other grandson, saw them." He stroked his beard. "I'm not sure if they want to talk to you. They probably will just clam up if you mention the giant ants. People said what they saw were probably demons. Or perhaps they'd been sipping too much juice. Why do you want to know about that anyway?"

"There've been reports of giant ants in other parts of Aurora. My partners and I are investigating these reports. We are taking them very seriously."

At that moment the door into the house and a woman stepped out. She held a rifle in her hand, which she aimed at Falcon. "What do you want?" She spoke harshly, but she couldn't hide the fear in her voice.

"They want to speak to Eric," the old man told her.

"What for?" The barrel of her rifle never wavered.

"I'm interested in hearing more about the incident with the giant ants," Falcon explained. "My name is Jeremy Falcon. My friends are Wesley Newman and Alita. We mean you no harm. Had we wanted to kill you, you'd be dead already."

"Where did you hear about the giant ants?"

"From your son Vic. We met him in Harristown."

"You'll have to talk to Eric and Dean. I know nothing about it. They are working in the field right now. They'll be home late."

"We are willing to wait. It is very important that we speak to your husband. We won't bother you. If you don't mind, we'll have our horses drink from your water trough. It's been a long day even for them."

She finally lowered her rifle but didn't put it away. "Go ahead. If you want to wash up, you can use the pump by the trough. The water is clean." Before she went back into the house, she warned him, "Don't get any fancy ideas. I'll be watching you. And don't think I can't use this rifle."

They led the horses to the trough. "I hope her husband is friendlier," Newman remarked. "We may not get permission to sleep in one of their barns."

It was close to getting dark when they heard the creaking of wagon wheels coming down the road. Soon after that, a farm wagon pulled by one horse rolled into the yard. Two people sat on the bench. When they saw their visitors, the older man grabbed a rifle but just held it in his hands. "You are trespassing on my property."

"Our apologies," Falcon called back and began walking toward the cart, his arms away from his body. "Your wife allowed us to water our horses."

"It seems you've done that. Is there anything else you want except for using my water trough?"

"Yes, there is. We came here from Harristown where we met

your son Vic. We want to discuss the incident about the giant ants with you."

"The ants? That's old history. Nobody believed us. What makes you want to know now?"

"You are not the only ones coming across these giant ants. They are not mystical creatures or demons. They are called Osirians, and they may be on Aurora to invade your planet. We are traveling to different states to talk to people who had a similar experience with them. If need be, we must and will stop them."

"Who is 'we'?"

"The Solar Union."

"Since when is the Solar Union interested in us? Most people living on Aurora don't even know what the Solar Union is. In fact, they don't even know where we come from. Earth to them is just a legend."

"You seem to know."

"Yes, I do. I have a brother who works on the spaceport in Rima. He is quite knowledgeable about the worlds outside ours. I learned a lot from him."

"What did he say when you told him about the giant ants?"

"I haven't seen him for years. He used to visit once in a while, but he got disgusted with all the ignorance that exists everywhere." He snorted. "The majority of people in Brettany and some of the other states are zealots and ignorant halfwits, believing in evil spirits, witches, and dark forces." He stopped talking suddenly. "I've said too much already."

"No, you haven't. By now you may already have guessed that I am not a native of Aurora." Falcon smiled. "Mr. Mallory, I won't report you as a non-believer or of spouting heresy. You have nothing to worry about. I am Major Jeremy Falcon of the Interstellar Secret Service of the Solar Union. My colleagues and I are here to investigate the presence of the Osirians on Aurora."

Mallory climbed from the wagon. "I guess I don't have to introduce myself. You seem to know who I am already. It is getting dark. Let's all go into the house where we can talk. My son and I are hungry and have to eat supper. Perhaps you and your colleagues will join me for supper. I'm sure you are hungry, also."

"Thank you for the invitation. Are you sure your wife won't object? We don't want to create any work for her."

Mallory laughed. "Don't worry about that. My wife always cooks enough to feed a whole village."

[18]

THE NEXT DAY, MALLORY TOOK THEM TO THE SPOT WHERE HE AND his son had encountered the Osirians.

"In which direction did they take off?" Falcon asked.

"Northeast, but they may have changed direction soon after. They loaded the meat onto a cart that just floated above the ground. I didn't see any wheels. Once they loaded up everything, all four ants climbed onto the cart and then they took off at high speed. Just like magic. I've never seen anything like it." He chuckled. "Just because I don't know how they managed to make that thing move, means nothing. All I know is there was no magic involved."

"You are right. Not magic but science. They probably used what we call an anti-gravity generator to power their craft."

"You know, if that thing would have had wheels like a regular cart, they would have left tracks behind and we could have followed it, but like this...not a chance," the farmer deliberated.

"Not all is lost," Falcon assured him. "We may be able to track them." He looked at Alita. "I guess it is time to make use of some of the gadgets we brought along."

She nodded. "The Bloodhound. If their camp isn't too far away, we should be able to sniff them out."

"Bloodhound?" Mallory obviously had no idea what they were talking about.

"Everyone calls it that, but it isn't an animal. It is a tiny sphere, a seeker, with a built-in camera and detection devices that can be programmed to search for certain objects. We can follow its progress on a computer screen. It will tell us in which direction the target lies and how far away it is."

"You lost me after sphere, but I have confidence in your ability to find this camp." Mallory sighed. "You have no idea how good you make me feel. It's like a weight has been lifted off my shoulders. Finally, somebody who doesn't call me an imbecile or one touched by the demons."

"Ignorant people will do that," Newman said. "You are one of the few people on Aurora with an open mind."

"Thank you for your cooperation, Mister Mallory." Falcon held out a hand. "Tell your wife thank you for feeding us and tell her we apologize for coming unannounced to your farm and scaring her."

"Are you not coming back with me?"

"No. We'd lose too much precious time. We should be in Rowarra right now. Coming to your farm was not a scheduled stop, but it was not a waste of our time. The information you gave us helps our investigation immensely."

Mallory shook Falcon's hand. "I am happy you came and I'm glad I was able to help you. I hope you find these giant ants and put them out of business."

Falcon stayed serious when he spoke. "It may not be as simple as it sounds. The Osirians are an advanced race with superior weapons. It depends how large their camp is and how many of them are in that camp. Once we find them, we will have to decide how to proceed. We have a battlecruiser with a large team of soldiers waiting for my orders on one of the moons.

Should we engage in a battle with this group, or should we try to negotiate with them? We don't want to start a war with the Osirians."

"I don't blame you. Well, I am sure you'll do the right thing." Malory mounted his horse. "Good luck and may the Lord protect you."

"Thank you." Falcon smiled. "We rely on our wit and weapons not an invisible entity."

Malory clucked softly and rode away.

Falcon looked after him. "In a way I envy him," he said to Newman and Alita. "He lives in his simple world, doesn't worry too much about the future, and puts his trust in a god that may or may not exist to protect him."

"Some people say the gods are created by believing in them," Newman said.

"Do you believe that?"

Newman shrugged. "I don't know what to believe. I actually grew up in a religious family, but as I grew older, I became more and more disillusioned with the universe. I am not saying I'm a non-believer because I do believe in a higher power. Don't ask me what I envision."

"What do the Accilla believe?" Falcon looked Alita.

"We have no gods, not anymore. Gods are for primitive societies. They have no place in a high-tech universe."

"Religion is not something that can be discussed between people that have different beliefs, especially if each is convinced that what they believe is the only truth," Newman stated. "They will never agree on anything, and it will only end up in a stalemate and possibly in conflict."

"I won't argue," Falcon agreed. "That's why we should drop the subject. Let's get the Bloodhound programmed and launched."

Alita removed a package from the packhorse and opened it. Inside was a cube. She touched it to make a screen appear. Then she removed a small pellet from a box and pressed it against the cube. Moments later she took the pellet and launched it into the air.

The screen lit up and, on the screen, appeared the three-dimensional image of what the seeker transmitted.

"I guess, now we wait," she said.

In many ways, it was easier to find a certain target on a primitive, low-tech planet. Falcon knew that she had programmed the seeker to locate the nearest device emitting electronic impulses.

It took less than an hour to discover the base camp of the Osirians.

It was only thirty miles away.

All three of them studied the picture the seeker transmitted.

"There is something wrong with this picture," Newman said. "I expected to see one or more domes, but all we see are houses, obviously built by humans. I assumed the ants live in domes, not houses."

"You are right. This looks like a human village, not like the base camp of the Osirians," Alita agreed with Newman.

"Can you control the movements of the seeker and is it possible to zoom in on certain objects?" Falcon wondered.

"Sure can." She did something to the screen and the scene changed.

"There," Falcon said. "Bring that closer."

The picture grew in size, and they looked at a group of people inside a fenced-in area in front of a large building.

"Those are Suries," Newman said.

Falcon cursed. "I think we've stumbled upon another camp where somebody is keeping prisoners."

"But these are Osirians," Newman protested.

"The reports we have included disappearing of cattle as well as people, all supposedly committed by the Ants."

As Falcon spoke, two ants came out of the building. They carried trays which they put onto the ground. A closer look revealed chunks of meat on the trays.

"They are feeding their prisoners like they were animals," Alita said.

The picture above the cube changed as she moved the seeker to another part of the village. It displayed two disc-shaped objects resting on the ground.

"This makes little sense," Falcon pondered. "These are the same type of aircraft as the one the Apovians used to visit us when we camped by the river."

"Is it possible that the ants are working together with the Apovians?" Newman pondered.

"It is not impossible, but to me, that seems highly unlikely." Falcon rubbed his chin. "Nothing we see here adds up."

"We need to travel there and take a closer look," Alita suggested.

"I agree. Depending on the terrain, we should be able to make it there before sunset," Falcon said. "Let's move."

The landscape was mostly prairie and the occasional forest, with no road to follow, but they made good time and arrived near the village in the late afternoon. The village was surrounded by forest that provided cover, but Falcon warned, "They may have lookouts or surveillance cameras to warn them of intruders. We'll have to watch out for them."

It was dark when they decided to make their move. Falcon produced a gadget that detected any large warm-blooded creature. It would also warn them of an electronic surveillance system.

"I didn't think we'd have to use any of these sophisticated devices on a backwater planet like this one," Falcon mused. "We are dealing here with an advanced race. Soldiers by all appearances. We can't go against them with our small lasers. This calls for heavy artillery."

He went to their packhorse and unloaded a big leather bag. Opening it, he took out a few bundles which he unwrapped. Then he began to assemble the pieces. When he was done, he held three proton beam rifles. He handed one to Alita and another one to Newman. "Let Alita show you how to work this thing. The most advanced weapons in the Union. We may need them."

They walked stealthily toward the village, mindful of any danger that could pop up from anywhere. They realized they were up against an enemy they knew little about. They had no idea what kind of sophisticated defence system they might come across. What kind of weapons did they possess?

The village lay in darkness. The only light came from the stars above. When they arrived at the first building, they carefully approached it, weapons ready, expecting anything. From up close it was obvious the house was in bad shape. The boards of the walls were showing signs of rot. The window frames were without glass and the door hung only on one hinge.

"Nobody has lived in this house for a long time," Newman concluded.

The second house was in no better shape.

"This is a ghost town," Alita observed. "A perfect place for any shady business."

"It seems it was abandoned a long time ago. It isn't on the map," Newman said.

Not every part of the village was dark. The corral they had seen through the seeker's eye was lit up. The wire fence around it was about ten feet tall. A single wire ran along the top of the fence.

"I bet that wire will give you a nasty shock, even kill you, if you touch it," Falcon speculated. "Nobody in their right mind will try to climb over that."

In the dim light, they saw shapes sitting on the ground, huddled together. From the pictures the seeker had transmitted, they knew those shapes were people. At first, they assumed all of them were Suries or Suman, but looking at them through the fence they saw also many humans among them. Everyone was naked.

A small group of humans sat near the fence. Falcon threw a small pebble at them, hoping he'd get their attention. One man lifted his head and looked around. When he looked in the direction of Falcon's team, Falcon waved his arms above his head. The man gaped, obviously he had seen him.

"Hey," Falcon called in a voice as loud as he dared. Then he indicated for the man to come closer. At first, he hesitated, but then he got up from his sitting position and advanced toward the fence. He stopped on the other side and stared at Falcon. "Who are you?"

"I am Jeremy Falcon. These two are Wesley Newman and Alita."

"Did you come to rescue us?"

"Sorry. We found this camp only by pure chance. What is going on here?"

"We've been captured by these giant bugs and brought here. We don't know what is going to happen to us. Sometimes, they take a few of us and load them into their flying discs. We don't know what happens to them." He stood in front of them, shivering. "They treat us like animals. Is there any way you can get us out of here?"

"I'm afraid not. We didn't come equipped for any rescue mission. Aside from those big ants have you seen any other species?"

The man shook his head. "No, the ants are the only ones."

"One more thing. Are there any of them inside that barn?"

"That's where they are. They are not numerous. We could take them, but they have terrible weapons we've never seen before. We have no chance against them." The man hung his head. "When I saw you, I suddenly was hopeful, but it seems I was wrong. Be careful and don't let them catch you." He turned and walked away.

"Those ants don't expect to be attacked by anyone," Newman contemplated. "They feel safe and probably smug inside that barn. Couldn't we use that to our advantage?"

"We don't know how many there are. Don't forget, they also

have highly efficient weapons. Ours may not even be a match to theirs."

"We need to do something," Newman insisted. "We are here. We can't just walk away again. What good are these modern rifles if we can't use them?"

"We won't walk away, Newman," Falcon assured him. "We just have to be smart about it and not rush into something we can't control."

"So, what do you suggest?"

"Perhaps, there is a backdoor into that barn. I want to check it out."

They pulled away from the fence back into the darkness. Under cover of the shadow between the trees, they advanced toward the other side of the barn. They didn't find a door but a few loose boards. Trying not to make any noise, they carefully pried the boards away from the studs, until they had an opening large enough for them to squeeze through.

It was dark inside the part of the barn they entered. Falcon donned a pair of nightglasses, as did Newman and Alita. Carefully, they made their way through the obstacles strewn across the floor.

When they came to a wall, they searched for a door.

"Over there," Alita whispered, pointing.

The door was closed. Looking at the rusty hinges, Falcon hoped it wouldn't make noise when he tried to open it. Slowly, he pulled on the handle. The door swung into their room. It creaked softly and he stopped. Then he pulled again, carefully and gently. After opening it a crack, a splinter of light fell into the room.

Listening for any noises or voices, they heard nothing, but he didn't let that fool him. Putting his face against the opening, he looked into the room. An old farm wagon stood near an outside wall not far from his location. There were tools and other farm equipment either hanging on a wall or strewn across the dirt floor. Letting his gaze wander around the room, he spotted three ants lying on the ground. He didn't know if they were sleeping or just resting.

Another two were busy doing something further down. He realized they were butchering a couple of animals hanging from the rafters. Suppressing a loud curse, he pulled his face away from the opening and pushed the door close.

He stood for a moment trying to digest what he just witnessed.

"What did you see?" Newman gave him a questioning look.

"Barbarians!" Falcon cursed. "They are a bunch of fucking barbarians!"

"What did you see?" Newman asked again.

"Look for yourself."

Newman pulled open the door and looked. It took only a moment before he closed the door again. "The ants are slaughtering humans," he said hoarsely. "We need to do something."

"Are there any live humans in there?" Alita looked from Newman to Falcon.

Newman shook his head. "I didn't see any, but that doesn't mean there are none."

"How many Osirians did you see?"

"I saw three lying on the floor and two butchering," Falcon told her.

"There could be more then?"

"It is possible." Falcon suppressed all feelings of compassion and pity. He'd seen a lot of horror in his life as a soldier. Violent death was not a stranger to him. However, it did not make it easier. Seeing two bloody, headless human carcasses hanging from hooks in the ceiling was not something to be written off as just another act of violence.

"We have to keep our heads," Alita warned. "We must control our emotions and not do something rash."

"They will pay for what they are doing," Falcon spoke with a calm voice. There was no emotion left inside him. No anger and no pity. He had slipped into combat mode. His mind was clear and cold.

Alita sensed his state and touched his arm. Then she turned to Newman. "Remember what I taught you about these weapons?"

He nodded. "Aim at a living target only and squeeze the trigger."

"We'll be facing trained soldiers that we know nothing about. Don't try to be a hero. You are not used to combat. Stay in the back, promise?"

"I will, but I also will use this weapon," he said fiercely.

"The room is well lit from torches hanging on the walls. As soon as I open the door we'll start shooting," Falcon instructed them. Then he pulled open the door completely.

The bright flashes from the proton beam rifles were silent and deadly. It was over in moments.

Falcon looked at the five dead Osirians on the floor. "They felt secure in here. That was their downfall. I feel almost disappointed. No alarms and not even a living guard."

"It almost seems that they weren't even soldiers," Alita ventured.

"Something is happening to the bodies," Newman said loudly.

They watched the five dead bodies change from their ant-form into snakes.

"Apovians," Falcon said and spat onto the floor. "They are not Osirians but Apovians. This whole thing is getting more and more confusing."

"It makes you wonder if the Osirians are actually on this planet," Alita mused. "Maybe all these reports about giant ants kidnapping people and raiding cattle are false. It is Apovians that are doing all those things and blaming the Osirians for that."

"You could well be right," Falcon agreed.

"What should we do with those two unfortunate bodies? We can't leave them hanging there." Newman's face looked pale.

It was apparent to Falcon he had never seen such savagery. "We'll give them a decent burial in the woods," he told him.

"Do you think the snakes ate them or did they feed them to the prisoners?" Newman wondered.

"It is best not to speculate," Alita suggested. "We should take the bodies down and put them into the other room before we bury them. No need to let the abductees see them."

They found the heads lying on the floor and it was easy to determine that both were Suries and not human. Suries males, to be exact. Falcon noted it with clinical detachment. Not that it mattered either way.

After the bodies had been moved, they opened the barn door and walked out into the yard. When the light from the open door flooded the immediate area in front of the door, a few of the captives rose from the sitting or lying position and watched Falcon and his companions stepping outside, carrying their rifles on their backs.

"You are free," Falcon told them. "Your captors are all dead."

"How many did you kill?" one of the humans among the group asked.

"We killed five."

"That's not all of them. Some of them are staying in houses."

"Do you know how many there might be?'

"At least ten more," another man said.

Falcon looked at Alita and Newman. "You heard. We'll have to hunt them down. We still have the element of surprise on our side."

"Then let's go," Alita said.

They walked stealthily down the old main road of the ancient town, their weapons ready, staying in the shadow of the tall trees. All the houses lay in darkness, showing no signs of life. Falcon wondered what caused the original inhabitants to leave their homes. Was it some kind of catastrophe? A plaque that killed all of them? He didn't believe that. There should have been signs, like skeletons of people and animals. Or abandoned farm vehicles.

"I see a faint light in one of the houses to our right," Newman reported.

"I hope they are as careless as the ones in the barn," Falcon whispered.

Weapons ready, they approached the house. The sudden hooting of an animal broke the silence of the night. All three froze and listened. An animal sound didn't necessarily mean an animal. It could be some kind of alarm. When nothing happened, they carried on, senses as tight as the strings of a musical instrument.

They chose the back of the house to, hopefully, enter. As expected, there was a back door.

Falcon pulled a gadget from his pocket and held it against the wall. A screen lit up to show three shapes inside the house, fortunately, close together.

Hoping there was no alarm attached to the door, Falcon slowly opened it. Pulling it open, they entered a small corridor. There used to be another door at the end of the corridor, but now it was gone. There was only an opening.

The corridor was dark, but they saw light beyond the door opening and heard voices. Not human voices. The sounds were guttural and hissing and originated from a throat not human but alien.

Falcon was the first one through the door. The Apovians didn't hear or see him. Alita was close behind him. Newman was still in the corridor when Falcon and Alita fired their weapons. The three Apovians in their original serpent form never became aware of the enemy entering the house they had felt secure in.

They had weapons, but they lay on the old wooden table in the center of the room.

Falcon almost felt guilty killing three unarmed entities without at least giving them a chance to defend themselves. That feeling disappeared quickly when the image of the two headless bloody corpses hanging from the rafters filled his mind.

This was an enemy that deserved no mercy or a second chance.

"Three down," he said to his companions. "If our information is correct there are seven more."

They found a second house with a shimmer of light falling through a window.

Falcon's gadget displayed four shapes inside.

Before they could open the door, it swung open. Something stepped outside, but it was not a serpent but a giant ant.

Too close to the house, they didn't have a chance to hide. The alien saw them and disappeared back into the house. The team rushed back into the shadows to take cover behind the thick trunks of the trees.

The door opened again, four Ants came out, carrying weapons. They moved fast and were out of sight before Falcon or any of his companions could get off a shot.

Standing behind the tree, Falcon listened but didn't hear anything. A sudden bright light lit up the darkness. Alita had released a fireball. Peering around the trunk, he saw a shape moving away fast. Bringing up his weapon, he fired and watched with satisfaction the shape go down.

Then it was silent again. He stood and waited.

"I think they fled," Alita said from her position.

"I'm moving to the street," he announced. "Be careful and cover me."

He moved in the darkness toward the street. One of the moons was beginning to rise into the sky and bathed the street with a pale light. He saw another large shape running down the street. It was gone in a moment. The Apovians were able to move fast in the ant form. He ran after it hoping to catch up with it.

When he came around the corner, he saw a disc-shaped

aircraft in an open space. As he stood and watched, it began to rise into the air.

By the time he brought up his rifle, it was gaining speed. The automatic zoom of his weapon displayed the craft on the small screen as it moved away. The crosshairs centered on it as he squeezed the trigger.

The craft exploded in a colorful display of light and seconds later the sound of the detonation disrupted the silence of the night.

"Well, that is done," Falcon said to no one in particular. He was quite confident that all danger had passed, but he still kept vigilant as he walked slowly down the street, back to where he had left Alita and Newman.

The moon had risen higher into the sky and the darkness was not as black as it been a while ago.

Tomorrow would be a good day.

He stopped and raised his weapon when he saw two figures in human form, dressed in battle fatigue, coming out of one of the houses.

[19]

THEY RAISED THEIR ARMS ABOVE THEIR HEADS WHEN THEY SAW HIM. Falcon didn't relax; if nothing else, he was doubly watchful. Carrying his rifle casually in his hands, he was ready to use it in an instant should they give him an excuse.

They stopped walking but didn't lower their arms.

"Don't shoot," one of the men called in a loud voice.

"I won't unless you give me a reason." He smiled savagely. "You made a good choice when you decided not to leave with your companions."

"They are not our companions. We are not like them." He pointed at himself and ran his hand down in front of him. "This is my real body."

Falcon stopped a short distance in front of them. "Are you saying you two are humans?"

"Not human like you. We are Trevorians."

"You appear to be human. Are you saying you are not descended from Earth-humans?"

"Before we came through, we've never even heard of Earth or of the humans occupying this sector of the Galaxy. Our home planet is called Laazar. That's where our race was born. From there, we spread to neighboring worlds."

"I can't say I've ever heard of Laazar." He scrutinized both men. Unless their bodies were different inside their outfits, he didn't notice anything that would set them apart from any other human, except possibly their ears. They were long and pointy. "What is your relationship with the Apovians?"

"We are...were their slaves. My arms are getting heavy. Can I put them down?"

"Go ahead but do so slowly. Do nothing rash. If you are hiding a weapon, don't try to reach for it. I am still wired, and my reactions are faster than yours. You'll be dead before you finish your move."

"We are unarmed. They didn't give us any weapons."

Falcon allowed himself to relax, especially, when he saw Alita and Newman appearing on the street. He lowered his rifle, but still kept his attention on the two men. "What did you do for the Apovians?"

"We both are engineers and maintained their aircraft. After all, it is our technology. The Apovians are a violent race, but they are dying. That is the reason they capture young males and females from other races in an attempt to revive their own race. So far, they have not been successful."

"I am a little confused here," Falcon said. "Why haven't we heard anything about the Apovians and your race before this? You say you are Trevorians? Are you occupying only one planet or more?"

"The Trevorian Empire is spread over a dozen star systems," he said proudly. "We are feared by all the minor races."

"If you are so fearsome, why did you become slaves to the Apovians?"

The Trevorian glanced at his partner. "We are fugitives from our own people. I don't want to get into it."

"They are criminals," Alita said. She and Newman had joined them a few moments before.

"I suspected that." Falcon gave the two men a thoughtful look. "You still haven't told me what I want to hear. Where is this huge fearsome Empire?"

"On the other side of the gate. We came here through the star-portal. I thought you knew."

"If I did, I would not have asked," Falcon said, annoyed with the other man's arrogant attitude, especially since he had no idea what the Trevorian was talking about. "Where is this star-portal?"

The man spread his hands. "They did not give us the location for fear we may escape. All I know is that the portal is somewhere in the mountains north of here."

"One more thing. Obviously, Inglis is not the language spoken among the Trevorians. How and where did you learn to speak our language?"

The man gave Falcon a curious look. "I am baffled you even ask. It is not difficult with a mind transfer device. It can be done within a few hours. Everybody knows that."

"Of course, they do, except me," Falcon said drily. "I don't know what to do with you two. To just kill you would be the easiest solution, but I won't do that. I'm not a murderer. However, I can't let you go. Not just yet. We'll put you into the compound with the other slaves. Tomorrow morning, we will make a decision."

―――――

THEY SLEPT INSIDE ONE OF THE HOUSES. IT WAS MORE CONVENIENT than erecting their tents and safer than sleeping outside. Before they bedded down, Falcon and Newman took the time to bury the two corpses, while Alita went to get the horses.

It was still early morning when they went to the enclosure to talk to the captives and find out what they wanted to do. In daylight things were different. Five of the captives were Suries and four Suman, and there were seven humans. They also found a young Moyan couple among them. They kept to themselves and didn't mingle with the others.

Alita went to talk to them. They didn't question her ability to talk their language. They told her that they wanted to join their tribe. They left soon after Alita explained to them that they were free.

Newman showed the others his crude map and suggested they should make their way to Rowarra, which was south from the old town. From there, they could take the train either to Rima or Harristown. Or they could walk on foot to wherever they wanted to go.

When Falcon asked the two Trevorians what kind of plans they had, they indicated that in a way they were lost. Unless they could find the star-portal they would be stuck on Aurora.

"We have a problem," Falcon told them. "All these captives want to go home, but it is a long walk to the next large city. Some of them are malnourished and they may not be able to walk for days without food or water."

"We might be able to help them," one of the Trevorians said. "There are two air-sleds in one of the barns. They are large enough to transport all of them. We know how to control the sleds. We might even find someone who is willing to help us. After all, we are strangers on an alien planet we know nothing about. It would be good to have friends."

"It might work, except there still is the problem with food," Falcon mused.

"How far is this city from here?"

"According to this map, it is probably three days ride on horseback."

"With the sleds we can make that in two days, unless we have to stop too often."

When Falcon presented the plan to the captives, some were hesitant but most of them accepted the idea. All agreed that anything was better than vegetating in an old, abandoned village. They knew they could not stay here.

"The idea is great, but all of us are starving. We need food to get our strength back before we attempt the trip," one of the men said.

"I know that, and I've been searching for a solution," Falcon told them.

"You have weapons," another man said. "There are plenty of animals out there and you could go hunting. We know how to prepare meat."

"We could search for edible tubers and fruit in the forest," a young woman suggested.

"How about clothing? It would be nice to find something to wear."

"There is a pile of clothing in the barn," Alita told them.

All greeted the news with excitement and soon they entered the barn to look for clothing.

Falcon brought his attention back to the two Trevorians. "It looks like I don't have to shoot you after all," he said with a little smile. "I still don't know if I can trust you with the lives of sixteen people."

"As I've said, we are strangers here with few choices. I promise to take care of these people. I will defend them with my life. We have nothing to gain by breaking our word."

"I will trust you and hope you are honorable men. These sixteen people will show their gratitude. You will be heroes to them. They will tell their children how two strangers saved them from a miserable life, possibly even death. I don't know what you did before you were abducted, but now you have a chance to redeem yourself. Not many get a chance like that. Count yourself lucky." Falcon looked for Alita. "Let's go back to the house," he said to her. "We have things to discuss."

"What about us?" Newman wanted to know. "How do we proceed from here?"

"I don't know. I haven't made up my mind. That's why we need to talk about it."

Once in the house, he said, "Both of you heard those two. They claim to have come to this planet through a gate, a star-portal they called it. Has any of you ever heard anything about such a portal?"

With a shake of his head, Newman said, "Never. Did they imply that there is a large gate on another planet and when they stepped through it they landed here in Aurora? I am not a scientist and wouldn't even know how such a thing could work."

"I have to admit that I've heard rumors about an ancient race that used a system of gates to travel from one planet to another, but that's all they were...rumors," Alita confessed. "As far as I know, nobody has ever found such a gate. If they have, they will not disclose that discovery. Can you imagine the power a government will have if they find and control one? It would change the whole mode of travel in the Galaxy."

Falcon pursed his lips. "As crazy as it sounds, I am inclined to believe these two. How do you explain the presence of the Apovians and their quest to abduct young humans and other humanoids to, apparently, save their race from extinction? Nobody has ever heard of another species that can change their shape. The only one we know are the Accilla."

"We are not like the Apovians. We don't kidnap people," Alita said.

"According to what those two told us, the portal is north of here. Somewhere in the mountains," Falcon mused. "I would venture that the Apovians have a base nearby from which they operate."

"We need to find this base," Newman suggested. He spread the map on the table.

"That's like finding a grain of sand in a dust storm." Alita studied the crude map Newman had produced. "We've had reports of the Ants also raiding cattle in this region." She traced a finger across the map and pointed at one spot. "This is the town of

Tuson. It is closer to us than Rowarra. I suggest we forget about Rowarra and make Tuson our next destination. There should be farms on the way there. We might find out more from them."

"I agree." Falcon rubbed his chin. "It means we have to forget about visiting the Scouts Outpost in Rima." He looked at Newman. "You had your own agenda to get there. You don't have to come with us. You could join the others to get to Rowarra and take the train to Rima."

"Don't ask me to do that. I promised to stick with you, and I won't abandon you now. I can always take the train from Tuson to get the Rima. It just will take a little longer."

"Okay." Falcon nodded. "I appreciate your loyalty. Then it is settled. We go to Tuson." He opened his pack and took out a small box. Inside was a short needle, which he inserted into his wristband. It released a cube of light that floated above the wristband. It took only a moment and then a face appeared inside the lightcube.

"Major Falcon, we've expected your report sooner than this."

"There was nothing to report until now," Falcon said, already irritated.

"Go ahead."

"I won't make a detailed report now. Nothing of interest really happened. Here are the most important news flashes. The reports about the Osirians are false. So far, we found no evidence that they want to invade Aurora. We've discovered a race of shapeshifters. They call themselves Apovians. In their original shape they are giant serpents. They are the ones abducting people and killing cattle. We've also discovered a human-like race. They are the Trevorians. The Apovians and the Trevorians claim to come to Aurora from another part of the Galaxy. They came here through a portal. I am not aware of such a portal, and I want to know if there is any evidence such a portal exists. End of report."

"Thank you, Major. There have been new developments. Your orders are to go to the military base in Tuson in the north of

Ontura, where you will report in detail everything you've learned. You will receive information you need to proceed."

"I was not aware of a military base in Tuson."

"It is not advertised as such. The Base is disguised as a Ranger Station."

"Alright. We will travel to Tuson and look for that station. Anything else you want to tell me?"

"In Tuson, you will be given all the information you are cleared to know."

"Cleared to know? I probably already know more than I'm cleared for. I may just keep everything I'll discover on my own to myself," Falcon said angrily.

"Careful, Major. This conversation is monitored."

"So what? All this secrecy can cost lives. If anything is known about these star-portals and that information was kept from me on this mission, somebody in the upper ranks is a total moron."

"Watch what you say, Major Falcon. We can pull you from this assignment at any time and put you in front of a court and charge you with inappropriate behavior and uttering insults."

"To pull me at this stage would be insane. I've come this far, and I am close to solving the problem on Aurora. Only an idiot would give the order to take me off this mission." Falcon knew he was skating on thin ice, but he was too angry to let that stop him. Somebody in the upper ranks had screwed up and if things went the wrong way he would be made the fall guy.

"All your question will be answered in Tuson, Major. I suggest you stop from making comments. Don't dig yourself in deeper."

"Thanks for the advice, Lieutenant. End of transmission."

Falcon collapsed the cube of light. "What an idiot!"

"Who was that?" Newman asked.

"Lt. Wagner. He is the communication's officer on the battle-cruiser stationed on one of the moons. He is also the liaison's officer between me and High Command. No sense of humor and a stickler to regulations. And a prick. That's Lt. Hugh Wagner."

Newman chuckled. "I get a feeling you don't like him."

"The feeling is mutual." Falcon stowed away his device with a deep sigh. "It seems we made the right decision. We'll go to Tuson."

———

Two days later they rode out of the ghost town. Before they left, Falcon had gone hunting with a couple of the human men. He shot a big antlered animal and dragged it behind his horse back to the camp.

"That should keep you fed for the next few days," he said. He didn't care what they did with the animal. It seemed, humans and Suries knew what to do and that was good enough for him.

They rode all day, passing a few farms. They saw large herds of cattle and a few fields of grain, the golden heads swaying gently in the breeze like waves on the surface of a calm lake. They also saw a herd of wild horses, and Falcon had to admit it was one of the most beautiful sights seeing these majestic animals running free across the grassland, their long manes flowing in the wind.

By late afternoon it had begun to rain. When they came across another farm, they decided to stop and ask the farmer to sell them some fresh food. Newman volunteered again to go and talk to the farmer.

After banging on the thick wooden door, it opened. An older woman stepped out. Falcon and Alita didn`t hear the conversation, but after a few moments, Newman gave them the okay sign. They slid from their horses and walked to the door.

"Sorry to bother you," Falcon said. "We'll try not to be a burden to you and your family."

The woman laughed. "I am Marinda. Don't worry about bothering us. I was getting lonely anyway. This is a welcome interruption. My husband and our two sons are out looking for stray animals. They may be back tomorrow some time, if I'm lucky. Now it is just my daughter and I. Come in and take shelter from the rain."

They entered the house. The air inside was somewhat musky, the way old houses smell, but it wasn't unpleasant, more like a friendly welcome odour. There was a large room with one old looking chesterfield, a couple wooden benches and chairs. They were covered with thick cushions.

"Make yourselves comfortable," Marinda invited them. "You must be hungry after traveling all day. Do you want me to make something to eat for you?"

"I won't say no to that," Falcon said. "If it isn't too much bother."

"No bother at all. My daughter is the one that cooks. She won't mind. In fact, she's been cooking all day, getting ahead of tomorrow's supper. She always cooks plenty."

She disappeared through a door into what probably was the kitchen. Moments later, she came back and said, "Supper is ready. Come and sit at the table."

The kitchen was roomy with a crude wooden table, large enough to seat half a dozen people without crowding them.

"Sit down, sit down," the old woman said.

She had put a few small wooden bowls onto the table. Two metal pots containing what looked like some kind of stew also sat in the center of the table.

The three travelers took their seats. Falcon ladled some of that stew into his bowl. "Would you by any chance have some ale?"

"Of course, I do. My husband makes it himself."

"Then it must be good," Falcon said with a little smile.

She went and brought three mugs filled with a dark liquid and sat them onto the table. "How is the food?"

"Very good," Newman remarked. "You can't beat homemade."

"Anything is better than the gruel we get on the ships," Falcon agreed. He laughed softly. "I guess there are a few perks we can enjoy on these missions to backward planets." He took a sip from his mug.

"How is the ale?" the old woman asked.

"It is strong. I can feel it go to my head," Newman confessed.

The old woman snickered. "My husband loves it that way." With a sidelong glance at her daughter, she added, "It lends him stamina, if you know what I mean." She cackled and emptied her own mug.

The daughter's name was Leena. Tall and thin, her face narrow and her eyes rimmed with dark circles, she was not what one might call attractive. Wearing a constant frown, Falcon wondered what made her that way. She seemed shy and didn't take part in the conversation.

"Are you married?" Falcon asked her.

She shook her head, barely looking at him.

"Never been married?" He pushed on.

This time she looked at him. "No. Can't find a husband in this godforsaken place."

"Why don't you move? I'm sure your parents can get along without you just fine."

"Nobody wants her," the mother said. "Look at her. She's no beauty. One might say she is useless."

Falcon didn't know how to respond. Leena certainly wasn't much to look at, but useless?

"Beauty is overrated," Newman joined the conversation. "I'm sure you have other attributes. This stew is the best I've eaten. I'll bet there is a man out there who would appreciate a talent like that."

"Why don't you marry her then?" The mother chortled.

"I'm not the marrying kind." Newman laughed. "No woman would want me, anyway. I'm never home."

"It seems you and I will die two lonely people," Falcon growled. "I'll have another mug, if you don't mind."

By the time they were ready to move on, Falcon was feeling good. So was Newman. Both men talked loud and laughed a lot.

"Are you sure you want to leave now?" The old woman looked concerned. "It is late in the evening and there isn't much between here and Tuson. You'd have to spend the night outside under the stars, unprotected. It is dangerous out there."

"We sleep in tents and we can protect ourselves."

"Against the night-ghouls?"

"Night-ghouls?" Falcon repeated.

"They live in caves in the mountains. The only time they come outside is during the night. Flocks of them. Almost as tall as men, they swoop down on their intended victim, sink their long fangs into the victim's neck and inject some kind of paralyzing poison into the victim's body. Then they carry them back into their caves and slowly drain them of their blood. Not a noble way to die."

Falcon looked at Newman. "Have you ever heard of those creatures?"

Shaking his head, Newman said, "I haven't, but that doesn't mean a thing. There are many creatures on this planet I've never heard of. It doesn't mean they don't exist."

"You could stay in my place overnight and travel on in the morning," the old woman offered.

"Do you have room for us?"

"With my husband and the two boys gone there is plenty of room."

"What do you think, Alita?"

"Whatever you decide is fine with me." She didn`t seem to care one way or another.

"Then it is settled. We'll stay here until tomorrow morning." Falcon chuckled merrily. "In that case I'll have another mug of ale."

When it was time to settle down for the night, Marinda suggested Falcon sleep in her sons' room. Since there was only one wide bed in the bedroom of the two boys, she said Newman should sleep in the living room on the chesterfield, and if Alita agreed she could sleep in the same room as Leena. There were two beds in the room. One bed hadn't been used for a long time. It had belonged to Leena's older sister, but she died years ago from some kind of illness. Nobody knew from what. One day she just died.

Falcon was happy to be able to sleep in a warm bed instead of the hard floor inside a tent, especially since hearing the news about night-ghouls sucking the blood out of their victim's body. He didn't know how much of that he could believe, but he felt safe and protected inside four solid walls.

In reality, Falcon was not overly worried about the possibility of being attacked during the night. As a soldier, he was used to facing danger night or day and sleeping under the stars in a hostile environment. However, he saw nothing wrong with taking advantage of an offer of comfort and safety.

Having consumed a few mugs of the potent ale, he was tired and fell asleep almost the moment his head hit the pillow. He woke up in the middle of the night feeling the urge to go outside to empty his full bladder.

When he stepped into the living room, he became aware of a creaking noise. At first, he thought the floorboards created the sound as he walked across the wooden floor, but when he heard the soft cries of a woman and the grunting of a man, he stopped to look around. It was dark in the room, but the pale light of one of the moons falling through the window revealed two figures thrashing on the chesterfield. The light seemed to concentrate on them, and he saw quite clearly a naked woman lying on the chesterfield and a man, also naked, moving between her spread legs.

He didn't have to guess that the man was Newman. It was also obvious to Falcon that the woman could be no other than Leena. While Falcon stood in the shadows watching, they changed position. Newman lay down on the chesterfield and waited for her to straddle him. Falcon was more than surprised when he saw the woman was not Leena but Marinda, her mother. The old woman had her hair undone and it spilled down her back to her buttocks. She let out little mewling sounds as she moved her lower body vigorously in Newman's lap.

Falcon couldn't help but grin. 'Newman, you old dog. Seems to me you are not immune to the temptations of the flesh'.

As he watched, the couple changed position again. The woman got onto her knees and Newman moved behind her. She arched her back, raised her posterior to let him enter her again. He moaned deeply as he did. Marinda cried out and pushed back against him, whipping her buttocks furiously back and forth.

Walking slowly toward the exit, Falcon didn't want to be seen by them. Not because he though what they were doing was wrong, but to avoid being embarrassed for watching them.

It had stopped raining, and the two visible moons flooded the countryside with their pale light, creating an eerie dreamlike feeling. He walked to the edge of the small stand of trees in the back of the house and studied the alien night sky. The sky looked different from the sky over Icarus. None of the constellations were familiar. He felt a short pang of home sickness. When he was a little boy, he loved lying on his back after dark and dream of traveling to the tiny flecks of light in the night sky. He knew they were planets like his own. In his imagination, he saw strange and wondrous beings, battled ferocious beasts and rescued beautiful alien girls.

Here he was on one of those alien planets, looking at the sky the way he did when he was a boy. This was reality. Somehow it was not as exciting as it had been in his imagination. The ground he stood on didn't feel any different. The sky he looked at may not be the same, but there was no magic on it. It was just another sky peppered with tiny lights.

He looked at the house. It looked like any other house he'd seen on other planets populated by humans. A tall tree with wide-spreading branches grew beside the house. He stopped and lay down, staring at the sky.

Opening his eyes, he realized he must have fallen asleep for a moment. With a sigh he got up and walked back to the house.

When he entered the house, he saw Newman and Marinda still going at it. Marinda was again on her back, legs spread with Newman moving slowly between them.

Once in his bed, he lay awake for a while, hoping they had not seen him. Somehow, he couldn't get the image of Newman fucking the old woman out of his mind. The fact that she was cheating on her husband didn't even enter his mind. Actually, he could care less. He wondered though, what her neighbors would say if they knew. Most religions condemned cheating women and husbands, considering it a mortal sin.

When he fell asleep, he dreamed of lying naked outside under a tall tree with a woman writhing above him like a sinuous, bone-less serpent. The two moons illuminated her slender figure, and when he saw her ghoulish eyes staring into his he knew it was Leena. He reached up to touch her small breasts, kneading them gently. From her open mouth escaped loud sobs as she milked his stiff organ, pumping her hips furiously in his lap. Her slippery hot vagina caressed his engorged penis like a satiny, tight glove, squeezing it rhythmically with every stroke. Grunting loudly, he grabbed her lean hips and steadied her erratic movements, pushing deep into her.

He awoke with an almost painful erection and unfulfilled desire. When he found himself naked, he wondered if it had been just a dream or something else.

[20]

HE HAD A SLIGHT HEADACHE AND BLAMED DRINKING TOO MUCH OF the homemade ale the night before. He didn't feel as rested as he had hoped for. After climbing out of bed and dressing, he found Leena already in the kitchen making breakfast. She gave him a shy smile but didn't say anything, only looked at him for a quick moment with her dark, creepy eyes.

"Is there a place I can wash up?" he asked.

"There is a pump outside," she told him. Then she handed him a pail with the words, "Bring some water."

The water from the pump was cold but refreshing. When he came back into the kitchen with the pail full of water, Newman sat at the table. He gave Falcon a friendly nod and said, "Sleep well?"

"Can't complain. Even though my sleep was interrupted by strange dreams, I slept quite deep. I don't think a gunshot would have woken me. Must be the alcohol. That ale is potent."

"It sure is," Newman agreed. "I feel a little drained this morning, but otherwise I feel okay. Did you see Alita?"

"I saw her outside when I went to wash up," Falcon said. "She was studying the sky. She predicts it will be a nice day. We should get going as quickly as we can. By the way, where is Marinda?" His question was more meant for Leena than for Newman.

"She's still resting," Leena explained. "She said she feels tired this morning."

"Is she okay?"

"She is fine. She says to wait for her before you leave. She is happy that you stayed overnight. She was beginning to feel lonely. She wished you would stay another night."

"That could be arranged," Newman spoke up, looking at Falcon.

"I don't think it is a good idea," Falcon told him. "The husband and the two boys will probably come home today. I'd feel a little awkward. We should move on...today.

"I agree," Alita said as she walked into the room. "It'll be a nice day for traveling. We shouldn't waste it."

"Alright." Newman looked and sounded disappointed.

Everybody looked up when Marinda came into the kitchen. "Good morning," she said with a bright smile. "Sorry I am a little late, but I needed the rest. When you get to be my age it doesn't take much to sap your energy. I see Leena has everything under control. Let's have breakfast. I am starving."

It seemed to Falcon that she looked much younger and more energetic than the day before. Perhaps it was only his imagination. Even Leena seemed more chipper. She hummed a little tune as she served the food.

"I cooked up a few eggs and sliced up one of the sausages," she told her mother.

"How about the biscuits and the bread?"

"Still in the oven. Almost done."

"Nothing tastes as good as fresh baked bread," Newman announced.

"I hope everyone had a good night's sleep," Marinda

commented after they took their seats at the table. Looking at Newman, she asked, "Was the chesterfield comfortable?"

"Couldn't have been better." Newman began peeling the shell from his egg. "Best night I've had for a long time."

"I was hoping you'd say that. We aim to please. If you stayed another night you may get one even better that that."

Newman sighed and, with a glance at Falcon, he said, "I would love to stay, but Falcon wants to move on. He's the leader. I have no say in that."

"Too bad. Perhaps he'll change his mind if we offer him a special treat?"

"As tempting as your offer sounds, I'm afraid we have to decline. It was good to sleep in a bed, though," Falcon told her. "I hope the next place where we'll spend the night will be as comfortable as your home."

"I wish you that." She chuckled. "I doubt you'll get the personal attention you've received here."

"I can't agree more," Newman beamed. "I for one can't complain."

"I hope not." She gave him a toothless smile.

Falcon wiped his mouth and reached for another biscuit. "Would it be too much trouble to make us a few sandwiches for the road? We'll compensate you for everything, of course."

"If you stay another night, I won't charge you anything." Marinda smiled but he knew she was serious.

Leena, who sat across from Falcon, took a sip from her drink, but her strange, dark-rimmed eyes watched him over the rim of the cup.

Falcon shook his head. "Sounds like a good deal, but my mind is made up. We will leave as soon as we can get going. It will take us more than a day to get to Tuson, which means we are already falling behind."

"I didn't want to be the one complaining about wasting time

this morning, but I agree with you, Falcon," Alita spoke up. "I'll say let's get going."

———

BY THE TIME THEY FINALLY LEFT, IT WAS MUCH TOO LATE TO REACH Tuson by nightfall and Falcon wondered if they made the right choice not to stay one more day and night, but he suspected had they stayed it wouldn't have made much different the next morning. They still would have found a reason to dawdle.

The strange dream he had about having sex with Leena wouldn't leave him alone. Was it possible it had not been a dream? He remembered going to bed wearing his underwear, but when he woke up in the morning, he was naked. He found his underwear beside the bed.

He had been watching Newman having sex with the old woman. Had that been real or was that a part of his dream? He needed to find out more.

"Did you sleep okay last night?" he asked Newman when they stopped to eat something and give the horses a rest.

Newman gave him a surprised look. "What brings that up?"

"I was only wondering if your sleep was plagued by strange dreams."

"Strange dreams?"

"Yes. Mine was. We both consumed a lot of alcohol drinking that homemade ale. It would not be unusual for that to create hallucinations and crazy dreams."

Newman didn't say anything for a moment, seemingly concentrating on his sandwich. Then he looked up and queried, "What did you dream?"

Falcon decided to tell him and Alita the truth. "I dreamed I had sex with Leena. The problem is I'm not sure if it was just a dream or if it actually happened."

"Perhaps it is best to leave it alone," Alita suggested.

"It isn't that simple. There is more," Falcon continued. "I remember getting up at night and going outside to relieve myself. At least I think that's what happened. Maybe I dreamed it." He tried to avoid looking at Newman, instead he concentrated on Alita's face. "I saw something in the dark, something I found peculiar, but not impossible. Normally, I wouldn't even mention it, because it isn't my business. However, I am beginning to wonder if what I saw was real or if it was part of my dream."

"I must admit, I also had a strange dream," Newman said. He chuckled. "Not about you and Lena. About me and Marinda. She came to me at night. We had intercourse and it was amazing. I am still tingling thinking about it. I thought it was only a dream, but now I'm not so sure. If it was real I have to say that old woman had more stamina than some women half her age."

"I watched you having sex with Marinda," Falcon admitted. Then he added, "I don't mean I stood and watched you. I just happened to see you two when I went outside." He pursed his lips. "Here is the question. If you dreamed you had sex with Marinda, how could I have watched it unless it was real? If it was real, then I also had sex with Leena."

"There was something odd about those two," Alita mused. "I don't like to talk about certain things. You both know I can read the thoughts of other entities, but I don't broadcast it when I touch the mind of someone. I admit I do it when I suspect there may be a chance of danger or some kind of threat. I am very careful when I do it so I don't arouse any suspicion or give myself away. When I tried to touch their minds I encountered a barrier, a mind-shield."

"Is that abnormal?" Newman wondered.

"It is. Quite abnormal. They could be some kind of mutation or..." she paused as if deciding what to say next. "...they may not be human."

"They looked and behaved like humans. What else could they be?"

Shaking her head, she said, "I don't know. Some unknown

species we've never encountered before. Some kind of vampire creature maybe. How were you two feeling this morning?"

"Fine." They both answered almost at the same time.

"More tired than usual," Newman admitted, "but otherwise not much different than after a night of little sleep."

"May I check your neck?" She looked at Falcon.

"Sure." He opened his collar. "Go ahead."

After checking him, she did the same to Newman. Shaking her head again, she stared at Falcon. "I don't know what to make of it. I found nothing. It doesn't seem to be anything physical, like drinking blood, for instance."

"Perhaps the act itself is what they crave and need," Newman suggested. "Both of them appeared to be quite energetic this morning."

"Whatever it is, there seems to be no lasting damage. The only thing that puzzles me is the fact that both of you think it may have been only a dream."

"There is no evidence it wasn't. Maybe that's all it was...just a dream," Falcon suggested. "A lucid dream."

"No, I don't believe it was that. There is more to it. I think that Marinda and Leena induced that dream. Most likely they dreamed with you. They had sexual intercourse with you in some metaphysical realm. That is why you, Falcon, think you remember watching Newman and Marinda. Don't ask me to explain."

Newman let out a sigh. "Even if it wasn't real, it felt real, and I enjoyed it. In a way, it doesn't matter. I have the memory. I know it will fade, but that's okay."

"I will keep an eye on both of you," Alita said. "Just in case."

They finished their lunch and continued on their way to Tuson.

Somehow Falcon was not satisfied with the explanation they came up with. They may never know what really happened.

They didn't talk much most of the day. Falcon was still thinking about what may or may not have happened during the previous night. It was getting dark when they arrived at a small lake.

"I guess we'll spend the night here," Falcon suggested. "It is still a long ride to Tuson."

Alita and Newman had no objections. It would have made no sense to carry on. They set up their tents and made sure the horses were secured to trees not far away from the tents.

———

FALCON LAY HALF-AWAKE IN HIS SLEEPING BAG, LISTENING TO THE sounds of the night. Strange, how every planet was the same. The animals were different, but their habits were similar. Some creatures were awake during the day, and some preferred the darkness of the night. Most of them were hunters, finding it easier to hunt protected by the mantle of darkness. Their screams and roars of victory after bringing down their prey filled the night with terror and fear.

A loud roar close by, the scream of an animal in pain, and the immediate silence after brought him to full awareness. Crawling out of his sleeping bag, he reached for his rifle and went outside. Listening, he heard the snorting of the horses. Holding his rifle with both hands, he went to check up on them. They seemed uneasy, pawing the ground with their forefeet. He looked around and listened to the night but saw and heard nothing menacing.

Looking up into the sky, he focused his attention on the two moons. He didn't know on which one the team was waiting for his orders inside their battle cruiser. It may not even be one of these two. Smiling grimly, he wondered if this whole thing with the reports of giant ants raiding farms may have been nothing but a smokescreen. So far, they had not met even one Osirian. The giant ants they came across had turned out to be a race of shapeshifters from a world on the other side of a so-called star-portal. He wondered if important information had been kept from him. Was the existence of star-gates or portals already known but only by a certain group of privileged individuals?

What did the secret orders waiting for him in Tuson contain? The presence of a military base in Tuson was another fact they had forgotten to mention.

What the hell was going on?

Satisfied that everything was safe outside, he crawled back into the tent. Newman was snoring softly inside his sleeping bag. He stopped snoring for a moment and turned onto his side but never woke up.

Falcon finally managed to relax. He woke up to the sound of soft voices. Opening his eyes, he noticed that Newman's sleeping bag was empty. Crawling out of his and then outside, he saw Newman and Alita down by the lake washing up. Checking his timepiece, he realized it was still early in the morning. The air was crisp but fresh and clean, something impossible to find on most highly advanced planets where water and air was polluted from the by-products of civilization and technology.

Breathing deeply, he walked down to the lake. "Good morning," he called. "It will be a nice day."

"I'm happy to see you in good spirits." Alita gave him a friendly smile. "I have a feeling we'll be facing trial days ahead."

"Don't spoil my morning by reminding me of that," he told her.

"Sorry, didn't mean to. We were just trying to decide if we should go for a little dip. The water is cold but refreshing."

"I believe a short dip wouldn't hurt," he said. "I feel sort of grimy." With that, he took off his clothes. Naked, he ran toward the water and then into it without testing the temperature. Once submerged, the cold water hit him, but it was too late. He was already in it. Coming up, he shook his head to clear the water from his eyes.

"You sure are brave," Alita laughed. "How is it?"

"Like a tub." He grinned, trying to hide his shivering. "Join me if you dare."

"Nobody dares me and gets away with it," she exclaimed. Within moments she was naked, but she didn't jump into the water like Falcon did. Dipping her foot into the water, she looked at him with a mock frown. "This doesn't feel like a tub."

"It will once you're in it. Hey, Newman. Don't just watch. Join us. It'll do you good. We don't know what lies ahead."

When all three of them were in the water, they laughed and frolicked like three people on a holiday, but Falcon knew this was nothing but. Floating on his back, he stared into the blue sky trying to relax and think pleasant thoughts. Living on a planet like this, was so different from spending time inside the confines of a spaceship. Sure, they had pools, but you could not compare them with the vastness of a lake or a river. Nothing was the same. Here the sky was so high you could lose yourself in it. Even though a hologram did a pretty good job creating the illusion of depth it wasn't the same. It was still only an illusion.

They were on the road a short time later. If things went well, they might make it to Tuson by late evening.

It was shortly before noon, when they spotted a strange object appearing in the distance. It looked like something was heading in their direction. Falcon pulled out his binoculars and zoomed in on the object.

"What do you see?" Alita wanted to know.

"You won't believe this. It is too bizarre. I see a giant ant riding a two-wheeler coming our way."

"That makes little sense. Are you sure your eyes are not deceiving you?"

He handed her the binoculars. "You are correct," she said. "It is one of the Apovians disguised as an Osirian coming at pretty good speed toward us. He is sitting on a vehicle with two wheels."

"Should I get the rifle ready?" Newman was squinting against the bright sky.

Falcon held up a hand to stop him. "No. Let's wait and find out what he wants. He certainly is bold. There must be a reason he is trying to contact us."

Alita put down the binoculars. She didn't need them anymore to see that it was indeed a giant ant on a two-wheeler.

Before he came too close, he stopped and pulled something out of one of the packs in the back of the two-wheeler.

"It gets more and more bizarre," Falcon commented. "He's waving a white flag."

"Does that mean he is surrendering?" Newman uttered.

They watched the Ant stop again and get off the vehicle. Waving the white flag in front of him, he came walking toward them.

Something pulled in Falcon's head and then he heard a clear voice say, "I come in peace. I represent my hive and I want to make a peace offer. Please, come with me. My section leader wants to explain the truth to you."

After getting over the initial shock, Falcon asked, "Are you Apovian or Osirian?"

"I am Osirian. We have nothing in common with the Shapeshifters. Please, follow me."

He turned, stalked back to his vehicle and mounted it. Then he drove off slowly.

Alita looked at Falcon. "Well?"

"Let's follow him but be wary. It could be a trap."

They rode for about half an hour until they came to a wooded area. At the edge of the woods stood a large building constructed from tree trunks. A few smaller buildings surrounded it on both sides.

The Osirian stopped and got off the two-wheeler. Without waiting for them, he walked toward the large building and opened the door. Holding the door open, he made a gesture with his left hand.

They accepted the invitation and walked into the building.

Entering a large room with a high ceiling, they looked around, senses alert for any danger that may lurk behind any of the doors. When one of those doors opened and a woman dressed in a black body suit walked into the room, it took them by surprise.

"I don't have a name, but you may call me Ariana. I am the team leader of this hive. I am not a queen, but I am descended from a queen."

"Are you human?" Falcon asked.

She chuckled. "No. Neither am I a shapeshifter. What you see is only an illusion, not my real body. Only descendants of royal blood have the ability to enter another being's mind and make them believe they see what isn't there."

"What is this place?" Falcon asked.

"This is just a small post. We have only a few soldiers for protection. Most of the hive consists of scientists and engineers."

"What is the purpose of you being here?"

"We needed to be near the star-portal to study it."

The star-portal. They knew about the star-portal. "Are you here to invade this planet?"

Her laughter sounded amused. "We are not here to invade anyone. We just want to make sure we have access to the portal."

"Are there more of your people on this planet?" Falcon wondered if she would be telling them the truth.

"Yes. We are constructing a large permanent base more suitable for our species on what you call Drago Island. No humans live there, and it is the perfect location for our people. We will not interfere with the human population on Aurora and hope to be able to live there undisturbed."

"Tell me, how did you become aware of our presence?"

"After registering a huge explosion not too far from here, we sent out a monitor and found you. We discovered that you shot down one of the Apovians' air vehicles and became curious. From there, we tracked your journey and decided to make contact with you."

"Why?"

"We know that the Human Federation has a military base in Tuson. We've been monitoring their communication with the Scouts Base in Rima and lately with the battleship you have on one of the moons."

Falcon stood silent, trying to digest what she just told him. It seemed the Osirians were technologically more advanced than the humans. According to her, the Osirians were quite aware of the military presence of the Solar Union on Aurora, unlike the Solar Union's military who seemed to have been unaware of the Osirians. The only information they had were rumors about giant ants mutilating cattle. The star-portal was another matter. Did they know about it and kept the knowledge from him? Or were they ignorant of the existence of a star-portal on Aurora? Or anywhere else, for that matter. Did they know about the Apovians? So far, the indication was that they did not. He would have to find out.

The Osirian female had stayed silent while he tried to come to grips with what she told him. She waited for his response.

"You seem to know a lot about us humans while we know nothing about your species," he finally said. "Until now, you kept your presence here on Aurora a secret. Why are you making contact now?"

"We don't want conflict with the humans, but we want to be here on this planet, because of the star-portal. We won't allow anyone to prevent us from being here. We have a common enemy...the Apovians. They tried to hide their presence by pretending to be Osirians and blaming us for the mutilation of farm animals and kidnapping humans and members of other species living on Aurora. We did not do that. The humans need to know this. We want to live in harmony with the humans. When you are reporting to the military base in Tuson, you must tell them that."

"I will." He hesitated. "I hope they believe us."

"We will communicate a message to the military base after you make your report to confirm what I told you and to demonstrate our willingness to live in peaceful co-existence with the humans."

"Would that willingness include divulging the location of the star-portal?"

She answered without hesitation. "Yes. It would serve no purpose to keep that a secret. Not anymore."

[21]

It was already dark when they arrived in Tuson. They made the decision to rent a room for the night before contacting the military base. It could wait until morning.

Alita and Newman had been silent during the conversation between Falcon and the Osirian female, but they heard every word...inside their head, just like Falcon. The illusion of talking to a human woman had been complete.

"Can we trust her?" Newman asked when they sat in the dining room of the hotel having supper.

"I see no reason not to. They contacted us, trusted us by disclosing the location of their base, and letting us enter. They could easily have killed us." Falcon defended the action of the Osirians. "Of course, what we think and believe means nothing in the end. It is up to the higher ranks to decide what is going to happen." He focused his attention on Alita. "You haven't said much ever since we left the Osirian post."

"Just like you, I have a lot to sort out. The presence of a star-portal on Aurora opens up a massive number of problems for humans and Accilla. Not only for our two species but for everyone

252

else. It will bring about huge changes. Whoever controls this portal, controls powers not faced by anyone until now. My people will not stand by and hand such control over to the humans. If word gets out, there will be other races coming here, looking for a piece of the pie." Her eyes studied him. "You understand that I have a decision to make, don't you?"

He nodded solemnly. "I understand. You have to decide where your loyalties lie."

"The choice is not that difficult. I am Accilla and I will not betray my people. When I was sent to join you on this mission, it was a joint operation between my people and yours. Just like you, I will have to make a report to my superiors. I cannot suppress the existence of the portal. Aurora was, until now, considered a planet populated by mainly humans, but it was never part of the Human Federation, because of its location in a Neutral Zone. The star-portal changes everything."

"I know. We both also know that certain factions in our military will scramble to claim Aurora for the humans. You may not be safe anymore."

"I am aware of that. Fortunately for me, the Osirians will never allow that to happen. They don't want conflict with the humans or anyone else, but they will defend their status on this planet." She paused for a moment before saying, "So will the Accilla."

"What about me?" Newman looked from Alita to Falcon.

"As far as we know, the military is not aware of you being with us. Which means you are comparatively safe. This is what I'm thinking. I will not report to the base until the day after tomorrow to give you time. Newman, you will take the train to Rima and make your detailed report to the Scouts Base in Rima. Make sure they know how important your report is. Most importantly, they have to be made aware of the existence of a star-portal on Aurora. Even if we don't know the location yet. They in turn will send the report to your Scouts headquarters. Emphasize that this must be done in complete secrecy."

"I understand. When do you want me to leave?"

"As soon as possible."

"What do you suggest I do?" Alita looked expectantly at him. "It is no secret that I was part of this mission."

"I thought about that. It makes it a little more difficult, but not impossible. What I am going to suggest will border on treason, but there is too much at stake here. You were never here. You accompanied the captives from the ghost town to Rowarra. From there, you will make your way to Tuson."

"How is that going to keep me safe?"

"It is just a ruse. I suggest you travel to the Osirian Post and ask the Osirians for asylum. They must have a way to commute back and forth to Drago Island. On Drago Island, they surely have sophisticated communication equipment to send interstellar messages. From there, you may be able to get in touch with your people."

"What if we are only assuming the worst?"

"I don't think we are. Remember our orders? Our orders were to gather information and to 'Exterminate the Nest of the Giant Ants infecting Aurora'. It said nothing about communicating with them."

"What if we are wrong?" she insisted. "We don't want to create a panic or a volatile situation that may lead to consequences we won't be able to control. Nobody wants a war between the Osirians and the humans, much less between humans and Accilla."

"I agree. Do you have any suggestions?"

"I do. What if we program one of the seekers to act as a communicator between you and me? You can activate the seeker once you are being debriefed or interviewed. I will stay here in the hotel, and I will be able to learn what your military is planning. If what we fear is true, we can follow your plan."

"It may work, as long as they don't have any detection devices at the base."

"I am sure they don't. This is a low-tech planet where sophisticated devices like that are not needed."

Falcon mulled it over and had to agree Alita's plan may just work. They had to make certain that what they feared was real before they took action. One thing was clear, Alita could not take the chance to enter the human's military base here on Aurora. It might mean her certain death.

After breakfast the next day, Newman left for the train station. His only purpose now was to make sure his report was relayed to Scouts headquarters as soon as possible. Once the Scouts knew about the existence of a portal on Aurora everyone should be safe. The military would not be able to suppress that knowledge.

Falcon left for the military outpost the next morning. When he was ready to leave, Alita came up to him. "We've become friends, Jeremy. I cherish your friendship and I want to thank you for caring. I would do the same for you, you know that."

"I know. One more thing, once you've become aware of our military's plans you must leave immediately. Change your identity and don't look back. Don't worry about me. I'll be alright. Your secret is safe with me. They can interrogate me to get more information from me as long as they believe is necessary, it won't matter. I cannot be broken. It is part of my enhancement treatment."

She smiled. "I am not worried. You take care of yourself. If destiny wants it, we will meet again someday."

"It could happen." He grinned. "Perhaps, we can celebrate our reunion with me letting you drink some of my blood."

She gave him a gentle slap on the shoulder and laughed. "I hope it will be your desire to taste my passion and not because I am near death." Putting her arms around his neck, she pulled him close and kissed him gently. Letting him go, she whispered, "Good luck, my friend."

As he had been told, the military base was disguised as a Ranger's station. There was no indication from the outside that it was nothing but a Ranger's station, except when he entered the building. Inside the front entrance stood a trooper on guard.

"I am Major Falcon," he introduced himself.

The young man nodded. "We've been waiting for you. I will take you to Captain Jackson."

They walked down a narrow corridor and through a door at the end. In the room they entered, sat a middle-aged man behind a desk. He frowned when Falcon walked in. "You are one day late, Major. We expected you yesterday." He moved his head to look behind Falcon. "Where is the Accilla woman?"

"You mean Captain Alita?" Falcon took the seat in front of the desk without being invited. "She is not with me. She decided to accompany the human and Suries captives we rescued in that old, abandoned town to make sure they arrived safely in Rowarra."

"You never communicated that to us. This complicates things."

"I don't see why. We didn't think it mattered. She'll be here eventually. It will just take a few days for her to get here from Rowarra. Why would that complicate things? There is no need for both of us reporting the same thing. My report should be enough. No?"

"I guess it will just have to be enough. The Brass won't be happy."

"Let me ask you a question, Captain Jackson. How long has this base been here on Aurora?"

"Two years?"

"And you?"

"The same. What does it matter?"

Falcon leaned back in his chair. "I'm just wondering. Why would they send you, a captain, to vegetate on a low-tech planet like Aurora? There is no chance of advancement on this forsaken place. This is where old soldiers with no future retire."

Jackson looked agitated. "I don't believe my career is any of your business, Major Falcon. Let us worry about yours."

"I suppose you are right, Captain." Falcon allowed himself a smile. "Why would I have to worry about my career? Unless there is something you know, and I don't." He dismissed that with a wave of his hand. "Not important. How long have you known about the star-portal?"

Jackson's eyebrows went up. "What star-portal? I know nothing about a star-portal. I want to know what you found out about these giant ants. Where is their hive? How large is it? How many of them are on Aurora?"

Not believing his ears, Falcon bent forward and stared at Captain Jackson. "I was told I would be briefed on new developments. Isn't that the reason I am here?"

"You will be, but not by me."

"By whom then?"

"General Strathon. He will also be the one you will file your report with."

Falcon shook his head, not quite understanding this whole thing. "Where is this General Strathon?"

"He is not here, not in person. You will be talking to his hologram."

"That seems highly unusual. How do I know I am talking to a real general and not an artificial creation of someone that doesn't exist?"

"He exists. It is your own man Lt. Wagner that will control the communication."

With a deep sigh, Falcon said, "Alright. Let's get this thing over with."

Jackson did something to a device on his desk. A cube of light appeared and then the face of Lt. Wagner filled the cube. "Major Falcon. Good to see you again."

"I wish I could say the same," Falcon growled.

Ignoring Falcon's remark, Wagner continued, "I will monitor the connection between you and General Strathon." The image of his face washed away to make room for another person. The head and part of the shoulders of a square-jawed man in the uniform of the Solar Union Space Navy took form.

Falcon saluted and said, "General Strathon. I am a little confused here. I expected to make my report to my superiors at the ISS. Why am I talking to you?"

"You are talking to me because of the importance of your discovery. I am taking over Operation Aurora. From now on, you will only talk to me and nobody else."

"Since when is there an Operation Aurora? My mission was to investigate the reports about a possible invasion by the Osirians. As I reported to Lt. Wagner, there is no such thing taking place on Aurora. The Osirians are not here to invade the planet. They are here because of the star-portal and are no threat to anyone. The Apovians that are coming here through the portal might be a threat. However, that is only speculation. They may also have no plans for an invasion. What they do is abduct humans and other species making Aurora their home and enslave them. What I would like to know is this: Are there other planets that have a star-portal? Are there more or is Aurora the only one? If there is knowledge of other portals, why is that kept a secret? Was that knowledge purposely kept from me?"

The General's face was immobile as he looked at Falcon, as if making up his mind what to say next. "Many questions. And they will be answered in time, but not now. However, you don't have clearance for most of the information. Your real mission was to locate the hive of the Osirians, those giant ants, and erase it from the face of Aurora. The discovery of a star-portal changes the original mission. The order to destroy the Osirian hive still stands, but only after they reveal the location of the portal, which you will relay to me. Only to me. The execution of my order should present no problem. You have a battle cruiser with twenty-two trained soldiers standing by. Use them. You are not to contact anyone in the Union, especially not the ISS. We cannot trust anyone. The knowledge of the portal on Aurora must be kept top secret. No other species must know. What happened to your partner, the Accilla female?"

"She is Captain Alita." He made a point of emphasizing it. "She stayed behind in the ghost town where we destroyed an aircraft of the Apovians. She stayed to help and protect the captured humans we rescued from the Apovians. Once that is done, she will report to the military base."

The General's eyes were hard when he looked at Falcon. "She is Accilla and therefore represents a threat. As soon as she makes contact with you, you will eliminate her immediately."

The order did not come unexpectedly but still came as a shock. It confirmed beyond a doubt that his suspicion had been correct. He knew that everything that was said here, was transmitted via the seeker to Alita. "Let me understand this correctly, sir. You are asking me to murder someone who has been working for the ISS in cold blood?"

"She is not one of us," General Strathon said with a cold voice. "In the end, her loyalty lies with her people, the Accilla. I am not asking you to murder her. Major Falcon, I am giving you the explicit order to execute her. If you refuse, you yourself may face the firing squad. Understood?"

"You've made that loud and clear, General. May I point out that there may be repercussions?"

"This project is much too important to worry about such small details."

"What about the Apovians?"

"What about them?" It almost seemed to Falcon the General didn't know what exactly he was talking about.

"How are we supposed to deal with them?" Falcon wasn't taking any chances second-guessing the General.

"Forget about them for now. We'll discuss that problem later."

"One more question, sir. Talking to a hologram is so impersonal. Will you be coming to Aurora?"

"I am on my way, but I am still at least a week out. That,

however, should not stop Operation Aurora. I expect to find everything done by the time I get there."

"I will try my best, sir." Falcon saluted. "You can put your trust in me."

The face of the General faded away and then the light-cube collapsed.

Falcon stared at the empty spot, slowly shaking his head. Looking up, his eyes met Captain Jackson's eyes. "He didn't say anything about what should be done with you."

Jackson gave him a startled look. "What are you talking about?"

"As you admitted yourself, you are ignorant of what we discovered here. You knew nothing about the star-portal supposed to be on Aurora. Neither did you know anything about the Apovians. That knowledge is above your paygrade. Incidentally, also above mine." He allowed himself a mocking chuckle. "Unfortunately, just by listening in on my conversation with the General, you are privy to information you should never have heard about. This means you are a security risk, and I may have to kill you."

"You must be joking, Major."

Seeing the sudden fear in Jackson's eyes made Falcon smile grimly. "Relax, Jackson. I have no such desire. I am not a cold-blooded murderer. There is something fishy about this General Strathon and I will have to find out what. Unfortunately, we have little time and time is of the essence." His words weren't really meant for Jackson, but mainly for Alita. Everything he and she had discussed had turned out to be true and she knew the gravity of the situation.

"How long does it take to get to Rima by train?"

"Nearly a day. That train isn't very fast, but it is faster than a horse buggy. Why are you asking?"

"I want to take a ride there," Falcon told him. "Is there a way to take a horse with me?"

"There is. They have special wagons for that."

"Good. I will leave in the morning. Do you know of a place nearby where one can get a good meal?"

"There is a fine restaurant not far from here." The change of subject seemed to have a calming effect on Captain Jackson. "Williams can point you in the right direction."

"That would help, but I have a better idea. Will you have lunch with me, Captain? I hate eating alone."

———

HE PUT HIS HORSE INTO ONE OF THE STALLS IN THE LAST WAGON. IT would be good to have his own transportation once in Rima.

The train was not as sophisticated or comfortable as the ones on high-tech planets. The wooden seats were not padded and there were no separate compartments for the passengers. Looking out of the window at the passing landscape was boring and frustrating. At the speed the train was traveling, it was no wonder the journey would take hours. But then again, it was more relaxing and faster than sitting on the back of a horse.

One thing about traveling like this, there was nothing to do, except sleeping or watching the scenery outside the window. One could not be in a hurry or anxious to get anywhere. Traveling in a train taught patience.

Falcon used the time to catch up on some much-needed sleep. He shared the wagon with perhaps a dozen other travelers. He never counted them. It didn't matter.

"Where are you going?"

Half asleep, he didn't realize somebody tried to talk to him. Opening his eyes, he saw a young man sitting across from him. Judging by the way he was dressed, he was most likely a farmer or farmhand. When he saw Falcon's open eyes, he said, "I'm on my way to the spaceport."

Falcon wasn't really interested, but seeing the young man's

eager face, he knew he couldn't be rude to him. "I'm going to Rima."

Laughing, the young man said, "Then you're on the right train. We are heading for Rima." He bent forward. "Isn't it marvelous to be traveling in such luxury without worrying about bad weather or getting robbed because somebody wants your horse? This is high-tech stuff."

"It sure is," Falcon agreed.

"This is the future of traveling. I am excited by all of this. Unfortunately, so many people are against anything that changes their way of life; they are stuck in the rut and will carry on like that until they die." He gave Falcon an inquiring look. "What about you? You look like a man that has seen and done many different things. You wear simple clothing, but you must have some funds to be able to afford taking the train to Rima." He drew himself up. "It took me two years to save up enough to pay for this."

"What are you going to do in Rima?" Falcon was actually curious.

"I want to get a job on a freighter and travel among the stars. I need to get away from this dreary life on a planet where people are stuck in the past, believing in demons and evil spirits that suck the life out of you when you sleep. Did you know that our ancestors came here hundreds of years ago looking for a better life? They didn't have to do the seeding of grain by hand, for instance. They had machines for that. They didn't use candles to light their houses. They had globes floating in the air that lit up a room like it was daylight. They had so many wondrous things, but nobody remembers them anymore."

"You know about them. How did you discover this?"

"I was out hunting one day and rode too far. I sort of got lost and stumbled upon this dead village in Brettany. I spent the night there and next morning I visited the church or whatever was left of it. Every village has an old church. That's where I found this dusty old book. It had pictures of how things were a couple of hundred years in the past. That was about two years ago and that's when I made up my mind to get off this planet with no future."

Falcon gave the young man a thoughtful look. "What is your name?"

"William Forester." He smiled. "My friends call me Will."

"I know we are not friends, not yet, but I'll call you Will. Is that okay?"

"Sure is."

"How old are you?"

"Just turned nineteen."

"Alright, Will. You seem to be an intelligent and ambitious young man, but, sadly, it won't get you onto that freighter. They will never hire somebody from a planet like Aurora, because most of you will never last. The gap between a primitive planet like Aurora and the far-advanced life in space is just too great."

Forester's face had fallen while Falcon talked. "I can adjust," he said weakly.

"I don't doubt that, but you have to deal with old, wizened Captains. They won't take a chance with someone like you, no matter how eager you are."

Forester sat staring at his hands. When he looked up, he seemed to have aged. "What am I going to do now?" His voice was cracking. "I had my heart on this. I'll die on this world if I can't get away."

"Not all is lost, Will. Perhaps I can help you."

"How? What can you do?"

"Let me introduce myself. My name is Jeremy Falcon. Major Jeremy Falcon. I am a soldier. As you can guess, I am not a native of Aurora."

Forester looked at him with large eyes. "You are a soldier? Where are you from and what are you doing here?"

"I was born on a planet much like this one, only the people that colonized it hundreds of years ago did not fall back into savagery. It is a modern world with all the wondrous things you probably read in that book of yours and more. My father is a farmer, but he uses high-tech machinery to help him with the work. I joined the Space Navy when I was about your age. I won't go into that. I am here because there is a great danger facing Aurora and I must try to prevent it. I can't do it alone and I need help. You can help me save this planet from a terrible disaster. Would you be interested?"

The young man stared at him. It was difficult to guess his thoughts. Most likely he was thinking Falcon was some kind of conman, trying to take advantage of him.

"How would that involve me?" he finally asked.

"I can get you onto that freighter with one condition. You will have to deliver a message from me to my unit. A most important message. I will trust you with my life. Are you willing to do that?"

He could see the hope in Forster's eyes. "What happens to me after I deliver the message?"

"Your life will change. From now on I will be your sponsor. I have that much faith in you. You will experience all the adventure you hunger for. And more. My people will take you in and protect you. You will be part of an organization, a brotherhood that takes care of its own. You will never be alone again."

"You are not pulling my leg, I hope?"

"No. Will. This is much too serious and important. Think it over. You have until we get to Rima. By then you will have to decide. I will understand if you are scared and bail out. I hope you will accept my offer. An opportunity like this will never come your way again, I can guarantee you that."

[22]

THE SCOUTS OUTPOST IN RIMA WAS IN A BUILDING MORE MODERN even on the outside than the one in Riwarda. Falcon didn't have any problem locating it.

"The people you will meet are not soldiers," he advised Forester. "They are scouts. Perhaps one of them will explain the difference to you. All of the scouts are from some planet far away, but they are a close-knit family just like soldiers. They will protect each other with their lives."

"Sounds wonderful." Forester seemed a little intimidated by all the new things he was learning, but Falcon could sense the eagerness and excitement in him. The young man knew he stood on the threshold of a new and exhilarating future.

Newman greeted Falcon with a hug. Surprised and a little embarrassed, Falcon pushed him away very gently. "What's up?"

"I am happy to see you, Falcon," Newman said. "I feared they had arrested you and stuck you into some god-forsaken rat-hole and never let you see the light of day again."

Falcon laughed. "Why would you think that?"

"I worried, that's all. Can't I worry about a friend?"

"If you think I'm your friend then I guess it is alright." Falcon smiled.

Newman became serious. "Tell me what happened. Is it as bad as we feared?"

"Worse. Much worse."

"You must fill me in later, but won't you come in? Introduce me to your young friend here."

"Sorry. This is William Forester. He is going to become one of the most important pieces in the chess game we are about to play. But first, I want to meet every scout on this post. I will give all of you my report, so you know what we are facing here. We need to come up with a plan to win this game."

Aside from Newman, there were seven scouts stationed on this Outpost. Five men and two women.

Ronald Silver, the oldest of them, held the title of Master Scout. One of the women, Dr. Anya Novac, was not actually a scout. She was the medic and looked after their well-being.

After Falcon introduced William Forester to everyone, he said, "Do you have a room where he can wait until you've all heard my report? A place where he isn't bored to death with nothing to do?"

"We have quite a library of adventure holograms we watch to keep us entertained. He could watch one of those," Dr. Novac suggested. "He might find them fascinating."

"Sounds good to me." Falcon chuckled. "Perhaps some space adventure of an agent on a mission on a hostile planet, if you have those. Or something about scouts mapping out a newly discovered planet?"

Dr. Novac laughed softly. "We actually have those. I hope it won't be too scary for him."

"He has an open and inquisitive mind. He'll enjoy it."

When Forester heard about watching space adventures, he was quite eager to experience such entertainment and didn't argue about sitting in a room all by himself. Falcon assured him that he was still a part of the big plan.

After Falcon finished his report, all of the scouts sat in stunned silence.

"This is bad," Scout Wu Hung finally commented.

"We could be looking at a full-scale war," Scout McMillan said. "With the Osirians and the Accilla."

"What do we actually know about these giant ants, the Osirians?" a dark-skinned scout wondered.

"Nothing," Falcon admitted. "We don't know their capabilities. They might be much more advanced than the human race. To attack them without provocation is pure insanity. They haven't done anything to justify such an act."

"You aren't really contemplating executing that command?"

Falcon gave the scout a grim smile. "McMillan, isn't it?"

The scout nodded. "That's correct. Frederic McMillian."

"Well, Scout McMillan, that thought hasn't even entered my mind." He chuckled. "I like your choice of words. Execute. I was ordered to execute my Accilla partner, Captain Alita. That wouldn't happen in a million years. I'd rather face a firing squad than betray a partner who hasn't done anything to even warrant such a directive."

"What happened to her?"

"Before I answer that question, I must remind you that everything you hear in this room is top secret and must not be repeated anywhere. Just by sharing my conversation with General Strathon with you I am committing high treason, punishable by death. I hope you are aware of that."

"We all are," Master Scout Silver assured him. "There is something though, I need to tell you. The existence of a star-portal on Aurora comes at a surprise, but the knowledge about star-portals or star-gates isn't really such a secret. Sure, it is kept from the masses, but there are plenty of scientists and others who know about them. There are three portals I know of. One is on Aregon, one on Savanna, and one on Salamander. That one is working. The legendary Master Scout Derek Stonewall and his team went through and, apparently, ended up on the far side of the Galaxy."

"How do you know all of this?" Garcia asked. "Why haven't we heard of it?"

"Because for some reason the existence of the star-portals is not something the masses are supposed to know about. What reasons? I don't know, but by now there are more people that know about them than the military would prefer. Like everything it is a political thing. I found out when I became a Master Scout. One of the other candidates confided in me with the promise I would not broadcast it."

"But now you are telling us," Hung said.

"It would make no sense if I kept silent now."

"What about the young man Major Falcon brought with him? How much does he know?"

"He knows nothing except what I choose to tell him," Falcon assured them.

"And the Accilla woman? How much does she know?"

"Everything."

"Where is she now?"

"I don't know, and I don't want to know. We agreed that she would seek asylum with the Osirians. If everything went according to plan, she is safe with them, and they are aware of this ridiculous and evil plan General Strathon and the people behind him have concocted." He gazed at Newman. "Scout Newman, did you manage to send your report to your headquarters?"

"I did, but it was incomplete. They know nothing about General Strathon and his evil plan because I didn't."

"Can you send a follow-up report? It is important that we contact as many people as possible."

"I can," Newman confirmed. "That young man? How does he fit into the picture?"

"He is a local farm boy with big dreams." Falcon smiled. "He is smart and curious, reminding me of myself when I was his age.

When he told me about his plan to hire on with one of the freighters, I realized here was an opportunity handed me on a platter. I promised to get him onto one of the freighters, but I told him it would come at a cost. I want to use him as a messenger to get everything I recorded and more to my direct superiors."

"How?"

"The Frigate that brought me and my crew to Aurora is only a few days out. Something General Strathon does not seem to know, otherwise he would have mentioned it. It will take the freighter nearly one week to reach it. I will arrange with the captain of the freighter to deliver Forester to the Frigate. Once that has been achieved, things will progress from there. I need to know who this General Strathon really is, who he is associated with, and if the Solar Union Space Navy backs him up. I just wish we had some more time."

"A good plan, providing everything falls into place and runs smoothly. Is this young man with big dreams agreeable?"

"I explained to him that this was the opportunity of a lifetime, and it would never again be presented to him. He knows what he is facing, and he is looking forward to it. I know he won't be sorry."

Master Scout Silver wondered about something. "Everything sounds plausible and not too difficult, but I foresee one huge hurdle. How will you convince one of the captains to hire someone from Aurora, a kid with no experience and no idea what waits for him in that jungle among the stars?"

"Enough gold buys a lot of things. Especially, if I promise him a huge award after he delivers the kid to the Frigate."

"Who will pay him this huge award?"

"The message and information William Forester will carry on his person has no price tag. My superiors and the Union will gladly pay any amount to avoid a disaster."

"The information he will deliver," Newman wondered. "How will you make certain it doesn't get lost on the way?"

"I thought about that. I used a seeker to record my conversation with General Strathon. The seeker transmitted the recording as it happened to Alita. The information is still stored on the seeker, every word. I want to transfer everything onto a memory pin, including my message. I have a few of these tiny pins in my survival kit. They are no larger than a short needle." He looked at Dr. Novac. "This is where you come in, Doctor. I want you to insert the memory pin under Forester's skin. It will take only a tiny incision to do that. His skin will heal within a couple of days with the help of a little healing cream. Will that present a problem? I could do it myself."

"It will be no problem," Dr. Novac assured him. She smiled. "I must say that is a brilliant idea. The whole thing could work."

"Not could, Doctor," Falcon corrected her. "It will."

———

WILLIAM FORESTER STOOD IN AWE, STARING AT THE HUGE FREIGHTER on the tarmac. It sat there like a squat shiny beetle.

"Hard to believe a massive metal construction like this even gets off the ground," he said. "What kind of power makes this possible?"

Falcon chuckled. "I am not an engineer and wouldn't even dare to start explaining that to you. If you think this freighter is huge, wait until you see one of the big starships. It could swallow this freighter. They are too big and heavy to land on the surface of a planet. Instead, they use shuttles to transfer people and materials from the ship to the surface."

"I can't wait to see one of those," the young man said eagerly.

"And you will. I promise you that. However, first we have to convince the captain of this freighter that he will make a huge mistake if he doesn't hire you."

"How will we do that?"

"I will buy his services. The biggest problem right now is to find the man. Come on, let's talk to one of the guards. They might be able to point us in the right direction."

Falcon saw only three guards walking slowly in a circle around the ship. They carried laser rifles, but nothing as sophisticated as the proton beam rifle he carried in a case across his shoulder. The guard Falcon approached stopped walking and watched him coming toward him. He held his laser casually in both hands, but Falcon saw the sudden tension in the man's behavior.

Lifting his laser to aim at Falcon, the guard called, "That's close enough. Nobody allowed near the ship."

Falcon stopped. "I just want some information. Where can I find your Captain?"

"You can't find him unless he wants to be found," the guard said with a loud voice. "He doesn't take on passengers. We are not equipped for that. This is a freighter."

"I know. I am not looking for passage. I want to hire his services."

"Are you a merchant?"

"No. I am Major Falcon of the Solar Union Space Navy. It is important I talk to your Captain."

The guard stood silent for a minute, trying to make up his mind. Then he said, "You should find him in the tavern near the spaceport. If you're lucky he'll be sober."

"What is his name?"

"Harrington. Captain Harrington."

"What does he look like?"

"He's short and stocky. His face red and swollen from too much alcohol and he's boisterous. You can't miss him."

Falcon tipped his hat. "Thank you. What's your name?"

"Jorg Benson."

"Take care, Benson. I'll be seeing you." He walked back to Forester. "Come, let's find Captain Harrington."

It didn't take long to locate the captain. He sat at one of the tables with a girl in each arm. Half a dozen empty glasses cluttered the table in front of him. When Falcon walked up to the table, he looked at Falcon with a big grin. "Want to join me? I don't know if I can still handle two girls. How about you take one off my hands?"

Falcon sat down in one of the empty chairs. "Thanks for the offer, but perhaps another time. Right now, I have a proposal for you."

Harrington broke into loud laughter. "A proposal? Listen, I'm not that kind of a guy. I love women." He pulled one of the girls to him and kissed her on the cheek.

Falcon joined his laughter. "What a coincidence! So do. I'm talking about gold. Lots of gold."

Harrington reached for one of the glasses and put it to his lips. Throwing it onto the table again, he mumbled, "Empty. I need another drink."

"I want you to be sober for this, Captain Harrington. I am serious. I want to hire your services and I am willing to pay you with gold. More gold than you've ever seen."

Harrington looked at Falcon with small eyes. "Who are you anyway?"

"My name is Jeremy Falcon. I am a Major with the Solar Union Space Navy. We need you to perform a small service for us, Captain Harrington, and we are willing to compensate you generously." Falcon pulled a large leather bag out of his pocket and opened the top for the Harrington to see. "This is gold, Captain, and it is yours if you want it."

The Harrington's eyes lit up. Suddenly he didn't appear so drunk. "All of it?"

"All and more, but we need to talk about that in private. Not here. Too many ears that can listen in."

"There is only one private place I trust," Harrington said, still slurring his words a little. It could be an act, but Falcon didn't think so. This man was drunk, and he needed to sober up to fully understand what Falcon was going to ask of him.

"Where is this private place?"

"Oh, right. The only place I trust is on my ship." Turning to the girl on his left, he gave her hip a squeeze. "I'm afraid we'll have to continue this tomorrow. Business is calling." He tried to get up from behind the table but seemed to be stuck.

Falcon gave Forester a sign with his head. "Go, help the Captain."

The young man pulled the table away from the corner to give Captain Harrington room to free himself. Staggering to his feet, Harrington looked at Forester. "Who are you?"

"That is William Forester. He will be part of the deal. We'll discuss that in your office. Now, let's go, Captain." Falcon grabbed the man's arm and guided him outside.

"That's my ship over there," Harrington said proudly. "Isn't she a beauty?"

"For a freighter that ship is a classic," Falcon said and thought 'Just another spaceship that has seen better days.'

When the guard Falcon had spoken to, stopped them, Harrington waved him away. "It's okay, Benson. We'll be in my office, discussing some business. Make sure nobody disturbs us."

"No problem, Captain."

They took the elevator to the upper deck. Forester was looking around with large eyes. This was all new to him and he seemed almost overwhelmed.

"If things go well, this will be your home for a week or so. Make the best of it," Falcon said to Forester with a muffled voice.

Captain Harrington's office was just a small cubbyhole with a desk and a couple of chairs in it. There would have been more room had it not been for all the clutter.

"Find yourself a place to sit," Harrington suggested and sank into the chair behind his desk. "Let me see that gold again."

Falcon showed him. "This is just part of it," he said. "If we come to an agreement there will be more."

"What do I have to do to get all that gold?"

"I want you to hire this young man. Like I already said, his name is William Forester."

Harrington lifted both hands. "I don't need another crewmember. Especially one as green as he is."

"Don't jump to conclusions, Captain Harrington. He will be with you only for a week. He is carrying valuable information in his head which I need to get to my superiors. Now listen, carefully. The Frigate Star-Hawk is about a week from here on its way to an unspecified location. You will contact the ship and let them know that you have vital information about Aurora from a Major Falcon that you must personally bring on board. All you have to do is deliver William Forester to the Captain of the Frigate. That is all there is to it."

"When will I get my gold?"

"As soon as Forester is safe onboard the ship." Falcon let the case he had been carrying slip from his shoulder. "And to sweeten the deal I have a present for you, Captain."

"I wondered what you were carrying."

Falcon opened the case. "This is a proton beam rifle," he explained. "Better, more powerful and more reliable than any laser rifle you can buy on the market. The best the army and navy are using right now. It is yours. This is my gift to you, Captain Harrington."

"Is it legal for a citizen to own a weapon like that?"

"Not really, but what do you care?" Falcon smiled. "I am willing to bet that if I search your ship, I will find a few items that you are not authorized to possess."

"And I am willing to bet you won't find anything like that. I am an honest merchant."

"I don't doubt that, but sometimes stuff ends up in your possession just by accident. It happens." Falcon closed the case. "Nobody will ever find out about this weapon. This is strictly between me and you. I am sticking my neck out to give it to you, but what I am asking from you is more important than quibbling over the legality of a small item like a proton beam rifle. Wouldn't you say so?"

Captain Harrington was staring at the case. He nodded. "I totally agree with you, Major Falcon. I am not quibbling." He held out a hand. "We have a deal. I will protect this young man with my life. I will deliver him safely to that Frigate Star-Hawk. You have my word. Just so you know. We will leave in two days. Make sure this boy is on board by noon tomorrow."

Falcon rose from his seat. "He will be. We will go over the details again just to make sure things will run smoothly." 'And to make sure you are completely sober.'

"What about my gold?"

"Tomorrow. I will bring the gold and the rifle tomorrow. Remember, it is only a down payment. See you then."

[23]

FALCON WENT OVER EVERYTHING IN HIS HEAD TO MAKE SURE HE hadn't missed anything. Forester was safely tugged away on the freighter and on his way to the Frigate with the memory pin under his skin close to his heart. Once on board of the ship, it was going to be a minor thing for the ship's doctor to remove the tiny needle. He had transferred the conversation between him and General Strathon to the memory pin with his own comments and instructions to forward everything to the headquarters of the Interstellar Secret Service. He also emphasized the need to find out who this General is and who he is working for.

Now the only thing left to do was wait. That was the worst part.

Hoping Alita had made contact with the Osirian Post and been able to send a message to her superiors about the existence of the star-portal on Aurora and the looming danger of a war with the Osirians. If Strathon managed somehow to destroy their base on Drago Island it would not go unnoticed. The Osirian Empire would retaliate.

There was also the problem with the Apovians that could not

be ignored. That problem would not go away by itself. They seemed to be far advanced, and they might pose a greater threat than anyone could imagine. Nobody wanted to start a war with another species, especially one with unknown capabilities and weapons.

They told Falcon that their race was dying and not very numerous, but they could have mighty and powerful allies. Nothing was known about what existed on the other side of the portal.

As far as he knew.

Rumors of an ancient star-faring race existed, maybe more than one race, but if there was evidence of those races it had faded away in the passage of time. Some explorer might find such evidence on an obscure planet and not even recognize it as such.

Falcon had spent the last few days on the Scouts Base in Rima, waiting for a message from Scouts headquarters with possibly some kind of news about General Strathon. If nothing else, just to confirm they received the report about the star-portal.

It was on the fifth day when the scout's detection satellite registered the arrival of a spaceship. It landed in the early hours of day six on the spaceport in Rima.

Falcon and Newman watched it settle on the tarmac. Within an hour five military vehicles rolled out of the loading doors, followed by a small tank.

All of the vehicles carried the symbol of a yellow sunburst on a black background inside a red circle.

"You know that symbol?" Newman asked.

Falcon shook his head. "I don't but I'm sure we'll find out. One thing I know for certain, they don't belong to any branch of the Solar Union Space Navy or any division of the Solar Union land forces."

"Private army. In other words...mercenaries," Newman stated.

All vehicles including the tank traveled north.

"I am curious where they are headed," Falcon said.

"So am I. I'd say we get the horses and follow them."

The vehicles didn't travel far. They stopped in the small village of Sundown. Falcon and Newman watched in disgust as a score of soldiers in fatigues went to a few of the houses and brutally evicted the people living in them. In one instance, when two of the men resisted, they were shot and killed. After that, everyone ran away in a panic, heading for Rima.

"Bastards!" Newman was visibly angry. "Bunch of murderers! We should have done something."

"There is nothing we could have done or can do now. We'd only manage to get ourselves killed," Falcon warned. "These are not Union troopers. They are mercenaries with no ties to anyone. It is just a job, and they love killing. Human lives mean nothing to them. Most of them are criminals and should be sent to a prison planet."

"If I had something to say I would shoot them all," Newman cursed.

"It looks like this is going to be their headquarters," Falcon said. "I believe we've seen enough. Let's return to the base."

Back at the Scouts Base, he contacted his battle cruiser on the moon. When Lt. Wagner's face appeared in the light-cube, he asked, "Do you know whose ship just landed on the spaceport in Rima?"

Instead of answering his question, Wagner said, "Major Falcon. You haven't contacted us."

"No, I haven't. I didn't see the need. Let's skip the formalities. Do you know whose ship that is?"

"Of course, I do. It belongs to General Strathon."

"Is he on board?"

"Yes, he is. He wants you to report to him immediately."

"I'll give it some thought. The ship is not a military ship of the Union. Are you aware of that?"

"I am not at liberty to divulge that information. General Strathon will reveal all to you."

"You seem to be pretty chummy with this general."

"General Strathon and I are not strangers. He likes to keep his distance from the lower ranks and prefers to be called 'General' Strathon. Protocol is important to him." Wagner sounded almost like a lecturer scolding a student.

"I guess that is another thing we don't have in common," Falcon said, not hiding his sarcasm.

"Are you going to report to the General, Major Falcon?"

"Like I said, I'll think about it." He cut the connection without giving Wagner a chance to reply. He just learned something curious about the lieutenant he had not known, filing if away for later.

Lt. Wagner contacted him again the next day. "I spoke to General Strathon, and he orders you to see him today. He is in his office at his new headquarters north of Rima in the village of Sundown. He is expecting you." This time Wagner broke the connection without any fanfare, something that suited Falcon just right. He had no desire to talk to Wagner any longer than necessary. He was beginning to dislike the man.

"I have to report to my General," Falcon told Newman with a grim smile. "I would appreciate if you accompanied me there."

"No problem. I'm curious to see what they are doing to that place."

It only took them about an hour to reach Sundown. "I'm going in alone. They don't have to know about you, anyway," Falcon told Newman. "I want you to be my observer. I don't know what is going to happen. I might get shot and you will never see me again. Be alert. There is a good chance I will need you."

"Do you have some kind of plan if things go wrong?" Newman wanted to know.

"No plan. I'm going in cold, but I will be cautious, I promise." He grinned. "They don't have any idea what I actually am. Surprise is on my side."

Newman gave him a puzzled look. "I don't have the faintest

idea what you are talking about. What actually are you? Something I don't know about you?"

"I am a specially trained soldier with extraordinary abilities. The ISS sends soldiers like me on missions that require a different kind of soldier. We didn't know what to expect when we received reports about giant ants possibly invading Aurora. We know nothing about them. There may come a situation where we needed to hit fast and hard. Regular soldiers would be useless. All the soldiers on the battle cruiser are like me. That's all I can tell you."

"I still don't quite know what all that means, but, good luck and come back alive."

Falcon left Newman with the two horses inside a small bushy area where they were hidden from view. He walked briskly across a meadow covered by tall grasses toward the new camp.

The five military vehicles were parked in an open circle with the tank inside. It seemed the mercenaries claimed three houses that were close together. When Falcon walked around the last vehicle, he was challenged by one of the soldiers.

"This is private property," the soldier said with a harsh voice. "I suggest you turn around and walk away as fast as you can before I shoot you."

Falcon gave him a cold look. "Go ahead and shoot me. I don't think General Strathon would appreciate that. He is waiting for me."

"Who are you?"

"I am Major Falcon, you moron. Weren't you told to watch out for me?"

"Sorry, Major. The soldier saluted sloppily and then pointed to one of the houses. "I didn't recognize you. Go right ahead. The General is in his office in that building."

After Falcon walked through the main door, another soldier directed him. He had no trouble finding the indicated room. Two soldiers stood guard on either side of the door.

General Strathon sat behind a plain metal desk when Falcon entered his office. He looked up and gave Falcon a stare. "It's about time you show up, Falcon. I don't like to wait for anyone."

"Well, I'm here now. What's happening?"

"What's happening? What kind of talk is that, Major?"

Falcon shrugged and perused the room, registering every piece of furniture and the location of the two soldiers in the room, judging the distance between him and them. He had switched his awareness from normal to high alert. Things slowed down around him, his mind was as clear as a crystal, resonating with everything he saw and heard. He was one with the room and all its contents.

"Just making small talk, General."

"I don't make small talk, Falcon. What progress have you made? Did you get in contact with those ants? How about the location of the star-portal?"

"Actually, I haven't made any contact with the Osirians. That's what those giant ants call their species. As far as the location of the star-portal? I have no idea where it is."

"No idea? What have you done these last few days?"

Falcon shrugged. "To be honest...absolutely nothing."

Strathon's expression was priceless, as far as Falcon was concerned. He almost smiled when the General burst out, "What do you mean when you say 'nothing'?"

"Nothing, that's what I mean. I've done nothing."

Strathon leaned back in his chair. "This is unbelievable! I had a bad feeling about you, but this beats everything. This is not the way a soldier of the Solar Union behaves. The lower ranks obey the upper ranks without questions. Are you aware that I am a General?"

"Actually, I don't know if you are a General in the Solar Union military. I've never heard of you, and I don't know anyone who can vouch for you. The soldiers in your unit are not Union troopers but mercenaries for hire. The spaceship you came in is not a

Union ship. I don't recognize the symbol on your trucks. Who are you, General Strathon?"

Strathon rose in his chair, his face red. "Your own man, Lt. Wagner, can vouch for me, but that is irrelevant. I don't have to prove to you, a major, that I am a general. I can see that you will be trouble and therefore useless to me. It is a good thing that I came prepared for such an eventuality. I will replace you with Major Tanner. You are done. Major Falcon, I am placing you under arrest. Hand over your sidearm."

"I didn't come unprepared, either General Strathon," Falcon said calmly. "I will not hand over my weapon. This is what is going to happen. I will walk out of here now and nobody will stop me, not in this room and not outside. There will be consequences should I be stopped or attacked."

Strathon pointed at one of the soldiers. "Major Tanner. As your first assignment you will arrest Major Falcon. You will take him to the ship and put him into the brig," he thundered.

Falcon watched Tanner reaching for his sidearm, but before he could free it from its holster, Falcon has his gun already in his hand. From the corner of his eye, he registered that the other soldier was faster than Tanner. He had his gun halfway up when Falcon shot him. Whirling around, he shot Tanner between the eyes, while running toward the exit. He saw Strathon pulling his gun, but he was already out of the door.

The two guards in the corridor had their weapons in their hands, when Falcon came out, but too late, they could not match his speed. He shot the first one in the neck from the side, dropped and rolled away, came up and shot the other one.

Coming around the corner, he slowed down and, casually, kept on walking. The two guards by the entrance, watched him with curiosity. "Something is going on back there," he told them. "Some kind of argument. I got the hell out of there. Maybe you want to check it out."

He walked through the entrance. Once outside, he looked

around and didn't see any of the soldiers. There were two houses on each side of the building he came out of. He could only guess how many soldiers, or more to the point, how many mercenaries were in those two houses. He didn't waste time speculating and sprinted at top speed to the spot where he left Newman.

Newman had anxiously been waiting. "What happened?"

"Later," Falcon said, getting onto his horse. "Let's go. Things will be moving fast from now on."

They drove the horses to run as fast as they could. They cut the time to get back to the Scouts Base by half. Once inside, Falcon asked Olivia Rossi, who was the communication's expert on the base, to put in a call to the battlecruiser on the moon. When Lt. Wagner answered, he bellowed, "Put Captain Stone on the com! Now!"

Stone was his second in command. When his face and head appeared in the light cube, Falcon said with an urgent voice, "Listen closely, Captain Stone. Don't ask any questions. I want you to arrest Lt. Wagner immediately! Charge him with treason. Do it now. I'll wait. If he resists, shoot him!"

Falcon heard the protesting voice of Wagner and then sounds of a scuffle. It wasn't long before Stone's face showed up in the light cube again. "It is done, sir. What do you want me to do with him?"

"Put him in the brig for now. I'll decide what to do with him later." He paused. "I've just shot and killed four of General Strathon's mercenaries. Right now, I'm a fugitive, but I need you to trust me. General Strathon is not who he pretends to be. I am waiting for orders from headquarters to confirm my suspicion. I have sent a detailed report to the Frigate Star-Hawk with a trusted courier. They should have received it by now and I hope to get answers soon. These are my orders: Stand by and accept communication and orders only from me, no matter what happens. Do you understand what I am asking of you?"

Stone saluted. "I understand clearly, sir. You can count on me and the men."

"I have no doubts. Good Luck, Captain Stone." He saluted and cut the connection.

"Are you sure you can trust those men?" Newman had been listening in on the conversation. He was as eager and anxious as Falcon to get some answers.

"Captain Stone and I have been on a couple of other missions before this one. I trust him with my life, literally."

Newman let out a deep breath. "Good to hear. After all, your Captain is in command of a weapon that could melt our base into a puddle of lava in a matter of seconds should he be so inclined."

Falcon gave Newman a grim smile. "You worry too much, Newman. That is never going to happen. However, it could have happened with Lt. Wagner in charge. Why do you think I was in such a hurry to have him arrested?"

———

THEY DETECTED THE ARRIVAL OF A SHIP THREE DAYS LATER. IT dropped out of Over-Space not far from the satellite where his battle cruiser was hiding. By all appearances, it was large but not the Star-Hawk, as Falcon had been hoping for.

The light-cube of the Scout's communication's device lit up a few hours after the ship's arrival, displaying the image of Captain Stone. "Major Falcon, I've been contacted by the Warship 'Flames of Justice'. They want to talk to you."

"Put them through."

The head of a stern-looking, square-chinned man with a thin mustache in the uniform of the Solar Union Space Navy took form in the light-cube. "I am Commander Williamson of the Flames of Justice. Am I talking to Major Jeremy Falcon?"

"Yes, sir. I am Major Falcon. I hope you bring good news, Commander."

"I am not certain if it can be called good news. The report you sent was disturbing, to say the least. Is there any way you and I can talk person to person?"

"That may be difficult, Commander. I am a fugitive and stuck on Aurora. I have no way to get back into space without putting myself in danger."

"Who are you in danger from?"

"If you've watched and listened to my report, you will know that a General Strathon is determined to take control of this planet. His warship is sitting on the tarmac of the spaceport in Rima. He has established his headquarters in a small village north of Rima. He commands a large army of mercenaries in that camp and there surely are many more still on his ship. I have no doubt that the spaceport will be watched. Can you arrange to come down to the surface and meet me at a specified location?"

After a short pause, Williamson agreed to meet with Falcon. "We'll have to figure out the details. I will get in touch with you at 900 hours local time."

"One more thing, Commander. How will I know you are the real thing or not just another imposter?"

Williamson gave him a grim smile. "You don't know. I could say the same thing about you. We just have to trust each other. That is the reason I want to meet with you in person. We have a lot to discuss."

The image of the Commander faded away to make room for Captain Stone. "I will be meeting with Commander Williamson tomorrow at a time and place still to be determined. He will be coming down to the surface of Aurora. Tonight, under cover of darkness, I want you to take a shuttle and land it near a small town called Mosk. Bring two troopers with you. I can reach Mosk by train in a few hours. I will send out a beacon you can track to find me. The shuttle should be small enough to be undetectable by General Strathon's forces."

"Why did you tell Commander Williamson that you can't leave

Aurora? We could pick you up with the shuttle and then you can meet the Commander on his ship."

"Call me paranoid, Captain. I want to meet him on neutral ground where I am in control."

"Understood, Major. See you later tonight."

Falcon didn't waste any time. He and Newman boarded the train an hour later. He had already decided to ask Commander Williamson to meet him in Mosk.

Mosk was a quiet small town with about a couple of thousand inhabitants. The houses didn't look much different from the ones in other towns and villages, but unlike Rima, the town was more laid-back. Since it was located in Ontura, they didn't see as many churches, either.

They found a small tavern at the edge of town. Falcon picked it as their meeting place. It couldn't be any more neutral. They had supper and then they took a walk away from the town until they found a small grove of trees, a perfect place to land a shuttle unobserved, especially, in the dark.

Falcon initiated the beacon and then they waited.

"You are sure there is enough room for us to sleep in the shuttle?" Newman wondered.

"Plenty of room," Falcon assured him. "We'll be sleeping in bunks. It won't be as comfortable as sleeping in a hotel room in a nice bed, but better than spending time in a sleeping bag under the trees."

The shuttle landed without fanfare a couple of hours after they arrived at the designated spot. Captain Stone jumped onto the ground, looking around, with his hand on his laser. Falcon and Newman watched him from the safety of the trees.

Falcon smiled. Stone followed protocol. *Never trust the silence and assume it is safe.* Especially not on an alien planet. Stepping out of the shadows, he called, "Captain Stone. I am over here."

"You are not alone," Stone observed.

"No. Scout Newman is with me. He can be trusted."

After Stone determined everything was safe, another trooper jumped out of the shuttle. Falcon recognized Corporal Martin Bernard. Bernard saluted smartly and relaxed after Falcon told him to do so.

"We set up the com in the shuttle to be able to communicate with Commander Williamson," Stone informed him.

"That's good. I'm expecting his call at nine hundred hours tomorrow. I've decided to meet him here, also. Who else is in the shuttle?"

"Corporal Ramses. He is in charge of communications." He gave Falcon an inquiring look. "Have you decided what to do about Lt. Wagner?"

"He will be charged with treason. I suspect he has leaked secret information to General Strathon. We will investigate the charges later. Now, let's get into the shuttle and wait until morning. I am quite tired and would like to get into my bunk as early as possible."

Williamson's call came at exactly nine hundred hours. "Did you come up with some ideas, Major?"

"I have. I hope you agree. Let's meet tonight near a small town called Mosk in the state of Ontura," Falcon suggested. "It is halfway between Rima and Rowarra. The railroad runs right through it. Come in a shuttle. It is small enough to avoid detection. You will be able to follow my beacon."

"Highly unusual this cloak and dagger game you're playing," the Commander said with a chuckle. "I'll play along. It should be fun. I hope you're not wasting my time. I would have preferred to meet you here on the Flames of Justice."

"It is better this way, Commander." Falcon smiled. "Look at is this way. You will experience firsthand what it is like to live on a non-tech planet. If only just for a couple of hours."

The Commander's shuttle arrived a short time after the sun had disappeared below the horizon. Falcon and Newman waited in the open for the Commander to step onto the, for him, alien planet. Captain Stone and Corporal Silver stood in the shadows among the trees, weapons in their hands, while Corporal Ramses watched everything from inside the shuttle, his hand near a switch that controlled a laser, in case things went sideways.

Falcon had to give the Commander credit for bravery. He came out alone. Seeing Falcon and Newman standing there, he headed for them without hesitation. Falcon had no doubt that inside the Commander's shuttle at least three troopers sat with their fingers on the weapon's console.

Falcon and Newman had chosen their positions very carefully. They were clearly visible in the pale light of one of the moons.

Commander Williamson was a big man, much bigger than Falcon who stood five feet eleven inches. He stopped and saluted, then he said with a booming voice, "Major Falcon, it is an honor to meet you."

Falcon returned the salute. "Likewise, Commander Williamson. I apologize for asking you to meet me here and making everything seem difficult. I've selected a small tavern in Mosk for the meeting. It will be more convenient, and we won't have to worry about being interrupted. And it is safe." He gave the Commander a little smile. "You can sample the local fare. You may even like it."

Williamson looked at Newman. "You don't look like a navy man." Turning his attention back to Falcon, he asked, "Who is this man? Why is he here?"

"This is Scout Wesley Newman. He is my partner on this mission. He knows what I know. I want him present. He may even be able to throw more light on everything than I can. Now, if you are ready, let us get going."

"Are we walking?"

"It is a pleasant twenty-minute walk. Better than being cooped up inside a spaceship," Falcon explained with a soothing voice. "By the way, we won't be the only ones going. Two of my people,

Captain Stone and Corporal Silver will be joining us. They are waiting over there." Falcon pointed into the trees.

Stone and Bernard left the darkness under the trees and came closer. Stone saluted and said, "Just making sure everything is safe, Commander."

The Commander chuckled. "In that case I will ask my aides to join us, too. Like you said, Captain, making sure everything is safe."

His two troopers climbed out of the shuttle. They held rifles in their hands.

Falcon stiffened and reached for his sidearm. He saw Stone do the same. "No need for weapons," Falcon said sharply.

"I will decide that, Major." Williamson's voice seemed suddenly cool. "You may trust this silence and seemingly idyllic scenery. I don't. I am on an alien planet I know nothing about. I take no chances. Ever."

Falcon relaxed. He made a motion with his hand to indicate Stone do the same. "I guess, I can't blame you, Commander. Maybe I'm getting too complacent after spending so long on this planet. It is almost beginning feel like home." He knew that wasn't true, but he said it just to cool down the moment.

"Alright, then. Let us get going. I am anxious to taste some of this local cuisine."

[24]

MOST OF THE TABLES IN THE TAVERN WERE OCCUPIED, BUT THEY managed do get two tables adjacent to each other. Falcon insisted that Captain Stone join him, Newman, and Commander Williamson at their table.

They ordered food and ale. After getting permission from the commander, the two troopers from Williamson's shuttle ordered food but nothing to drink. Corporal Bernard also ordered food only. Falcon gave him permission to order a mug of ale, but he declined.

"I don't drink when on duty," he told him.

Commander Williamson clearly enjoyed his meal of venison and steamed tubers. "This ale is surprisingly good," he announced and ordered a second mug.

After swallowing his last bite, he wiped his mouth and leaned forward. "Now, Falcon, tell me more about these shapeshifters and those humans from the other side of the portal."

He took Falcon by surprise. "I put everything into my report, Commander."

"I studied your report until I could practically recite it. Everything seems to be there, but you never really elaborated on the possible danger we may be facing from the other side of the star-portal."

"The Apovians and the Trevorians are not the immediate danger we are facing right now. Neither should we worry about the Osirians. They are no danger to us, because they have no interest in starting a war with the Human Federation. It is General Strathon we need to deal with. Who is he really and who does he represent?" Falcon looked at Commander Williamson with watchful eyes, waiting for a response.

"General Strathon will be dealt with at the appropriate time, Major."

"When Commander? He is the clear and present danger. He ordered me to destroy the Base of the Osirians on Drago Island. I refused because that act would have had dire consequences. He is still bent on doing that. That must be prevented under all circum-stances as quickly as possible." When Williamson stayed silent, he asked again. "Who does Strathon represent?"

The Commander heaved a deep sigh. "You are a persistent man, Major Falcon. I cannot give you a detailed answer, because you don't have the clearance for that kind of information."

In a fit of anger, Falcon smashed his fist onto the table, making the mugs jump and bang into each other and guests on other tables turn their heads. "Commander Williamson, I am sick and tired playing this, as you called it, cloak-and-dagger game. This is not a game. I was sent to this planet to investigate a problem. I put my life on the line many times. I discovered two alien races from the other side of a portal I never knew existed. Next thing you will tell me is that I am not privileged for that information, either. I know about the portals now; Scout Newman knows about them. So does my partner, the Accilla Captain Alita. By now, the Accilla will know about the portal on Aurora. I believe I am entitled to be included in the circle of people who know about these star-portals."

He stopped to take a breath, suddenly realizing he may have broken protocol, but he didn't care. "Who the hell is this General Strathon and for whom does he work? I certainly hope he is not supported by the Solar Union."

Commander Williamson gave him a long stare. Then he nodded with a serious expression on his face. "You certainly have a violent temper, Major Falcon. Don't forget who you are talking to. However, how can I blame you? I would probably react the same way were I in your position. I can assure you, General Strathon is not a general in the Solar Union nor is he backed by the Union. He used to be. He even made it to Colonel, but he was dishonorably discharged years ago. He is a powerful man and has enormous influence with military terrorist groups. Right now, he is backed by a company called Black Star Explorations, which is a subsidiary of Interstellar Sunburst Conglomerate, which in turn is controlled by one of the most powerful cartels."

"Does that mean he can't be touched?"

"It does look like that on the surface, but if he were to suffer an unfortunate accident here on Aurora, who would know about it?"

The Commander's face didn't show any emotion when he made that statement, but Falcon understood the meaning. "How about the portals?" he insisted. "What, if anything, is known about them?"

Williamson glanced at Newman. "Plenty. Normally, I would not be able to keep Scout Newman in the loop, but from what I found out, the Scouts know more about them than the military."

"Interesting." Falcon leaned back in his chair. "I am all ears, Commander."

"To make you feel better, Major, until now I was as ignorant as you when it comes to the star-portals. You must have heard rumors about an ancient star-faring race that didn't use ships to travel between the stars. Instead, they had a web of portals throughout the Galaxy, which they used to travel instantly from one star-system to another. These rumors are not suppressed by anyone."

He paused to let that sink in. Then he continued, "Those rumors are true. The portals exist. Only a handful of scientists and members of the higher ranks know about their existence. We have a working portal on Salamander. Colonel Stonewall, a Scout Master, and his team of scientists and explorers stepped through it. They ended up on the far side of the Galaxy. Another portal exists on Savanna. Scientists are still trying to uncover its secret. The portal on Aregon is in partial use already. The news about a portal on Aurora has created quite some excitement and the Union will do anything to protect it from falling into the hands of the cartels or any other interest group. That is why we need to know what we are facing when it comes to this race of shapeshifters and others that came here from the other side."

"I agree about protecting this portal, but we cannot prevent the knowledge of its existence from other races. As I already mentioned, the Osirians know about it and so do the Accilla. The news will spread to others. The Spiders, for instance, have their spy net everywhere. You can't hide anything from them. Let's face it, Commander, the secret is out."

"A question, Falcon. Do we know where exactly this portal is located?"

"No, we don't. That is the reason we must be on good terms with the Osirians, because they know its location."

"We could always torture one of the shapeshifters to find out," Williamson said.

Falcon didn't know if he was serious. "First you have to catch one. With their ability to take on any shape it will be a challenging task." He smiled. "For all you know, I could be one of them."

"I don't find any humor in that, Major. How about that Accilla female? Do you know where she is?"

"Captain Alita? I don't know. Possibly, with the Osirians. I haven't been in touch with her since we decided to stop General Strathon. Why?"

"Just wondering. She might know more about the portal. Is there any way you can contact her?"

"I'm afraid not. We didn't make any contingency plans in case things went wrong for the sake of security."

"Too bad." The Commander drummed his fingers on the tabletop. "Any ideas how we should proceed from here?"

"No."

"The problem is my hands are tied in many ways. You see, Interstellar Sunburst has interests everywhere. They finance and control huge companies that employ thousands of people on many planets. They have politicians in their pocket and own hundreds of banks. Nobody knows who sits on the Board of Directors. Hypothetically, I could be on the Board of Interstellar Sunburst Conglomerate or one of its subsidiaries. Who would know?" He seemed to enjoy himself. "You made a joke before. How do you know I'm not making a joke now?"

"I don't, but I hope it is a joke, Commander." Falcon's tone was icy. "You are on an alien low-tech planet. Anything can happen here? It would be easy for a skilled assassin to make you disappear without a trace. Hypothetically speaking, of course."

"A veiled threat, Falcon?"

"Not a threat, just an observation."

"Well, we don't have to worry about that. I am not a board member." He chuckled. "I got you going there for a moment, didn't I? That is actually a good thing. It tells me that you are a loyal member of the Union and willing to do what is necessary. We need to discuss what should be done with General Strathon."

"I have a feeling you are waiting for me to take action." Falcon watched Williamson's reaction and was not surprised when the Commander lifted both hands.

"If you think I will give you any orders, I won't. Like I said, I cannot get involved, not directly. All I can say is you do what must be done. I am giving you full powers. That is the best I can do."

"No questions asked?"

"None. You are on your own." Williamson looked at his empty mug. "All this talking made my throat raw. I think I'll have another tankard of this excellent ale."

The Commander left with his shuttle a short time later. Before he walked out of the door, he said, "Good Luck, Major Falcon. I know you'll do the right thing. We need more good men like you." He smiled. "Try to get that temper of yours under control."

———

THE FLAMES OF JUSTICE DEPARTED A FEW DAYS AFTER FALCON'S meeting with the Commander. Falcon realized he had been abandoned on Aurora, left to fend for himself and to prevent a disaster from happening. The knowledge that he was not completely alone, gave him confidence that things may just work out. He had a battlecruiser with twenty-two loyal men he could rely on hiding on the moon, waiting for his orders. Actually, only twenty-one. Lt. Wagner had turned out to be a traitor, which was unfortunate and disappointing.

He decided to launch a blitz attack on General Strathon's headquarters, but he needed more information about the number of soldiers stationed now in the village of Sundown and which houses they occupied. He was quite certain that all the inhabitants of Sundown had fled and there would be no danger any of them would be injured.

He needed at least two people Strathon and his men would not recognize. Newman agreed to ride to the town to snoop around. Falcon wanted one of his soldiers to accompany Newman. Lt. Stone suggested to use Corporal Bernard. Apparently, he was familiar with horses since he grew up on a farm.

Newman and Bernard left early in the morning. They were

dressed in local garb, wearing the sloppy, grey hats most farmers wore. They didn't carry any weapons in case they were captured and searched.

"Be careful," Falcon warned them. "Don't take chances and don't try any heroics. I need you two to come back alive with the information we seek."

———

RECONNAISSANCE MISSION REPORT BY SCOUT WESLEY NEWMAN:

Corporal Bernard and I left Rima just before sunrise. Our destination: the headquarters of General Strathon. Our mission: to find out as much as we could about the camp.

Dressed in plain clothing, we should be able to get into the camp without arousing suspicion. Just a harmless couple of local farmers.

We rode into the small village of Sundown still in the early morning hours. As we had suspected, the houses were empty. All the locals were gone. We saw the occasional goat and a few chickens running around free, but no horses or cattle. They were also gone.

We found five military trucks parked in a semi-circle and one tank. As we came closer, a soldier in camouflage outfit stopped us. "This is a military zone," he said with an authoritative voice. "No civilians are allowed past this point."

I pretended not to comprehend the meaning of what he said. "I didn't understand a word of what you told me. Who are you people? I know nothing about a military zone. We don't have an army on Aurora."

"Well, you have now," the soldier told us, waving his weapon around.

"Where are all the people that lived here in Sundown? This used to be a bustling little village. We were planning to have breakfast in the cozy restaurant a little further down."

"It seems you'll have to change your plans. We are occupying this village now." The soldier grinned. He turned around when he heard another soldier coming to see what the commotion was all about. It seemed to me these guys were bored.

"What is going on here," the second soldier asked.

"Nothing, really," the first one told him. "Just a couple of local comedians wondering what happened to their quaint little village."

"Nothing happened to the village. It is still here. The people left, that's all." The second soldier looked us up and down. "What do you two want here? There is nothing here for you anymore. Where are you from?"

"West of here. We own a farmstead there. My brother Daniel here and I decided to go to Rima for a couple of days. Take a few days off from farming. I'm sort of interested in the spaceport. Maybe there'll be some ships we can look at."

The soldier laughed. "What do you know about spaceships?"

"Nothing. You don't look like locals. Did you come here in a spaceship?"

The guard pointed a finger at me. "Now you're getting warm. I guess you are not as dumb as you look. Yes, we came in a space-ship. You may be able to get a close look at it in Rima."

"No kidding. That would be wonderful. What's it like out there in space? It must be exciting to travel to other worlds. I wish I could do that. How big is that spaceship of yours?"

"Not very big but big enough for our group."

"How many soldiers are in your group?"

"Thirty-two. Now." The soldier made a face. "We were more, but we had a bit of an incident here where four good soldiers lost their lives."

"That's horrible. What happened?"

"It is none of your business," the first soldier snapped. He looked at his companion. "Don't give away secrets!" He looked back at me. "You should leave. By the way, your brother hasn't said a thing. Does he have nothing to say?"

"He's got plenty to say. At home on the farm. He never shuts up, but he is difficult to understand. He got kicked in the head by a horse when he was young and hasn't been the same since then. He's a good worker, though. Strong like a horse and never complains. You should see his muscles."

"I don't think I'm interested. But I think it is time for you two to leave before we have to arrest you for trespassing."

I gave him my best smile. "You are too nice to do that. Who lives in the big house?"

"The General." He made a motion with his hands. "Turn your horses around, take your muscular brother, and get lost before the General comes out. He is not as friendly as we are. Go to Rima like you planned."

I tipped my sloppy hat. "We will. Thank you for talking to us. It was highly informative. I am so excited to have met two real spacemen."

We left before they got suspicious. I was happy but Corporal Bernard was not. Can't blame him. "Kicked by a horse?" he said. "I was never kicked by a horse."

End of Report.

———

MAJOR FALCON LOOKED UP FROM THE SHEET OF PAPER NEWMAN HAD handed him. "You did alright under the circumstances," he said with a smile. "Was it necessary to make Corporal Bernard look like an imbecile?"

Newman shrugged. "I didn't mean any harm. It sort of popped into my head. A spur-of-the-moment thing, you know. He was kind of silent all the time."

"That is his nature. He is a quiet man, but very capable. One of the best men I have." He looked at the report again. "Thirty-two soldiers against my twenty-one. We should be alright, though." He gave Newman a thoughtful look. "My men are superior to those mercenaries. All of them have been enhanced and specially trained. We will hit them fast and hard in the middle of the night. It will be over before they realize what is happening."

"What about that General Strathon? Will you arrest him?"

Falcon shook his head. "No."

"What will happen to him? Will he go free?"

Falcon smile grimly. "I shouldn't tell you this, but he will be shot dead in the frenzy of the battle. We can't let him live. He is too dangerous and has too many friends."

Newman nodded slowly. "It makes sense. I am glad I am not a soldier. To make a decision like that can only be made by someone with a different mentality. Scouts try to save lives, not take them. I admit, there is a need for men like you, Falcon. Who else would take care of men like General Strathon?"

"You are right, Newman. Who else but men like me? We are the hunters and the executioners. We are a necessary evil."

[25]

THEY HIT THE CAMP AT TWO-HUNDRED HOURS. IT WAS A DARK NIGHT, but the men wore night-glasses. As expected, the camp was quiet. There were only two sentries guarding the camp. One was sitting on the steps of the large house, which were General Strathon's quarters. He was half asleep with his rifle across his knees. The other one was leaning against the tank, looking at the stars.

Neither of the two saw his killer coming up from behind him.

Falcon's men entered all three houses at the same time. They surprised the mercenaries sleeping in their beds and left them to bleed out with their throats cut. None of them got a chance to even reach for the guns lying on the floor or sound the alarm.

General Strathon was the only one still awake. He was standing beside his desk, studying a map of Aurora his monitor projected against one wall. He was concentrating so much on his task he never heard Falcon come into his office. He swung around when Falcon said, "Good evening, General."

Strathon stared at him in surprise, completely caught off guard. "What the hell!" he cursed, reaching for his sidearm.

"Don't!" Falcon warned him.

Strathon didn't finish the move. "How did you get in here?"

"I walked in." Falcon smiled. "All of your men are dead. You are the only one left alive."

"I don't believe you."

"Believe it. My men are occupying every room and every corridor. You are alone, General Strathon. Your dream of becoming the man who controls the star-gate ends here and now."

Strathon walked around his desk and sank into his chair. "I am a powerful man, Major Falcon. I have influential friends everywhere. If you play your cards right, you can be rich beyond your wildest dreams. You could retire on any planet of your choice, surrounded by luxury you never knew existed. There is no reason for you to spend the rest of your life as a slave of the Solar Union, enduring hardship and misery on planets like this one. This could be the opportunity of a lifetime, something you will never be offered again. Take me to my ship and let me go free. I will see to it that you will live a life of luxury as a private citizen."

"I have to admit, you do make it sound wonderful and tempting. It all sounds great, but you know that it won't happen, even if I let you go free. You are as much a slave to your masters as I am to mine. There is only one way this can end, General Strathon. You know that. I will give you a chance to defend yourself, a chance to die as a warrior. I will let you draw your gun. Maybe, you will be faster than me."

Falcon saw the sudden desperation in the General's eyes. He let Strathon draw his gun before he even reached for his. Strathon never had a chance. Falcon shot him between the eyes. The General died with his gun lifted halfway. His body slumped forward and hit the desk with a thud.

With one last glance at the projected picture of the planet Aurora on the wall, Falcon walked out of the room.

The executioner's job was done.

His men had moved all the dead bodies into the street and into a large pile. Even though they left them there to rot, Falcon knew that the carrion eaters would find them soon enough.

"What should we do with the trucks?" Lt. Stone asked.

"Leave them. The residents of the town will be back. I'm sure they'll figure out how to use these vehicles. They will be put to good use and maybe propel them a little into the future."

His men were gathered in a group, waiting for new orders. "You know that our task isn't over yet. We still have to take care of the spaceship sitting in the spaceport. I want to get it all done tonight. We'll ride back to Rima and finish the job."

They rode in silence, arriving at the spaceport near morning. The entry to the spaceship was closed, but one guard was on duty. Falcon walked boldly up to him and said, "I am Major Falcon. You may have heard of me."

The guard gave him a surprised look. "You are a wanted man, Major." He lifted his rifle, but Falcon had his own gun already in his hand.

"How many men inside the ship?"

"Only four."

"Good." He signaled his men. One of them disarmed the guard and tied his hands behind his back with a magnetic band. "No need for all of you to go inside," Falcon told Stone. "You will have to deal with only four soldiers. Take four of the men and clean up the place. Take them into custody if you can. We've spilled enough blood already today."

———

There wasn't any reason for the battlecruiser to hide on the moon anymore. Falcon made the decision to have it brought down to the surface and park it on the spaceport's tarmac in Rima until it was decided what their next move would be. The threat of the Apovians still existed. The location of the star-portal was still unknown.

The original mission had been to stop the invasion of the Osirians. The threat of an invasion by giant ants had never been real, instead Falcon discovered the existence of a gate to the far side of the Galaxy and a different threat...a possible invasion by an unknown alien race of shapeshifters from beyond the star-gate. The Apovians had insisted that they had no plans to invade Aurora, but could they be trusted?

When the Scout's surveillance satellite reported the arrival of a large spaceship, Falcon knew the race for the star-gate had begun. A few days later, a shuttle landed on the spaceport. Its insignia identified it as belonging to the Accilla. That meant Alita had been able to contact her people.

Falcon wondered when the Solar Union would be sending a ship with a team of scientists and specialists to investigate the star-portal.

Two weeks later, a Frigate of the Solar Union Space Navy dropped out of Over-space. The military wasn't taking any chances to possibly have some other alien race take control of the space-portal by force. Even though Aurora was considered part of the Human Empire, it was too far away from all the trade routes to be easily defended. It was more or less a sitting duck. A ruthless enemy could easily invade it without much resistance. The presence of the Frigate would be warning enough to tell everyone to stay clear.

A couple of days later, a call came in for Major Falcon. He had expected a call at some time and had moved into the cruiser.

The head of a heavyset man in uniform materialized in the light-cube. Falcon recognized him immediately. "Commander Kennedy. What took you so long?"

The Commander nodded solemnly, but then his lips formed a thin smile. "Major Falcon, still so little respect for age and rank, I see."

"You know that is not true, Commander. I have nothing but

the greatest respect for you, sir. Let me say this, I am overwhelmed with joy to see you."

"Don't overdo it now, Major. I am happy to see you, also. Happy to see you alive and well. I will send a shuttle to pick you up. I want to talk to you in person. The initial report you sent in such a unique way only scratches the surface of what is going on here. By the way, that young man you used as your courier is a fine lad. With a little bit of molding, he will make a dedicated trooper with a promising future. I will make this short, but we will talk at length when I see you. Looking forward to it. Expect the shuttle some time tomorrow."

His image faded away and the light-cube collapsed.

Falcon sat for a moment, staring into thin air. To have Commander Kennedy coming in a Frigate to this planet proved that the Solar Union was taking this seriously.

The shuttle landed the next day. Falcon boarded it and it took off again. A few hours later, flanked by two troopers, he walked down a long corridor on the Frigate.

Commander Kennedy looked up from the screen he seemed to have been studying when Falcon entered his office.

Falcon saluted with the words, "Major Falcon reporting, sir."

The Commander returned the salute and said, "Relax, Major. It is just you and me right now." He got up from behind his desk and walked around to the front. Then he opened his arms and pulled Falcon close to hold him for a moment. Letting him go, he stepped back and smiled. "How many years has it been?"

"Five," Falcon answered.

"That long? I've been told you have gone through the enhancement program. I am proud of you for what you have achieved."

"Thank you, sir. How is Aunt Elizabeth?"

"She is fine. We communicated just before I left for this mission, but I haven't been home now for six months. When was the last time you saw your parents?"

"Almost two years now, sir."

"A long time to be away from family, but that is the lot of a soldier. It's what we chose." He went back to take his seat again behind his desk. "I've arranged to have supper tonight with you and a couple of my strategists. After supper, we will take your detailed report and decide what is going to happen next."

"Looking forward to that, sir." Falcon saluted again.

"Good. You're probably eager to check out the Frigate." He chuckled. "Perhaps someday you will command one of these ships. I'll have my aid Captain Johnson show you around a little."

As if on cue the door opened and a young woman, dressed in uniform, walked in. She gave Falcon a friendly smile. "Come, follow me."

———

THINGS BEGAN TO CHANGE. IT DIDN'T TAKE LONG BEFORE A SPIDER ship arrived. One of their shuttles landed and set down on the spaceport, right beside the Accilla shuttle and the one Commander Kennedy sent down days before, along with twenty troopers.

Besides the Solar Union's Frigate there were now the space-ships of the Spiders and the Accilla in Aurora's orbit. Falcon knew more would be coming soon.

The troopers of the Solar Union's Special Forces claimed the five trucks and the tank parked in the village of Sundown. Then they drove them to Tuson and took over the Military Base. It was going to be their headquarters.

No orders had come in for Falcon and his men yet. He and the men felt left floating in limbo. When Falcon confronted Commander Kennedy, he told him to be patient and wait.

With the help of Newman, Falcon found a huge empty house and decided to rent it for himself and his men. He called it their temporary headquarters. He hired a couple of Suries females as housekeepers and cooks. His men were happy. They had been cooped up in the battlecruiser for weeks and this was a welcome change for all of them, almost like a holiday.

"Have you heard from Alita?" Newman inquired.

"Not a word. I hope she is okay. I am beginning to worry about her."

"You liked her, didn't you?"

"Not the way you make it sound." Falcon smiled. "I care for her, but that is where it ends. I admit, though, we bonded and formed a special friendship." He knew there was a bit more to it than just friendship. Something happened between them the day they had sex, even though it happened because she needed him to save her life. They had not only joined bodies but their minds also. She left something of herself behind, there was no denying that.

"Do you think she got the location of the star-portal from the Osirians?" Newman wondered.

"If she did, the Accilla will be the only ones knowing where it is. It will give them an advantage," Falcon speculated.

"Not for long. They will all be watching each other, and nobody will be able to make a move without everyone else knowing about it."

Falcon made a decision. "What would you say if you and I ride out to the Osirian's Post? Hopefully, they can tell us what happened to Alita?"

"Not a bad idea. Sure. When do you want to leave?"

"Tomorrow, if you're up for it."

They took the train to Tuson. From Tuson it was only a few hours on horseback to the Osirian Post. They had no trouble finding it. Riding slowly, waving a white flag, they approached the collection of houses.

"I hope they are as friendly as the first time," Newman said.

As they came closer, one of the doors opened and a giant ant came out. It waited until Falcon and Newman were close enough to speak. "You found us again."

"We did," Falcon agreed. "Are you the one who greeted us on the cycle?"

"I am. May I inquire your reason for being here?"

"Yes, you may. We are looking for the female Accilla that came to you for help. Is she here?"

"No, she isn't, but I invite you to come in and speak to our leader."

Like the first time, they followed the Osirian into the room with the high ceiling. It didn't take long until another Osirian walked into the room.

"We expected to find Ariana," Falcon said.

"You have found her." Her ant body began to fade away and then they looked at the woman in the black bodysuit. "I am Ariana," she said with a little smile.

Falcon made a little bow. "I am happy to see you again. We are looking for our companion, the Accilla that came to you seeking sanctuary."

"She was here, but now she is gone."

"What happened to her?"

"We took her to the island. She may still be there."

"You don't know? Is she safe? Is there any way we can get in touch with her?" Falcon knew he sounded desperate, worried.

"We will let her know about you."

"Thank you. There are other things we want to tell you. As you must know by now, much happened since we were here. Word of the existence of the star-portal is spreading among the races. Ships are coming to this planet to find out more about this portal. But the most important news I have for you is that your people are safe. We have eliminated the man that gave the order to destroy your base on the island. There is no danger of that ever happening."

"I appreciate you telling me that, but we were never in such danger. Our base on the island is protected by an impenetrable force field."

"I see. The only other thing to tell you is that we humans have the desire to live with the Osirians in peace. We will not challenge your presence on Drago Island. No humans will try to interfere with you making it your base."

"It is my turn to thank you. Perhaps, my people and yours will be able to trade with each other someday."

"I will let it be known." He didn't know what else to say except for, "We'll be leaving with the knowledge that you will get in touch with your people on the island and forward this message to the Accilla female: Contact Jeremy Falcon at the Scouts Post in Rima."

"I will. I hope she will answer your request."

Her human body dissolved and then he was looking at a tall ant. She turned around without another word. He and Newman left the building and rode back to Tuson, where they boarded the train again to take them back to Rima.

"One thing I have to say about the Osirians, they are not easy to get warm to," Newman commented.

"They are different from us humans," Falcon agreed. "Quite similar to the Spiders. Their mentality is not like ours, either."

Another week went by. Falcon was getting bored waiting for something to happen.

Then one early morning Newman came to Falcon's temporary headquarters. "Yesterday, another ship landed at the spaceport. The ship is one of ours. This morning, we received a message. An important Scout is coming for a visit. There was also a message for you. Whoever it is, he wants you to be present. It is most important you be there."

"I don't understand. Why would they send a message for me with a Scout's ship?" Falcon wondered.

"They didn't say, and Olivia didn't ask."

"When am I supposed to be there?"

"This afternoon. Why don't you come for lunch, just to make sure you are present when they come?"

"Alright, I'll be there. I am very curious what this is all about."

It was already late afternoon; Falcon happened to look out of the window, when a sleek military-type vehicle decorated with the Scout's symbol pulled up in front of the Scouts building. Out stepped four people. They wore the uniform of the Scouts, but something about them set them apart from regular Scouts.

They stood beside the vehicle, looking around. One man decided to come to the door.

Master Scout Silver opened the door to greet him. Falcon didn't hear what was said, but Silver came back into the main room and announced with some excitement in his voice, "You won't believe who that is."

"Well, don't hold us in suspense. Spill it," McMillan said.

"It is Master Scout Derek Stonewall. Do you get it? The legendary Scout. The Scout at the door announced him as *Colonel* Stonewall."

"Colonel?" Falcon wondered. "I had no idea you have military ranks in the Scouts organization?"

"It looks like we do. Colonel Stonewall is here. Waiting outside our building."

"Why not just invite them in?" Scout Suchina suggested.

Silver rushed to the door to open it again. He came back with four people in tow.

The first one was a tall, elderly man. His chest was decorated with a couple of colorful bars. He smiled and said, "I am Colonel Stonewall of Scouts Security, and this is my staff. He pointed at one of the Scouts who was clearly a woman, "This is Salabet, and this is Captain Gorona of the Anorian Space Force. Last but not least, this is Robert Lee." He smiled. "He is actually a human. So am I."

"We are honored to have you, Colonel Stonewall," Silver said. "What brings you here?"

"To your outpost or to Aurora?" Stonewall asked with a chuckle.

"Both, I guess. Can we offer you some refreshments?"

"You can, but a place to sit would also be appreciated."

"Well, of course. We can go into our meeting room, sir."

Stonewall looked at Falcon. "You must be Major Falcon." He held out his hand." I have a message for you, but we'll get to that a little later."

Falcon shook the offered hand. "I am a little perplexed, Colonel. Where do these orders for me come from?"

"Directly from your headquarters of the ISS. The message is too important to trust it to a transmission. Now, let us all sit down and have a drink." He rubbed his hands. "You wouldn't have a barrel full of the local ale, would you?"

"Sorry, Colonel," Silver apologized. "All we can offer is fruit juice. Tonight, if you want, we could all go to the tavern not far from here and enjoy a few tankards of ale."

"Sounds wonderful. I want you all to relax and think of me as just another scout. I've never been big on protocol. Let's go into that meeting room."

There was a long table, large enough for all of them. Once they were seated, Stonewall said, "The answer to your question is quite simple. I am sure you all can guess the reason. I am here because of the star-portal. We will have plenty of time to discuss everything in detail, but in short, I am taking over the control of the portal. From now on, I will be the highest authority on Aurora. On my ship, I have a team of scientists and engineers that will take the portal apart until we know all of its secrets."

"Does that mean the Solar Union is claiming the star-portal for the Union?" Falcon asked.

"No, Major. We are only claiming the right to investigate and study it. We will allow access to the portal to everyone. Salabet here, she looks human, but she is a Kraach in human form." He smiled. "She doesn't like the word 'Spider' by the way. She represents the Kraach. Captain Gorona, as already mentioned, is an Anorian. The Accilla have a spaceship at the spaceport. We are anxious to talk to your partner the

Accilla Captain Alita, Major. Is there any way we can contact her?"

Falcon shook his head. "No, sir. I am waiting for her to get in touch with me."

"Good. Also, I wouldn't mind communicating with the leader of the Osirians. Can that be arranged?"

"Hopefully, with the help of Captain Alita it may be possible."

"In your report, you mentioned the alien species from the other side of the portal, the Apovi. Salabet had a run-in with them on Aregon. They are a nasty bunch. Dangerous because of their shapeshifting ability." He gave Falcon a thoughtful look. "Now to you, Major. This is a direct order from Colonel Washington of the ISS. You and your men have gone beyond your call of duty and proven yourself to be a strong and effective force. You, Major Falcon, have shown initiative and impeccable character when you dealt with the situation. You prevented the Union from getting drawn into a war with the Osirians and the portal from falling under the control of the Cartels. You and your men will stay on Aurora, and you will be under my command."

"How can that be? Nothing against you, sir, but you are not military. You are scouts. It has been proven that scouts are not military material because of your different mental attitude; your dislike of violence, for instance. You are not strategists and planners. The military and the scouts don't really get along well."

"You seem to have gotten along well with Scout Newman," Stonewall injected.

"That is true. I admit, we've come to like each other." Falcon glanced at Newman. "We've become friends."

"What more proof to you want, Major? Scouts and soldiers can work together quite efficiently."

"Okay, that is so. It still doesn't explain why a scout was given the job of defending Aurora and the star-portal when there are plenty of generals out there who would be able to do the job better because they have the training and experience."

Stonewall sighed heavily. "I am not surprised by your skepticism. I probably would have been disappointed had you meekly accepted. Let me explain something to all of you. The High Senate created Scouts Security. We are beyond politics. We don't belong to any political or other organization. We owe allegiance to nobody. Scouts Security answers only to the High Senate, no matter who is in power in the government. We have our own task force. All of us are highly trained in warfare, combat, and strategy. As far as our dislike of violence goes, it doesn't stop us from using violence if it is necessary. Does that answer some of your questions?"

Falcon tightened his jaw, not sure how he should react. "Some," he finally conceded. "What happens to the military base in Tuson? We have a few Special Forces people there now. Are they staying? Are they also under your command?"

"They will stay. We have to make sure we have a strong military presence on Aurora. And yes, they will also be under my command. Just to give you a glimpse into my plans. I have arranged for a builder ship to come here. It will build a compound which will become Scouts and Military Headquarters on Aurora. We will have our own spaceport, independent from the other two. Any more questions?"

When all were silent, he said, "In case any of you didn't really grasp it. I will say it again. From this day on, I will have total control over every military base and every Scouts Post on Aurora. All of you will report to me." Stonewall smiled. "Let us put it in simple words: I am your boss."

The End

Don't miss out on your next favorite book!

Join the Melange Books mailing list at
www.melange-books.com/mail.html

———

THANK YOU FOR READING

Did you enjoy this book?

We invite you to leave a review at the website of your choice, such as Goodreads, Amazon, Barnes & Noble, etc.

DID YOU KNOW THAT LEAVING A REVIEW...

- Helps other readers find books they may enjoy.
- Gives you a chance to let your voice be heard.
- Gives authors recognition for their hard work.
- Doesn't have to be long. A sentence or two about why you liked the book will do.

ABOUT THE AUTHOR

Herbert lives near Winnipeg, Canada. He spends his free time spinning tales about imaginary worlds and the strange creatures inhabiting them. His first published story `The Anniversary Gift' appeared in `Sweet Revenge' published by Midnight Showcase. Even though he writes in other genres, his love is Science Fiction. He enjoys building alien worlds and societies. Most of his stories contain an element of Erotica. All of his books are available from Melange Books.

Website: www.fictitioustales.weebly.com
Blog: hegro.blogspot.com
Blog: hergros.blogspot.com
Email: hegro@shaw.ca

ALSO BY HERBERT GROSSHANS

Operation Stargate Series

Codename Salamander

Savanna

The Aregon Files Volume 1

The Aregon Files Volume 2

Mission Aurora

Mystery Novels

Bullet of Revenge

A Matter of Justice

Mark of the Cobra

Sci-Fi Novels

Orola

Orion

Rhodar Series

Clouds Over Maridaan

Seeds of Chaos Duology

Eden's Gate

Hell's Gate

Stardogs Duology

Return to Redsky

Redemption